THE LOCKED ROOM

THE LOCKED ROOM

A RUTH GALLOWAY MYSTERY

Elly Griffiths

MARINER BOOKS

Boston • New York

HarperCollins books may be purchased for educational, business, or sales promotional use. For information, please email the Special Markets Department at SPsales@harpercollins.com.

Originally published as *The Locked Room* in Great Britain in 2022 by Quercus.

FIRST MARINER BOOKS EDITION PUBLISHED 2022.

Library of Congress Cataloging-in-Publication Data has been applied for.

ISBN 978-0-358-67139-8

22 23 24 25 26 LSC 10 9 8 7 6 5 4 3 2 1

To all the friends who have helped me through lockdown, especially: Frauke, Julie, Lesley, Mel, Nancy, Rob, Stephany, Veronique and William.

He said not 'Thou shalt not be tempested, thou shalt not be travailed, thou shalt not be diseased', but he said, 'Thou shalt not be overcome.'

Julian of Norwich
Revelations of Divine Love
(published 1670 but probably written during the plague outbreak of 1373)

PROLOGUE

At first, she thinks that he'll be coming back. It's all a mistake, she thinks. He can't mean to leave her locked in the dark for ever. And it is dark. She doesn't have her phone. Where did she leave it? There are blanks in her memory which scare her even more than the locked room.

She tries to pace it out. Eight paces forward, eight paces across. When she reaches a wall, it's cold and clammy. There's no window. The door is metal. She heard it clang behind him. She can't remember entering the room. Did he drug her? She thinks, from the cold and damp, that she must be underground. She imagines earth above her head, fathoms of it. Is she in the basement of a house? Is anyone above her?

What did he say? That he'd be coming back later? Why can't she remember any more than that?

Does he mean to leave her in the dark for ever?

1
___

Saturday, 22 February 2020

It feels strange being in the house on her own. When she was growing up here, her mother always seemed to be in possession, even – mysteriously – when she wasn't actually present. Ruth remembers coming home from school and feeling guiltily relieved when the double-locked front door meant that Jean Galloway was out at her part-time job. But, even as Ruth turned on the TV and raided the biscuit tin, there was always the sense that Jean was watching her, not just from the black-and-white wedding photo over the set – Jean in an uncomfortably short sixties dress, Arthur surprisingly dashing in a thin tie and Mod suit – but from every corner of the neat, terraced house. And now, even though Jean has been dead for nearly five years, there's still the same sense that she's hovering somewhere on the edge of Ruth's consciousness.

Maybe Jean is hovering because Ruth is currently in her mother's bedroom going through a shoebox of photographs marked 'Private'. Ruth's father has gone away for the weekend with Gloria, his new wife. When they return, Gloria wants to redecorate so Ruth has offered to go through her mother's belongings. Gloria (however much she likes her, Ruth can't think of her as her stepmother) has been very tactful about the whole thing. She hasn't changed anything in the house since she moved in two years ago, living with Jean's clothes in the spare room wardrobe and Jean's pictures on the walls. It's only natural that she would want to redecorate a little and, frankly, the house could do with it. Now that she doesn't live there, Ruth notices the peeling paintwork, the faded wallpaper, the outdated furnishings. Once these were just part of what made up her home but, looking at the place with Gloria's eyes, Ruth can understand the desire to freshen things up a bit. And, if Gloria has managed to persuade Arthur to get rid of his comb-over, there's no limit to her powers.

Ruth is alone because her sister-in-law Cathy has taken her daughter Kate to the zoo, reluctantly accompanied by Kate's seventeen-year-old cousin Jack. Kate loves animals and has been looking forward to the treat all week. Ruth hasn't been to London Zoo for years but she has a sudden vision of the Penguin House, an art deco marvel of curves and blue water. But didn't she read somewhere that penguins were no longer kept there because it turned out not to be suitable for them? She has the uncomfortable feeling that zoos, especially in the city, aren't suitable for any animals. She braces herself for a debate with Kate on this subject when she returns. Kate is a great one for philosophical debate. Ruth can't think where she gets it from. Kate's father, DCI

Harry Nelson, is allergic to the word philosophy. See also: art, archaeology, spirituality, yoga and vegan.

So far the photographs in the shoebox have not lived up to their intriguing label. There are a few pictures of Jean when she was young, as a schoolgirl in plaits and as a young bank clerk in a dark suit. Ruth peers at the faded prints, trying to detect any resemblance to herself, or to Kate. Ruth has often been described as looking like her mother, but she has always thought this was just because they both had a tendency to put on weight. Now, looking at the young Jean, she thinks she can see a faint likeness to Kate in her direct gaze and defiant stance, even in pigtails. It's a real sadness to Ruth that Kate never really got to know the grandmother whom, she now realises, she rather resembles in character.

A picture of a fluffy dog is a mystery. Jean always refused to have a pet and thought that Ruth's acquisition of two cats in her late thirties was a sign that she had, in her words, 'given up'. Next there's a picture of an older Jean in a long white dress, like a nightdress. What on earth? Then Ruth spots the grim-looking building in the background. Her parents' church. This must have been Jean's second baptism, when she was 'born again'. Ruth doesn't share her parents' faith and, when she was growing up, she had bitterly resented the church's influence on their lives. Finding God seemed to mean that her parents lost touch with everything else. For the truly righteous, religion is a full-time job. But the years have softened Ruth's stance and she was particularly glad that her father had the church's support after her mother died. In fact, the Christian Bereavement Group is where he met Gloria.

She shuffles through several adult baptisms until there's only one photograph left in the box. It shows three cottages surrounded by flat marshland. Ruth looks again. It's her cottage! Her beloved, inconvenient home, miles from everywhere, facing the Saltmarsh, inhabited only by migrating birds and the ghosts of lost children calling from the sea. Jean always disliked the house. 'Why can't you live somewhere more civilised?' she used to say, a south London girl born and bred. 'Somewhere with shops and a proper bus service?' Why on earth would Jean have kept a photograph, a rather scenic one too, of the despised cottage?

But there's something wrong with the picture. The cottages are painted dull pink rather than white and are surrounded by a low hedge rather than a picket fence. The car parked in front of the last house looks boxy and strange. Ruth turns the photo over and sees, in her mother's characteristically loopy handwriting: *Dawn 1963*.

Ruth was born in 1968. She looks again at the picture, taking in the sepia tones and the rounded edges. There's no doubt about it. Her mother had a picture of Ruth's cottage, taken thirty years before Ruth ever saw the place.

Ruth takes the shoebox of photos into her room and puts it by her case. She's sleeping in her old childhood bedroom, barely big enough for a bed, bookcase and wardrobe. Kate has Simon's old room which was bigger because he was older *and* a boy. 'Boys need more space,' Jean used to say, in answer to Ruth's regular complaints. But Simon, unlike Ruth, was a neat, contained creature and would have fitted comfortably in the box bedroom. Ruth remembers that he never expanded to fill his room in the way that Kate has done over one night, clothes on the floor, open books on the bedside table. Ruth picks up the clothes, though she knows she should make Kate do it herself. Kate is eleven, after all.

Ruth has packaged her mother's clothes into two bin bags, one for charity and one for recycling. There was nothing she wanted to keep. Arthur has already given Ruth her mother's gold watch on a chain and her diamond engagement ring. Ruth keeps these in a wooden box with Kate's pink hospital bracelet from when she was born ('Girl of Ruth Galloway') and a shepherd's crown, a fossilised sea urchin meant to bring good luck. This last was a present from her druid friend Cathbad.

Looking through her mother's belongings has made Ruth feel sad and restless. She needs some fresh air. The house is in a residential part of Eltham, rows and rows of Edwardian terraces and thirties' semis, slightly smarter than in Ruth's day but still presenting a rather grey and forbidding aspect. There's nowhere very exciting to walk, unless you make the trip to the park or the cemetery. Ruth decides to go to the local shops. It's a depressing little parade but it has a Co-op where she can buy a *Guardian* and a cake for tea. As Ruth walks, she thinks of taking this route with her schoolfriend Alison. When they were children, they went to the newsagents every Saturday to buy comics. Later, they both had paper rounds, slogging through the early morning streets delivering the *South London Press*. Later still, they lied about their age to buy alcohol from the sleazy off-licence on the corner. On impulse, as she passes this shop, now a Tesco Metro, Ruth takes a selfie and texts it to Alison. She's not very adept at doing this and cuts off half her face but Ali will get the message.

When she gets back to the house, Cathy, Kate and Jack have returned from the zoo. Kate is full of information about tigers, sloths and an okapi called Meghan. Jack is quieter but, in between mouthfuls of cake, tells them a quite frightening number of facts about spiders. Cathy shudders but Ruth says that Cathbad apologises if he disturbs a spider's web. 'They are great works of art,' he says.

'Is that your wizard friend?' says Cathy. She has refused cake because 'it's a five hundred calorie day' but she's not a bad sort really.

'He's a druid,' says Kate.

'What's the difference?' says Jack.

'Druids are real,' says Kate. She specialises in unanswerable replies which can sound rude if she's not careful. Ruth is just about to plunge in with more questions about the zoo when her phone pings. It's from Alison.

R U in Eltham?

Ruth types back 'yes' though she knows Kate wants to remind her about the 'no phones at the table' rule.

OMG. It must be a sign! School reunion tonite! U up for it?

Is she?

2

Nelson is looking at a photograph of a dead woman. This is not normally something that he would do at home, on a Saturday, but his wife, Michelle, has taken their youngest child on holiday to their native Blackpool and so he has the house to himself. He had decided on an afternoon of watching rugby and drinking beer, but this was spoiled by his German shepherd dog, Bruno, who stood in front of the television, sighing. Eventually, Nelson took Bruno out for a walk and, when they returned, Nelson didn't seem to be able to recapture that Saturday afternoon feeling. He thought about Michelle and Georgie. They were visiting Michelle's mother and Nelson was pretty sure that they would be at the Pleasure Beach today. It wasn't Nelson's favourite place and he spent several minutes worrying about safety harnesses and passing child molesters. Then he thought about Ruth and Katie in London. Ruth had said that she was packing up her mother's belongings which must be a sad task. Nelson can't imagine life without his mother, although he's glad she lives two hundred miles away. But thinking of his mother makes him think of a conversation he had with her at Christmas and a decision he needs to make. He can't think about that now, not with Bruno staring at him trustingly and Georgie's toy garage in the corner of the room. So he takes refuge in work.

Samantha Wilson was found dead yesterday at six p.m. She was lying on her bed beside an empty bottle of pills. Her body was found by her adult son, Brady, who had called in to the semi-detached house in Gaywood when he became concerned at Samantha not answering her phone. There will have to be a post-mortem but all the signs point to suicide. And yet . . .

Samantha was fifty-two, Nelson's age. She was divorced with two adult children: Saffron, a beautician, and Brady, a personal trainer. Samantha worked part-time at the local library. The scene was attended by two uniformed PCs who reported no signs of forced entry or struggle. The photograph, taken by one of the officers, shows a woman lying, fully dressed, on a flower-patterned duvet. Her face looks peaceful, her ash-blonde hair neatly arranged. Brady, who'd been too shocked for a proper interview, said that his mother had not seemed depressed or worried. This, in itself, is no reason to suspect foul play. Children, even grown-up children, don't always know what goes on in their parents' minds. No, what worries Nelson is the description of the kitchen. Sergeant Jane Campion has done a thorough job: *Daily Mail* on the table next to an empty coffee mug, vase of tulips, empty water glass upside down on the draining board, ready meal in the microwave. This last is what's making Nelson wonder if the Serious Crimes Unit should be involved. Because who puts a Weight Watchers' chicken and lemon risotto in the microwave if they're planning to kill themselves?

His phone buzzes. Jo Archer. Why is Nelson's boss ringing him at home?

'Hi, Nelson,' says Jo. 'Look, it's nothing to worry about.'

'What isn't?' says Nelson, worrying.

'I've been thinking about coronavirus.'

Even Nelson hasn't been able to avoid hearing about the deadly flu that apparently started in China. The news has been full of cancelled flights, holidaymakers trapped on a cruise ship like some modern-day re-enactment of the *Flying Dutchman*. Nelson is sorry for anyone caught up in it, of course, but it does slightly confirm his view that it's better to avoid holidays altogether.

'Have there been more cases here?' he asks. 'In the UK?'

'Thirteen more today.'

'That's still not that many though, is it?'

'There'll be more,' says Jo, with what Nelson thinks of as ghoulish relish.

'It's just flu though, isn't it?'

'People die of flu,' said Jo. 'Remember the Spanish flu?'

'I'm not that old.' He knows Jo wants him to retire but this is ridiculous. Wasn't the Spanish flu just after the First World War?

'I think we ought to be prepared,' says Jo. 'I'm calling a meeting on Monday.'

Jo loves meetings. Nelson bets that she'll conduct this one

in a full hazmat suit, complete with Darth Vader mask. He thinks she's overreacting but he can't really say so.

'I'll be there,' he says.

'And we should tell everyone to carry hand sanitiser with them. I've ordered extra.'

Hand sanitiser. Jesus wept.

'I've been thinking about the Gaywood suicide,' he says. 'Something's not quite right about it.' He explains about the microwave meal.

'Maybe she just forgot to eat,' says Jo. 'I often do.'

One of the many differences between them.

'So I think we've got enough ingredients to make our own bread for several weeks. We can grow potatoes, leeks and carrots in the garden. I wonder if we should get some hens?'

Judy looks at the jars of flour and yeast in the pantry. When they bought the cottage, she hadn't even known what the little room off the kitchen was for. But Cathbad, she realises, was always secretly prepared for the apocalypse.

'Do you really think it'll come to that?' she says. 'Shops running out of things? There have only been a couple of cases in the UK.'

'People always panic about food,' says Cathbad. 'Food and loo paper.' They get their lavatory paper specially delivered from an ethically sourced company. Judy approves in principle but she wishes the boxes weren't labelled 'Who Gives A Crap?'

'Are you panicking?' she asks.

'No,' says Cathbad. 'But I like to be prepared.' And he does look quite happy, humming under his breath as he sorts jars of pasta. But all the same, despite the everyday noises of Michael playing the piano, Miranda watching TV and Thing, their bull terrier, whining gently from the hallway, Judy feels slightly jolted. Could this coronavirus thing be more serious than everyone thinks? She's not a catastrophist but she does trust Cathbad's instincts.

'Super Jo has called a meeting for Monday,' she says.

'Good for Jo,' says Cathbad. 'What does Nelson say?'

'He says,' Judy consults her phone. '"Jesus wept. What a lot of fuss about nothing."'

'I'm afraid Nelson is wrong this time,' says Cathbad. 'I'm going to put a circle of protection around the house.'

'Things must be serious,' says Judy. She means it lightly but Cathbad says, almost to himself, 'I just hope it'll be enough.'

3

Cathy has to go home for her low-calorie meal, but Jack offers to stay and babysit Kate while Ruth is out. 'We'll get fish and chips,' he says. Kate looks delighted.

'Thank you,' says Ruth. 'I'll drive you home when I get back.' It's a good excuse not to drink.

Alison says they're meeting in a pub in Blackheath. 'There'll be a few people from our year. Paul Edwards. Dave Rutherford. Kelly Prentis. Kelly Sutherland as was.'

'Is Fatima coming?'

'She said she'd try but I think it's hard. With work and the kids.'

Fatima was the third of their triumvirate at school. Ruth vaguely recognises the male names but she definitely remembers Kelly Sutherland, who was the acknowledged queen of their year, cool and fashionable with a boyfriend who waited for her outside the school gates on a motorbike. Ruth doesn't think they ever exchanged more than two words together. Also, she still can't understand why women change their names when they get married.

Alison, like Ruth, has never been married. At school, Ruth, Alison and Fatima were 'the clever ones', collecting prizes every year and studying in the library when their contemporaries were experimenting with drugs behind the gym. The Three Amigas, they called themselves. At a plate-glass comprehensive in the eighties, it wasn't assumed that most people would go on to university. By the time they took their A levels, the three girls were part of an elite group who had special lessons on completing UCCA forms and applying for grants. Full grants still existed in the eighties; Ruth couldn't have gone to university without one. Ruth and Alison had been at primary school together, Fatima joined them in the third year of secondary, noticeable for her elegance (which transcended her inevitable nickname, 'Fatty') and for being one of the only black students. Eltham was a multiracial area but this wasn't yet evident in Ruth's school. Eltham was later to become infamous for the murder of Stephen Lawrence, a young black man killed by white thugs as he waited for a bus, but, even in the early eighties, there was a racist undertone to daily life that Ruth might not have noticed if it hadn't been for Fatima. 'They mean eloquent for a black person,' Fatima explained when collecting a debating prize. 'They're surprised I'm not speaking patois.' In fact, Fatima's father, Reginald, had the poshest voice Ruth had ever heard. He was a doctor, something that even impressed Ruth's mother.

Ruth went to UCL to study archaeology, Alison to Bristol to study English and Fatima to Edinburgh to study medicine. Ruth and Alison both won prizes at the final assembly but it was Fatima who was Student of the Year in 1986. Fatima is now a GP in north London, married with two children. Alison did a post-graduate degree at Columbia and lived in New York for over twenty years, teaching and working as a freelance journalist. She is now back in London, but Ruth hasn't seen her since a hasty drink after Jean's funeral. Ruth had been very touched when Alison turned up at the church.

Ruth finds a parking space near the pub. Alison says she'll meet her outside. 'It's awful going into a bar on your own.' Ruth had thanked her but she thought that, if Alison really feels self-conscious about going into a south London pub, then she must have changed. This was the woman who had lived on her own in Manhattan, after all.

When Ruth first sees Alison, standing huddled in a red, fake-fur jacket under the twinkly fairy lights of the Black Lion, she thinks that her friend hasn't changed at all. Same short hair, same glasses, although these have trendy black frames, unlike the battered specs of childhood. They hug and go into the pub. The Eltham Park reunion is in a private room upstairs and Alison says she needs a drink first. It's only when Ali takes off her coat that Ruth realises that she *has* changed. She looks diminished somehow and, close up, her face is gaunt and lined. Was Ali always this small? Ruth is only five foot five, yet she seems to dwarf the figure beside her.

Ruth buys red wine for Alison and lime and soda for herself.

'To us.' They clink glasses.

'You look well, Ruth.' Ruth feels underdressed. She didn't bring any smart clothes with her so is wearing jeans and a blue jumper that's slightly too big for her. She did wash her hair though; it's still damp at the back.

'So do you,' she says.

'Thank you,' says Alison. Then, 'I've lost quite a lot of weight.'

So that's it. Alison isn't shorter, she's thinner. Without the coat, she is twig-like, her head with its oversized glasses almost too big for her body.

'I went to Lean Zone,' says Alison. 'I lost three stone.'

'Great!' says Ruth. She knows this is what you are meant to say when someone has lost weight. After all, 'Have you lost weight?' is universally considered to be a great compliment. Ruth never feels that it is, though. Partly it's the word 'weight', so solid and uncompromising. Also it's the implication that the speaker feels that this diminution is devoutly to be wished, if not long overdue.

'I just wanted to feel healthier,' says Alison, almost defensively.

'That's great,' says Ruth again. 'I really must lose some weight.'

'I'll send you a link to the website,' says Alison. Which wasn't the answer Ruth wanted.

'Shall we go and join the reunion?' she says.

For one panicky moment, Ruth thinks that she doesn't know anyone in the room. There seem to be middle-aged men everywhere, grey-haired or balding. To her surprise one of these old men – these *dads* – immediately comes up to talk to them.

'Ruth?'

Ruth still doesn't recognise him. It's Alison who says, 'Daniel? Daniel Breakspeare?'

'Danny. Yes.'

Ruth looks dumbly at the bald man in a suit. In the sixth form Daniel Breakspeare had been her boyfriend. They went out together for almost a year. Her mother had liked him and never failed to tell Ruth that he'd 'done very well for himself' since school. He's a plumber, Ruth seems to remember, and now runs his own company. That explains the suit and the Rolex watch protruding subtly, but not modestly, from Danny's shirt cuff. Ruth wouldn't have been able to pick him out in a police line-up.

'How are you, Ruth? I didn't know you were back in London.'

'I'm just here for the weekend. Do you live in London?'

'Yes. In Blackheath. Just around the corner from here.'

Jean would be very impressed. For most people living in Eltham, Blackheath is the promised land. Alison says that she's living in Clapham after years in the States. She and Daniel chat about New York ('one of my favourite cities' says Daniel) and Ruth finishes her lime and soda with an embarrassing sucking noise.

It's a couple of seconds before Ruth realises that Daniel has left Manhattan and is addressing her. Alison has drifted away to talk to another grey-haired group.

'Are you married, Ruth?'

'No, but I've got an eleven-year-old daughter.'

'Lovely age. I've got two grown-up daughters and now I've got a baby. It's a nightmare going through all those sleepless nights again.'

The grown-up daughters and the new baby remind Ruth of Nelson but she's willing to bet that Daniel's new baby is the result of a new marriage. Sure enough, Daniel says that he met Ruby a few years ago and it was a 'whirlwind romance'. The name alone tells Ruth that she's in her twenties. Or her eighties.

'I met your mum in Waitrose a few years back,' says Daniel. 'Actually, it must be six or seven years ago now. She said you were famous. Appearing on TV, writing books.'

Ruth loves the way Daniel name-checks the upmarket supermarket in case she should imagine he shops at Morrisons. But she's touched to think that Jean stood next to the fresh sushi and the cheese of the week and showed off about her daughter.

'I'm an archaeologist,' she says. 'I teach at a university in Norfolk and I've written books about bones. Nothing anyone would actually read.'

'You always were clever, Ruth. You and Alison and . . .'

'Fatima. She's a doctor now. My mum told me that you were very successful too.'

Daniel laughs. 'Mums, eh? How's yours? I always liked her.'

'She died five years ago.'

'Oh, I'm sorry,' says Daniel. And he does sound it. He was always very kind, Ruth remembers. He hadn't been bad-looking in the old days either. She would have slept with him if she hadn't been terrified of getting pregnant and being trapped in Eltham. As it was, they had done what was euphemistically called 'everything else'. She thinks of this now and knows that she is blushing. Luckily the upstairs room is very dark.

'My dad died last year,' says Daniel. 'He was in his eighties but it was still a shock. I don't think you can ever be prepared.'

'I think that's right,' says Ruth. There's a brief, but not uncomfortable, silence, as if they are both acknowledging the fact that they are older and their parents are dying.

'That's why I'm in London, really,' says Ruth. 'I've been sorting out my mum's stuff. My dad has married again and they want to redecorate.'

'That must have been tough,' says Daniel.

'It was,' says Ruth. 'And mysterious too.' She starts to tell Daniel about the box marked 'private' and the strange photograph but suddenly there's a glitter of gold and someone shouts, 'Danny! Darling!'

A woman dives between them, kissing Daniel on both cheeks with an *Ab-Fab* flourish. She has blonde hair, tanned skin and lots of gold jewellery. Ruth has noticed that, as a general rule, the women present tonight look younger than the men. This is partly because the women have tended to go blonde, rather than grey, with age. This woman seems burnished all over and the effect is quite dazzling.

'Kelly, you remember Ruth. From our year?'

So this is Kelly Sutherland, the Queen of Eltham Park.

'I remember you, Ruth,' says Kelly unexpectedly. 'You used to go out with Danny.'

'That's right,' says Ruth, 'for a few months in the sixth form.'

'For a year,' says Daniel.

'I got him next,' says Kelly. 'Did you know?'

It turns out that Kelly and Daniel dated for two years. 'But it didn't work out,' says Kelly, 'we were babies really.' Daniel went on to marry Fiona, by whom he has grown-up daughters, and then the youthful-sounding Ruby. Kelly has been married three times and her current husband is none other than the school-gates-haunting boy on the motorbike.

'My first love,' says Kelly, laughing rather loudly. 'Romantic, eh?'

'Very,' says Ruth. She is wondering whether she can make her excuses to Alison and go home.

Daniel offers to buy more drinks. Kelly asks for Prosecco but Ruth says no, thank you. She doesn't think she could take any more soda water. While Daniel is at the bar, Kelly puts a red-nailed hand on Ruth's arm. Ruth pulls away slightly, she's getting a headache from the glare of Kelly's hair.

'You know, Ruth, I used to envy you at school.'

'Really?' This is the biggest surprise of the night.

'You always seemed to know what you wanted. You weren't bothered about clothes and boys and all the rest of it.'

'I was bothered about them,' says Ruth. 'I just wasn't very good at them.'

'Danny was mad about you. He was so upset when you finished with him.'

As Ruth remembers it, she and Daniel had drifted apart when she went to university. Although she had only crossed London to go to UCL, she had moved into halls and consciously started a new life.

'Well, he seems OK now,' says Ruth lightly.

'We're all OK now,' says Kelly. 'Have you seen Alison? She must have lost five stone.'

4

Ruth is keen to leave after breakfast on Sunday. Arthur and Gloria aren't due back until the evening but Ruth has explained that she needs to be back in Norfolk by midday in order to prepare for the next day's teaching. Although, now she's head of department she finds that she spends as much time juggling timetables and listening to complaints from students – and lecturers – as she does teaching. Besides, she wants to see her cat, Flint. Both her neighbours are away so she's had to rely on Cathbad coming round to feed him. She knows that Cathbad will have discharged his duties faithfully. He gets on well with Flint and claims that they have a psychic bond. It's just that she doesn't like to think of her cat alone in the cottage with no humans in sight. Ridiculous, she knows; this is probably Flint's idea of heaven. She remembers her mother saying, 'It's not natural, living in the middle of nowhere.' But why had Jean kept a picture of the unnatural dwelling place amongst her private papers?

'What would Granddad do on Sundays?' asks Kate, who is sitting at the kitchen table eating toast and Marmite. Ruth is sure that this room will be high on Gloria's redecorating list, the blue Formica cabinets haven't changed since she was a child and the lino is threadbare in places. Nevertheless, it's the cosiest room in the house. After Jean and pre-Gloria, Arthur used to spend most of his time in here, watching a black-and-white television set balanced on top of the microwave.

'I suppose he'd go to church,' says Ruth, making herself a second cup of instant coffee. She bought her father a cafetière once, but he had clearly been baffled by the gift and there's no sign of it in the cupboards. Gloria thinks caffeine is a poison.

'Shall we do that?' asks Kate brightly.

'I don't think so.'

'Can we visit Grandma's grave then?'

Kate obviously wants some sort of Sunday activity, something wholesome and slightly boring. Well, maybe she's right. If Ruth packs up the car, they can leave as soon as they have paid their graveside respects.

Ruth and Kate walk to Eltham cemetery and buy flowers from the opportunistic stall at the gate. It's a bright, cold morning. Last week high winds, given the inappropriately cosy name of Storm Dennis, ravaged the country but today the trees that line the paths are almost completely still. Jean's grave looks very white amongst the older models. Ruth wonders whether her father, or maybe even Gloria, comes to clean it.

Jean Galloway
Beloved wife and mother
At rest with the angels
1938–2015

There's a rose in a pot at the foot of the stone. Ruth places their carnations next to it.

'Shall we say a prayer?' says Kate. Ruth gives her daughter a look, wondering where she's getting this religious stuff from. Kate's school is secular in a 'let's all be nice to each other' way. Nelson's a lapsed Catholic but Ruth can't imagine him ever talking about prayer. Cathbad? His inclination is always to light a ceremonial fire rather than say an Our Father.

'OK,' she says. 'Let say a prayer quietly in our heads.'

She thinks Kate looks disappointed.

'Hi, Mum,' says Ruth silently, 'I miss you. I never thought I'd miss you this much. There's so much we didn't talk about. Daniel Breakspeare's a successful businessman now. You were right about him. Kelly Sutherland has been married three times and I haven't even married once. I did give you a granddaughter though. I wish you could see her. And, Mum, why did you have a picture of my cottage dated 1963?'

'Mum?' Kate is tugging at her arm. 'Have you finished? Can we go and see the tiny pilot?'

In the older, more overgrown, part of the graveyard there's a half-sized statue of an airman killed in 1938. The little figure is dressed in overalls that look oddly like a post-apocalyptic radioactivity suit. The inscription says that

Ernest Francis Bennett was killed in a flying accident at Auchengilloch Hill, Scotland. He has a sweet, childlike face and Ruth had once imagined herself going back in time and falling in love with him. She remembers shedding sentimental tears at the vision of herself receiving a telegram containing the tragic news of her boyfriend's death. When she and Alison were sixteen they had drunk a bottle of Blue Nun in front of Ernest's grave and tried to talk to his spirit. Ruth wonders if Ali remembers it.

Kate picks daisies and puts them at Ernest's booted feet. Richmal Crompton, the author of the Just William books, also rests in Eltham Cemetery, although she doesn't have a gravestone because her ashes were scattered in the crematorium rose garden. Ruth wonders what Ms Crompton would have made of Kate and the children of the twenty-first century. She has a feeling that, excluding things like TikTok and Instagram, nothing much has really changed.

They reach Norfolk at two, having stopped on the way for a service station lunch. It's a beautiful afternoon, the yellow grasses brushing the bright blue sky, the seagulls calling from the shore. Flint is waiting by the gate, looking disapproving, but what catches Ruth's eye is a van by her next-door neighbour's house. She knew that Bob was renting out the place while he spent a year in his native Australia but she hadn't realised that the new tenant would be moving in so soon.

She tries not to stare at the objects being carried into the house but can't help making a few value-judgements:

tea-chest marked 'Books' (good), birdcage (bad), chaise longue (perplexing). Kate rushes upstairs to 'do homework' which Ruth suspects consists of texting her friends. Nelson bought Kate a mobile phone two Christmases ago and, although Ruth had disapproved at the time, it has proved a lifeline for a pre-teen living miles from any of her class-mates. Ruth feeds Flint – who makes it clear that the food still in his bowl is no longer acceptable – and sits down by the window to do her own work. Should she go next door to say hallo? What would Cathbad do?

She has just decided that Cathbad would knock on the door with a bottle of locally sourced wine when she sees a figure walking down her path. Ruth hurries to open the door.

Her new neighbour is a pleasant-looking woman of prob-ably Ruth's own age. She has brown hair pulled into a messy bun and is wearing paint-stained dungarees.

'Hi. I thought I'd come and say hallo. I'm Zoe.'

'Ruth.' Ruth extends her hand. 'Would you like to come in for a cup of tea or coffee?'

'That would be lovely if it's not disturbing you.' Zoe nods towards the open laptop.

'No, it's OK. Just answering a few work emails.'

'What do you do?' asks Zoe, following Ruth into the house.

'I teach archaeology at the University of North Norfolk. UNN.' Ruth always thinks that her institution has a very unpleasing acronym. It looks even worse written down.

'That must be so interesting. I'm a nurse.'

'Will you be working at the Queen Elizabeth?'

'No, I'm a practice nurse. I'm starting with a GP surgery in Wells. Westway.'

'Sounds great. I've got some good friends in Wells.'

'It's beautiful there. Well, it's beautiful everywhere in Norfolk.'

Ruth warms to her neighbour. She likes people who appreciate her adopted county. Unlike Nelson who never stops moaning about the dullness, flatness and general lack of northern grit. And unlike Ruth's mother, who thought Norfolk was godforsaken. And, in her case, she meant it literally.

Ruth and Zoe chat about work and family and pets. Zoe is from Lincolnshire, divorced with no children. She has a Maine Coon cat called Derek. Ruth explains about Kate and Flint.

'Oh, I think I saw Flint in the garden earlier. Is he ginger? He's gorgeous. Derek was a house cat when I lived in Lincoln but I'm hoping he can go out here.'

'I'm sure he'll be able to. It's a very quiet road. It only leads to these three houses.'

'I love the quiet,' says Zoe.

'Me too,' says Ruth. It occurs to her that she might have found a friend but, before she can say more, Kate bounds in with demands to have a frog costume by tomorrow. 'We're doing an assembly about the environment.' Zoe smiles and says she had better go. At the door, she adds that she can sew and would be happy to help with any future costumes. Better and better, thinks Ruth.

'. . . and making sure to wash your hands thoroughly whenever you come in. Experts suggest singing "Happy Birthday" twice over while you do it.'

Jo beams around the room. Nelson groans inwardly. Is this what his life has become? Listening to a woman in jogging clothes ('athleisure-wear' according to his woman officers) telling him to wash his hands? Jo asks if there are any questions and Judy would like to know if there are contingency plans in the event of the virus taking hold in the UK. Nelson shoots Judy a reproachful look. *Don't encourage her.* Jo says importantly that she is on a coronavirus working party. Then, thank goodness, she leaves the room and Nelson can get on with his briefing.

'There are a couple of things that bother me about the Gaywood suicide,' he says. 'I'd like you, Judy, to speak to the adult children. See if you can get a sense of the mother's mood in recent months.'

'Do you really think it could be foul play?' asks Tony

Zhang. He's the newest member of the team and manages
to get an unseemly relish into the words 'foul play'.

'There's no sign of it,' says Nelson, repressively. 'There'll
be a post-mortem. That's routine in cases like this. But,
like I say, there are a couple of things. A ready meal in the
microwave, for one thing.'

'People don't always act logically before taking their own
lives,' says Judy. 'There are plenty of cases of people buying
return tickets, that sort of thing.'

'I know,' says Nelson. 'But it can't hurt to check up.' He
stops himself from adding 'there's a good girl'. He has three
daughters, two of them adult professionals, and knows
where the line is. Judy is a detective inspector. She should
really be leading her own team but, to do that, she would
probably need to move from Norfolk. Nelson dreads that
day although he knows he should be encouraging Judy to
look for jobs elsewhere. Or retire himself.

When the briefing is over, Nelson goes to his office to
prepare for a tedious meeting on regional crime targets.
His secretary, Leah, brings him coffee and then, unusually,
seems disposed to chat.

'I heard you talking about the Gaywood case,' she says.
'That's quite near me.'

'Is it?' Leah must live somewhere, Nelson supposes, but
he's never really thought about where.

'I think my mum knew her. The woman who committed
suicide.'

'Samantha Wilson?'

'Yes. Mum was very shocked when she heard.'

'Was she?' Nelson is listening now.

'Yes,' says Leah, heading towards the door. 'But you never know when people are desperate, do you?'

And she is gone, leaving the door swinging gently behind her.

Ruth is looking into a grave. Council workers digging up a street in the centre of Norwich have found what looks to be a human skull. Ruth is not too surprised by this. The road is in Tombland, the ancient area around the cathedral, and human skeletons have been found here before. She has decided to bring some of her students so that they can watch the excavation at first hand. They stand in a nervous and expectant group by the 'Road Closed' sign while Ruth and Ted Cross from the field archaeology team consult the foreman.

'I knew it was human at once,' he says, 'so we stopped work immediately.'

'Thank you,' says Ruth. 'We'll excavate as quickly as we can.' She knows that the delay will be costly and inconvenient for the council.

'Do you think it's been here a long time?' asks the foreman, whose name is Cezary. The yellowing skull is clearly visible in the earth, lying beside a broken pipe. The skull itself looks undamaged and Ruth feels an excavator's thrill.

'Probably,' said Ruth. 'There was a medieval cemetery nearby.'

'Is that why it's called Tombland?' asks Cezary.

'Tombland comes from a Danish word meaning empty space,' says Ruth. 'I know that's disappointing.'

'Plenty of tombs here though,' says Ted. 'We've found skeletons before, haven't we, Ruth?'

'Yes,' says Ruth. 'The graveyard of St George's once covered this whole area. There are rumours that there's a plague pit here too, although nothing has ever been discovered.'

'Plague?' says Cezary, rather nervously.

'There were several outbreaks of the plague in Norwich in the fourteenth, fifteenth and sixteenth centuries. So many people died that there wasn't room in the graveyards,' says Ruth. 'It's thought that the bodies were probably thrown into pits. Mass graves.'

'The outcast dead,' says Ted. There's a service of this name every year, to remember the bodies buried in unmarked graves. Ruth always tries to attend, despite not believing in an afterlife.

Ted climbs into the trench and Ruth beckons her students nearer.

'Human bones must always be treated with great care and respect,' she says, as Ted brushes away the soil from the skull. 'Every bone and fragment must be preserved. When I was excavating war graves in Bosnia, my mentor used to say that if you leave a bone uncharted, then you are an accessory to the crime.'

The students, who are only in their second term, look at each other nervously.

Ted only needs to work for a few more minutes before it becomes clear that an entire skeleton is present. Cezary goes to tell his workforce to go home for the day.

'See the way the body is laid out,' Ruth tells her students.

'This suggests a formal burial. The corpse may have been shrouded. There may even have been a coffin.'

'What's happened to the coffin?' says someone. It's an obvious question but Ruth is glad it's been asked.

'It would have rotted away,' she says.

Erik, Ruth's mentor at university, used to say, 'Wood returns to earth, only bones and stone remain.'

Ruth takes a measuring rod and lays it next to the emerging bones.

'It's important to photograph the bones in situ next to a suitable scale,' she says, in lecture mode. 'We need to take samples from the context – the surrounding soil – too. That will help with dating.'

'How do you know it isn't recent?' says someone, a man with a full-face beard. Ruth doesn't do much teaching now that she's head of department, and the students are starting to look very much alike.

'Very recent burials are comparatively easy to spot,' says Ruth. 'You can tell by the grave cut, for one thing. But it can be hard to differentiate between bones that are fifty years old and those that are a thousand years old. That's why we need carbon-14 testing. But, in this case, it's an established medieval site so I think we're looking at skeletal matter from that era. I could be wrong, of course.'

No one thinks this is likely.

By three o'clock, the skeleton has been excavated. It's not very tall and, from the pelvic bones, Ruth thinks that it is female. She allowed the students to help with the final stages and they are in a state of high excitement as they load the numbered paper bags into a box marked 'Archaeology Lab'. Ruth is in a more sombre mood. She always feels that she should handle the bones as if the dead person's relatives are watching her and that's no different if they died ten years ago or in the fourteenth century. Besides, her back is aching.

Ruth walks back to the car park with Ted. It's been a grey day and is already getting dark. Lights shine in the cathedral close and the church itself looms above them, birds circling the tower and steeple. An omen of something, Cathbad would say.

'Are you OK to take the bones back to UNN?' asks Ruth. 'I've got to pick up Kate. Her childminder can't make it today.'

'No problem,' says Ted. He's carrying the box under his arm. A human being weighs very little in the end.

'Ruth!' A figure appears from one of the many secret archways that surround the cloisters. A woman, wearing a grey cloak that flutters dramatically in the uncertain light.

'Blimey,' says Ted. 'It's the Grey Lady.'

The Grey Lady of Tombland is a famous Norfolk ghost but Ruth has recognised the apparition. It's Janet Meadows, a local historian who also works as a cathedral guide.

'Hi, Janet.'

'Hallo, Ruth. Have you been involved in the excavation?'

Ruth nods towards the box in Ted's arms. 'Just finished.'

'Do you think it's a plague victim?' says Janet.

'It's possible, I suppose,' says Ruth, 'but I think we might just have come across a cemetery that used to belong to one of the churches.'

'Can I talk to you?' says Janet. 'Have you got a minute?'

'I've got to collect Kate from school. Could we get together another day? Have coffee or something?'

'Of course,' says Janet. Ted loads the bones into his van and drives off with a cheery toot of the horn. The birds fly squawking into the air and the two women watch him go.

'What did you want to talk about?' says Ruth.

'The plague,' says Janet.

6

Judy faces Saffron Evans and Brady Wilson across their mother's grey and pink sitting room. It's a pleasant space, furnished with the kind of decorating flourishes that Judy never quite achieves: multiple cushions, fringed lamps, framed photographs in tasteful clusters. Even the books are arranged by colour, their spines unbroken. Judy's living area includes Cathbad's driftwood collection, Michael's piano and Miranda's artwork pinned onto the walls. Their books are dog-eared and arranged by psychic connection. Judy doesn't possess any chenille cushions and, if she did, Thing would eat them.

'I'm so sorry,' Judy says. 'This must be very hard for you.' She has told the family that this is a courtesy call, to explain the police procedures for investigating an unexpected death. She won't mention Nelson's suspicions, unless the siblings give her reason to suppose they share them.

'It's just a shock,' says Saffron. She's probably in her late twenties, as immaculate as the room, blonde hair in a French plait, nails a perfect shell-like pink. Brady is tall and muscular, looking as if he is about to burst out of his black tracksuit. They look more like actors in a soap opera than real-life people.

But Saffron's tears are real enough. 'I just can't believe it,' she says, taking a tissue from the floral-printed box on the table.

'You were saying your mother's death was a shock,' Judy prompts gently. 'Had you any idea she was feeling depressed?'

'Mum wasn't depressed,' said Brady. 'She just didn't do depression. She got on with things.'

Judy doesn't answer that depression does not stop people getting on with things, that it's an illness that many people live with all their lives. Instead she says, 'When did you last see your mum?'

'The day before,' says Brady. 'The day before . . . she was found. I usually pop in on my way home from the gym. I wasn't going to be able to come on Friday so I texted her and then phoned. I thought it was odd that she didn't answer. So I came round.'

'Mum always answers texts immediately,' says Saffron. 'Usually with a row of emojis. Smiley faces, hearts, cry laughing. I used to say I regretted showing her where to find them on her phone.' She holds the tissue up to her eyes.

'And Samantha seemed her usual self on Thursday?' asks Judy.

'Yes,' says Brady. 'She was going to photocopy some more personal training leaflets for me. She used the machine at the library. We talked about that. And about Poppy. My little girl. She's three. Mum doted on her.'

'We all do,' says Saffron.

Judy knows that Saffron is married but doesn't have children. Brady lives with his partner, Claire, and they have one daughter. They seem a close family. Samantha was divorced but remained on good terms with her husband, Nick. Brady called in most days on his way home from the gym where he works. Saffron saw her mother at least once a week. Samantha often collected Poppy from school and the little girl sometimes stayed over at her house. Why would this happy, fulfilled woman kill herself?

Judy asks about the sleeping pills and Saffron says that her mum sometimes suffered from insomnia. Except it seems that, this time, Samantha took the pills in the middle of the day.

'I always knew when she couldn't sleep,' says Saffron, 'because she'd send me all these YouTube videos in the middle of the night. Mostly about animals.'

'Did your mum have a pet?' There's nothing in this pristine room that suggests the presence of an animal.

'Not now. She used to have a cat called Trudy but she died at the end of last year. Mum was devastated.'

Judy loves animals but surely losing a beloved cat is not enough reason to drive a person to despair? Besides, it happened last year. She doesn't want to ask any more intrusive questions so she talks the siblings through the process of the post-mortem and inquest.

'Will we have to wait until the inquest before we can have the funeral?' asks Brady.

'No,' says Judy. 'You can plan the funeral as soon as you have a death certificate. Did Samantha leave any specific instructions?'

'No,' says Saffron. 'And she didn't leave a will either. Mum was such an organised person. I'm sure that, if she'd meant to die, she would have made some plans, written something down.'

Judy has made a will and even Cathbad has left a long list of his burial requirements, including a funeral pyre and ritual chanting. She thinks it's strange that someone who colour-coded their books didn't draw up a will. Strange, but not necessarily suspicious.

'She would have wanted a church funeral,' says Brady. 'Will that be allowed?'

'Of course,' says Judy. Suicides were once denied burial on hallowed ground. Thank goodness this is a thing of the past. Judy asks if Samantha attended a local church.

'She went to evensong at St Matthew's sometimes,' offers Saffron. 'And she used to go to that special service at the cathedral.'

'Which service? Christmas? Easter?'

'No. The one for the dead,' says Saffron. 'The outcast dead.'

Ruth gets held up in traffic and is ten minutes late to collect Kate. She finds her daughter sitting smugly in the secretary's office pretending to read a library book.

'I'm so sorry,' says Ruth, half to Kate and half to Mrs Chambers, 'I got held up on a dig.'

'I know,' says Kate. 'You're all muddy.'

Ruth looks down and sees that she's left dirty footprints on the grey carpet. She starts apologising again but Mrs Chambers says that it's no problem. 'I'll just pop the hoover over it.' This makes Ruth feel worse than ever.

In the car, Kate embarks on a long description of the Year 6 trip in the summer term. She's in her last year in primary school and, from the PTA newsletter, it looks as if her final term will be full of valedictory events: picnics, discos, rounders matches, concerts, even a prom. Ruth always feels slightly guilty, knowing that she won't be able to get away from work for all these festivities. Nor will Nelson, although he'll want to come to Kate's final assembly and will embarrass everyone by taking too many photographs.

Kate's next educational step has also proved controversial. Ruth was determined that Kate should have a comprehensive education, as she did. 'But she's so bright,' said Nelson. 'So was I and I did OK,' countered Ruth. 'Comprehensives are for everyone, that's the whole point.' Nelson wanted Kate to go to the private girls' school attended by his older daughters. In the end, Ruth consented to take Kate to the open day at St Faith's. She'd been slightly afraid that Kate would be swayed by the facilities, especially the theatre with real swishing curtains, but Kate announced that she preferred the comprehensive. 'Why?' asked Ruth, masking her relief. 'Because it's got boys in it.' Ruth had filled in the forms that night.

Is Ruth sacrificing Kate's prospects for her own political beliefs, as Nelson clearly thinks? No, she tells herself. Kate would do well anywhere, and Ruth wants her daughter's schoolfriends to be socially diverse, and to include boys. She thinks back to the reunion at the weekend. Ruth's old classmates are certainly a mixed bunch: hard-working GP Fatima, successful plumber Daniel, much-married Kelly. Would they have been different if she'd attended a private school? Did Ruth's parents ever consider another option? They couldn't have afforded private school fees but there might still have been the odd grammar school around. Ruth has an opportunity to ask her father about this because he rings later that evening, after Kate has gone to bed.

'Hallo, Dad. How was Eastbourne?' Arthur and Gloria were staying with Gloria's eldest son, who runs a restaurant.

'Fine. Very pleasant. Cleaner than Brighton.'

'That's nice.' Ruth loves Brighton but she can see why it wouldn't be her father's favourite town.

'Thank you for what you did, Ruth. For taking care of . . . of Mum's stuff.'

It still makes Ruth's heart contract to hear her father say 'Mum' without the determiner, as if Jean is still there somewhere. Mummy, Daddy and two children. Just like an old-fashioned reading book.

'That's OK. Happy to help. Dad, I was going through some of Mum's old pictures and I found one of the cottage.'

'Cottage? Which cottage?'

'This cottage. Where I live.'

'She must have taken it when we visited.' Those visits were few and far between. Jean always refused to stay the night at Ruth's house because she thought the stairs were unsafe.

'It was taken before I moved here. On the back it said, "Dawn 1963".'

There's a silence. Then Arthur says, '1963. That's before you were born.'

'Yes.'

'You were born in 1968. Simon in 1966.'

'I know, Dad.'

'Then why would Jean have a picture taken in 1963?'

'I don't know. That's why I was asking you.'

'Well, I don't know.' Arthur sounds confused and rather upset.

Ruth decides to change the subject: 'I went to a school reunion while I was in Eltham. Alison invited me. You remember Ali?'

'Of course I do.' Arthur sounds relieved to be on firmer ground. 'Funny little thing. But she had a good heart. I'll always remember her coming to Mum's funeral.'

'Me too. Well, Alison told me that there was an Eltham Park reunion at the Black Lion in Blackheath.'

'Nice pub.'

'Yes. Daniel Breakspeare was there. Do you remember him?'

'Yes. Your mum always liked Daniel.'

'She did. Dad, did you ever think of sending me to another school?'

Another pause. 'Why would we have done that? Simon went to Eltham Park. Everyone went there.'

'I don't know. I suppose I was just thinking about secondary schools because of Kate.'

They talk about Kate for a comfortable few minutes, then say goodnight. Ruth suddenly feels the need for a drink. She goes to the kitchen and pours herself a glass of red before sitting down at her laptop.

There are three new emails. The first is something of a surprise.

To: Ruth Galloway

From: Daniel Breakspeare

It was great to see you on Saturday. Maybe it's old age (!) but I've been thinking a lot about school. And about you. Do you ever come to London? It would be good to have lunch one day. And you can tell me more about the mysterious box.

All best

Dxx

Ruth looks at this missive for some time, sipping her wine. Why does Daniel want to see her? Is he just feeling nostalgic? Is it a symptom of age, with or without the jaunty exclamation mark? Is it surprising that he has remembered Ruth's half-finished tale of the box marked 'private'? And which should she believe: the more formal 'all best' or the D followed by two kisses?

The second email is from Alison.

It was good on Saturday, wasn't it? So strange to see everyone again. Some people I wouldn't have recognised but Kelly was unchanged! Daniel seemed very pleased to see you. Asked for your email address afterwards. What would your mum have said??

Hope to see you soon. Maybe next time we could get together with Fatty? Have a Three Amigas reunion??

Lots of love

Ali xx

PS here's the link to LZ as promised.

The third email is from her colleague David Brown. Subject: *Tombland Dig*. Ruth knows she should open this but instead she presses the link to enter the Lean Zone.

7

Ruth's day starts with a department meeting. Her predecessor, Phil, avoided group gatherings, preferring to waylay his staff in the canteen, where it was easier to get them to agree with him. Ruth hopes that having monthly meetings will create a sense of camaraderie and teamwork and will also stop the AGM taking what seems like days.

Camaraderie seems thin on the ground today. Bob Bullmore, the anthropology expert, is determined to talk about the new unisex toilets. Fiona Green, Conservation and Bioarchaeology, wants to tell them about her recent paper on gender bias. David Brown, prehistory lecturer and Ruth's personal irritant, disagrees with both of them. Peter Llewellyn (Cultural Heritage) says nothing. Eventually the meeting draws to a cantankerous close because lectures are starting. David remains behind. He's very tall and he seems to cast a shadow over the whole room.

'How was the Tombland skeleton?' he asks. 'I sent you an email last night.'

Ruth doesn't apologise for not responding. She wants to

break David of the habit of emailing at all hours of the day and night.

'It was an interesting find,' she says. 'A complete skeleton, probably female, laid out as if for formal burial. I've sent off samples for carbon-14 dating and isotope analysis. We might even get DNA.'

'Unlikely, if it's an articulated skeleton,' says David. This is one of the things that annoys Ruth about him. She knows very well that the process of putrefaction can destroy DNA and it seems to work faster with articulated remains. David does not need to point this out to her, the forensics expert.

'Was there anything else?' she says.

'You know I'm on the board of the Friends of Tombland?'

'Yes.' Ruth had actually recommended David for the post, because she didn't have time herself. She feels like reminding him of this.

'Your friend Janet Meadows is on the board too.'

'I know.'

'She wants to put on a plague festival.'

'A plague festival?' This must have been what Janet wanted to talk about yesterday.

'Well, an exhibition about the Norwich plague pits. But it's nonsense. They haven't found any plague pits in Norwich.'

'I thought there was one near the coach park at Black-friars?' Ruth suddenly thinks of her school reunion in the Blackheath pub. She read once that the area took its name from plague pits dug there during the Black Death. She doesn't share this nugget with David, who is still talking about Tombland.

'Why would anyone bury their dead in the centre of the city? It's just pandering to the ignorant. Tombs, plague, the Grey Lady, ring-a-ring-a-roses. It's sensationalising archaeology.'

'I thought you were keen on plagues.' It's one of David's pet theories that, when the Beaker People came to Britain in the Bronze Age, they brought with them a deadly virus that wiped out the native population.

'That's different,' says David. 'Janet Meadows just wants to dress up as the Grey Lady and frighten tourists.'

Ruth thinks of Janet in her cloak and of Ted's comment. *Blimey, it's the Grey Lady.*

'That's unfair,' she says. 'Janet's a serious historian.'

'There'll be a fight about this,' says David, sounding as if he relishes the prospect. 'And I hope you'll be on my side.'

'I'll be on the side of truth,' says Ruth, but only in her head. She doesn't need Cathbad to tell her that truth can be a very slippery concept.

'On balance, I think Samantha Wilson committed suicide,' says Judy. 'We may never know why.'

'What about the ready meal in the microwave?' says Nelson.

'We can't know what was in Samantha's mind,' says Judy. 'But there's no sign of forced entry. No suggestion that anyone was in the house with her. All the evidence points to her lying down on her bed and taking an overdose of sleeping pills. It's very sad but it's not suspicious. In my opinion.'

'I've got the post-mortem results here.' Nelson turns his screen to face Judy. 'Chris Stephenson agrees with you. Cause of death: respiratory failure due to chemical overdose.'

'The daughter said her mother suffered from insomnia,' says Judy. 'Hence the sleeping pills.'

'Did the children say anything else?' asks Nelson. Judy knows that he's not about to give up. His persistence is one of the things that makes him a good detective but it's rather trying when you're on the receiving end of it. 'Had their mother seemed depressed recently?'

'No,' admits Judy. 'They were very shocked. They seem a close family. Samantha was devoted to her children and to her granddaughter. The son, Brady, saw his mother the day before she died when she seemed in good spirits.'

Nelson is silent for a minute, tapping a pen against his desk. Then he says, 'Have a word with Intel. See if there have been any other suicides in the area recently. See if there's a pattern.'

'What sort of pattern?'

'A suicide where the person wasn't previously known as depressed. Something that came out of the blue. Like this one.'

'OK, boss.' Judy will talk to her friend Liz, a civilian data analyst. At least that will get Nelson off her back.

At the door she says, 'Did you hear about the body in Tombland?'

'No,' says Nelson. His tone is neutral, but she can see his fingers tighten around the pen.

'I just saw it on yesterday's report. A body was found where they're digging up the road to make cycle lanes. Thought to be medieval. Ruth did the excavation.'

'That's all I need,' says Nelson. 'Another bloody Stone Age body.'

Judy doesn't explain the difference between the medieval and Neolithic periods. She knows that, as soon as she is gone, Nelson will be on the phone to Ruth.

'If you bite it, write it. If you nibble it, scribble it. If you lick it, Bic it.' Jacquie smiles round at the women sitting in a circle around her. A few smile back, old hands who have been to many Lean Zone meetings. What worries Ruth is that these stalwarts look no thinner than the rest of them.

Ruth is already regretting the impulse that led her to click on the link at the end of Alison's email. A link that took her to this village hall, smelling of damp and instant coffee. Lean Zone products are arranged on a trestle table by the door, the Zs on the low-sugar chocolate and diet drinks merging to create one long, soporific ZZZZZZ. Ruth feels pretty tired too after a rather fractious day at work, but she doesn't have to collect Kate until six and she has already filled out the forms to join, her untidy academic handwriting sprawling out of the tiny boxes provided.

Is she here because Alison has lost three stone and everyone at the reunion said how well she looked? Well, partly. And partly because she thinks that, at nearly fifty-two, she should make one last effort to become slimmer and healthier. After all, her mother had a stroke in her seventies and Ruth has always been told that she resembles her. And how hard can it be to lose weight? If Jacquie is to be believed, it's simply a matter of writing down everything you eat. Oh, and never eating carbohydrates or drinking alcohol.

Ruth is woken out of a miserable low-cal doze by the swing doors opening and shutting. A woman is apologising for being late whilst taking a seat in the circle.

'Hi, Zoe,' says someone.

Ruth turns around to see her new next-door neighbour stowing her handbag under her chair. Zoe straightens up and mimes pleasure and surprise at seeing Ruth. Ruth herself feels rather embarrassed. Guilty of the terrible crime of being overweight. But, at the same time, Zoe's presence makes her feel slightly better. Although built on the same lines as Ruth and her mother, Zoe looks very attractive to Ruth. She's wearing a green dress and low-heeled brown boots and manages to look smart without being overdressed. Her brown hair, which was in a bun last time, is now loose around her shoulders. Maybe it's not, after all, the law that you must have a neat bob after the age of fifty.

When Jacquie has told them who is Slimmer of the Week and exhorted them to keep a food diary, they are free to go. Zoe comes over to Ruth.

'Great to see you here,' she says.

'It's my first time,' says Ruth, feeling rather foolish.

'I've been coming to this group for a few months,' says Zoe. 'I belonged to a different group before.'

'I've never tried anything like this before,' says Ruth.

'Oh, I've done them all,' says Zoe. 'Weight Watchers, Slimming World, Lean Zone. I'm a yo-yo dieter.' She grins as if this is a wonderful thing to be.

'I've just got to get weighed,' she continues. 'Have you got time for a coffee afterwards?'

Ruth had watched in alarm as the women lined up before Jacquie's talk to stand on the scales and have the results recorded in their 'Lean Journal'. But Zoe makes this sound like it's not an ordeal at all.

'I'd love to have a coffee,' says Ruth.

But what she really wants is a large slice of cake.

8

There's only one café in the village. It's rather bizarrely designed to look like an American diner, with bench seats and a lot of chrome and neon, but it's still open at five o'clock, which makes it a mecca for Ruth and Zoe. They sit opposite each other in a booth and drink strangely frothy cappuccino.

'It's not horrible,' says Zoe, 'but it doesn't taste like coffee.'

'It is slightly horrible,' says Ruth.

'Cappuccino is two points in Lean Zone,' says Zoe.

'Do you have to write down drinks too?' asks Ruth.

'You have to write down everything,' says Zoe. 'Didn't Jacquie do her thing about "if you drink it, ink it"?'

'I think I stopped listening after a while,' says Ruth.

'She does the same spiel every week,' says Zoe, 'but she's not a bad consultant. I've had a few that were terrible. And some of the other women are nice.'

'Are they always all women?'

'Not always. In my last group there was a man who used to come. Most people ignored him though. Poor chap.'

'Why do you keep coming?' asks Ruth, before she can help herself. 'I mean, you look terrific.'

'Thank you,' says Zoe. 'But it's how you feel inside, isn't it? I've been fat and I've been thin and there's no doubt in my mind that people are nicer to you when you're thin.'

Is this true? Ruth has always felt that she was too big, in the eyes of society anyway. Would people have treated her differently if she'd been as slim as, say, Shona, her glamorous friend and fellow lecturer? Ruth remembers how Kelly had talked of Alison's weight loss, almost with awe.

'That's depressing, if so,' she says.

'Isn't it?' says Zoe cheerfully. 'Anyway, I'd like to be thinner.'

'So would I,' says Ruth, 'but I've never wanted it enough to stop eating.'

'Why did you decide to come today?' asks Zoe. She's spooning out the last of her froth. Ruth has given up on hers.

'I don't know,' says Ruth. 'I went to a school reunion at the weekend and one of my old schoolfriends had lost lots of weight.'

'And you thought she looked good?'

'No,' says Ruth. 'Actually, I thought she looked better before.'

They both laugh so loudly that the café owner, who is stacking chairs in a passive-aggressive manner, looks over in alarm.

'I've never been to a school reunion,' says Zoe. 'Though I liked it when I was there.'

'It was rather surreal,' says Ruth. 'I met my old sixth-form boyfriend. He's now a successful businessman with two wives and no hair.'

'I married my sixth-form boyfriend,' says Zoe. 'Sounds like you had a lucky escape.'

'Did you really?' says Ruth. She remembers Zoe telling her that she was divorced.

'Yes. I was mad about him. Patrick was a couple of years older than me and one of the really cool boys at school. Football team and all that. Long blond hair like a pop star. You know the sort of thing. We got married when I was twenty and he was twenty-two. Our parents thought we were mad and we were, really. But we stayed together for ten years. I trained as a nurse and he did his apprenticeship to be an electrician. He's very successful now too. Not bald but completely white-haired. Still long though, like an aging rock star. We've stayed on good terms. I sometimes think, if we'd had children, we'd still be together.'

Ruth doesn't want to ask why Zoe doesn't have children. She says, 'I've never been married and I've never lived with Kate's father. He's married to someone else. It's complicated. Or perhaps it isn't.'

She stops, wondering if she's said too much. She doesn't usually tell almost-strangers about Kate's parentage. But somehow Zoe doesn't seem like a stranger.

'Kate's lovely,' says Zoe. 'I'm looking forward to getting to know her.'

'Me too,' says Ruth. 'I mean we both are. Looking forward to getting to know you, I mean.' She realises that she's rambling, also that it's five thirty and she needs to leave to collect Kate.

Ruth tries to pay for the coffees but Zoe won't let her. The café owner seems relieved to see them go.

It's dark by the time Ruth and Kate get home but, as Ruth approaches the cottages, the security light comes on and she sees a familiar battered Mercedes outside her gate. How long has Nelson had that car? Ever since she's known him, which is over twelve years now.

'Dad!' shouts Kate in delight.

'So it is,' says Ruth. Her own emotions are rather more complicated. She hasn't seen much of Nelson since he was injured last year. In the emotional aftermath of that day, both had revealed rather too much of their true feelings for each other. Now Ruth thinks that Nelson is worried that she expects him to leave Michelle for her. But she doesn't; she never expects that to happen. Besides, Nelson's mother visited him for Christmas and was sure to have been preaching the virtues of Christian marriage.

Kate rushes over to the car and is soon dragging Nelson towards the house. Ruth follows more slowly. From the window she can see Flint regarding Nelson with disapproval.

'I saw the woman next door,' says Nelson. 'She said you'd be home soon. I didn't know you had a new neighbour.'

'She only moved in on Sunday. Why didn't you ring to say you were coming?'

'I tried to,' says Nelson, 'but your phone was switched off. At the university they said you'd left early.'

Guiltily, Ruth realises that she switched her phone off during Jacquie's homily. And she did not leave work early. She arrived at eight and left at four. She wonders who said she did? Her PA, Prisha, is far too discreet.

'I was at a Lean Zone meeting,' she says. Why be embarrassed about it, she tells herself.

'A what?'

'A meeting about losing weight.'

Nelson looks positively appalled. 'Why would you want to lose weight?'

Ruth has no answer to this. She lets Nelson into the house and makes tea while Kate describes the Year 6 trip in exhaustive detail.

'Where is this activity centre?' asks Nelson. 'Have the school done health and safety checks?'

'I'm sure they have,' says Ruth. It's a good thing that Nelson is so annoying sometimes. It stops her fantasising about them living together.

'What about coronavirus?' Nelson asks Kate. 'Have the school been telling you about hand sanitiser?'

'I never thought I'd hear you talking about hand sanitiser,' says Ruth.

'Yes,' says Kate. 'They tell us to sing "God Save the Queen" while we're washing our hands.'

'What if you're a republican?' asks Ruth.

'I don't suppose many eleven-year-olds are republicans,' says Nelson.

'That's what's wrong with this country,' says Ruth, only half joking.

Kate decides that Nelson needs to see every piece of artwork she has produced in school this term and goes to collect them. Ruth takes advantage of her absence to ask Nelson why he has been ringing her at work. And why he's driven all the way out to the Saltmarsh to see her.

'I wanted to know about the body in Tombland,' says Nelson. 'Dead bodies are my business, after all.'

'This one has been dead a long time. I think it's medieval. I've sent samples for carbon-14 testing.'

'Was it a plague victim?'

'That's what everyone asks. It's possible but it may just be a body that was buried at St George's. The graveyard probably stretched all the way to the roundabout.'

'How was your weekend in London?'

'OK,' says Ruth. 'I went to a school reunion. I saw my ex-boyfriend. He's completely bald.'

Nelson laughs but Ruth notices that, unconsciously, he raises a hand to his hair which, while greying, is still thick. Kate reappears and Nelson settles down to admire paintings, pottery owls and pieces of slightly grubby cross-stitch.

'Do you want to stay for supper?' asks Ruth. 'It's just pasta. Or something.'

'Thanks, but I'd better get back for Bruno. The dog-walker brings him home at six. Michelle's away.'

In that case, thinks Ruth, there's nothing to stop Nelson coming back later. He could even bring Bruno with him (sorry, Flint). She wonders if Nelson is thinking the same thing. But neither of them says anything and, after admiring Kate's art extravagantly, Nelson gets up to leave.

Cathbad has also cooked pasta although, in his case, it comes adorned with courgette spirals and broccoli florets. The children eat quickly, they are used to their father's culinary prowess, but Judy savours each mouthful. She finds cooking very tedious and she knows that preparing meals every day would soon drive her to distraction. But Cathbad actually seems to enjoy it. Thing is leaning against Judy's legs, looking up at her lovingly, although he's not much of a broccoli fan. It's dark outside but there are signs that spring is returning; a bunch of daffodils on the table, a school newsletter trumpeting about Easter bonnet competitions.

When Michael and Miranda have drifted away, Cathbad pours Judy a glass of wine and asks about her day.

'It was OK. I had to tell the boss that I thought his potential murder was probably still a suicide. And Ruth excavated a skeleton in Tombland.'

'Really? A medieval skeleton?'

'I think so. I just saw the report. I'm pretty sure Nelson will follow it up.'

'I'm certain he will,' says Cathbad.

There's a short silence while they both think about Nelson and the reasons why he will be interested in this particular archaeological discovery.

'It's a very haunted place, Tombland,' says Cathbad. 'Very spiritual but also very troubled.'

'I know about the Grey Lady,' says Judy. 'And the ghost that haunts the Maid's Head. Is that grey too? The Grey Maid?'

'I had a friend who worked at the Maid's Head,' says Cathbad. 'And he says the Maid is a friendly presence. There's a former mayor who's more troublesome. The Grey Lady is a sad spirit though. I saw her once.'

Judy isn't surprised by this sort of thing any more.

'When was that?'

'It was when I was first in Norfolk. I took a shortcut through Tombland Alley on my way back from the pub. It was autumn and there were leaves on the ground. A woman in a long, grey dress was walking in front of me. I assumed she was in fancy dress – it was near Hallowe'en – but then she turned and seemed to go through a door. When I got to the place, there was no door there, just a brick wall. Then I realised that her long skirt hadn't made any noise as she walked through the fallen leaves.'

The detail in this story makes it unexpectedly chilling: the pub, the leaves, the door that wasn't there. Judy says, 'Maybe there was another door that you didn't see.'

'Maybe,' says Cathbad equably. 'But there isn't always a rational explanation, you know.'

Judy secretly disagrees. 'Didn't the Grey Lady live in a house that was boarded up because of the plague?' she says. 'That's a horrible story. Thank God things like that don't happen any more.'

But Cathbad doesn't answer this. He changes the subject

and starts to talk about Thing. After a few minutes' dog chat, they clear the table and go to join the children.

Nelson can hear Bruno barking as soon as he turns into the cul-de-sac. The wretched animal has been on his own for barely more than an hour. He hopes the neighbours won't start to complain.

Bruno gives him a hero's welcome, whining ecstatically and running upstairs to find a suitable gift. He comes back with one of Michelle's bras. Nelson thanks him and extracts the garment, which he hangs on the banister. Then he goes in search of food.

Michelle went to Blackpool two days after George's fourth birthday on February the fifteenth. She left Nelson with enough ready meals to last two weeks. As he extracts a chilli con carne from the freezer, he thinks of Samantha Wilson putting her Weight Watchers' meal in the microwave. What was she thinking when she pierced the plastic wrapping? 'Ensure food is piping hot before eating.' Piping hot. A curiously old-fashioned phrase, like something Nelson's mother might say. Why didn't Samantha eat her hot food? Why did she go upstairs, lie down on her bed and take an overdose of sleeping pills?

Nelson thinks of Ruth inviting him to supper. 'Pasta. Or something.' He doesn't get the impression that Ruth is much of a cook. Has he ever eaten a meal prepared by her? He doesn't think so. What would he have done if Ruth had invited him, not just to eat, but to stay the night? There's nothing stopping him. Except Bruno, who is still looking at him expectantly. Nelson lets the dog out into the garden, which will satisfy him for a few minutes. He could have taken Bruno to Ruth's. That grumpy cat would get used to him eventually. But it still doesn't seem right. Not until he has had *that* conversation. Is it the thought of the complications ahead that is making him feel uneasy tonight? No, he thinks it's something else. Something connected to his conversation with Ruth. Nelson broods, watching the container revolving under the electronic spotlight.

It's a few minutes before he realises that his phone is buzzing. Michelle.

'Hallo, love,' says Nelson. 'Is everything OK?'

'Why do you always think something's wrong? We're all fine. We took George for a donkey ride on the sands today.'

Katie had loved the donkeys in Blackpool, thinks Nelson. But, of course, he can't say this.

Michelle talks about George for a while and then says, 'Harry? Are you worried about coronavirus?'

'Not really,' says Nelson, wondering if this is true. 'It's just the flu, after all.'

'I'm a bit worried about Mum.'

'Why?' Michelle's mum is young and active in her early seventies. She's the perfect grandmother. And mother-in-law. Nelson's mother, Maureen, seems like she comes from a different generation.

'She's diabetic,' says Michelle. 'Remember?'

Nelson had forgotten.

'They say people with diabetes might be at risk. And people over seventy.'

'Try not to worry, love. I'm sure she'll be fine.'

Michelle sounds comforted though she must know that Nelson doesn't know the first thing about this mysterious virus. She puts George on the phone to say goodnight. He wants to talk to Bruno but the dog is still in the garden, so Nelson has to improvise whining and panting sounds. He thinks that George is convinced.

After supper, Ruth sits down with her Lean Journal.

'Tuesday 25th February,' she writes. 'Breakfast: two slices toast and marmite. Cup tea. 11am: Cappuccino. Blueberry muffin. Lunch: Hummus and roasted vegetable wrap. Apple. Supper . . .'

She sighs and thinks of Kelly saying Alison must have lost five stone. Of Zoe saying, 'It's how you feel inside.' Of Nelson's face when he asked, 'Why would you want to lose weight?'

And she tears the page into tiny pieces. Then she puts the journal in the bin.

9

When Nelson gets into work the next morning – later than usual because he has had to wait for the dog walker to collect Bruno – he knows that the team have something to tell him. Tony Zhang looks exactly like Bruno when he's discovered something to deposit at Nelson's feet.

'There's been another one,' says Tony, as Nelson makes his way through the open-plan area.

'Another what?' says Nelson. He wants to get into his office and have his first coffee of the day. He still can't get used to not seeing Cloughie at his desk, demolishing a McDonald's breakfast. But Clough is a DI now and has his own team in Cambridgeshire. Rumour has it that he's even given up junk food. The team also still feels the loss of Tim, who died five years ago. For Nelson, thoughts of Tim resurrect so many different emotions that he tries to keep them suppressed.

'Another suicide that looks slightly suspicious,' says Judy, giving Tony a quelling look. 'I'll tell you at the briefing.'

'You do that,' says Nelson. Leah brings him a coffee and

he drinks it while deleting most of his emails. Then he summons the team in.

'Avril Flowers,' says Judy, 'aged sixty. Found dead yesterday in her bungalow near Hunstanton, probably from an overdose. She was in her bedroom, which was locked.' She looks at Tony, daring him to give away the punchline. 'From the outside.'

'From the outside?' says Nelson. 'She was locked in?'

'That's what it looks like,' says Judy. 'Her body was found by her cleaner at midday yesterday. The pathologist thought she'd probably been dead for twenty-four hours. Case was passed to the Serious Crimes Unit this morning.'

'We should interview the cleaning lady,' says Nelson.

'Who says the cleaner is a woman?' says Judy.

'But is she?'

'Yes.'

Nelson breathes deeply. 'Did this Avril Flowers have any family?'

'A daughter,' says Judy. 'She lives in Scotland but she's coming down today.'

'We should talk to her too,' says Nelson. 'I'll send SOCO in now. The scene will have been contaminated by the emergency services but they might find something. With any luck they'll have finished by the time the daughter gets there. Did you find anything about cold cases from Intel?'

'I spoke to Liz Forbes, the information analyst, ' says Judy, 'and she's been going through suicides recorded in the last six months. I think there are three that we might look into.'

She opens her laptop and props it on Nelson's desk. Her screensaver, Nelson notes, is her crazy-looking bull terrier.

Karen Head, aged 48. King's Lynn. Cause of death: overdose.

Rosanna Leigh, aged 55. Snettisham. Cause of death: hanging.

Celia Dunne, aged 59. Terrington St Clement. Cause of death: suspected overdose.

'I've chosen these three,' says Judy, 'because the deceased were all of a similar age and from the King's Lynn area. Information is quite sketchy, but it appears that all three had jobs and families. Therefore, suicide might be seen as unexpected.'

'Hanging's very different from taking an overdose though,' says Tanya, peering to look at the screen.

'That's true,' says Judy, with just a touch of impatience. 'But the other factors are there. Age, location, date of death. It's about triangulation.'

'Good work, Judy,' says Nelson. 'Tony, you can look into these. Talk to the families but be sensitive. These are recent tragedies. They'll still be grieving. Judy and Tanya, you take the Avril Flowers case. Find out about the locked room. There may be an innocent explanation, but I can't think of one right now.'

The team file out. Judy closes her laptop and seems to have something to say.

'Yes?' says Nelson, not very helpfully.

'I was just wondering,' says Judy. 'Is Leah OK?'

'I think so. Why?'

'She seems a bit quiet, that's all.'

'She's not one for chatting,' says Nelson. But, as he says this, he remembers Leah talking to him about Samantha Wilson. *You never know when people are desperate, do you?* He resolves to pay more attention to his PA.

Ruth is in the café attached to Norwich Cathedral. It feels like skiving on a work day but, she tells herself, she has just visited the site where the body was found on Monday and she is talking to Janet Meadows about local history, something that might be seen as valid outreach work. True, she and Janet have also discussed children, pets and coronavirus but now Janet is asking about the Tombland skeleton.

'I haven't got the results back from the lab,' says Ruth, 'but I think it's a woman. Probably medieval. The graveyard of St George's would have covered that area.'

'I had a student of yours in yesterday asking about it,' says Janet.

'Really?' says Ruth. 'Which student?'

'I can't remember his name,' says Janet, 'but he had one of those Victorian beards. A Lytton Strachey beard.'

Ruth remembers the student asking her about the plague. Victorian is a very good description. She pictures an intense face, dark eyes above facial hair like a mask.

'I wonder why he didn't ask me,' she says.

'He said his personal tutor was David Brown,' says Janet, as if this explains everything.

'David said that you and he had been having some discussions,' says Ruth.

Janet laughs. 'That's one word for it. He doesn't agree with my ideas for the exhibition.'

Ruth now knows that Janet is planning an exhibition entitled *Norwich: the plague years*. Janet launches into a description now, leaving Ruth to concentrate on her lunch. They are in the modern refectory attached to the ancient cathedral. Ruth remembers the first time she met Janet, in this same café, when she had been on the trail of a long-dead archbishop. Janet had shown her the cleric's statue, hidden in one of the mysterious alcoves of the church, and they had become friends. Ruth feels instinctively on Janet's side against David.

Janet talks about the plague while Ruth eats falafels and salad. In defiance of Lean Zone, she has also bought a chocolate brownie.

'There was an outbreak of the plague in Norwich in the thirteen hundreds. It's thought that Julian of Norwich contracted it and that her near-death experience is what inspired the *Revelations of Divine Love*. An eighteenth-century historian called Francis Blomefield said that fifty-seven thousand people died in Norwich in 1349. That figure seems far too high. There were only about twenty-five thousand people living here then but some sources say that, by the end of 1349, only six thousand people remained. Some will have escaped to the country, of course. There was another outbreak in 1578 when Elizabeth the First visited with her entourage. This time there were officially 4,800 victims but the real figure could have been twice that.'

'A royal visit to remember,' says Ruth. She thinks: so much for singing 'God Save the Queen.'

'Your friend David Brown thinks we're making too much of the plague,' says Janet.

'Well, he can't deny it happened,' says Ruth. She wonders if she can remind Janet that David is not her friend but her employee.

'Can't he?' says Janet darkly. She takes a bite of her sandwich.

Ruth doesn't know why she should defend David but, in fairness, feels she has to say, 'I think David was just worried by the mention of plague pits because none have been found in Tombland.'

'Where are all the bodies then?' asks Janet.

'It's possible that they were all just buried in local churchyards,' says Ruth. 'You can see how high they are around here, St John Maddermarket, for example. They may have been raised to accommodate the extra dead. David makes a good point about Tombland being too busy, too full of people. The Maid's Head was already a hotel in 1349. It seems unlikely that anyone would bury plague victims here. And, you know, even the so-called plague pits they discovered on the Crossrail dig in London were actually rather orderly. Nothing like the mass graves in Bosnia.' She stops. She doesn't often talk about the time when, as a graduate student, she had helped to unearth the remains of men, women and children, hundreds of them, thrown together into a ghastly human soup, but she knows she mentioned it quite recently. Oh yes, it was when she was talking to her students on Monday, excavating the skeleton beneath the roadworks. She remembers carrying the bones back to

Ted's van in the gathering twilight, Janet appearing out of the gloom.

'Tell me about the Grey Lady,' she says. 'She seems to have come up a lot in conversation recently.'

Janet laughs. 'She's not very popular with David either. I think he thinks I'm obsessed with her. But it's such a strange and awful story.' She pauses. Ruth finishes her last falafel and thinks about her next course.

'She haunts Augustine Steward's House,' says Janet. 'You know, that crooked, timbered building opposite the cathedral? Next to Tombland Alley? I'll show you on our way out. Well, in the sixteenth-century plague, the one supposedly caused by Elizabeth's entourage, the house was boarded up. That's what they did in those days. Sealed the house with the occupants still inside. They'd draw a cross on the door and sometimes the words "Lord have mercy" and they'd leave the household to die. I suppose it was a way of containing the outbreak. When they opened the house again, they found the bodies of a man, a woman and a young girl.'

'How sad,' says Ruth. It seems rather callous to eat her brownie now.

'Very sad,' says Janet. 'But that's not the worst thing. The man and the woman had teeth marks on their bodies. Human teeth marks. It was thought that they'd died first and the girl had kept herself alive by eating their flesh. Maybe she died by choking on it rather than of the plague.'

'Oh my God.' Ruth pushes her plate even further away.

'The daughter is the Grey Lady,' says Janet. 'She's often seen in the alley, walking through walls, opening doors that aren't there. Sometimes you just see the light of her candle reflected in the window panes. She's a sad spirit. Maybe she's exiled from heaven because she consumed her parents' flesh.'

'That seems very unfair,' says Ruth.

'There's nothing fair about this life or the next,' says Janet. She's another lapsed Catholic, Ruth remembers. Like Nelson. And Cathbad too, come to think of it.

'There have been lots of sightings of the Grey Lady,' Janet continues. 'Even by a former vicar of St George's.'

'Have you ever seen her?' asks Ruth.

'I've often sensed something,' says Janet. 'A shadow, a presence, sometimes just a feeling of intense sadness. The tourist information centre is in Steward's House, you know. People don't like to work there after dark.'

Ruth is not surprised. She doesn't like to hear this story in the daylight, in a brightly lit café, with a school party jostling in through the doors, carrying activity books and Disney lunch boxes.

'Cathbad's seen her,' says Janet, with a slight smile.

That doesn't surprise Ruth either.

Avril Flowers lived in a neat bungalow on the edge of Hunstanton. Tanya immediately awards it a score out of ten. She and Petra are house hunting.

'Seven,' she says as Judy parks by the gate. It's usually the junior officer who drives but Tanya's car is in for a service. Judy never minds driving though. Tanya is always surprised by how much of a petrol head she is.

'So high?' says Judy.

'Two points for the garden,' says Tanya, 'and I like the veranda.'

The house has a wrap-around porch that reminds Tanya of American films. There are plants in pots and one of those swing seats. The garden is well kept with a large pond and a willow tree. It looks like a place where someone once enjoyed spending time. The scene-of-crime team have finished, and the only sign of their presence is some plastic sheeting leading to the front door.

Avril's daughter Bethany is meeting them at the house. There's a smart hatchback on the drive which looks to Tanya as if it's owned by someone called Bethany.

The door is opened by a blonde woman who is probably in her mid-thirties. She introduces herself as Bethany McGarrigle. She shows them into a sitting room that has a distant view, thanks to the elevated site, of the sea.

'What a lovely house,' says Tanya. She wonders if she can ask how much it costs.

'Mum loved it,' says Bethany, her eyes filling with tears. 'I wanted her to come back to Scotland to be near me, but she said she had her life here. She worked at the library and volunteered at the school, listening to children read. And she was really involved with the local church.'

'How did your mum seem when you spoke to her last?' asks Judy. Tanya notes that she's swapped 'mother' for 'mum', the sort of detail Tanya always forgets.

'She seemed fine,' says Bethany. 'I spoke to her on Sunday.

That was our ritual. We'd chat when Mum got back from church.'

'And her health was good? No worries?'

'Her health was better than mine,' says Bethany. 'Sixty's young these days and Mum took care of herself.'

'I'm sorry,' says Judy. 'I know this must be a terrible shock for you, but can you bear to tell me what happened when you got the call about your mum?'

Bethany takes a few deep breaths but, when she speaks, her voice is quite controlled. 'Tina, the cleaning lady, called me at midday yesterday. She'd arrived to clean at her usual time. At first she thought Mum wasn't in but that wasn't unusual. Like I say, she was a busy lady. Tina had her own key and she started work as normal. But, when she went to Mum's bedroom, it was locked.'

'From the outside?' says Tanya.

'Yes. The key was still in the lock. Tina opened the door and she . . . she found Mum, lying on the bed. Dead. There was a bottle of pills beside her. Tina called an ambulance, but she said she knew that Mum was already dead.'

'I'm so sorry,' says Judy.

'It was just such a shock,' says Bethany, taking more deep breaths. 'I never thought . . . Mum was the last person to . . .'

'You mentioned a bottle of pills,' says Judy. 'Was your mother on any medication?'

'Not that I know of,' says Bethany. 'She didn't believe in that sort of thing. She was always so well.' She covers her face with her hands. Judy asks if she can get Bethany a glass of water. Bethany shakes her head.

'Can we have a quick look round the house?' says Tanya. 'While you . . . compose yourself.'

'The police have sealed off the bedroom,' says Bethany, dabbing her eyes hard.

'We'll just get a sense of the place,' says Tanya. Judy gives her a look but Bethany says that's fine.

It's a small house, just kitchen, sitting room, two bedrooms and a bathroom. The bigger bedroom, where Avril was found, has police tape across the door but they can see a double bed and mirrored wardrobes. This window, too, has a view of the sea, framed by blue velvet curtains. The small bedroom obviously doubles as an office and contains a computer and printer as well as a sewing machine which looks well-used and an exercise bike which doesn't, as though the wrapping had just been removed. The bathroom has navy blue tiles and a walk-in shower. Everything looks very neat and clean. Clearly Tina the cleaner does a good job. Tanya is tempted to stand on the high-tech scales to check that she is still at the perfect BMI. She says as much to Judy but is greeted by a blank look. The kitchen is galley style, with white units and the same navy tiles. There are pots of herbs on the window sill and magnets on the fridge. A calendar shows the Beauties of Norfolk with many appointments scribbled in for February. Again, it feels like a place where someone has been busy and happy.

Bethany doesn't have much more to tell them. She has no idea how the bedroom came to be locked from the outside. She doesn't know if anyone else, apart from Tina, had a key to the house but she thinks it's unlikely. They take Tina's address and the names of Avril's closest friends, her next-door neighbour, Jean, and Maggie from the church.

'There was also a man called Hugh that she used to see at the library,' says Bethany. 'I'm sorry, I don't have an address for him.'

'We'll ask at the library,' says Judy. 'Thank you. We'll leave you in peace now, but we'll stay in touch, keep you updated on any developments. And, if you need anything, don't hesitate to call me. You've got my card.'

'Thank you,' says Bethany. 'You've been very kind.'

They decide to call on Jean first. The house next door is bigger than Avril's but, Tanya notes, it doesn't have the veranda.

'I can't believe it,' says Jean. 'Avril, of all people.'

'Were you close?' asks Judy.

'As close as neighbours can be,' says Jean, gesturing towards the garden wall as demonstrating the physical distance between the houses. In fact, by Tanya's standards, the houses are quite far apart, set within large gardens. It's not like the suburban street where Tanya grew up, where she could lean out of the window of her semi-detached house and pass notes to her friend Rachel – in retrospect, her first crush.

'How long did you know Avril?' asks Judy.

'Ever since she moved here,' says Jean. 'It must be five years ago now. I've been here almost thirty years. I knew the previous couple well too. This is a friendly area.' Jean is probably older than Avril, thinks Tanya, but what her mother would call 'well preserved', with tanned skin and short white hair.

'How did Avril seem when you last saw her?' asks Tanya.

'Fine,' says Jean. 'We talked about the weather. You know, like you do.'

It doesn't sound to Tanya as if the two women had a very close friendship. She asks if Jean saw anything unusual yesterday morning.

'Unusual?' says Jean, bridling slightly. 'What do you mean, unusual?'

'Just anything out of the ordinary,' says Judy, with a quick glance at Tanya. 'Any callers. Anything unexpected.'

'I just saw the cleaning lady going in at about eleven,' says Jean. 'But I don't spend all day looking out of my window. The first thing I knew was when the ambulance arrived. I went next door then to see if I could help but Tina said that Avril had . . . well, passed.'

'Passed' is Tanya's least favourite euphemism for death. It seems far too casual somehow.

'Do you know Tina Prentice, the cleaner?' asks Tanya.

'Everyone knows Tina,' said Jean. 'She was devoted to Avril.'

10

Tina Prentice is certainly very upset about Avril's death. She tells Judy and Tanya this whilst preparing lunch for two children, who look about two or three, feeding a white fluffy dog and making coffee.

'I have the grandkids on Wednesday and Friday,' she explains. 'And my daughter's dog. I clean on Tuesdays and Thursdays. On Mondays I work in a care home. Oh, and I take in ironing.' She gestures at a pile of neatly folded clothing on the kitchen table. Tina lives about ten minutes' walk from Avril's bungalow in a semi-detached that Tanya at once categorises as 'ex-council'. It's very comfortable, though, with a cheerful yellow kitchen and wooden floors. Tanya can see chickens in the garden. She gives the place a solid six.

'When do you have a rest?' asks Tanya.

She means it seriously, but Tina laughs and says, 'I'll relax when I'm dead. I have Saturdays off. On Sundays I usually do a roast for the family.'

'How long have you worked for Avril?' asks Judy, sitting

at the table. The children, a boy and a girl, in their booster seats, eye them solemnly. Tina moves the clothes and puts sandwiches and fruit in front of them. Tanya feels her stomach rumbling and hopes Tina hasn't heard.

'Like a sandwich?' asks Tina.

'No thanks. We're fine,' she says. She'll have to get Judy to stop off on their way back to the station. Tanya is very keen on eating regularly. It's the best way of burning calories.

'I've worked for Avril since she moved here from Scotland about five years ago,' says Tina. 'She and her husband, Tony. Such a lovely man. They wanted to retire on the Norfolk coast but Tony died only a year after they moved here. Cancer.'

'That must have been tough for Avril,' says Judy.

'Very tough,' says Tina, now preparing chicken feed. 'But she got on with things. That was the sort of woman she was. She got involved in the community.'

'Could you tell us what happened yesterday?' says Judy. 'Sorry, I know this must be hard.'

Tina shoots a glance at the children, but they are still busy with their lunch.

'I went round to Avril's at eleven as usual,' she says. 'I remember it was a lovely day and there was a heron by Avril's pool. I took a picture of it. Avril and Tony loved birdwatching. It was one of the reasons they moved here. Avril wasn't in but that wasn't unusual. She worked part-time at the library and did lots with the church. I cleaned the kitchen and hoovered the sitting room but when I went to Avril's bedroom it was locked.' She looks again at the grandchildren. 'Do you two want to feed the chickens?' she says. She helps them down and sends them into the garden with a pail. Then she turns back to Judy and Tanya.

'The key was in the lock,' she says. 'All the rooms have keys but I was surprised to find it locked. I opened the door and Avril was there on her bed. I went over to her and took her pulse. I work in a care home so I know first aid, but I could see it was too late. I rang an ambulance though, just in case. Even tried CPR. But, like I say, it was too late. Her body was cold.'

Tina sounds sad but her voice is quite steady. She's seen death before, thinks Tanya.

'Can you think of any reason why the door might have been locked?' asks Judy.

'No,' says Tina, now sounding troubled. 'At first I didn't think anything of it. I was just concentrating on Avril but later, when the policeman called, the one in uniform, I started to think about it. I even wondered if I'd imagined it, but the door was definitely locked. I remember turning the key.'

'And there's no way Avril could have done it from the inside?' asks Tanya.

'I don't think so,' says Tina. 'And why would she do that?'

So she couldn't change her mind, thinks Tanya. She is starting to think that lovely community-minded Avril, who didn't believe in medication, knew exactly what she was doing when she lay down on her bed in front of the mirrored wardrobes. She wonders if Judy has come to the same conclusion.

Judy doesn't give anything away but, after a few more questions, Tina says, 'Excuse me,' and rushes into the garden where her grandchildren have begun pelting each other with chickenfeed.

Time to go. Judy calls out her thanks and they leave.

When Ruth gets back to the university, she finds someone waiting outside her door. This is unusual these days when most students prefer to email their requests for essay extensions and complaints about the curriculum. Ruth composes her face into a welcoming smile although she was looking forward to a few minutes' peace before her meeting on 'Pandemic Precautions'.

'Hi,' she says. 'Were you waiting for me?'

Her visitor is a girl. A young woman, Ruth corrects herself. But the figure in front of her really doesn't look much older than Kate and has the same long, dark hair. It predisposes Ruth in her favour.

'Yes,' says the girl. 'I hope you don't mind. I'm Eileen. Eileen Gribbon. I was at the excavation on Monday. I just wanted to ask you about it.'

This must mean that she's one of the first years. Ruth unlocks her office and ushers Eileen inside. Within a few minutes she has learnt that her visitor is from Guildford, she went to Spain on her gap year and that she loves hip-hop and modern dance.

'But my family were originally from Norfolk,' she says. 'Gribbon is an old Norfolk name.'

In Ruth's experience, people either live in Norfolk for

ever or get out as soon as they can. She asks why Eileen chose to study archaeology.

'I think it was watching *Time Team* with my dad when I was a little girl,' says Eileen.

Ruth has lost count of the number of students delivered to her by Tony Robinson and *Time Team*.

'It was a great programme,' she says. 'Though things happen a bit more slowly on real digs.'

'That's what I wanted to talk to you about,' says Eileen. 'People are saying that there's going to be a dig in Tombland, and I wondered if I could be part of it.'

Ruth sighs. 'I'm not planning a dig,' she says. 'Tombland's a popular tourist destination. I'd never get funding.'

'Aren't you looking for a plague pit?' says Eileen, sounding disappointed.

'There's no evidence for a plague pit,' says Ruth, thinking of her conversation with Janet. 'The skeleton I excavated on Monday was probably originally buried at St George's.'

'I've been thinking about that,' says Eileen. 'If the skeleton was buried away from the other graves, do you think it was someone who committed suicide?'

Ruth looks at Eileen's open, youthful face. What gave her that idea? she wonders. It's actually not a bad theory. Suicides used to be buried on so-called unhallowed ground, outside the church walls. She's not sure of the theological reason. To prevent them posthumously infecting other, less desperate, souls?

'It's an interesting thought,' she says. 'We'll do some more research into our skeleton when I have the carbon-14 and isotope results back. Isotope analysis will tell us where she grew up. I think it's a woman, by the way.'

'A woman?' says Eileen.

'Yes, from the pelvic bones I think the skeleton is female. Also, from the shape of the skull. I've sent off for DNA testing but I'm not hopeful given the age of the bones. I'll send you the isotope results though, if you're interested.'

Eileen looks pleased by this and Ruth manages to bring the conversation to an end. She's almost late for her meeting. At the door she thinks to ask Eileen the name of her bearded classmate.

'Oh, that's Joe McMahon,' says Eileen. 'He was the one who told me about the plague pits.'

Ruth does not know why this information makes her feel uneasy.

Judy and Tanya drive straight to a chip shop. Tanya will do an extra circuit of the gym tonight to compensate. Eating the comforting carbs in the fug of the car, Tanya says, 'Tina Prentice seemed more of a friend to Avril than her next-door neighbour was.'

'You don't always know your neighbours well,' says Judy. 'I hardly ever talk to mine, though Cathbad does, of course. I'd be hard put to tell you their names.'

'My neighbour keeps referring to Petra as my flatmate,' says Tanya. 'However many times I say "wife" she still does it. Mind you, "wife" is a terrible word.'

'It really is,' says Judy. 'It's one reason why Cathbad and I haven't got married. I was a wife once. Never again.'

'Do you think Avril Flowers killed herself?' says Tanya, licking salt off her fingers. Forbidden foods really are delicious.

'I don't know,' says Judy. 'Suicide does sometimes seem to come out of the blue like that. I've been reading up on it. But there are some similarities that bother me. Avril went to church. Like Samantha Wilson. She worked in a library. Like Samantha Wilson.'

'Lots of old people go to church,' says Tanya. 'And to the library.'

'If there's a pandemic, churches and libraries will shut,' says Judy. 'What will old people do then?'

'There won't be a pandemic,' says Tanya. 'It's just the flu. People should take vitamin C tablets and stop complaining.'

11

Ruth collects Kate from Sandra, the childminder who has looked after her since she was a baby, and drives home. Kate is chattering about the Year 6 trip ('We've got to choose who we want in our cabin. Four people have chosen me already. I'll need new leggings') but Ruth is worrying. The worries keep pace with the car as they cross the Saltmarsh, rather as the clouds chase across the flat marshland, turning the grass indigo blue and purple. Ruth's meeting on Pandemic Precautions was far from reassuring, partly because the universities have had no guidance from the government. Should they provide lessons online? But how would that work, in practice? Would all the students be confined to their rooms, only communicating electronically? That's not the university experience that Ruth wants for them. And what about staff, already worried about vulnerable family members and their own health?

'Look, Mum. There's that lady,' says Kate.

Zoe is standing in her garden, leaning on a rake. There's no barrier between the two front gardens and Ruth's is full of bindweed and startlingly tall yellow ragwort. The third house in the row is owned by Sammy and Ed, known to Ruth as 'the weekenders', who use it as a holiday home, though they've been visiting less regularly since their children grew up. They have concreted over the space at the front of their house, which they need because everyone in the family seems to own a monster jeep. The weekenders have also built an extension and landscaped the back garden. Ruth always feels that their cottage now looks embarrassed to be joined to hers. She thinks back to her mother's photograph. The gardens had been neat and uniform then, behind their box hedge. She really must do some research into the history of the houses.

'Doing some gardening?' asks Ruth, as they get out of their car. It's an inane question really but she's still a little shy with Zoe. They had bonded over Lean Zone but Ruth hasn't told Zoe that she won't be going to any more meetings.

'I'm just trying to clear some weeds,' says Zoe. 'It would be nice to have some old-fashioned cottage plants here.'

Ruth has a vision – she thinks it's from a long-forgotten Rupert the Bear annual – of hollyhocks and rambling roses. Oh, yes there's a bear in a pinafore coming out of the door.

'I'll help,' she says. 'I'm afraid I've let my garden get into a state.'

'Mum never gardens,' says Kate disloyally.

'I'm a London girl,' says Ruth. 'I don't really know what to do.'

'I can help,' says Zoe. 'My mum was a keen gardener.'

'Are your parents still alive?' asks Ruth, noting the past tense.

'No,' says Zoe. For a moment she rakes away at the brambles. 'They both died some time ago. Within a few weeks of each other. What about you?'

'My mother died five years ago,' says Ruth. 'We didn't always get on, but I'm surprised how much I miss her now. She was such a constant in my life.'

'What about your dad?' says Zoe.

'He still lives in London,' says Ruth. 'He's married again.'

Kate wanders inside in search of Flint. Zoe asks if Ruth will be going to Lean Zone next week and Ruth manages to say that she didn't think it was quite her thing.

'No problem,' says Zoe. 'I don't know why I keep going really.'

Ruth and Zoe chat for a few more minutes and Ruth goes indoors to start supper. When she looks out of the window, distracted by the six thirty Radio 4 comedy, she sees that Zoe has stopped gardening and is staring back at the houses. Her expression is hard to read.

Tanya and Judy get back to the station at three. Nelson asks them if they've been eating chips.

'Can you smell them?' says Judy.

'It's the vinegar,' says Nelson. 'I can smell it a mile off. Reminds me of Blackpool.' He says it longingly. 'Find out anything interesting?'

'Everyone seems shocked and surprised about Avril,' says Judy. 'Doesn't mean it's not suicide though.'

'Team meeting in half an hour,' says Nelson. 'Young Tony's going to talk us through the cold cases.'

Tanya wonders how long it will be before Tony stops being officially 'young'.

Tony looks slightly nervous, thinks Tanya, but he speaks well. She notices that he has made notes on his phone and she approves. She's had enough of Judy's iconic notebook and Nelson's aversion to technology.

'Karen Head was a teacher, divorced with one child. I spoke to two of her colleagues at the school who said that she didn't seem depressed. They'd been out for a staff party the night before she died. Karen's ten-year-old daughter was staying with her father. He found Karen's body when he brought her home. Cause of death recorded as paracetamol overdose.' Tony scrolls down with a practised thumb, hardly pausing for breath. 'I spoke to Rosanna Leigh's mother. Rosanna was a retired midwife. Apparently, she had suffered from depression in the past. She'd come off antidepressants because she was worried about the side effects.'

One of the side effects was suicide, thinks Tanya. But she doesn't say this aloud.

'Celia Dunne lived on her own. Sounds as if she was a bit of a recluse. I haven't been able to talk to anyone who knew her. It was some days before her body was found, hence the uncertainty over cause of death.'

Nobody says anything about this because they can all visualise the scene.

'Well done, Tony,' said Nelson. 'I'd say that Karen Head, at least, fits the pattern.'

'Maybe Rosanna and Celia as well,' says Judy. 'Rosanna took antidepressants. That doesn't necessarily mean she was suicidal.'

'Hanging yourself does though,' says Tanya, realising, too late, that this sounds rather callous.

'What about Avril Flowers?' says Nelson. 'What did you learn about her?'

'Both her daughter and her cleaner thought that suicide was completely out of character,' says Judy. 'Avril sounded active and happy. Very involved in her local community. There were a couple of interesting connections to Samantha Wilson too. Both worked at a library, both were church-goers.'

'Neither of those things is exactly suspicious,' says Nelson. Tanya is tempted to disagree. She thinks churches and libraries are both rather creepy.

'What about the locked room?' says Nelson. 'Any theories about that?'

Tanya decides it's time she spoke. 'The cleaner, Tina Prentice, said that the door was locked from the outside,' she says, 'though she did say that, afterwards, she wondered if she'd been mistaken. It was one of those old-fashioned keys. It's possible Avril could have manipulated it from the inside.'

'We'll see what SOCO have to say,' says Nelson. 'At the least they'll be able to tell us if anyone other than Avril and the cleaner touched the door. We should talk to the libraries and the churches. See if the women had any acquaintances in common. Judy, you're in charge but keep it low key. The other cases might well be suicide, but Avril Flowers is different. If the room was locked from the outside that points to homicide.'

'It's a locked room mystery,' says Tony. 'Like in the books.'

'Nothing,' says Nelson, 'is like it is in the books.'

———

12

The post-mortem results show that that Avril Flowers, like Samantha Wilson, died from 'respiratory failure due to chemical overdose'. The scene-of-crime report comes in the next day. The most interesting finding, as far as the team is concerned, is the presence of a third set of fingerprints – besides Avril's and Tina's – on the handle and key of Avril's bedroom door.

'So someone did lock her in,' says Tony. He seems fascinated by the case. Judy is finding it rather trying although she tells herself that being keen is not a crime. She was the keen youngster herself once.

'There was no sign of a struggle,' says Judy, scrolling through the report on her laptop. 'Avril was lying peacefully on her bed.'

'It's a bungalow,' says Tanya. 'Avril could have locked the door and climbed in through the window. It would have been easy with the veranda running all the way round the house.'

Tanya really is obsessed with that veranda, thinks Judy.

'Why would she do that?' she says. 'If Avril was going to commit suicide, why bother to make it look suspicious? And who did the third set of prints belong to?'

'They don't belong to anyone on our database,' says Nelson. 'That's all we know. We need to talk to more of Avril's friends and acquaintances. Judy, did you say she worked part time in the local library?'

'Yes,' says Judy. 'I've got an appointment to see the librarian this morning. Avril was a regular churchgoer too. I'm seeing the vicar this afternoon.'

'Good work,' says Nelson. 'Take young Tony with you as he seems to like locked room mysteries so much. Tanya, can you organise some door-to-door? Someone might have seen a stranger hanging around. It's a nice area. There might even be CCTV.'

'The average house price is £275,000,' says Tanya.

Hunstanton Library is a low, modern building in a residential area. It's nothing like the solid Carnegie-built library in King's Lynn that Judy remembers from her school days. It looks more like a doctor's surgery or a primary school.

'I used to love visiting the library when I was a kid,' says Tony. 'My mum took us after school on a Thursday. I remember, when you were ten, you got a green library card which meant you could get six books instead of just three. It seemed the most exciting thing ever.'

Tony always keeps up a steady flow of chat, unless specifically requested to shut up. It's like wading in his stream of consciousness. Judy knows that Tony was brought up in

London and came to Norfolk to attend university. His parents are first-generation Chinese immigrants and he has a brother, Mike, who's a junior doctor. Tony once told her that he had a sister who died of meningitis as a child, but Lily rarely features in the reminiscences.

'My parents weren't big readers,' says Judy. 'I can't remember them ever taking us to the library. I went with the school though.'

'My parents read in Chinese,' says Tony. 'We used to go to Charing Cross Library on Saturday mornings because they had a big Chinese books collection. Sometimes we'd go to the cinema afterwards.'

'Sounds great,' says Judy as she parks in front of the library. 'Remember to let the interviewee get a word in edgeways, won't you.'

Tony lapses into silence but is soon chatting to the librarian, Emma, about green library cards and Charing Cross.

'I worked for Westminster Libraries for while,' says Emma. 'A funny little place in Mayfair. Interesting readers though.'

Emma is originally from Scotland.

'It was a bond I had with Avril,' she says. 'We were both from near Edinburgh. I just can't believe she's gone.'

'Avril's death must have been a shock to you,' says Judy. They are in the children's section because the library isn't open yet. It feels odd, talking about death whilst sitting on squashy cubes surrounded by primary-coloured book covers: *Elmer the Patchwork Elephant, Spot, Dear Zoo, Happy Birthday, Tiger Twins.*

'It was a terrible shock,' says Emma, the words bringing out her Scots accent. 'Avril always seemed so cheerful. I looked forward to her days.'

'How many days did she work in the library?' asks Judy.

'Just two days a week. Usually Mondays and Thursdays. She was a volunteer. We're relying on them more and more these days. There aren't enough trained librarians to go round.'

'What do the volunteers do?' asks Judy.

'All sorts,' says Emma. 'Sometimes they deliver books to housebound readers or help with children's activities. Avril did general administrative work – putting protective covers on books, that sort of thing – but she also helped out with IT support. She was proud of being a silver surfer.'

'How did she seem when you last saw her?' says Judy. 'Did she seem anxious or depressed?'

'Not at all,' says Emma. 'I saw her on Monday. She seemed her usual self.'

According to the post-mortem, Avril died sometime on Monday night or early on Tuesday morning. She was found by Tina the next morning. In a locked room.

'Can you remember what you talked about?' asks Tony. Obviously aimless chat is one of his specialist subjects.

'We were laughing about something we saw on TV,' says Emma. 'I can't remember what.' She looks from Tony to Judy. 'Is it true? That she committed suicide? That's what people are saying but I just can't believe it.'

'We're still investigating,' said Judy. 'I'm sorry. I know it must be distressing. Did Avril ever mention anyone or anything troubling her? Anyone hanging around the house, for example?'

'No,' says Emma, wide-eyed. 'Avril got on with everyone.'

'Is there anyone that we should be talking to? Her daughter mentioned someone called Hugh that Avril used to meet here?'

'Oh, Hugh Baxter. He's another volunteer. A lovely man. Very interested in local history and all that. I think he's a bit sweet on Avril. He'll be devastated when he hears.'

'Do you have an address for Hugh?' asks Judy.

Lovely man or not, he's going on their list.

Hugh Baxter lives nearby so Judy and Tony leave the car and walk. It's midmorning and the streets are very quiet. Tony stops to talk to a cat sunning itself on a wall but otherwise there is not a living creature to be seen. Is everyone staying inside because of the threat of coronavirus, thinks Judy, or is Hunstanton always like this?

Hugh's house is an end-of-terrace cottage. The brickwork looks slightly shabby but the garden is immaculate. A bird-bath stands in a perfect circle of lawn and early daffodils are pushing their way up through the soil.

'My uncle Wang Lei loves gardening . . .' Tony begins but Judy silences him with a look. The door is opened by a white-bearded man in the sort of clothes Judy's grandfather wears for relaxing: shirt, tie, cardigan, neatly pressed trousers and slippers.

Judy had thought she would have to break the news about Avril. This is something she has been trained to do but it's never pleasant. However, it's clear that Hugh already knows. When Judy says why they have come, he rubs his eyes.

'Poor Avril. Such a tragedy.'

Bad news travels fast, thinks Judy.

'I'm so sorry,' she says. 'Do you feel up to answering a few questions?'

Hugh ushers them into a small sitting room smelling strongly of furniture polish. 'The cleaner's just been,' he says. 'That's why everything is so tidy.'

'Who does your cleaning?' asks Judy. Though she thinks she can guess.

'Tina Prentice,' says Hugh. 'She's wonderful.'

'Was it Tina who told you about Avril?'

'Yes. She rang yesterday. She knew Avril and I were close.'

'How long have you known Avril?' asks Judy.

'About three years,' says Hugh, picking imaginary fluff from the arm of the sofa. 'When she started working at the library. We had a lot in common. She'd just been widowed. I lost my wife, Doris, ten years ago. We were both interested in gardening and local history.'

'Your garden is lovely,' says Tony.

'Thank you,' says Hugh. 'It's a great comfort. I like watching the birds too.'

Judy gives Tony a look to warn him not to start talking about Uncle Wang Lei.

'We're talking to everyone who knew Avril,' says Judy. 'Trying to get an idea of her state of mind. When did you last see her?'

'I think it must have been on Monday morning,' says Hugh, 'after the library. We went for a walk on the beach.'

'And how did she seem?'

'Her usual self,' says Hugh. 'Avril was always cheerful, always put a brave face on things. Look.' He fetches a framed photograph from the mantelpiece. It shows Hugh and Avril laughing on a pier. Cromer, Judy thinks. Avril is wearing a blue and white striped dress. Hugh is debonair in a panama hat.

'She thought that dress made her look fat,' says Hugh. 'But I loved it. She looks bonny.'

He uses the Scottish word unselfconsciously. Emma was right; Hugh was sweet on Avril.

'Isotope analysis,' says Ruth, 'is a particularly useful tool for archaeologists. Many different materials, such as bone, hair or organic residues, can serve as substrates for isotopic analysis. Teeth are particularly important. Can anyone tell me why?'

She looks at the earnest faces of her students. On the screen behind her is a photograph of the Tombland skeleton, still lying in the middle of the Norwich roundabout, measuring rod beside it. She has decided to use this case as a way of teaching stable isotope analysis to the first years. After all, they were there when the body was discovered, that should make the information more relevant. Also, David is always moaning that the course doesn't have enough on the latest forensic techniques.

It's the bearded student, Joe McMahon, who answers. 'Because once we get our adult teeth, they're there for life.'

'Exactly,' says Ruth. 'Bones renew themselves, teeth don't. Isotope analysis of teeth gives us a good idea of where a person lived. In this case, our skeleton seems to have had a diet that was high in meat and dairy, which suggests that she was a fairly high-status individual.'

Eileen Gribbon puts up her hand. 'Does that mean that she was buried in the churchyard and not in a plague pit?'

Ruth sighs inwardly. She blames herself for first mentioning the P word but some of her students really seemed obsessed. She answers, patiently. 'The location of the body, and the way it's laid out, does suggest a formal burial. We also found some fibres which could indicate the presence of a linen shroud. Wrapping the body in cloth would also limit the movement of the bones as the cadaver decomposed, which could account for the skeleton's well-preserved appearance.'

The deceased. The cadaver. The skeleton. As always, Ruth feels the inadequacy of words for the dead. But at least they know the sex. She clicks onto her next slide.

'We've been able to extract DNA from the bones,' she says. 'Until quite recently, DNA extracted from skeletal remains often turned out to be from the parasites that fed on the soft flesh.' She looks at her students to check for signs of squeamishness, but they are all listening intently. 'But then it was discovered that the petrous portion of the temporal bone,' she points, 'is the best place to take samples for DNA testing. We did this with our skeleton and, as I suspected from the pelvic bones, she is female. What's more, we think that she had dark hair and blue eyes.'

The students gasp. Ruth smiles; she, too, can never get over the fact that DNA can yield such intimate secrets. At the end of the session, she suggests that they give their subject a name.

'Ruth,' says someone.

'Martha,' says Joe, with such emphasis that all the other students immediately agree with him. So the Tombland skeleton is now named Martha, the sister of Lazarus, who rose from the dead. It's quite fitting, thinks Ruth.

The vicar calls herself Mother Wendy. When she invites them to use this form of address, Tony has a sudden choking fit.

'It's the dust,' says Judy, slapping him – hard – on the back. But the church isn't particularly dusty. Maybe Tina cleans here too? St Andrew's is a handsome building, with a square tower and Gothic windows. Like a lot of Norfolk churches, it looks rather too grand for its surroundings. Wendy says that, these days, it's only full for weddings and funerals. Will Avril Flowers be buried here? Judy assumes so.

'We have our regulars, of course,' says Wendy. 'Some people come to the Eucharist every day.'

'Was Avril one of your regulars?' asks Judy. They are sitting at the back of the church by a display showing the repairs needed for the tower. Judging by the graphs, the work will be completed some time in the next century.

'Yes, she was,' says Wendy. 'She was very devout in her quiet way.'

'Did she ever seem worried about anything?' asks Judy.

'Of course she was worried,' says Wendy. 'That's what the church is here for. For worried people. That's why we'll always be here.'

'Was she worried about anything in particular?' asks Judy.

'I can't really say,' says the vicar.

Is this because she doesn't know, wonders Judy, or because of the seal of the confessional? Do Protestants even go to confession?

'Avril seemed like a very nice lady,' says Tony. Judy sees that his guileless charm is the right tack to take. Mother Wendy visibly relaxes.

'She was. She was the sort who always kept busy. Doing the flowers, helping with the cleaning rota, collecting for charity.'

'My mum's the same,' says Tony. 'Always doing things for other people. I think she forgets to look after herself sometimes.'

Is this too heavy-handed? No, Wendy is smiling mistily at Tony. 'That's just it. Sometimes we forget to love ourselves.'

'Is that what Avril was like?' says Judy. 'A bit hard on herself?' She remembers Hugh saying that Avril 'put a brave face on things'.

'A bit,' says Wendy. 'She came from the Scottish Presbyterian tradition, of course. It's all very Calvinistic and strict. Unlike us lot in the C of E.' She laughs, sending a pigeon flying from the rafters.

'Did Avril ever have suicidal thoughts?' asks Judy.

'She never mentioned suicide to me,' says Mother Wendy, serious again. 'But that doesn't mean that she didn't think about it.'

'Do you know if Avril ever attended the service for the Outcast Dead in Norwich?' asks Judy.

Wendy looks surprised. 'Yes. There's a group of us from the church who go every year. Such a lovely idea. To remember all those poor plague victims.'

'Avril's daughter mentioned a friend called Maggie,' says Judy. 'She said she was another churchgoer. Do you know who she meant?'

'Poor Maggie,' says Mother Wendy. 'It was such a shock when she went.'

It turns out that where Maggie 'went' was to the afterlife. To heaven, if that's the way your mind works. She died suddenly of a heart attack in January. 'I think Avril was very upset about it,' said Mother Wendy. 'We all were.'

'How old was Maggie?' asked Judy.

'Seventy but that's no age these days,' said Wendy, 'and she was as fit as a fiddle, always exercising. Not a couch potato like me.'

'Do you think that Maggie's death might be suspicious?' asks Tony as they drive back to the station.

'I think we ought to investigate a little,' says Judy, 'but the coroner obviously didn't see any cause for an inquest.'

'Maybe losing Maggie is what pushed Avril over the edge.'

It's rather a violent image, thinks Judy. She sees a figure

teetering on a precipice. A shadowy figure appears behind them and sends them tumbling to their death. She suddenly thinks of Samantha Wilson and the demise of her cat, Trudy. According to her daughter, Saffron, Samantha had been 'devastated'. Could these two bereavements have been triggers for suicide? Thinking of Samantha reminds Judy of something else.

'Samantha Wilson went to the service for the Outcast Dead,' she says. 'Like Avril Flowers.'

'What does that mean though,' says Tony, 'other than they were both religious?'

'Suicides could be considered outcast dead,' says Judy. 'Their graves used to be unmarked, outside consecrated ground. It could show that Avril and Samantha were already thinking that way.'

'Mother Wendy talked about plague victims,' says Tony. 'That made me think about coronavirus.'

Judy gives her colleague a sharp look. It's unlike Tony to be so melodramatic but, then again, his family are originally from China where, it seems, the virus originated. He might know more than she does.

'It's hardly the bubonic plague,' she says.

'I expect that's what they thought about the bubonic plague once,' says Tony.

The rest of the drive passes in silence.

13

————

Monday, 23 March

Ruth can't believe how quickly things have changed in the past four weeks. One minute she was lecturing, excavating skeletons, having coffee in fake American diners, the next she is driving home with her car full of files and dividing her sitting room into part-office, part-schoolroom. On 19 March, Prime Minister Boris Johnson said that he was confident that coronavirus could be 'sent packing' in twelve weeks. On the evening of 23 March, Ruth sits with Kate on the sofa and watches Johnson saying that the country is going into lockdown. 'Stay at home, protect the NHS, save lives.' Ruth thinks the prime minister sounds slightly more coherent than normal, although his hair could still do with a good brush.

In a way, his words come as a relief. The last few days have been a nightmare of planning and cancellations. Staff started to panic. Some claimed pre-existing medical conditions and refused to do any face-to-face teaching. Others were clearly so nervous that they were unable to teach at all. When it became clear that virtual learning was the way forward, Ruth tried to put training in place. Over the last few weeks she has observed her colleagues' online lectures and has had to tell David to remove an empty bottle of wine and Fiona to discourage her cat from sitting on her shoulder. Students have enough to distract them as it is.

The students became increasingly twitchy, probably receiving constant messages from concerned parents. Ruth has gone from reassuring her students, promising them social distancing and good hand hygiene, to sending them home. Now she'll have to deal with demands for fee rebates and requests for webcams and extra screens. Kate's school is closed. There are over 2,600 cases of coronavirus in the UK and more than a hundred people have died. At least, thinks Ruth, putting her arm round Kate and holding her close, she now has only one priority: to keep herself and Kate alive. From the armchair, Flint watches her intently.

She's not too surprised, as soon as the broadcast ends, to see her phone vibrating with the word Nelson.

'Hi, Nelson.'

'Did you watch Boris's announcement?' Why do we all call him Boris? thinks Ruth. He's not our mate. Other prime ministers were referred to by their surnames. She grew up with Thatcher and briefly rejoiced with Blair. It now looks as if she's entering the plague years with Boris.

'Yes,' she says.

'You can't go outside, you know. Except once a day for exercise.'

'Nelson, I said I watched it. I know.'

'You can go to the shops for food. But you should wear a mask.'

'A mask?' For a moment Ruth has a vision of herself wearing one of those Venetian carnival masks that only cover your eyes and yet, in classical plays and operas, render you completely unrecognisable.

'Jo's telling us all to wear masks covering our nose and mouth. It's not official advice yet but they've been doing it in other countries.'

'Where do I find a mask?'

'I'll send you some.'

'What's this going to mean for you and the team?'

'I'm not sure yet,' says Nelson. 'The police might have to provide back-up for the other emergency services. My team will go on with their work, but it'll be difficult with everyone in lockdown. We've got a rather sensitive investigation going on at the moment, lots of interviews and softly-softly stuff. It's going to be hard if we can't get within two metres of anyone.'

Ruth knows that Nelson finds the softly-softly stuff hard at the best of times. His preference is always for action and it looks as if the next few weeks (months? years?) are going to be low on action.

'If you need anything,' Nelson is saying, 'just call me. I'm on my own at home. I can come round any time. Even if I have to stay two metres away.'

There are many thoughts in Ruth's mind. Why is Nelson

on his own? Is Michelle still in Blackpool? Why? How far away is two metres anyway?

'Mum,' says Kate, who is trying to interest Flint in one of his cat toys. 'Is that Dad? Can I talk to him?'

Ruth hands the phone over.

'My school is closed,' says Kate. 'Mum's going to teach me at home.' A pause. 'I suppose so,' says Kate dubiously. Is Nelson saying that Ruth will be a good teacher? She knows she should be, in theory, but teaching maths and literacy to an eleven-year-old is very different from teaching archaeology to eighteen-year-olds. And Ruth will have to do both at the same time. She prays that schools will open again soon. Apart from anything else, it breaks her heart to think of Kate missing out on all the end-of-Year-6 celebrations.

After Nelson has rung off, Ruth calls her dad. He sounds a bit bemused but says that the church is organising food deliveries for older people. 'Gloria's helping out although Ambrose says she's one of the older people herself.' Ambrose is Gloria's eldest son. Ruth gives thanks for Gloria and her extended family and, for the first time in her adult life, she gives thanks for the church too.

Opening her emails Ruth sees that her brother Simon has forwarded something saying that coronavirus is a hoax. There are also three messages from David Brown. Ruth does not feel able to cope with them right now. She goes into the kitchen to make supper and stares at the contents of her cupboards. Four tins of tomatoes, three sorts of pasta, rice, baked beans and some ancient packets of cereal. That won't get her far in the face of the apocalypse. She needs to go shopping, probably wearing a mask. Can she take Kate with her? What's more dangerous, the supermarket or being home alone? Ruth has no idea and she can feel panic rising. Flint wanders in looking expectant. He only has three sachets of his gourmet cat food left. That settles it. Ruth and Kate can make do, Flint definitely can't. She will have to go shopping tomorrow.

Ruth puts on a pan of water for pasta and pours herself a glass of wine. Only half a bottle left. On the back of Kate's latest school newsletter Ruth starts a list.

Cat food
Wine

Priorities.

Later, when Kate is in bed, Ruth pours herself a second glass and goes out into the back garden. The dark seems very comforting. Everything is the same here as it always is. She can hear the wind in the apple tree and, from the marshes, a night bird calls. Her security light comes on, illuminating grey grass and the spectral tree. Flint or a fox?

'Ruth?'

Ruth jumps. The voice is so close, almost as if her own thoughts are speaking to her. Then she sees Zoe standing by her back door, also with a glass of wine in her hand.

'Great minds,' says Zoe.

'Yes,' says Ruth. 'It's all rather scary, isn't it?'

'I'm actually quite relieved that we're in lockdown at last,' says Zoe. 'Most of the doctors at the surgery think we should have done it weeks ago.'

'Will you still be going in to work?' asks Ruth.

'Yes,' says Zoe. 'We're hoping to do a lot of telephone consultations, but we've got pregnant patients, patients with cancer, people with chronic conditions. They'll still need to see doctors and nurses. Thank goodness we've got PPE. There's a real shortage, you know.'

'PPE?' says Ruth. Isn't that something politicians study at Oxbridge?

'Personal Protective Equipment,' says Zoe. 'Respirators, face masks, aprons, gloves, that sort of thing. We buy directly from the suppliers but there's so much demand at the moment. The government are talking about ordering centrally but it's already too late for that.'

It's beginning to dawn on Ruth that everything is happening too late. Her worries about wine and cat food start to seem embarrassingly insignificant.

'I'm only in work three days a week though,' says Zoe, 'so, if you need anything, just call me.'

She uses almost the same words as Nelson but, unlike Nelson, Zoe is actually here, on the other side of the garden fence.

'That's very kind,' says Ruth. 'I need to go shopping tomorrow. Can I get you anything?'

'I'm OK,' says Zoe. 'I did a big shop last week. Are you taking Kate with you?'

'I don't think so. All the advice says to shop alone.'

'I'm home tomorrow,' says Zoe. 'I'll keep an ear out for her. Just text me when you're going. What's your number? I'll send you mine.'

'Thank you,' says Ruth. 'If you're around, I'd feel happier.'

'I'll be here,' says Zoe.

14

Nelson's drive to work feels very strange, almost surreal, as if in a dream world where everything is the same yet subtly different. Nelson often dreams about driving and usually it involves not being able to get to where he wants to be, hampered by road-blocks and traffic jams and Norfolk drivers in Nissan Micras. But, today, the roads are almost completely empty. Nelson finds himself gliding through junctions where, normally, he'd be grinding his teeth and accusing other drivers of being followers of Onan. When he has to stop at a red light, it seems almost like a bizarre ritual. There are no commuters, no children jostling for school buses, no taxis, no old men in hats driving in the centre of the road. It should feel like heaven but, as Nelson drives through the old city gates, he's reminded of science fiction films where towns have been taken over by lizard people or filled with replicants. If this is the future, he doesn't like it.

His day had started with a call from the dog walker, Maura. Was she still allowed to work for him? Was she a key worker? Nelson hastily assured Maura that she was but he thought he might have to make alternative arrangements for Bruno. He has no idea how busy he'll be and maybe he shouldn't be encouraging Maura to come to the house. The thought of being locked down without Bruno makes him feel even more depressed as he climbs the stairs to his office.

Even here, everything has changed. The cleaners have been hard at work and the clump of desks in the open-plan area has been wrenched apart and the furniture placed at strategic intervals, reminding Nelson of a game that he'd played as a child with his sisters where you have to get across the room without stepping on the floor. There are arrows indicating the way that you should walk to the loos and kitchen. Judy is standing in the middle of the room. She's wearing a black mask which looks shockingly wrong, as if she's been gagged.

'Hi, boss,' she says. Her voice is, at least, unchanged.

'Should we be wearing masks?' Nelson has a pack in his office. He must remember to send some to Ruth.

'Cathbad says it's a good idea to wear one inside,' says Judy, 'so I thought I'd get used to it. It's very strange. I keep thinking that I can't see or hear with it on.'

'Is Cathbad in charge of Covid regulations now?'

'Well, he is a scientist,' says Judy. Her tone is defensive but it's strangely hard to tell with the mask on.

He *was* a scientist, thinks Nelson. Now he's a freelance druid. But he doesn't say this aloud.

'Team meeting when everyone gets in,' he says.

'Jo says we should only have Zoom meetings from now on.'

'What the hell's *zoom*?'

'Didn't you read her email?'

Nelson lets his silence answer this.

'It's a video conferencing platform,' says Judy. 'A bit like FaceTime on your phone.'

Nelson's grown-up daughters like to use FaceTime. Nelson prefers a phone call. He rang both girls last night. Rebecca, living in Brighton with her boyfriend Asif, sounded quite upbeat about lockdown. They would both work from home and go for long walks by the sea. They might even get a dog. Laura, a primary school teacher living in King's Lynn, was more nervous. She wasn't sure how she could teach eight-year-olds online. She wasn't sure how she'd get on with her flatmates when they were all in the house all day. It's going to be one of the hardest things, thinks Nelson, being so close to Laura and not being able to see her. It'll be hard for Michelle too, he knows. She'll feel torn between her mother and her daughters. Even so, says a little voice in Nelson's head, it's strange for Michelle to have stayed away so long. She could have come home before lockdown was announced. Now she's trapped in Blackpool.

'We'll have a proper meeting in the open plan area,' says Nelson. 'I'll even wear a mask.'

Cathbad and his children are doing yoga in the garden. Miranda, aged seven, spends most of her time trying to stand on her head. Michael, aged ten, takes it more seriously. He dislikes games at school but is actually well-coordinated with a good sense of balance. Maddie, Cathbad's grown-up daughter, has unexpectedly joined them and she is like a poster for yogic prowess, standing on one leg in tree pose, her golden hair shining in the weak sun. The rescue hens, Darcy, Shirley and Motsi, watch her admiringly. The children chose the names although Cathbad still secretly thinks of the chicken sisters as Alecto, Tisiphone and Megaera, after the Eumenides, or Furies, the Greek goddesses of vengeance.

Cathbad has a pretty shrewd idea why Maddie has materialised this morning, but he says nothing until he has finished the session, raising his thumbs to his third eye and lowering them to his heart. Michael copies him. Miranda has wandered off to find Thing, who is excluded from yoga because he finds downward facing dog unbearably exciting. Maddie whispers a reverent 'namaste'.

'We're going to start every day with yoga,' Cathbad tells Maddie, as they walk back to the house. 'I'm trying to make home-schooling a real adventure. We'll tell a continuing story and illustrate it with things that we find on the beach or on our nature walks. The school have sent some work sheets but I don't think we'll bother with them. Michael and Miranda can learn science, history and geography from the world around them.'

'I can help,' says Maddie. 'I'm good at telling stories.'

'Have you come to stay then?' says Cathbad, measuring coffee carefully into his Italian espresso machine. The children have already got out the flapjacks. Thing is hoovering up crumbs.

'If that's OK with you and Judy.'

'You'll have to ask Judy but I'm sure it will be. We'd love to have you.' Cathbad feels an atavistic satisfaction at the thought of having all his children with him during lock-down. With the hens and the vegetable patch they'll be almost self-sufficient. There's no need for any of them to venture into the terrifying world of coronavirus. Except Judy, of course.

'I think I'll go mad if I stay at the flat with no outside space,' says Maddie. 'The lease is up next month and Jody's going to move back home too.' Maddie's flatmate Jody is a nurse. Cathbad thinks that she'll need all the creature comforts she can get in the weeks ahead.

'I expect I'll be furloughed,' says Maddie. 'But I can still do freelance work.'

'What's furloughed?' says Cathbad. The word has a baleful agricultural sound, a cross between furrow and plough.

'You keep your job, but on less pay,' says Maddie. 'I suppose it's better than nothing. But it'll leave me time to help with the home-schooling. We can start our own newspaper. The *Cathbad Chronicle*. The *Norfolk News*.'

'The *Weird Times*,' says Cathbad.

'These are weird times, all right,' says Maddie.

Nelson holds his meeting, in defiance of the new regulations. He does wear a mask though and is surprised how claustrophobic it makes him feel. You can breathe, he tells himself, it's all in your mind. He remembers Ruth telling him about a panic attack she once had whilst swimming.

'Suddenly I just forgot how to breathe.' He realises now that he never asked what Ruth had been panicking about.

It's a shock to see the team wearing masks too. Tony's, like Nelson's, is standard NHS issue but Tanya's is a rather jaunty tartan affair. 'Petra made it for me,' she says. 'Masks are going to be in short supply.' Nelson has already had a memo about shortages of PPE. It makes him feel slightly guilty about planning to send masks to Ruth.

He tells the team that the investigation into the death of Avril Flowers is still a priority. 'Just do as much on the phone as you can,' says Nelson. 'We'll keep looking into the other suicides too. We can't expect much back-up. Uniform might be required to help the emergency services.' He doesn't add that, according to Jo, one of the tasks that might fall to the police force is 'burying the dead'.

'What about civilian staff?' asks Leah. 'I've heard of people being furloughed.'

'Some will be furloughed,' says Nelson. 'But you're a key worker in my eyes.'

'Who else would work the printer for you?' says Leah.

Everyone laughs a lot at this, glad at the release of tension, but Nelson sees something else in his PA's face, something that makes him feel a little worried. He identifies it later: relief.

15

It's still dark when Ruth wakes up. The green numbers on her alarm clock say 6.05 a.m. Ruth resolutely closes her eyes but she knows there's something there, just on the edge of her consciousness, something waiting to pounce, zigzagging its way across her synapses. Ah, there it is. Pandemic. Lockdown. Virus. Death. Ruth sits bolt upright, reaching for the soothing tones of Radio 4. 'Health Secretary Matt Hancock announces that a temporary hospital called NHS Nightingale will open in London to cope with the rising tide of coronavirus cases . . .' Ruth switches off the radio. Her phone pings. 'GOV.UK CORONAVIRUS ALERT,' says the message, in stress-inducing capitals. 'New rules are now in force. You must stay at home . . .'

Ruth tries to breathe mindfully, the way Cathbad taught her. In for four, out for eight. Don't have a panic attack, she tells herself. You're quite safe as long as you never leave the house. But Ruth must go to the shops today to buy Flint's gourmet cat food. Strangely, the thought of doing something actually calms her. She gets up and puts on her dressing gown. She'll go downstairs and have a cup of tea. Then she'll start planning her day's teaching. She's getting to grips with the dreaded Zoom. At first, she treated it like a recorded lecture but now she's able to be more interactive and is even able to send the students into breakout rooms. Preferably for ever.

Ruth treads carefully across the landing. She doesn't want to wake Kate. She has a feeling that it's going to be very hard to occupy Kate all day, especially when Ruth has her own work to do. The worksheets the school has sent seem very dull and, besides, Kate will dash through them in minutes. Thank goodness for the Saltmarsh, miles of blessedly empty marshland full of educational possibilities. They can collect grasses and shells. They can search for Neolithic flint flakes. When the weather gets better, they can paddle or even swim. Surely this nightmare will be over by the summer? But, even as Ruth dreams of shell and grass collages, she imagines Kate refusing to go outside and rolling her eyes at the thought of Neolithic flakes. She must ask Cathbad for some advice. She's sure that he will have an imaginative curriculum worked out.

Flint is waiting for her in the kitchen, staring pointedly at his empty bowl. Ruth feeds him while she waits for the kettle to boil. Then she takes her tea into the sitting room. The sun is rising over the marshes, turning the distant sea to gold. The Saltmarsh is coming to life, like a photograph developing, the grasses turning from grey to brown to green, the birds ascending from the reedbeds to wheel across the rosy sky. Dawn. Ruth thinks of the picture she found in her parents' house, 'Dawn 1963'. Out on this very eastern edge of England, the sunrises are spectacular. Is that why Ruth's mother took that photo, all those years ago? The shoebox is still by the front door, where Ruth left it when she came back from London. So much has happened in the weeks since then. Ruth clears a space on her desk, which is overflowing with files and books from her office, and rifles through the school photos and adult baptisms until she finds the picture of the cottage. Flint jumps lightly onto the table and starts sniffing the box. Maybe he can just smell Eltham mice, but Ruth takes his interest to be a sign that this is a mystery worth pursuing.

The picture shows all three cottages. To take it the photographer must have been standing on the other side of the road, in the rough grass that segues into the marshes. Was it taken at sunrise? It's hard to tell because the colours have faded so much. There are no people present, just the three houses and a car. Ruth has no idea of the make. She could ask Nelson or Judy but she thinks they have enough on their plates on the moment. The houses are painted pink and there's a hedge in front of them. A tree in the garden of the right-hand house seems to be in blossom, which means the picture was taken in spring. The tree's not there now. The weekenders cut it down when they paved over the front garden.

Ruth moved into her house, 2 New Road, twenty-two years ago. She had been part of a dig that had discovered a Bronze Age henge buried in the nearby sands. The excavation turned out to have long-lasting and devastating consequences, one of which, for Ruth, was a passionate love of Norfolk. Ruth applied for a lecturing job at the University of North Norfolk and bought the cottage, which was then uninhabited. Who had owned it? She has the title deeds somewhere, but she remembers that the previous resident had been an elderly man who had died on the premises, probably in Ruth's bedroom with its view of the ever-changing marshes. She tries not to think of this fact too often. The house was then passed to his children who had been anxious to sell it as quickly as possible. Ruth got the place very cheaply and had loved it from the first. Even though she had first co-habited with her then-boy-friend, Peter, the cottage had seemed always and only hers, although nowadays Kate and Flint would probably claim joint ownership.

'What are you doing, Mum?'

Ruth jumps. Even Flint looks up guiltily. Kate is at the foot of the stairs in her Peppa Pig pyjamas, which are slightly too small for her. Her dark hair is standing up around her head. She looks very grumpy and very young.

'Looking at this picture,' says Ruth, showing Kate. She's interested in her reaction.

'That's our house,' says Kate. 'Why's it pink?'

'I think it was taken a long time ago,' says Ruth. 'Can you tell why?' It's never too early to start home-schooling.

'Because of the car,' says Kate, as if it's a stupid question. Which perhaps it is. 'And there's no satellite dish on Sammy and Ed's house.'

Ruth hadn't even noticed this. Kate likes the weekenders

who sometimes invite her in to watch their superior home entertainment.

'Let's have breakfast,' says Ruth, in her new jolly lockdown tones (lightly tinged with hysteria). 'Then maybe we can go for an early morning walk.'

'I hate walks,' says Kate. She and Flint look at Ruth with identically mutinous expressions.

At nine o'clock Ruth sets out for the supermarket. She leaves Kate watching a Harry Potter DVD. So much for the 'no screens before lunchtime' rule Ruth devised last night. But Kate finds the wizarding world very comforting and Ruth hopes it will make her forget that this is the first time she has ever been left alone in the house. At least Kate has Flint, sitting on the sofa watching Dumbledore narrowly, and Zoe next door. Ruth has texted Zoe and put her number in Kate's phone. 'NP,' Zoe texts back. 'Here if you or Kate need anything'. Ruth is halfway to Lynn before she realises that NP means 'no problem'.

At the supermarket she is momentarily distracted by the people standing, spaced at odd intervals, around the periphery of the car park. Then she realises that they are queuing. The shop is only allowing a few shoppers in at a time, so the rest are waiting patiently, resting their legs like weary horses, for their turn amongst the consumer durables. Ruth joins the line. She is wearing a scarf tied around her nose and mouth and feels rather ridiculous. Most people are not wearing masks although some have plastic gloves, which immediately makes Ruth think that the handle of her trolley is crawling with coronavirus germs. She must make sure that she doesn't touch her face before she has a chance to wash her hands whilst singing a suitably revolutionary song. Right on cue her nose starts to itch.

Once inside the shop Ruth catches the panic-buying bug and starts loading her trolley with cat food, toilet roll, wine and other things that suddenly seem essential. Calm down, she tells herself. Most items are in stock, although the pasta and rice aisle is almost empty. She can shop once a week and order things online. She can't stop herself adding two paperbacks and a jigsaw puzzle of Norwich Cathedral. It takes a long time to get through the checkout but Ruth finds herself feeling almost tearfully grateful to the smiling woman who scans her groceries. She's not wearing a mask which strikes Ruth as very remiss on the part of the supermarket.

'Thank you,' she says, as she pays an eye-watering sum of money on her debit card. 'It's so good of you to keep working.'

'I haven't got much choice,' says the woman. 'But thank you. It's nice to have some appreciation. People have been shouting at me all morning.'

Ruth drives home feeling grateful that she doesn't have to go out to work and despairing at the state of the world. Kate, deep in *The Prisoner of Azkaban*, hardly notices her return. Ruth goes to wash her hands (they already feel chapped and sore) and then starts to put away the shopping. It takes some time because there's so much of it but, eventually, most things are stowed away. Ruth gives Flint some of his new Kitty Treats, which he ignores, and makes herself coffee.

The film has ended so Ruth prints out a maths worksheet and gives it to Kate.

'I don't want to do maths,' says Kate. 'I want to read my book.'

'Oh, all right,' says Ruth. It's only eleven o'clock and already she's failing at home-schooling but she needs to get ready for her eleven thirty lecture.

She feels a rush of satisfaction when she manages to sign into Zoom and another when she sees the faces of her first years appearing. They pop onto the screen, some in kitchens and studies, some clearly still in bed. One youth looks like he's on a tropical island. 'You can get special backgrounds,' he explains in the comment box. Ruth has taken the trouble to angle her laptop so there's a studious backdrop of book-cases. Unfortunately, it makes her face look huge. She'll just have to try not to meet her own eyes. Two squares remain black. Does this mean those students haven't switched their videos on? It's curiously disconcerting.

At least Ruth knows now to tell the students to mute when they're not speaking. Her first Zoom session was a nightmare of competing voices, students appearing in startling close-up if they so much as coughed. They are getting better at listening too, though some are clearly on their phones at the same time.

Today's subject is Artefacts and Materials. Ruth projects pictures of pottery, ceramics and stone tools onto the shared screen and sends the students into breakout rooms to discuss them. Whoosh. It's like a particularly satisfying magic trick. In real life, even post-graduates make a huge fuss when asked to divide into groups. 'Can I be with Annie? I need the loo. Have I got time for a coffee?' Now, one click and they disappear. In the ten minutes' peace before she summons them back, Ruth checks the attendance list. Everyone is here. Who are the students who won't show their faces? Ruth checks the list again.

Eileen Gribbon and Joe McMahon.

16

Judy sits at her desk, feeling self-conscious in her mask. Should she take it off? Tony is sitting at least two metres away but he is still wearing his. Suddenly, Judy misses Clough who would have brought some normality to this abnormal situation simply by being himself, eating junk food and pretending to be an American gangster. On impulse she sends him a text, 'Strange times eh?' Two minutes later, Clough replies: 'Im bulk buying frankfurters. Its a wurst case scenario.' Judy sends back an eye-roll emoji but she does feel very slightly better.

Nelson said to carry on with the Avril Flowers investigation but that's going to be hard when everything is locked down. Judy looks at her notes. She has spoken to the people closest to Avril and is no nearer to understanding what happened that night in February. The vicar has said that Avril had been worried but seemed unable, or unwilling, to be more specific. Judy thinks of Mother Wendy saying, 'That's what the church is here for. For worried people. That's why we'll always be here.' What is Mother Wendy doing now?

Judy wonders. The churches are all closed. She was surprised how shocked she'd been to hear this news. Judy might be a lapsed Catholic, but she'd always assumed that, all her life, mass would be carrying on somewhere. Thinking of the silent churches, the unconsumed communion wafers, the empty chalices, makes her feel strangely panicky. What about her grandma, who goes to mass every day? But Judy's grandmother, an eighty-year-old diabetic, has been told to 'shield' and stay in her house. Judy doesn't know when she will see her again.

The last item in her notes is a reference to Maggie O'Flynn, Avril's friend who died in January. There didn't, on the face of it, seem anything suspicious about Maggie's death, which was apparently due to 'myocardial infarction'. But Maggie was another woman on her own, someone who went to church and did good works in the community. And now she is, unexpectedly, dead. It's still part of the pattern.

Judy decides that the best use of her first day in lockdown would be to follow up on one of Liz's suicide cold cases. She starts, as they always do these days, with Facebook. There are no results for Rosanna Leigh or Celia Dunne. Either their pages were closed when they died, or they are in the minority of people who are not on the social networking site. Even Judy has a profile, although she hasn't posted in five years. Cathbad doesn't have a personal page but he does have one for his yoga teaching. Miranda is already asking to join and lots of Michael's friends are already there, despite the age limit. Maddie has hundreds of Facebook and Instagram friends who all post identical pouting pictures of themselves. Clough posts pictures of his dog and his children. Tanya shares fitness tips. Almost the only people Judy knows who aren't on Facebook are Ruth and Nelson. Perhaps they have more in common than they realise.

Karen Head does have a page though. Her family have kept it open as a memorial to her. Judy supposes it's a new kind of immortality but it's still disconcerting to see Karen's smiling face looking out at her. Judy scrolls through the messages.

> Rest in peace angel.
> Sleep well Kaz sweetheart.
> Can't believe you are gone.
> We love you Miss Head.

This last reminds Judy that Karen was a teacher. She makes a note to talk to the school. Presumably, even if schools are closed, there is someone to take messages? Michael and Miranda's school is still open for the children of key workers, which presumably includes Judy. She's not going to suggest that they go to school, though, when she knows that they'll have a wonderful time being educated by Cathbad. As if prompted by an otherworldly power, her phone buzzes. Maddie.

'Hi, Judy. You busy?'

'Not really. It all feels very surreal.'

'I know. The streets are deserted. You could have a picnic in the middle of the A149.'

'Please don't.'

'I won't. I popped in to see Cathbad and he was doing yoga with the kids in the garden.'

Judy can imagine the scene. It makes her wish that she was at home and not in this weird socially distanced work-space.

'I was wondering,' says Maddie. 'Could I come and stay with you for a bit? Just while we're in lockdown. The lease is almost up on the flat.'

'Of course,' says Judy. 'Your room is waiting for you.'

'I can help Cathbad with the home-schooling.' Maddie always calls her father by his name, or rather by his alias.

'It would be good if you could remind him to do some,' says Judy.

Judy's hunch is correct. Karen's school, Gaywood Juniors, is still open and the headteacher himself answers the phone. 'Yes, we've got about fifty children here,' says Richard Parsons, 'some of them very vulnerable. It's been a nightmare making everything Covid-safe.'

'It's the same here at the police station,' says Judy. 'Though I suppose it must be harder making children stay two metres apart.'

'It's impossible,' says Richard. 'And it's difficult for teachers too. Some of them are shielding or looking after elderly parents. I'm having to live apart from my family because my youngest has asthma.'

They talk for several minutes before Judy can mention Karen. Richard's voice changes immediately. 'Poor Karen.

That was such a shock. She was a lovely woman and a great teacher.'

'You say it was a shock,' says Judy. 'Did you have any idea that she was depressed or having suicidal thoughts?'

'None at all,' says Richard. 'I knew she'd been hit hard by her divorce, but she seemed on good terms with her ex and was devoted to her daughter. Karen was always such a sunny presence around the school, organising get-togethers and what have you. She even got us to have a sponsored slim last year. I lost two stone. I've put it all on again since though.'

'Karen was at a staff get-together the night before she died, wasn't she?'

'Yes. We went out for a meal then on to a karaoke bar. Karen seemed on great form.'

Judy doesn't say that a karaoke bar would be her idea of hell. She asks who would have been the last person to see Karen that night.

'I think that was Sue Elver. They shared a taxi together.'

'Have you got a phone number for Sue?'

'I think so. She left the school after Karen died. Left the profession entirely. But I think I have a number somewhere in my phone. Yes. Here it is.'

Judy takes down the number, thanks Richard for his time and wishes him good luck with the rest of term.

'It's not so bad,' says Richard. 'I love teaching and it's good to be back in the classroom. It's not the same for everyone. I've already had parents on the phone begging me to take their children back.'

'My partner seems to be enjoying home-schooling,' says Judy.

'That won't last,' says Richard cheerfully. 'Bye now.'

Sue Elver also answers the phone quickly. 'I'm at home with my teenage children.' she says. 'Any diversion is welcome.'

'Must be tough for teenagers.'

'It is. My son was meant to be taking his GCSEs in the summer. Now they've been cancelled. It's all going to be based on teacher assessments. He's regretting now not having done any work for the past five years.'

Judy has already explained that she's investigating the death of Karen Head. Now she asks Sue about her friend.

'I still can't get over it,' says Sue. 'It was why I left teaching really. Just couldn't imagine school without Karen.'

'Tell me about her,' says Judy, knowing that this is the best way of asking this question.

'Karen was great fun,' says Sue. 'That's what I remember most. We laughed all the time. It's the only way to survive teaching really, finding things funny. But it was a nice school and Richard's a good head. I was happy there. Karen was happy.' She pauses.

'Was there anything that made her unhappy?' prompts Judy. 'Her divorce . . .'

'Her divorce was as amicable as these things can be,' says Sue. 'She still got on well with Chris and they were devoted to Maisy, their daughter.'

Chris had discovered Karen's body, Judy remembers. She must talk to him next.

'Can you think of anything that was worrying Karen in the weeks before her death?'

There's another pause. A more significant one this time.

'She was seeing someone,' says Sue. 'And she said I'd disapprove.'

'Did she say why?'

'No, but I got the impression there was an age difference. Something like that.'

'Did she say anything else about this person?'

'No,' says Sue. 'But I was a bit worried. I wish I'd asked more.'

But people don't always ask those questions, thinks Judy. And now it's too late.

By six o'clock, Ruth is exhausted, her head thumping, her vision blurred. This feels more tiring than driving to work and back in the rush hour. Ruth has done two Zoom lectures and three tutorials. She has also overseen Kate's schoolwork and tempted her out for a walk to the sea. They came back with a pile of 'interesting stones' that will probably never move from the middle of the kitchen table. Ruth has also made lunch and sundry snacks for Kate and Flint. Now they are both making noises about supper.

Ruth looks down at her emails. There seem to be even more of these than usual: students asking for reassurance, lecturers unable to log onto Zoom, opportunistic companies wanting her to spend money. Three messages immediately catch her eye. The first is from Janet Meadows saying that the plague exhibition will now be a virtual event. Ruth sends a quick reply commiserating and congratulating. She adds a quick PS. *Do you know anything about researching the history of a house?*

The next two missives are blasts from her romantic past. The first is Daniel saying that he is thinking of her 'in this strange new world of ours'. The next is from another ex-boyfriend, Peter Snow.

Hi Ruth. Interesting times, eh? Px.

Ruth met Peter when they were excavating the Bronze Age henge. It had been a magical summer, long days digging and long evenings by the camp fire watching the birds wheeling across the Norfolk sky. Peter wasn't an archaeologist; he was a historian who turned up one day and offered his help on the site. He had been enthusiastic, so enthusiastic that he almost drowned in quicksand trying to reach the buried timbers. Erik had saved him, crawling over the treacherous ground with his hand held out. That night, Ruth realised not only that Peter had nearly died but also that she loved him. Life was suddenly very precious. Erik's wife Magda seemed to read her mind and suggested that Ruth and Peter go and collect samphire together. There, by the water's edge, they had, simply and sweetly, walked into each other's arms. Peter had encouraged her to apply for the job at UNN and to buy the cottage. They were together for nearly five years and Ruth was so used to Peter that she didn't at first notice that

she'd fallen out of love with him. She ended the relationship, to her mother's horror, and, apart from a strange,
abortive reunion twelve years ago, Ruth hasn't seen Peter
since. She knows he's now married with a child. There's
no mention of either in his email. Ruth's finger hovers
over the reply arrow.

> Hi Peter. Hope things are OK with you. This is a strange, scary
> time, isn't it? I'm still working at UNN, though struggling to teach
> my students online at the moment as well as home-schooling my
> daughter, Kate. Peter – this might seem odd but do you remember
> anything about the people who had the cottage before me? I've been
> doing a bit of research. Ruth.

Ruth wonders whether Peter will respond but, when she
opens her laptop later that evening, after Kate is in bed,
there's another email from him.

> Hi Ruth. Great to hear from you. Funnily enough, I've been thinking
> a lot about the cottage. We had some fun times there, didn't we?
> I remember when we first bought the cats. Flint used to climb the
> curtains but Sparky was scared of everything. I don't remember
> anything about the previous owners. You always made it very clear
> that the purchase of the house was nobody's business but yours.
> The only thing I remember is that it used to be called 'The Cabin'.
> We used to joke about that. *The Evil Dead* and all those horror story
> tropes.
>   How old is Kate now? Daniel is eighteen and hoping to go to
> university in September. As long as this wretched virus is over by

then. I don't know if you know that Victoria and I are divorced. I'm
living on my own and teaching at Nottingham University. It's a very
interesting town, historically. You must visit one day. When all this is
over etc etc.

Take care

Px

Ruth looks at this missive for some time. It brings back
Peter in all his lovable, annoying glory. He had loved the
cats and they had shared their kittenhood together. The
mention of Sparky still makes Ruth sad, even after all these
years. The comment about the purchase of the house being
nobody's business but hers seems rather pointed though.
There had been some talk of them buying the house
together, but Ruth had, even then, been determined that it
would belong to her alone. She must have known, at some
level, that she and Peter were not destined to be partners
for life. But she had forgotten about 'The Cabin'. There had
even been a sign with a lopsided drawing of a house. It had
seemed funny back then when 'horror story tropes' were an
amusing, academic joke.

She can't believe that Daniel, who was a little boy when
she last saw Peter, is about to go to university. She seems
to be haunted by Daniels. There's her childhood boyfriend,
Daniel Breakspeare, and she had a good friend at university called Dan Golding. Why has Peter, like the other
Daniel, chosen to contact her now? It's the pandemic, she
thinks, and the prospect of weeks (months?) with only a
laptop and memories for company. She should stop this

correspondence now. She knows that she will never visit Peter in Nottingham, no matter how interesting the town is 'historically'.

She's about to press 'shut down', when another email appears on the screen. The sender is identified only by an anonymous Gmail address and the message is brief.

Beware the Grey Lady.

17

Beware the Grey Lady. Ruth thinks about those words the next morning when she watches Zoe driving off to work, dressed in blue scrubs. She and Kate are on their own now, with only Flint for protection. Ruth waves from the window, remembering her parents' next-door neighbour, Mrs Grantham, who was housebound by some mysterious illness. Mrs Grantham was always at the window when Ruth returned from school. 'She likes to see you,' Ruth's mother used to say, and Ruth would always wave cheerfully before dismissing the lonely figure from her mind. After only a day of lockdown, Ruth is turning into Mrs Grantham.

Ruth is pathetically grateful when the postman knocks at the door with a delivery. It's an Amazon parcel from Simon. Ruth usually tries to avoid ordering from the online retailer, preferring to shop at local bookshops, but there is something very comforting about being sent a book. It shows that her brother is thinking about her. Maybe it's a crime novel, something by Ian Rankin or Val McDermid? Fictional murder is oddly soothing in troubled times. Ruth tears open the cardboard. *Government Conspiracies and How to Spot Them.* Hmmm.

Kate is having a Zoom lesson. Ruth admires the way that the Year 6 teacher, Mrs Obuya, manages to make grammar both interesting and entertaining. Ruth herself, despite having a PhD, has no idea what a 'fronted adverbial phrase' is. But online lessons mean that Kate needs the laptop, so Ruth can't do any of her own work. Ruth's scheduled lectures take priority, of course, but she doesn't want Kate to miss any face-to-face teaching, especially when these sessions are so rare. Maybe she should buy another laptop but she doesn't like the thought of Kate having her own computer. Besides, Ruth has already felt the disastrous pull of online shopping. PayPal doesn't seem like real money, but she has to be careful. She is lucky to be in full-time employment and not furloughed but who knows what the future holds for unfashionable universities teaching unfashionable subjects?

Ruth doesn't like using her phone for confidential university business, so her options seem to be reading Simon's book about faked moon landings, doing some housework or continuing her research into the history of the house. She goes into the garden to call Janet.

'I was just about to send you an email,' says Janet. 'This is all a bit scary, isn't it?'

'It doesn't seem real,' says Ruth. 'Words like pandemic and lockdown belong in a science fiction novel.'

'Or a history book,' says Janet. 'I keep thinking how it must have felt during the plague in Norwich. There were people called "keepers", appointed to make sure residents stayed in their houses. They used to carry red wands, about a metre long, to encourage others to keep their distance. There were "watchers" too.'

'Social distancing,' says Ruth. She wants to stop Janet before she goes any deeper into the fourteenth century. 'I've been thinking of doing some research into my house. That's why I sent you the email.'

'What's brought this on?' says Janet.

'I found a picture of the cottages in the sixties,' says Ruth. 'It made me think.'

'Pictures are very important artefacts,' says Janet. 'You live on New Road, don't you?'

'Yes.'

'I've got a great picture of those cottages from the nineteen hundreds. I'll email it. Otherwise it's best to work backwards in time. Look at street directories and electoral registers. The 1939 register is particularly good because there wasn't one during the war. Also try searching via address in newspaper archives. I'll send a link.'

'Thanks so much,' says Ruth.

'No problem. I'm at a bit of a loose end. There's no teaching work and all the tourist attractions have closed. And, to cap it all, I'm having to move house.'

'Are you?' says Ruth. 'That sounds very stressful.'

'My lease is up,' says Janet. 'And my landlord is being rather intransigent. But I'm sure I'll find somewhere.'

Ruth thinks that her friend is being very resilient. She'd hate to move house in the middle of a pandemic. It makes her feel very grateful for her four walls, whatever mysteries they are hiding.

Before she rings off, she tells Janet about the Grey Lady email.

'"Beware the Grey Lady",' says Janet. 'Who could have sent that?'

'I don't know,' says Ruth. 'It gave me a bit of a jolt, remembering the story you told me. The bricked-up house and the girl eating her parents' flesh. All that.' She shivers although the garden is sunny and the birds are singing from the apple tree.

'Don't worry, Ruth,' says Janet. 'The Grey Lady can't hurt you.'

When Kate has finished her lesson, they go out for a brisk walk across the Saltmarsh. Kate is in a better mood today and happily gathers 'interesting grasses' to go in her Nature Book. It reminds Ruth of collecting samphire with Peter. Maybe she should contact him again? They always got on well and it's time that Ruth stopped waiting for Nelson, consciously or not.

Back at the house, Kate embarks on some homework set by Mrs Obuya. Ruth opens her laptop to see the photograph sent by Janet. She has opened a new folder on her computer and has also allocated a yellow file marked 'House' which contains the original photograph plus several printed-out pages. Ruth is a born academic; nothing is real until it has a file.

Janet's photograph shows the cottages, brick-fronted, with a horse-drawn cart in front. The sign on the cart says

'Adnam's Beer' and this was clearly the focus of the picture. Ruth knows that the local ale – a favourite with her ex-partner Frank – was first brewed in the 1870s. Why was the dray standing outside her cottage? Were the owners big drinkers? Ruth prints out the picture and puts it next to her mother's photograph, the pink houses, the boxy car. Peering closely she can see a name plaque on the middle house. Does it say 'The Cabin'? She can't be sure. The plaque isn't there in the nineteenth-century photo. Who gave the house its cosy but slightly sinister name?

Ruth has discovered that the three houses on New Road were built in 1860 and were described, in the county records, as 'farmworkers' cottages'. Ruth purchased her house in 1998 from the estate of the late Alfred Barton. The 1939 census shows that the house was occupied by Alf Barton, described as 'labourer', his wife Dorothy 'seamstress' and two children – John, 16, and Matthew, 14. John and Matthew would be in their nineties if they were alive now. Ruth doesn't discount this; people in Norfolk seem to live for ever. It's also possible, of course, that one or both sons died in the war. The thought makes her sad. She senses a definite fellow feeling with the family who once lived in this tiny house. The question is, did Ruth's mother also have a link with them? And, if so, what was it?

Who would have been living in the house in 1963? Alf, judging by the title deeds, but who else? Ruth logs into the archives of the local newspaper, as Janet had suggested. She puts her address into the search box and, immediately, an article from 1970 pops up.

BIG-HEARTED FOSTER MUM DIES

Tributes have been paid to Dot Barton, of 2 New Road, Saltmarsh, who died of cancer at the age of 68. As well as being mother to two sons, John and Matthew, and grandmother of three, Dot also fostered more than a hundred children. 'Our door was always open,' says Dot's husband, Alf (70). 'Dot was so kind,' says Alma McLaughlin (24), who was fostered as a teenager. 'She really made a difference to my life.' Dot's funeral will be held at St Peter's Church, Gaywood, on Wednesday 17th June.

Hundreds of children? Ruth realises that this is over a period of at least thirty years but she suddenly has a vision of small figures swarming over the tiny house, like an illustration from *The Old Woman Who Lived in A Shoe*.

'Mum!' says a commanding voice. Ruth turns to face her one and only child.

'Yes, darling,' she says, trying to channel the caring spirit of Dot Barton.

'I'm bored,' says Kate. 'Can I watch TV?'

Judy is also working from home. It's been decided that only a skeleton staff will remain at the police station. The boss goes in every day, of course, and the rest of the team will take it in turns. Today Tony is sitting alone in the shared area, deprived of any outlet for his relentless sociability. Nelson will be closeted in his office – doing God knows what – and Leah will be bringing him cups of coffee and answering the printer's querulous demands for fresh paper.

Judy has set up a workstation in her bedroom. It's not ideal because the rooms in the cottage are small and hers and Cathbad's is almost completely taken up by their antique brass double bed. Judy has managed to fit in a small table and chair, but she is now wedged beside the window and her Zoom background shows only a flowered curtain and a portrait of Thing, painted by Miranda, stuck on the yellow wall. It doesn't exactly say 'modern police professional'. But Cathbad has commandeered the kitchen for home-schooling and the spare room is now full of Maddie and her myriad possessions.

Still, it is peaceful here. The window is open and the warm spring air floats in. It's strange how this helps with the anxiety. At night, Judy lies awake worrying about work, school and Covid. Waking in the early hours she becomes convinced that she can't smell anything (one of the symptoms of the virus) and goes into the bathroom to sniff the organic soap. Cathbad sleeps on, regardless, protected by The Goddess. But, when the morning sun streams in, it's hard to stay pessimistic. Now she can hear her neighbour mowing his lawn and smell the freshly cut grass. Downstairs, the children and Cathbad are laughing as they listen to *Horrible Histories* on the radio. In her room, Maddie is tapping away on her laptop. A hen squawks from the garden.

Judy turns to her notes on the Avril Flowers case. There's something she's missing here, she's sure of it. Some link between Avril's death and Samantha Wilson's. Maybe Karen Head too. Judy flicks through her trusty notebook. She has included a brief sketch of Avril's bungalow: main bedroom, spare bedroom, bathroom, kitchen, sitting room. Judy thinks about touring the premises with Tanya, who'd been more concerned with its specifications and with her own BMI. What was it she had said in the bathroom?

Nice scales. Should I test them out? Check out my BMI?

Judy hadn't answered at the time. The house was a crime scene and so the question could only have been rhetorical. Besides, Judy finds Tanya's obsession with weight and fitness rather trying. But now those words are sounding warning bells.

What did Karen's headteacher say? *She even got us to have a sponsored slim last year. I lost two stone.*

Karen Head had organised a sponsored slim for the teachers at her school. Avril Flowers possessed state-of-the-art weighing scales. Samantha Wilson had died with a Weight Watchers meal in the microwave.

Avril Flowers in a stripy dress on Cromer Pier. *She thought that dress made her look fat.*

She was as fit as a fiddle, always exercising. Not a couch potato like me.

Could slimming be the link between the dead women?

By the late afternoon, Ruth's head is swimming from trying to read old-fashioned handwriting on electoral registers and birth certificates. Alfred Barton was born in 1900. Dorothy 'Dot' in 1902. Dot died in 1970 but Alfred lived on until 1997, when he had died in Ruth's upstairs bedroom. In 1963, the house had presumably been home to Alf, Dot and numerous foster children. Where does that leave Ruth? Feeling slightly inadequate is the answer. She often complains about her life (usually to herself, it's true) but she has a good job, a car and enough space for her and her daughter to have a bedroom each. She also has hot water, electric light and the internet. Yet there must be people facing the current crisis without any of these things. She really should start counting her blessings, but she's had enough of maths for the day. She's relieved when her phone buzzes. Nelson.

'How are you finding lockdown?'

'Has it only been two days?' says Ruth. 'It feels like years.'

Nelson laughs. 'It's very strange. The roads are empty, and it was just me and Tony at the station today.'

'I would have thought you'd have liked the empty roads. You're always complaining about other cars.'

'I know but when they're not there you miss them. It's the same at work. The team drive me mad sometimes, but it doesn't seem right to be in the office on my own listening to Tony's constant chatter. Then, when I get home, there's no one but Bruno to talk to.'

There's a brief silence. Ruth digests the fact that Michelle is still away. The distance between them seems to contract. Ruth imagines Nelson in his stream-lined kitchen, opening the cupboards in search of fast food, Bruno watching from the hallway. Nelson's house has always seemed exclusively Michelle's but maybe that's just because Ruth doesn't like to think of the two of them choosing soft furnishings or deciding on paint colours.

'How's Katie?' says Nelson.

'She's fine. I think she'll find it quite boring after a

while though. The school don't send her much work to do although she did have a Zoom lesson today.'

'She's so bright. She'll catch up.'

'I'm not worried about her falling behind. I'm worried about her getting bored. I'm worried about me getting bored.'

'What about your new next-door neighbour? The woman I saw the other week?'

'Zoe? What about her?'

'Is she company for you?'

'Yes, she is but she's a nurse. She works three days a week.' Ruth has already seen Zoe come home, looking tired. Ruth had waved from the window, embracing her Mrs Grantham persona.

'I wish . . .' says Nelson and then he stops. What was he going to say? That he wishes that he was with her? Or that Michelle was back?

'I wish none of this had happened,' says Nelson.

'We all think that, Nelson,' says Ruth.

She knows this isn't what he was going to say.

18

Ruth's days acquire a new routine. After breakfast, she Face-Times Cathbad and Ruth and Kate join in with the garden yoga. She tried watching the YouTube PE recommended by the school WhatsApp Group but it's far too energetic for Ruth. This way, they can see their friends and practise gentle breathing in the sun. The one bonus of lockdown has been a burst of glorious spring weather, as if nature is enjoying its break from carbon emissions and vapour trails in the sky. After yoga, in theory, Ruth and Kate both get down to work. Ruth has heard, on the mother network, about private schools that are offering a complete online curriculum. Children sit down, often in full uniform, and are entertained and educated all day. Kate's school is rather more haphazard although Ruth appreciates that they are trying their best with limited resources. They offer some online lessons and these are a godsend. Otherwise they send worksheets which Kate invariably finishes in ten minutes. Ruth is left to set Kate a vague reading task or to encourage her to finish writing her continuing saga about a time-travelling cat. It's called Whittaker, after Jodie Whittaker, the star of *Doctor Who*.

Then it's lunchtime. Ruth finds preparing a midday meal rather a strain. She's running out of acceptable variants of beans on toast. Cathbad makes home-made soup every day but he's a shaman in touch with earth magic and she . . . isn't. After lunch Ruth and Kate have a walk across the marshes, collecting more items for their 'nature table'. Then Ruth works while Kate reads or entertains herself. Ruth's 'no screens until six' rule has already been abandoned. Suppertime happens rather earlier than usual. And, every day this week, Ruth has had a large glass of wine at six p.m.

On Thursday, after supper, there's a variant. Ever since the Prime Minster's announcement on Monday, Ruth has been obsessively scrolling for Covid news. She tries to stop herself but, late at night, she finds herself on news sites reading about death rates in Italy and China. Thank goodness she's not on Facebook or Twitter because she's sure that other people's anxieties would finish her off altogether. Not to mention the Simon types saying that it's all a conspiracy to kill off the elderly population. In one of her doom-scrolling sessions Ruth reads about 'clapping for carers', the idea that everyone should go outside at eight p.m. on Thursdays to clap the NHS heroes. There have been heart-rending stories in the news about doctors and nurses, clad in their inadequate protective clothing, struggling to cope with the rising tide of Covid cases, risking their lives to fight a virus that no one really understands, weeping over elderly patients dying alone because visitors are no longer allowed in hospitals, stopping at the supermarket after a twenty-four-hour shift to find that greedy shoppers have stripped the shelves of food.

'Let's clap too,' says Ruth.

'No one will hear us,' says Kate.

This is true and the words give Ruth an unaccustomed shiver. Somehow, in the last three days, she has felt their isolation in a way that she never has before. Which is why, when Ruth and Kate step out into their front garden, Ruth is disproportionately pleased to see Zoe in hers, holding a saucepan and spoon. The marshes are dark, but Ruth can hear the sea in the distance, the waves breaking on the far-off sandbank.

'I thought I'd make some noise,' Zoe says. 'Frighten the foxes a bit. Derek is terrified of them. He's still scared to go outside.' Ruth has only seen the beautiful Maine Coon cat in Zoe's window.

'We should be clapping you really,' says Ruth. Zoe has changed out of her scrubs but she's still a heroic figure to Ruth.

'It's eight o'clock,' says Kate, who likes to keep track of time.

Feeling slightly ridiculous, Ruth starts to clap. Zoe beats time on her saucepan and Kate adds a few whoops. Birds fly up out of the reeds and seagulls call overhead but otherwise the only sound is the echo of their own applause, rolling back to them out of the darkness.

Judy is surprised, when she steps onto her doorstep, to hear the cheers echoing along the street. Cathbad and the children are already there, blowing whistles and clattering saucepans. Maddie whoops from an upstairs window. Judy looks towards the next-door house and is rather touched to see Steve and Whatsit applauding loudly. On the other side Jill and Fred (or is it Ned?) are clapping in a more restrained way, as if they are at a tennis match. Judy remembers what she said to Tanya about her neighbours. 'I hardly ever talk to mine . . . I'd be hard put to tell you their names.' She resolves to do better. There is something very moving about this moment, when they are united in admiration and respect, despite being locked down in their separate houses.

'Isn't it great?' says Cathbad, turning to smile at her. 'It's real universal energy.'

'Will universal energy fund PPE?' says Judy, then feels churlish. She compensates by adding a whoop of her own to the dying chorus.

Nelson wonders why everyone in the cul-de-sac is standing in their front gardens. What are they playing at? What about 'Stay Home' don't they understand? When he parks outside his house, he can hear Bruno barking but there's another sound too, something that reminds Nelson of childhood football matches. Applause. It's hesitant at first, a few staccato claps on the night air, and then it rises and swells. There are whoops too and someone rings a bell. What in God's name is going on? Then he remembers. They are clapping for the carers. Leah was talking about it today. Nelson doesn't want to look unsympathetic, so he stands on his doorsteps for a few minutes, joining in. His daughters used to complain that he clapped too loudly at netball matches and school plays and there is something particularly sonorous about the sound his hands make. He has big hands which is why he often had to play in goal rather than his preferred centre-forward glory-hunting position.

'Well done, Harry,' shouts someone.

Has he gone back in time and scored the winning goal for Bispham Juniors? Then someone else says, 'Three cheers for the police.' Jesus wept – they are clapping him now. Nelson knows this is unwarranted. He isn't risking his life like doctors and nurses and hospital cleaners. But he knows, too, that people need an outlet for their sentiment. So, he raises his hand in a way that he hopes acknowledges the ovation whilst, at the same time, asking for it to stop. Then Nelson lets himself into his house.

Bruno comes racing to meet him, whimpering with happiness. He's been with Maura all day, but he clearly wants another walk. Nelson slightly dreads marching past his suddenly admiring neighbours. He doesn't want to take any of his usual routes. He wants to go somewhere wild and deserted.

He wants to see Ruth.

19

Kate gets bored and goes back into the house.

'Want to meet back out here in an hour for a glass of wine?' says Zoe.

'Yes please,' says Ruth.

She manages to persuade Kate to go to bed. 'What's the point?' says Kate, 'there's no school tomorrow.'

'We still have to work,' says Ruth. Is this all there is now? Work? The only incentive to propel them from one day to another. Everything else – family, friends, meals out, cinema, chance meetings in coffee shops – has disappeared into the darkness. In the end, Ruth lets Kate take her laptop so she can watch a film in bed. Flint arrives and makes himself comfortable on the duvet, just out of reach of Kate's hand. At least they still have pets and technology, Ruth thinks. They will have to get them through this. As long as the Wi-Fi connection holds up.

When Ruth steps outside, the security light is on and Zoe, wearing a thick, padded coat, is sitting on a chair by her front door holding a bottle of wine.

'I'll get a glass,' says Ruth, 'and a chair.'

She gets a kitchen chair and places it roughly two metres away from Zoe's. She puts her glass on the ground and Zoe fills it up. These machinations hardly seem strange to her now.

'Cheers,' says Zoe. The light is still on, making the whole scene feel unreal somehow, as if they are on stage.

'Cheers,' says Ruth.

Pets, technology, alcohol and neighbours.

The roads are almost completely clear. Nelson drives fast. Bruno, on the back seat, braces himself for the corners like an expert co-driver. Whenever Nelson looks in his rear-view mirror (which doesn't happen often) he can see the dog's big ears and alert expression. He really should ring Jan Adams, a friend who is a retired dog-handler, to see if she can look after Bruno during lockdown, but he finds himself loath to lose his companion. Bruno, Nelson thinks wryly, as he takes the turning for the Saltmarsh, is almost the only living creature who wholeheartedly approves of him. All the women in his life – Michelle, Ruth, his mother, his older daughters, Leah, Judy, Jo – have plenty of ideas for how he could be improved. Only Bruno and his two youngest children, Katie and George, think he's perfect the way he is.

On New Road, civilisation disappears. No more streetlamps or traffic signs. The only light is an eerie green shimmer on the horizon. Don't look at it, Nelson tells himself. He's heard enough of Cathbad's stories about will-o'-the-wisps and ghostly lanterns that lead you to your death. He keeps his eyes on the road in front, although even that seems to have vanished. His headlights reflect back only darkness and Bruno whimpers softly from the back seat.

When Nelson sees Ruth's cottage bathed in light, he's at first relieved and then, immediately, worried. Why is Ruth's security light on? Is it a passing fox or that ridiculous ginger cat, hunting for mice he's too fat to eat? But, in that case, why is it still on? Nelson drives even faster, although he knows that there are ditches on either side of the narrow road and that one false turn of the wheel could send him and Bruno spinning to their probable deaths.

When he draws up outside the terraced houses, he sees two women silhouetted in the light, as if they are in some sort of play. They are sitting on chairs two metres apart and holding glasses of wine. They both turn to stare at him. As Nelson gets out of the car, Ruth says, 'Nelson! What are you doing here?'

It's not the welcome he was imagining.

Nelson takes a step forward until a warning bark stops him. He lets Bruno out of the car and the dog bounds forward. A sudden movement in the bushes indicates the departure of Flint.

'Hi, Bruno.' Ruth pats the dog in a way that also requests he keeps his distance.

Nelson, too, suddenly remembers the two-metre rule. He stops, just inside the circle of light.

'Hallo, Ruth.'

'Zoe,' Ruth addresses the other woman. 'This is Nelson.' No other identifying information is offered.

'Hallo, Nelson,' says Zoe amiably. She's the neighbour Nelson met in February. The nurse. She's about Ruth's age, with dark shoulder-length hair. Like Ruth she is wearing an anorak.

'We were just having a drink,' says Ruth, sounding slightly defensive. 'A socially distanced drink.'

'It's the new normal,' says Zoe.

'I've come to take Bruno for a walk,' says Nelson, knowing how ridiculous this sounds. 'I fancied a change of scene.' Bruno, recognising the W word, barks encouragingly.

'Is Michelle still away?' says Ruth.

'Yes.'

For a moment they all stand there in silence. Nelson is again reminded of a play. One of those God-awful modern plays that Michelle likes, where you pay twenty quid to watch the actors stare at each other.

'I'll be off then,' he says.

'Be careful on the marsh,' says Ruth. 'Stay on the path.'

This reminds Nelson of taking this route with Cathbad, more than ten years ago. *There's a hidden way. Trust me.*

'I'll be careful,' he says.

After Nelson's abrupt departure, Ruth and Zoe finish their wine and say goodnight. Ruth wonders if she should try to explain Nelson's appearance and disappearance but what is there to say? This is Kate's father, he's here because his wife's away? This is DCI Nelson of the Norfolk Serious Crimes Unit, he's driven twenty miles in a pandemic to take his dog for a walk? In the end, Ruth just wishes Zoe a good day at work tomorrow. 'I'm off on Fridays,' said Zoe. 'Thank goodness. So I'm here if you need anyone to keep an eye on Kate.'

Ruth thanks her for the offer and the wine and pushes open her front door which she has left on the latch. She goes to stand by the window and looks out into the darkness. The security light has gone off and she can hardly see Nelson's white car, parked only a few metres away. Will he come back when he's taken Bruno for a walk? Is that even allowed? The rules say that you can only exercise within walking distance of your home. Of course, Nelson is, to some extent, above the law but Ruth knows that he doesn't like using his position for personal advantage. In her obsessive reading of Covid news, she has come across some discussion about divorced parents being allowed to see their children. Perhaps Nelson's visit comes under this heading? But Ruth knows that Nelson did not come to see Kate.

Flint, who ran away at the first sight of Bruno, now squeezes through his cat flap and meows loudly. Ruth feeds him and wonders about pouring herself another glass of wine. At this rate, she'll be an alcoholic by the end of the first proper week of lockdown. She compromises by putting the kettle on. I'll have a cup of tea, she tells herself, and then I'll go to bed. Nelson will drive home. The whole episode will be forgotten in the morning.

She is pouring boiling water onto a tea bag when there's a soft tap at the window. Ruth puts the kettle down and goes to the front door.

'Who is it?' she says.

'It's me.'

Bruno charges in and immediately knocks several books off the coffee table. Ruth shuts the kitchen door. Flint will be safe in there and can come and go through his cat flap. When she turns, she sees Nelson watching her from the middle of the room, his dog at his side.

'I'm not sure you should be here,' she says.

'I'm sure I shouldn't,' says Nelson.

Ruth knows that she should tell him to go. It's a pandemic and they are breaking all the rules, to say nothing of the other rules sanctioned by the state and the Holy Catholic Church. But, instead, she's the one who steps forward and puts her arms round Nelson's neck, raising her face to his.

20

Ruth wakes up knowing that something is different. For once the new normal worries – Covid, school, work – don't come rushing into her mind. But there's something else. And the bed feels different. Warmer. Uneven. Ruth reaches out a hand and sits bolt upright. Nelson is lying next to her. She can see the 'Seasiders' tattoo on his shoulder. He is deeply asleep, his dark hair somehow shocking on her white pillow. The last time Nelson stayed the night here, there was no grey in his hair. That was the night Kate was conceived. Kate! She mustn't come in and find a strange man in Ruth's bed. Well, not exactly strange – Nelson is her father, after all – but definitely unexpected. Ruth looks at the green numbers on her alarm: 8.04. It's years since she slept this late. Recently she's been waking up before dawn. Kate will be awake any minute. She's starting to sleep later in preparation for being a teenager but it's rare that she sleeps past eight.

'Mum?' The door opens. Just in time, Ruth realises that she's naked and clutches her sheet to her. The movement wakes Nelson who also sits up.

'Hallo, Dad,' says Kate. 'What are you doing here?'

'Hallo, love.' Nelson rubs his eyes. 'We were just . . .'

'Are we doing yoga with Cathbad this morning?' says Kate. 'It's five past eight.'

'Yes,' says Ruth. 'Get dressed and I'll be with you in a minute.'

'OK,' says Kate but, instead of going into her room, Ruth hears her feet on the stairs. Then there's a cry of surprise. Ruth pulls on her best dressing gown and follows.

The door to the kitchen is open and the sitting room is full of shredded cushions. Bruno and Flint are lying on the sofa, side by side. Bruno looks up as Kate and Ruth descend the stairs. Flint pretends to be asleep.

'I knew they'd be friends,' says Kate, putting her arms round the dog.

'They've destroyed my Votes for Women cushions,' says Ruth, looking at the shreds of green and purple fabric covering the floor.

'That's because they're male chauvinists,' says Kate. 'What shall we have for breakfast? Dad likes fried stuff.'

Ruth is impressed that Kate knows this expression, though less impressed at the thought that she might have encountered the accompanying attitudes. And she's rather taken aback by the ease with which Kate has accepted Nelson's presence in the house.

'Let's just make toast,' says Ruth. 'And coffee.' She needs caffeine. About a gallon of it.

Nelson appears while she's still waiting for the toast to pop up. He's fully dressed, his hair wet from a hasty shower.

'We're having breakfast,' says Kate from her seat at the table. 'I told Mum you prefer eggs and bacon. Then we're doing yoga with Cathbad.'

'Rather you than me,' says Nelson. 'I need to get to work, I'm afraid, love.'

'Have some toast first.' Ruth puts a piece in front of him. 'The coffee's on.'

'Thanks,' says Nelson. 'You're a lifesaver.' Their eyes meet and Ruth quickly turns away to check the percolator.

'I can do warrior one and two,' Kate is telling Nelson. 'And I can almost do crow. Can you do yoga?'

'No, I can't,' says Nelson, spreading butter thickly. 'I'm glad that Cathbad's found something useful to do, though.'

Ruth puts Marmite in front of Nelson. She has no idea if he likes it or not and finds herself holding her breath, only to release it when Nelson covers his toast and butter with the black spread. Flint stalks into the room, followed by Bruno.

'I've got nothing to give Bruno except cat food,' says Ruth. 'Is that OK?'

'He'll probably eat it,' says Nelson. 'Don't worry though. I'll drop him off with the dog walker on the way to work. She's got food for him.'

In the end, Ruth puts gourmet cat food down for both animals. Bruno eats his in seconds and then tries to put his muzzle into Flint's bowl. Flint hisses at him and Bruno backs away, looking hurt.

'He's scared of Flint,' says Kate.

'So am I,' says Nelson. He finishes his toast and drinks his coffee in one swallow.

'I'd better be off. Bye, Katie.' He stoops to kiss her head.
'Bye, Ruth.'

'Bye, Nelson.'

They look at each other.

'See you later?' says Nelson.

'Yes,' says Ruth.

Nelson walks out to his car, Bruno at his heels. Ruth doesn't come to the door, but he sees her neighbour, Zoe, at her window. He'd initially been pleased that Ruth had someone living next door at last but now he finds himself wishing that her house was on an island, or in a secret world that only he could visit. That's what it had felt like last night, seeing her light when he returned from his walk over the marshes. He hadn't really thought what he was doing when he knocked on Ruth's window, but he supposes it doesn't take Cathbad's sixth sense to guess what would happen. And, what's more, it looks as if it's going to happen again tonight.

Nelson knows that he should be worried. He has, technically, broken the Covid rules and he could get into serious trouble for it. He could even lose his job. But it's a beautiful morning and the marshes are full of spring flowers, the sea a line of blue in the distance. Nelson finds himself singing a Frank Sinatra song as he drives, something about two sweethearts, the summer wind and an umbrella sky. He can't remember the actual words, but he makes them up as he goes along. Bruno sways on the back seat.

He drops Bruno at Maura's house. He wears a mask when

he hands the dog over but, once again, he thinks that he really should be making other arrangements. Again, he considers whether he should ask Jan if she can look after Bruno, just until lockdown is over. He tries not to think about predictions from the Chief Constable that lockdown will go on for months, maybe even for a year. Will Michelle stay away all that time? George is due to start school in September. Nelson tries to put this out of his mind, but he doesn't sing as he drives the rest of the way to the police station.

Judy is in the shared area, her hand sanitiser and her water bottle, correctly labelled with her name, on the desk in front of her. Nelson is pleased that it's Judy's turn in the office because he likes working with her. On the other hand, she's the most likely to notice if anything is different in his manner. He must be careful not to mention Ruth.

'Sorry I'm late,' he says. It feels odd talking to Judy from across the room. Not that he's one for sitting chummily on people's desks or clasping their hands, à la Jo, but it goes against human nature to stand so far apart.

'It's only nine thirty,' says Judy. 'Can I have a word about the Avril Flowers case? I think I might have discovered something.'

'Of course,' says Nelson. 'I'll just grab a coffee first. Leah!' He raises his voice to a polite shout.

'She's not in,' says Judy.

'Really?' Nelson can't remember the last time Leah missed a day of work.

'She left a message on the answerphone.'

'Jesus. It's not Covid, is it?'

'She doesn't think so. Just a bug.'

'She should get a test, just in case.'

'There aren't enough testing kits. I was hearing something about it on the radio.'

'There's not enough of anything, if you ask me. I'll just go and get myself a coffee then.' Nelson follows the arrows to the break room but then tracks back to ask Judy if she wants anything.

'No thanks,' says Judy. 'Do you know, I think this is the first time you've ever offered to make me a drink.'

'These are strange times,' says Nelson.

Ruth finishes her toast, has a quick shower, dresses in her loosest trousers and joins Kate in the garden. The air is so sweet and pure that it almost takes her breath away. It's as if nature is conspiring to make lockdown a less terrifying experience. Ruth has already noticed herself becoming interested in the tracks left by the foxes and watching the progression of the blossom on her tree. She leaves food out for the birds and has secretly named a crow Corbyn. Ruth wouldn't normally think about her garden except on the one (usually rainy) day a year when she decides to have a barbecue. Of course, it's only been a week and Covid hasn't yet hit her or her friends personally. She'll feel differently when it does. But, today, she feels alive and invincible. Nothing to do with Nelson and last night, of course.

She props her laptop up on a garden chair. As she does so, a large animal appears in front of her. It's the size of a small dog but is striped like a tiger. Ruth takes a step backwards, but Kate says, 'That's Derek.' A voice says, 'Is he with you? It's the first time he's been outside.'

Zoe, wearing what looks like pyjamas, appears at the other side of the fence.

'Yes, he's here,' says Ruth. 'He's gorgeous.'

Derek is looking at the laptop with interest. Ruth feels that she has to explain, for his sake as much as Zoe's.

'We're doing yoga with my friend via FaceTime.'

'Can I join in?' says Zoe. 'I'm wearing the right clothes.'

Zoe may be in her pyjamas, thinks Ruth, but they are stylish ones, dark green with white spots. Zoe's hair is tied back with a matching scarf. When Cathbad appears on screen, Ruth explains that they have an extra participant.

'All are welcome,' says Cathbad graciously. He is dressed in loose white trousers and a T-shirt with chemical symbols on it. His grey hair gleams in the sunlight. Ruth can see Michael and Miranda in the background. Miranda is standing on her head.

'Let's start by greeting the dawn,' says Cathbad.

'Are you saying that these women died because of *slimming*?' says Nelson. He says the word like it's the most outlandish activity known to humankind.

'I'm saying it's a link,' says Judy patiently. 'I'm been checking, and Samantha Wilson, Avril Flowers and Karen Head all attended Lean Zone meetings. Maggie O'Flynn too, Avril's friend who died. Samantha and Karen were even in the same group.'

'Lean Zone,' says Nelson. 'That rings a bell.'

'Does it?' says Judy, surprised. She can't imagine that Michelle has ever attended a weight loss group in her life.

'It might be worth checking,' says Nelson. 'It's the first definite connection, any road.'

'I've got numbers for the consultants who run the meetings,' says Judy. She looks at her notes. 'Jacquie Maitland and Barb Blakeborough. I'll give them a ring later. At the very least they'll give us some more background information.'

'That'll be something,' says Nelson. 'I suppose we're no nearer to tracing the person whose prints were on Avril's bedroom door?'

'No,' says Judy. 'There's no CCTV that we can find, and Tanya didn't get anything from the door-to-door.'

There's a brief silence during which Judy's phone pings. She glances at it and laughs. 'Look!' She shows the picture to Nelson. 'Cathbad's taken a screen shot of his yoga session.' Ruth and Kate are in their garden, both in the lunging pose Judy recognises as warrior one. From the other side of the fence another woman is joining in, laughing as she raises her hands above her head.

Judy thought that Nelson would laugh too but he says, rather dourly, 'That bloody next-door neighbour gets in on everything.'

How does Nelson know about Ruth's next-door neighbour? thinks Judy. She looks more closely at the picture and, from somewhere, comes a tiny twinge of recognition. And disquiet.

21

That tiny chord of – memory? unease? – continues to play in Judy's head as she returns to the empty incident room to telephone Jacquie Maitland and Barb Blakeborough. Both women have, very conveniently, included their mobile phone numbers on the Facebook page about group meetings.

'Is this a convenient time?' says Judy.

'It's fine,' says Jacquie, who has a pleasant, slightly husky voice. 'It's not as if I'm doing anything else.'

'Is Lean Zone still going on in lockdown?'

'Well, we obviously can't have meetings,' says Jacquie. 'We've offered online meetings or Zoom but who wants to be weighed in a Zoom meeting?'

'Is that what happens?' asks Judy.

'Yes,' says Jacquie. 'You get weighed at the start of the meeting. Some women – some members – go home after that but most stay for my talk.' She laughs. 'I can't think why because I always say the same thing.'

'As I said in my text,' says Judy, 'I'd like to ask you about Samantha Wilson and Karen Head. I believe they both used to come to your group?'

'I've looked through my records,' says Jacquie. 'Karen only came to a few meetings in early 2019. Samantha was a regular. I was really sorry when I heard what happened to her.'

She sounds sorry too. Judy also thinks she detects an intake of smoke. Has Jacquie replaced eating with smoking?

'When did you last see Samantha?' asks Judy.

'I think it was the week before . . . it happened. She came to the meeting as usual. She'd maintained that week, but she didn't seem too down about it.'

'Maintained?'

'Stayed the same weight. That happens sometimes. It's dispiriting but it's not as bad as gaining.'

Nothing's as bad as that, she seems to imply.

'Was Samantha friendly with anyone else in the group?'

'She got on with everyone, as I remember, but I don't think she had a special friend. People do become very close sometimes. We've even had a few romances.' She sounds rather wistful. Judy wonders if Jacquie is spending lockdown alone.

'Well, if you can think of anyone, can you give me a ring on this number?' says Judy.

'Of course,' says Jacquie. 'Can I ask though . . . I thought Sam . . . took her own life. Is there more to it than that?'

'I'm just following up on a few loose ends,' says Judy. 'But suicide is still the most likely cause of death.'

'Did Karen commit suicide too?'

'Yes, she did,' says Judy. This was what was on the death certificate after all.

After yoga, Ruth gives a lecture on decomposition and then settles down to do some marking. With end-of-year exams cancelled, the third years will have to do an extra piece of coursework, which means yet more work for the teachers. In their last departmental Zoom, David said the students were lucky to miss finals, but Ruth feels sorry for them. They may have avoided the horror of a written exam, but they'll miss the joy afterwards. She remembers sitting with her friends Roly and Caz in Gordon Square after their last exam at UCL. They had drunk red wine from the bottle and gazed up at the dusty plane trees. Anything seemed possible then. Ruth's students won't have this moment and, the way things are going, they might not even have a graduation ceremony.

Kate is making Hogwarts out of Lego. She got the set last Christmas, made it on Boxing Day and destroyed it by Twelfth Night. Ruth doesn't know why the wizarding school has appeared again, but she's pleased that Kate is happily occupied. Besides, she tells herself, slightly defensive even in her inner monologue, it's based on a book so it must be educational.

Ruth is scrolling through another second-year essay on lithic technology when an email pops up on her screen.

Can I talk to you? Eileen.

Ruth hesitates. Eileen isn't one of her personal tutees and this sounds like rather a personal request. Should she direct the girl to her counsellor? But she remembers Eileen coming to see her and her interest in Martha, the Tombland skeleton. Maybe this is just another question about isotope analysis.

OK, when?

The answer comes back almost as soon as Ruth's fingers leave the keyboard.

Can we zoom now?

Intrigued now, Ruth sends a link and, in a few minutes, Eileen's face appears on her screen. Ruth's first thought is that the girl looks ill. Ruth remembers seeing Eileen waiting outside her office at UNN and being struck by her long dark hair (rather like Kate's) and by her general air of health and well-being. Now the hair is pulled back into a greasy pony-tail and Eileen's skin looks both grey and blotchy. Perhaps it's just a bad Zoom angle. Ruth has abandoned hope of looking good on screen and, most of the time, manages not to look at herself. The second thing she notices is the brick wall behind Eileen's head and the institutional-looking noticeboard.

'Are you in halls?' she asks.

'Yes,' says Eileen. 'They're still open for international students and for people who haven't got anywhere to go.'

Eileen clearly falls into the second category. Was this why she kept her camera off during the last Zoom lecture, because she was embarrassed about not going home?

'What's it like?' she asks. 'Are you able to get food?'

'I go to the shops,' says Eileen. 'There's a mini supermarket quite near and I don't eat much anyway.'

Alarm bells are now going off in Ruth's head.

'Is there anyone else you can stay with? Family or friends?'

'Not really,' says Eileen. 'My dad's dead and I don't really get on with my mum. I mean, she's OK, I just don't feel welcome in her house.'

This was the dad who watched *Time Team*, Ruth remembers. She feels the chill of 'her house'. Despite all Ruth's disagreements with her parents, the house in Eltham has always felt like her home.

'Is there anyone else in halls?' she asks.

'A few overseas students,' says Eileen, 'and Joe. Joe McMahon from my course. That's why I wanted to talk to you. I'm worried about him.'

And I'm worried about you, thinks Ruth.

'Why?' she asks.

'He's not answering his phone. His blinds are drawn and there's no answer when I knock on his door. I'm worried he might have . . . done something to himself. His mum committed suicide. He told me about it.'

'I'm going to get on to the police,' says Ruth.

Nelson has never visited the halls of residence at UNN but, as he drives through the maze of buildings, he's reminded of similar places in Brighton and Plymouth, where his daughters were students. There are the same apartment blocks, bookshops and cafés with tiny roads between them, like a child's version of a town. The only difference is that, when he was dropping off Laura and Rebecca, the miniature streets were full of students and their parents, carrying luggage and saying tearful goodbyes. There had been balloons at Brighton and 'student welcomers' at Plymouth. Presumably, there were similar festivities at UNN, when term started last September but, today, the campus is deserted. Cherry tree blossom blows across the courtyards, looking like confetti from a long-forgotten wedding. The shops are boarded up and, across the bolted door of Canary Café, someone has written, 'abandon hope all ye who enter here'.

On the phone, Eileen told him to go to 'Vancouver', as if its location was obvious. But, in the event, Nelson finds it easily. It's the largest building, almost as big as a small hotel and with the same anonymous feeling to it, stone cladding with a vertical line of plasticky-looking blue tiles, rows of windows all with the same dreary blinds. There's a girl standing under the blue porch. She's wearing a mask but Nelson can tell that she's anxious just from the way that she's standing, arms wrapped around her body. She's wearing jeans and a T-shirt, too flimsy for the breezy spring day.

'Eileen? I'm DCI Nelson.' He shows his identification and, keeping his distance, takes off his mask so she can see his face. Eileen barely glances at the warrant card. Nelson wants to tell her to look properly. What's she doing, living in this deserted place all on her own? What are her parents thinking?'

'Thank you for coming,' says Eileen breathlessly. 'When Dr Galloway said she was calling the police I didn't know . . .'

'Dr Galloway has a hotline to the Serious Crimes Unit,' says Nelson. He puts on his mask. 'She said you were worried about a fellow student.'

'Yes,' says Eileen. 'My friend Joe. He's not answering his phone and his blinds are drawn.'

'Are you sure he hasn't just gone home?'

'I'm sure. He's got nowhere to go. Like me.'

The girl needs a hug and a hot meal, thinks Nelson. Well, he can't supply either.

'Can you show me Joe's room?' he says.

Eileen leads him up a staircase that smells of plastic and neglect. Joe's room is on the first floor at the end of a line of doors, some of which still have names on them. Trixie Bell. Big Ed. The Cookie Monster.

Nelson knocks on the last door. 'Joe?'

He knocks harder. 'Police! Open up!'

No answer. His voice echoes along the empty corridor.

'Stand back,' says Nelson to Eileen, even though she is dutifully keeping two metres away.

He charges the door, which opens easily. The darkened room is completely empty. Nelson takes in bed, desk, chair and a collage of photographs, all showing Dr Ruth Galloway.

22

Judy rolls her eyes although there's no one in the room to see it. Once again, the boss has gone rushing off after a phone call from Ruth, something about a student possibly being at risk. The best thing to do, in Judy's opinion, would have been to call campus security but Nelson muttered that it was quicker to go himself. Then he charged out of the office, knocking over a small table on his way. Judy heard his car roaring in the car park – she recognised the slightly dodgy exhaust – and then everything was silent.

Judy sighs and goes back to her Lean Zone notes. She has texted Barb Blakeborough and arranged to call at eleven. Barb answers her phone immediately, obviously ready and waiting.

Judy explains about following up on the death of Avril Flowers.

'Poor Avril,' says Barb. 'I was so shocked when I heard. Do you know what happened to her?'

'It's an ongoing investigation,' says Judy, 'but I'm very

keen to find out about Avril's state of mind in the days and weeks leading up to her death. I understand that she used to attend your Lean Zone meetings.'

'Yes,' says Barb. 'She was one of those women who never really seemed to lose weight, but she said the group helped stop her putting too much on. Not like me. I lost six stone in 2015 and I've kept it off. Thanks to Lean Zone.'

She says this like she's said it many times before. It sounds like a huge weight loss to Judy. Six stone is a small child, isn't it? She wonders if Barb expects congratulations, or at least amazement.

'Did Avril have any friends in the group?' she asks instead.

'I'm not sure,' says Barb. 'I think there were a few of them that used to have coffee together sometimes.'

'Well, can you text me if you remember any names?' says Judy. 'How was Avril's mood when you last spoke to her?'

'She seemed very cheerful,' says Barb. 'She was going on a trip with her friend Hugh.'

'I spoke to Avril's vicar,' said Judy, 'and she thought Avril might have been worried about something.'

'Mother Wendy?' says Barb. 'She's a regular at my Friday morning group.'

It's only when Judy asks Barb's whereabouts on the 25th and 26th of February, that the breezy voice falters. 'I had a 7pm group on the Tuesday and a 9am on the Wednesday. Why do you need to know? There's nothing *criminal*, is there?'

Judy thinks of the way Tony had pronounced the words

'foul play', with ill-concealed excitement. Barb sounds more fearful than anything and is not reassured when Judy says again that it's an ongoing investigation.

Nelson steps closer to the noticeboard. Ruth's face stares up at him, from a newspaper cutting about the excavation of murder victims, from the UNN archaeology prospectus, from the dust jacket of one of her books. There's even a screenshot from the TV series *Women Who Kill*, where Ruth was a – sometimes unwilling – expert witness. More worryingly, there are some photographs that were clearly taken from a distance, one showing Ruth and Katie outside the cottage. In the middle of the display – or shrine – there is a yellow Post-it note. Nelson leans forward to read the words written on it.

> *Stone walls do not a prison make*
> *Nor iron bars a cage.*

Nelson turns to Eileen, who is still keeping her distance. 'Did you know about this?'

'No,' says Eileen. 'I mean, I knew he liked her, thought she was a good teacher but . . . I never came into his room. I didn't know about this.'

'I'm going to call campus security,' says Nelson. 'And I really think you should find somewhere else to stay.'

'I'll be OK,' says Eileen. 'There's a lock on my door.'

Nelson remembers how easily he was able to break into Joe's room. The young really are astonishingly stupid sometimes. If Michelle were home, he'd be tempted to offer Eileen a bed for the night. But she isn't and he can't. Besides, they are in the middle of a pandemic. And he's planning to slope off to Ruth's as soon as he's collected Bruno.

'I'll speak to the university,' he says. 'They've got a duty of care.'

'They did send me a food parcel,' says Eileen. 'It had a Cup-a-Soup and two cans of baked beans in it.'

'Pictures of me?' says Ruth. She looks round the room. Kate is constructing the tower containing Dumbledore's study. Ruth remembers that the spiral staircase is very tricky. Flint is stretched out in a patch of sunlight. He seems to like having them both at home all day. They are all safe, Ruth tells herself.

'It was like a bloody shrine,' says Nelson. 'Newspaper cuttings, stuff from the internet. Even some photos that look as if he took them himself. One had Katie in it.'

'Kate?' Ruth can't stop her voice sounding sharp and anxious. Kate looks up and even Flint twitches in his sleep.

'What do you know about this lad?' Nelson is asking.

'He's one of my first years. He seems keen. Intelligent.' Ruth sees the dark-bearded face. Lytton Strachey. She thinks about Joe going to see Janet to talk about the Grey Lady. *Beware the Grey Lady.*

'Have you got a home address for him?' asks Nelson.

'There'll be one on the files. I'll check.'

'There was a Post-it note too. It said: "Stone walls do not

a prison make. Nor iron bars a cage." Do you know what that's all about?'

'It sounds like a poem.'

'It is. I googled it. By someone called Richard Lovelace.'

'I've never heard of him. I'll ask Shona.'

'Don't tell her too much.' Nelson is not the greatest fan of Shona, Ruth's friend in the English department. Ruth is fond of Shona but has to admit that discretion is not her strongest suit.

'I spoke to the campus security,' says Nelson, 'but they were bloody useless. There's a warden but it turns out he doesn't even live on site.'

'Most wardens don't.'

'I spoke to him too. I'm a bit worried about the girl. Eileen.'

'Me too.'

'I spoke to some of the other students in the halls. There are only a few of them. One of them, a nice Chinese girl, offered to keep an eye on Eileen. As well as she can from two metres away.'

'I'll check in with her regularly too,' says Ruth. 'I wish she could go home but she says she doesn't get on with her mother. I don't think the government have thought about students like Eileen. They think everyone has a nice safe home to go back to.'

'Home isn't always safe,' says Nelson. 'I'd better get back to the station now. Text me Joe McMahon's address. He's not necessarily a danger to you but I'd like to have a word with him.'

Not necessarily. It's not the most reassuring phrase, thinks Ruth. But Nelson's next remark is better.

'See you later,' he says.

After lunch, Ruth and Kate go for a windy walk across the Saltmarsh. Kate finds some crab claws and is ghoulishly pleased at the thought that a bird must have dropped them after feasting on the creature's insides. Back at home, she goes to give them pride of place on her nature table. Ruth takes the opportunity to ring Shona.

'Hi. How are you?' She's guiltily aware that she hasn't contacted her friend since the start of lockdown.

'OK. I'm going mad trying to keep Louis and Phil entertained. When you think we should have been halfway across Thailand by now.'

Shona and her partner Phil – Ruth's ex-boss – had been planning to take a year off and go around the world with their ten-year-old son, Louis. Phil had taken early retirement after a heart attack two years ago and Shona had managed to secure a sabbatical. Strictly speaking, they weren't planning to leave until July, but Ruth forgives Shona the slight exaggeration.

'It's awful the way everything's on hold now,' she says.

'It's the not knowing,' says Shona. 'Will everything be back to normal by the summer? Phil says not but he's being very gloomy.'

Shona sounds thoroughly fed up and Ruth doesn't blame her. Being locked down with Phil must constitute cruel and unusual punishment. Louis is not exactly easy company either.

'Maybe Louis and Kate could do something on Zoom one day,' she says, although she knows that the two do not always see eye to eye.

'That would be lovely,' says Shona. 'And the English department are having an online quiz tomorrow. Perhaps you could join in with that?'

'Perhaps,' says Ruth. She needs to think of an excuse, but she can hardly say that she's out that evening. She's not keen on quizzes at the best of times and doesn't fancy the idea of listening to the English department one-upping each other on Shakespeare quotations. Still, it reminds her of the purpose of her call.

'Richard Lovelace,' says Shona. 'He was one of those Cavalier poets.'

For a moment Ruth thinks Shona means 'cavalier' in the sense of being offhand, but then she realises that Lovelace must have been writing at the time of the English Civil War between the Parliamentarians (Roundheads) and Royalists (Cavaliers). Ruth is a bit vague on the detail but she knows that King's Lynn was besieged first by the Royalists and then by the Parliamentarians, led by the Earl of Manchester who always sounds made-up. Who was it that called the Parliamentarians 'right but repulsive'? She questions Shona, who laughs.

'That's from *1066 and All That*. The Royalists were "wrong but romantic". That's pretty much how I see the two sides. Lovelace was a Royalist, imprisoned by the Parliamentarians. Why are you interested in him? He's a minor poet, really.'

Ruth knows that Shona has her own literary hierarchy,

headed by Sylvia Plath and Shakespeare. Other dead white men are near the bottom.

'One of my students quoted something by him,' says Ruth, which is more or less true. '"Stone walls do not a prison make. Nor iron bars a cage."'

'That's probably Lovelace's most famous poem,' says Shona. '"To Althea, from Prison". I'll email you a copy if you like.'

'It's not that obscure then?'

'God no. You can probably get it on a mug or embroidered on a cushion.'

'Did he die in prison?' asks Ruth. 'Was he executed?'

'Oh no,' says Shona. 'He lived to fight another day.'

Ruth feels oddly comforted by this. They chat for a few more minutes before Ruth rings off, promising to think about the quiz.

Kate has gone back to her Lego so Ruth goes into the kitchen to ring Janet Meadows. She opens the back door and looks out into the garden. Once again, the small patch of green is extremely soothing. She can hear Zoe talking to Derek in her garden. A blackbird sings loudly from the apple tree.

Janet, too, seems pleased to hear from her.

'I'm already fed up with lockdown. There's only so much yoga and baking you can do.'

Ruth remembers that she included yeast and bread flour in her mammoth shop on Tuesday. Had she really been intending to bake bread? Things aren't that desperate yet. But then it's only been a week.

'I wanted to talk to you about one of my students,' says Ruth. 'Joe McMahon. He was the one who came to see you about the Tombland skeleton.'

'I remember. Chap with a beard.'

'That's right. I just wondered if you remembered anything specific about the conversation.'

Janet must wonder why she's asking but, unlike Shona, she doesn't press the matter.

'He wanted to know why a skeleton would be buried on its own like that. He thought it might mean that she was an outcast. Or a suicide.'

Eileen had said something similar, Ruth remembers.

'I don't think it was a deviant burial,' says Ruth. 'The body was wrapped in a shroud and was probably just interred in the graveyard. I told the students that.'

'He was quite intense,' says Janet. 'He told me that his mother had died recently. I felt quite sorry for him. Actually, hope this doesn't make you feel old, but he said he thought of you as a mother figure.'

Old isn't what this makes Ruth feel.

'I showed Joe the original plans to Augustine Steward's House,' says Janet. 'He seemed very interested. He said he was thinking of writing his dissertation about Tombland.'

'He's only a first year,' says Ruth. 'It's a bit early to be thinking of dissertations.'

'Really? I thought he seemed older. But, seriously, I don't think there's any harm in him. He's just a bit sad and a bit intense. We've all been there.'

Ruth definitely knows what it's like to be eighteen and

intense. She thinks of the days when she was dating Daniel, reading *The Brothers Karamazov* in the library and dreaming of escape. Life for Janet, pre-transition, must have been difficult in ways that Ruth can't even imagine. Maybe she's being a bit hard on Joe. After all, it's his business what he puts on his walls. She decides to change the subject.

'Have you found somewhere to live?' she says. 'When we last spoke you said you had to move out of your flat.'

'Yes, I've found somewhere.' Janet gives a little laugh.

'Is it in the centre of town?'

'Oh yes,' says Janet. 'Dead centre.'

Isn't that the punchline of a joke? Janet doesn't seem to want to explain so, after a few minutes' desultory chat, Ruth says goodbye and rings off.

23

The trouble with lockdown, thinks Ruth, is that the evenings are so long. Kate has finished Hogwarts by five and is wandering around the room, picking things up and sighing. Flint is not much better. He keeps standing on Ruth's keyboard and inserting the letters 'ppppoooottt' into her comments column. Ruth gives up. She switches on the news and learns that Boris Johnson has tested positive for Covid. His statement says that he's working from home and 'continuing to lead the national fightback against coronavirus'. Fightback sounds as if the battleground is even, instead of the virus having all the weapons. Ruth hopes the Prime Minister recovers quickly. There's something frightening about the leader of the country being taken ill, whether you voted for him or not. She turns the radio off.

Ruth pours herself a glass of wine and contemplates supper. Should she make some for Nelson? What did he mean by 'later'? She doesn't think she's ever cooked for him before and has no doubt that she will show up badly compared to Michelle's culinary skills. She always imagines Michelle putting perfect meals in front of Nelson, like a 1950s house-wife. Well, things are a little different chez Ruth. She decides to cook a bolognaise sauce which can be heated up later with fresh pasta if necessary. Flint comes in to remind her that he likes uncooked mince. She cooks it for him all the same.

While the sauce is cooking, Ruth takes her wine into the garden. She doesn't want to join Kate in front of *Pointless* and she feels too restless to read. When she was at work, she would buy the *Guardian* from the campus bookstore and do the quick crossword in the evening. A daily newspaper is one of the minor casualties of lockdown. Ruth sits on the doorstep and watches Flint prowling through the long grass. She thinks of Eileen alone, or almost alone, in the empty halls of residence. She imagines Joe's locked room – she is sure that Nelson will have shoulder-barged the door – the dust covering every surface, the photographs on the notice-board. Photographs of her. A shrine, Nelson said. The word gives Ruth a slight shiver, one that seems to be echoed in the breeze ruffling the leaves of the apple tree. She thinks of Walsingham, England's Nazareth, a place of pilgrimage since the eleventh century, the Anglican shrine, the Slipper Chapel, the archway of the ruined monastery. She remem-bers a woman's body being found under that same archway. Shrines aren't always healthy places.

According to Janet, Joe thought of Ruth as a 'mother figure'. If he's about twenty (Ruth thinks he's slightly older than the other first years but it's hard to tell with the beard) then, biologically, it's perfectly possible. Even so, the words seem suddenly sinister. Presumably the Virgin Mary was a mother figure for the pilgrims at Walsingham. But not everyone worships their mother.

It's almost dark now, the sky navy blue behind the trees. The security light comes on as Flint appears, tightrope walking along the fence. Zoe's voice floats into the twilight. 'Derek, De-rek.' She must be anxious about her cat, unused as he is to the outside world. Ruth wonders whether to call out to her neighbour, to say that she's sure Derek is fine, but somehow she doesn't feel like talking. It's a comfort to know that there's someone on the other side of the fence though. A woman and a cat. The perfect combination.

Still, she can't sit on her back-doorstep all evening. Ruth goes back into the kitchen and stirs the sauce. It needs something but she can't think what. She adds some salt, pepper and a splash of her wine for luck. She puts on some water for the pasta. Then she goes into the sitting room where Kate is still watching the quiz show. Ruth thinks of the English teachers and their Zoom quiz tomorrow. *Which of Shakespeare's heroines said this?* Well, she's got better things to do. Or has she? Will Nelson still be with them tomorrow? If so, it'll be the first time she's ever spent a complete Saturday with him. What will they do? It's not as if they can have a day out after all. They can take Bruno for a walk, she supposes. They can have supper together and watch a film on Netflix. Don't think about it, Ruth tells herself, and then you won't be disappointed. She opens her laptop. She'll get some more marking done.

She sees immediately that she has new emails from Peter and Shona. She opens Shona's first, to put off the other.

Shona has sent the text of 'To Althea, from Prison' by Richard Lovelace.

> When Love with unconfinèd wings
> Hovers within my Gates,
> And my divine Althea brings
> To whisper at the Grates;
> When I lie tangled in her hair,
> And fettered to her eye,
> The Gods that wanton in the Air,
> Know no such Liberty.
>
> When flowing Cups run swiftly round
> With no allaying Thames,
> Our careless heads with Roses bound,
> Our hearts with Loyal Flames;
> When thirsty grief in Wine we steep,
> When Healths and draughts go free,
> Fishes that tipple in the Deep
> Know no such Liberty.
>
> When (like committed linnets) I
> With shriller throat shall sing
> The sweetness, Mercy, Majesty,
> And glories of my King;
> When I shall voice aloud how good
> He is, how Great should be,
> Enlargèd Winds, that curl the Flood,
> Know no such Liberty.

Stone Walls do not a Prison make,
Nor Iron bars a Cage;
Minds innocent and quiet take
That for an Hermitage.
If I have freedom in my Love,
And in my soul am free,
Angels alone that soar above,
Enjoy such Liberty

'Wrong but romantic,' thinks Ruth. It occurs to her that Lovelace is the ideal name for a Cavalier. She is sure that Richard loved his lace, not to mention his plumes and velvet. She's not sure what to make of the poem. 'Tangled in her hair' is quite an image. She imagines Althea with miles of golden hair, like Rapunzel. But being trapped in hair is another imprisonment of sorts. 'Fettered to her eye' is unpleasant too, when you come to think of it. There's lots of flying imagery, lots of wings. Even fish get a mention. Are they flying fish? Maybe Lovelace, too, found comfort in nature while incarcerated. Maybe he too had a pet crow called Corbyn. 'If I have freedom in my love And in my soul am free . . .' Ruth thinks of Nelson. Are they free because they are under lockdown?

To escape from this train of thought, Ruth clicks on the email from Peter. There's an attachment too. Should she open it? If so, there's always a danger of disappearing down one of those rabbit holes that seem to be one of the hazards of a solitary life. You run the risk of becoming tangled in the hair of memory. Too late, she has already clicked on the icon. *Thought you'd like to see this.* It's a photograph of Ruth in this very room, sitting on the sofa with a kitten on each shoulder. Flint and Sparky, ginger and black-and-white. Like the two ravens of Odin. The room hasn't changed much, the same sofa and bookshelves, although there were more gaps then. The television is smaller and boxier and there's a framed poster of Devizes on the wall. Peter, a Wiltshire boy, must have taken it with him when he left. Ruth herself looks almost unbearably young and happy. Her hair is longer and her cheeks rounder. She's wearing a UCL sweatshirt and jeans. Ruth can almost hear Peter laughing as he took the picture. The Cabin.

Ruth looks at the picture until Kate tells her that the water is boiling. She and Kate eat their pasta in front of another quiz show. It's not until Kate is upstairs having her bath that Ruth opens her laptop again. Now there's a new message.

The Grey Lady can walk through locked doors. You can never be safe from her hunger. Beware.

Nelson doesn't appear until nearly nine. Kate is in bed and Ruth is sitting at the window marking essays. She sees the white Mercedes parking outside and wonders if Zoe too is watching from her house. They are breaking the rules, even if you factor in the 'divorced father' clause. Lockdown is going to make adultery a lot more difficult, thinks Ruth, wondering where that Old Testament word has appeared from. Sent by divine email from her mother? A rhyme comes into her mind, even as she gets up to open the door. *Do not adultery commit. Advantage rarely comes of it.* Now, where did *that* come from? She'll have to ask the English department quiz team.

Ruth expects Bruno to come bounding up the garden path, but Nelson emerges from the car on his own, gives a rather furtive look around him, and strides towards the cottage, head down.

Ruth opens the door before he can knock. 'Safe from the adultery police?'

'Bloody hell. That sounds like something my mum would say.'

'Where's Bruno?'

'That's why I'm a bit late. I dropped him off with a friend. Jan Adams. She's going to look after him, just during lockdown. She used to be a dog-handler. Got a German shepherd too, Barney. He's a distant relation of Bruno's, actually.'

'As long as he's with family.'

Nelson laughs and sits down on the sofa. Flint immediately gets up to leave. It occurs to Ruth that Nelson could actually move in with her, at least while Michelle is away. That way they would be one household and so not breaking any rules. But she doesn't say this. She asks Nelson if he wants supper. He says that he's eaten.

'Sure?'

'Well, if it's no trouble.'

Ruth goes into the kitchen to heat up the sauce and put the water on for more pasta. Flint follows, complaining loudly, probably about Nelson. She placates him with more gourmet cat food and pours two glasses of wine. When she comes back into the sitting room, Nelson is reading the back cover of Kate's copy of *The Hunger Games*.

'Is this for kids? It looks terrifying.'

'Kids like to be terrified.' Ruth hands him the wine. She thinks of the email. *You can never be safe from her hunger.*

'Did you have any luck tracing Joe?' she asks.

'No. I tried the contact number you gave me. It was his dad but he says they're estranged. He hasn't seen Joe for almost a year.'

'His mother died recently,' says Ruth. 'Maybe that's why.' She tells Nelson about Janet Meadows and her meeting with Joe.

'A mother figure,' says Nelson. 'Jesus wept.'

'Well, exactly.'

'Mother wasn't the word that came into my head when I saw those pictures,' says Nelson. 'It was as if he was obsessed with you.'

'You'd better see this.' Ruth hands him the laptop and leans over to show the Grey Lady email.

'Who's this from?' says Nelson.

'I've no idea. I had another one a few days ago telling me to beware of the Grey Lady.'

'Why didn't you tell me about it?'

'I thought it might not be important.'

'Bloody hell, Ruth,' says Nelson. 'Of course it's important. Someone's threatening you. Who is this Grey Lady anyway?'

'She's the ghost of a woman who was bricked up during

the plague. Apparently, she ate her parents and then died herself.'

'Jesus wept,' says Nelson again.

Ruth goes to check on the pasta.

Much later, Ruth feeds the cat and double locks the front door. She can hear Nelson in the bathroom upstairs. The security light comes on outside but she knows that it's just a fox. Or Derek. Or the Grey Lady. Nothing can scare her tonight.

24

Judy is surprised when the boss says that he isn't going to work at the weekend. They are still meant to be investigating the Avril Flowers case and Judy expected Nelson to be at the station every day, chivvying and chasing every last scrap of information. Instead, he told her, when she was leaving for the day, that he was going to take Bruno to Jan's house and 'have the weekend off'. Why is Nelson choosing this moment to slacken off from work? It's not as if he has anything else to do. Has he?

Nelson has been strange ever since he got back from the halls of residence, thinks Judy. He kept ranting on about some student who had pictures of Ruth plastered all over the walls. They tried to trace this boy, Joe McMahon, but to no avail. Besides, as Judy ventured to say, it's no crime to have someone's photo on your wall. She's never been a student but her bedroom at home had been a shrine to Michael Praed as Robin of Sherwood. Come to think of it, that probably explains a lot, from her son's first name to her relationship with Cathbad.

Judy should be happy at the idea of having some free time. She, after all, is driving home to a house full of people. Cathbad will have cooked supper. Michael and Miranda will want to tell her about their day. Maddie will be on hand for some heavy-duty *Grey's Anatomy* viewing later. But Judy knows that, some time over the weekend, she will be looking over the files on Avril Flowers. And on Samantha Wilson and Karen Head.

The family are all in the garden. Judy goes into the downstairs loo to wash her hands several times and then she goes out to join them. Maddie is tapping at her laptop, protected by a parasol. Michael and Miranda are digging their vegetable patch and Cathbad is siphoning recycled rainwater into a watering can. It's such a peaceful scene, the air smelling of grass and newly turned soil, that Judy almost wants to stand and observe it without anyone seeing her. But Thing notices her immediately and rushes over to welcome her. Cathbad follows more circumspectly.

'Good day?'

'OK. Strange. I'll tell you later.' She doesn't want to discuss Joe McMahon or the Lean Zone breakthrough with Maddie in the background, probably online to the *Chronicle* at this very moment.

'We're making a bug hotel,' says Miranda, pointing at a ramshackle collection of boxes in the middle of the lawn.

'It's more like a bug homeless shelter,' says Cathbad.

Judy thinks of Nelson's description of the UNN halls of residence. 'Like a hotel in a war zone.' She is very glad, once again, that her children are still at home with her, surely too young to be traumatised by this weird limbo-like time. For them, right now, it seems more like paradise than limbo.

'And we're going to have a worming,' says Miranda.

'A worm bin,' corrects Michael. 'I'm going to grow peas and broad beans in my bit of garden.'

'I'm going to grow an enormous tree,' says Miranda, determined to outdo him. 'With silver bells and cockle shells. Like the rhyme.'

'That's about torture,' says Maddie. 'The silver bells are thumbscrews. I read it somewhere. "Mary, Mary, Quite Contrary". Mary is Mary Tudor.'

The boss had mentioned a poem too, Judy remembers. *Stone walls do not a prison make. Nor iron bars a cage.* It had been on Joe McMahon's wall, alongside the pictures of Ruth. She realises that Cathbad is watching her and forces a smile.

'Has anyone made banana bread? I'm starving.'

Banana bread, followed by a delicious supper, white wine and several episodes of Meredith Grey saving lives all put Judy in a better frame of mind. On Saturday morning they go for a walk on Wells beach, revelling in the miles of sand and the complete absence of tourists. I'm so lucky, thinks Judy, watching Thing run to collect a piece of driftwood. Imagine being locked down in London, or even Norwich. Surely you would go mad without this stretch of blue, this healing space between you and the horizon.

In honour of her work/life balance, Judy has left her phone at home. When she checks it, she's irritated to see that she's missed a call from Tina Prentice, Avril's cleaner. There's a voice message, somewhat breathless.

'Hallo, er . . . Judy. You did say to call if I remembered anything. Well I've just remembered that I did see someone at Avril's house that day. Can you give me a ring back?'

Judy does so and leaves a message. Later that afternoon, when the children are watching *The Lion King* on DVD, Judy rings again and, to her surprise, someone answers. It doesn't sound like Tina. This voice is younger. More anxious.

'Hallo? Who is this?'

Judy explains.

'Mum's been taken ill. This is Denise, her daughter. She's gone to hospital.'

'Oh, I'm so sorry. I hope she'll be better soon.'

Judy does not like to say the C word but Denise does it for her. 'They think it's Covid,' she says.

So, this is what it's like, thinks Ruth. This is what it's like to wake up with Nelson, have breakfast with him and discuss what they're going to do all day. And, at times, when they are all sitting in the kitchen, eating bacon sandwiches and laughing at Flint's attempts to ignore Nelson, it really does seem like the purest happiness. At other times, when Nelson turns on the television – without asking – and seems mesmerised by some football programme, it's less delightful. It's not even a recent match. There's no live football, or any other sport, because of the pandemic.

'Let's go out for a walk,' says Ruth.

'I want to watch the football,' says Kate, sitting next to her father on the sofa.

'Who's playing then?' asks Ruth.

'It's . . .' Kate stares at the screen. 'Mun and Ack Milan.'

Nelson laughs. Ruth looks at Flint and is sure that the cat raises his eyebrows.

'Well, we should go out when this fascinating match is over.'

In the end, they walk over the sand dunes to the sea. The haunted landscape is looking at its best today: the marshes are bright with secret expanses of water and flocks of birds rise up into the pale blue sky.

'Godforsaken dump,' mutters Nelson, but his heart isn't in it.

'Godforsaken,' repeats Kate, enjoying the sound of the word.

Ruth misses Cathbad who would surely say something about sacred spaces and liminal zones. But she can't suggest meeting them for a socially distanced walk because then Judy would see that Nelson is with her.

Kate cheers up at the sight of the sea and runs along the sand, arms outstretched like a toddler pretending to be an aeroplane. Ruth thinks of the moment, twenty-one years ago, when they discovered the timbers of a Bronze Age henge on this same beach. Erik, her mentor and then friend, had fallen to his knees in the centre of the sacred circle. Eleven years later, a child's body had been found buried in that exact spot.

'I still think about her,' says Nelson. 'Scarlet. Do you?'

Ruth is rather taken aback by this Cathbad-like clairvoyance.

'Yes,' she says. 'I think about her a lot. She'd be fifteen now.'

Ruth never met Scarlet Henderson in life, but she imagines her now, a laughing teenager, striding along by the water's edge. Cathbad's daughter, Maddie, was Scarlet's half-sister. Ruth wonders how often she conjures this same image.

'It's a lonely place,' says Nelson, looking out towards the sea. 'A lot of bad memories too. Do you ever think of moving?'

Ruth hesitates. This is dangerous ground, more dangerous than the shifting quicksand of the marsh. 'Sometimes,' she says. 'Now that Kate's growing up. But I love it here.'

'I know you do,' says Nelson, his tone implying that this reflects badly on her judgement.

'My mum hated it,' says Ruth. 'But, when I was going through her belongings, I found a picture of my cottage.'

'She must have liked it a bit then,' says Nelson.

'It was dated 1963,' says Ruth. 'That was written on the back, "Dawn 1963".'

'It's a mystery,' says Nelson. 'I know you like those.'

'So do you.'

'I'm a policeman. I hate mysteries.'

Ruth thinks of the photograph from Peter. The two kittens sitting on her shoulders. Sparky is buried in the back garden. Nelson actually dug the grave. Can she bear to leave those memories behind? And what memories did her mother have of the house, some thirty years before Ruth ever lived there? But, before she can say more, or argue with Nelson – she thinks he likes detection more than he admits – Kate comes galloping over to show them a mermaid's purse. Concentrate on the present, Ruth tells herself.

Nelson, too, has always imagined this day. What would it be like, in a parallel universe, to be married to Ruth? Restful, is one answer. Ruth doesn't feel the need to tidy up constantly – she has left Monday's *Guardian* on the table all week – and she seems to have no particular agenda for the weekend. Of course, all the places Michelle would frequent – gym, garden centre, shops – are shut but Nelson gets the feeling that they wouldn't figure in Ruth's plans anyway. They have a leisurely breakfast, eating bacon sandwiches and drinking coffee. Nelson tries to lure the demon cat with a bacon rind, but the animal simply turns its back on him. Katie laughs so much that orange juice comes out of her nose. Ruth laughs too, and it's pure joy to hear mother and daughter enjoying themselves so much, even if it is at his expense.

Ruth seems less happy when he settles down to watch the football, as he always does at home. She forces them to go out on a walk, across the dull, flat landscape, pitted with treacherous streams, all the way to the dull, grey sea. Nelson calls it 'godforsaken' and Ruth gives him one of her sideways looks. They have quite an interesting talk about Ruth moving house. Although she stamps on the notion, it's the first time she's ever admitted that it might be a possibility.

Back at the cottage, Nelson offers to make fish finger sandwiches for lunch and is astounded that Ruth does not stock this essential foodstuff. They have cheese on toast instead. Afterwards, Nelson helps Katie construct a Lego house. He's forgotten how much he likes this sort of thing, fitting the little grooved bricks together, looking at the baffling Danish instructions, searching for that elusive corner block. He asks Katie what they're making and she says 'Hagrid's hut' so he's none the wiser. Ruth sits at the table by the window working on her laptop but Nelson notices her looking over towards him several times. He asks her if she's had any more sinister messages and she says no. He'll look into it on Monday. He doesn't trust Joe McMahon, not one inch. The boy is obviously obsessed with Ruth and now he's God knows where, plotting God knows what. Nelson does not approve of suspects being where he can't see them.

Ruth cooks a curry for supper. She does it in a rather haphazard way, with a book propped up on the work surface and Radio 4 tuned to some interminable play about the end of the world, but the curry is surprisingly good. Nelson and Katie wash up (after Nelson spent several futile minutes searching for the dishwasher) and Nelson makes coffee. Then they settle down to watch *The Princess Bride*. It's a film Nelson's daughters loved so, for the first time today, he feels slightly uncomfortable. Katie is sitting very close to him and keeps telling him the plot but, even so, after half a bottle of wine with supper, he feels his eyes starting to close. Ruth, the other side of Katie, is surreptitiously checking her phone. Is she worried about more Grey Lady messages? Or is someone else calling her? That horrendous David from work, perhaps?

'Dad,' says Katie. 'Your phone's buzzing.'

Nelson's phone is on the table. He picks it up. Laura. Instantly, the sleepiness and content fall away and all that is left is guilt. Nelson takes the phone and goes into the kitchen where Flint is sitting on the table hoovering up crumbs.

'What is it, love?'

Laura is crying. 'It's just so awful here, Dad. I can't cope. Can I come home?'

25

Ruth watches Nelson getting dressed, pulling on his shirt
and jumper, ruffling his wet hair. She almost offers to make
him a cup of tea but decides against it. To be honest, it's
as if he already left last night, as soon as he got the call
from Laura. Ruth understands his concern for his daughter.
Nelson is a devoted father, it's one of the things she loves
about him. But is he always going to leave her, as soon as
he gets a summons from his other family?

'I hope Laura's OK,' she says now.

Nelson turns around, looking almost surprised to see her
there. You're still in my house, Ruth wants to tell him.
You've just got out of my bed.

'She will be,' says Nelson. 'It's just lockdown and being in
that flat. I think she just needs some space.'

'It must be hard,' says Ruth. She has too much space, she
thinks. Her cottage is surrounded by space, the marshes, the
sea and the sky. Sometimes it feels as if she and Kate are on
another planet. Well, at least she now has Zoe next door.

'I'm sorry, love,' says Nelson. Though he doesn't say what

for. He kisses her quickly, his lips hardly touching hers. And he's gone.

Laura arrives home at ten a.m. Nelson has already been back for three hours, trying to make the place look lived in.

'I think you should go now,' Ruth had said last night. Her voice was perfectly pleasant, and he couldn't tell if she was annoyed or not.

'Oh no, Dad,' said Katie. 'Please stay. We haven't got to the six-fingered man yet.'

So Nelson had stayed the night but he got up at six to drive home. Ruth had still been pleasant in the morning but it was as if all the intimacy had vanished. She sat up in their still rumpled bed, looking, in her white nightdress, like a statue of virtue. 'I hope Laura's OK,' she said, as if asking after an acquaintance.

Nelson had tiptoed in to kiss Katie goodbye then he'd walked out to his car. Looking back, he saw the devil cat at the window, obviously planning a party to celebrate his departure. Was there a flicker at the next-door window too, a hand pulling back a curtain, a white face looking out? Nelson still isn't sure. As he drove along the coast road, the mist lifted and the sea was smooth and clear, like a mirage. He didn't see a single other car.

'Where's Bruno?' says Laura as soon as she comes through the door.

'Jan's looking after him. I've got a lot on at work.'

'What about Maura?'

'I thought Jan was easiest. What with lockdown and everything. And she's got Barney too.'

'We could get him back now I'm here.'

'You'll be working too, won't you?'

He knows that Laura is still going into school, teaching vulnerable children and the children of key workers. The strain of this and coming home to a shared flat with no outdoor space is clearly what is making her feel stressed. Nelson has always worried about his eldest daughter who has struggled in the past with anxiety and eating disorders. She's hard-working, conscientious and sensitive and, five years ago, she saw a man die in this very room. It's no wonder that lockdown is proving hard for her.

'It would be nice to take Bruno for walks,' she says.

'You can take me for walks.'

'You! Go for a walk without Bruno! That'll be the day.'

I went for a walk yesterday, Nelson wants to say. *Katie found a revolting object called a mermaid's purse and I had to put it in my pocket along with several lucky stones.* But he just gives Laura a hug. 'It's good to have you home.'

'Were you lonely on your own?'

'Very lonely,' says Nelson.

'I'll look after you now,' says Laura. 'I bet there's no food in the fridge.'

Ruth is left to face Sunday, never her favourite day, on her own. Kate is whiny and bored, missing Nelson. Even Flint looks disappointed. Ruth is at a loss as to how to distract her daughter. Normally, they'd drive into Lynn, look at the shops or go to the cinema. Or they'd go to the swimming pool and race each other up and down the lanes before having frothy cappuccino and KitKats in the café. There's still the sea, Ruth tells herself, but Kate greets the prospect of another beach walk with disdain.

'You could take your wetsuit,' says Ruth. 'See if it's warm enough to swim.'

She knows the water will be absolutely freezing. Ruth doesn't have a wetsuit but will be forced to go in if Kate does. She's slightly relieved when Kate dismisses that idea. Ruth knows not even to mention homework.

They are eating a rather silent and grumpy breakfast when there's a knock at the back door. This is unusual enough to make mother and daughter look at each other. Ruth feels an actual twinge of fear. They are on their own, without the protection of Nelson. What if it's the person who's been sending her the messages? *The Grey Lady can walk through locked doors. You can never be safe from her hunger.*

The door is the stable type. Ruth opens the top half to see Zoe standing on the other side. She's wearing jeans and a pink jumper but still manages to look somehow chic, pulled together in a way that Ruth can never achieve.

'Sorry to disturb you,' says Zoe. 'But I'm going mad with boredom on the other side of the wall. Do you two fancy going for a walk? We could take tennis rackets and play on the beach. It's the perfect game for keeping two metres apart.'

Ruth is afraid that Kate is going to pull *that* face again but it seems that a walk with their fun new neighbour is far more exciting than one with just her mother. She agrees immediately and goes off to get dressed. Ruth makes Zoe a coffee and passes it over the door.

'Thank you,' says Ruth. 'You've saved our lives. Or rather you've saved our Sunday.'

'It's a funny day, isn't it?' says Zoe. 'Even if you don't go to church it feels different from other days.'

'My parents were very religious,' says Ruth. 'They spent almost the whole day at church. I hated it when I was a child, but I suppose it gave them something to do. I wonder what my dad's doing now that churches are closed.'

'Is your dad on his own? Oh no, I think you said he'd remarried?'

'Yes. It was a bit of a shock at the time but I'm just glad he's got someone to keep him company. And Gloria is very nice, which helps. She's religious too. In fact they met at church. This whole thing has made me a bit more tolerant of religion. Their church really does seem to be looking after its parishioners.'

'My parents went at Christmas and Easter,' says Zoe. 'I quite liked the ritual of it.'

'You must miss them,' says Ruth.

Zoe looks away for a minute. 'I was watching a programme about Romanian orphanages the other day,' she says, 'and I realised that I'm an orphan. It's like something out of a Victorian children's book.'

'There are lots of orphans in children's books,' says Ruth. '*Anne of Green Gables*. Mary in *The Secret Garden*. Harry Potter.'

'Why are you talking about Harry Potter?' Kate appears, fully dressed, even wearing an anorak.

'Are you a fan?' says Zoe. 'I am. Let's talk about it on the way. Who's your favourite character?'

Zoe really is the perfect neighbour, thinks Ruth, as she fetches her own cagoule. Ruth would be hard put to think of her favourite Harry Potter character though she does have a soft spot for Dobby the House Elf.

Judy waits until late morning to ring Tina's number again. There's no answer but she leaves a message.

'Hi. This is Judy Johnson. Hope you're feeling better. When you're up to it, please give me a ring. I'd love to hear what you remembered about Avril. Take care. All best.'

She feels twitchy all day, all through a long walk along the beach, Sunday lunch and Michael and Miranda's afternoon concert with Michael playing the piano and Miranda the recorder, accompanied by Maddie's unexpectedly beautiful singing voice.

When the children are in bed and Cathbad's listening to music on his headphones, Judy and Maddie settle down to watch *Grey's Anatomy*. They are just into the first soothing medical catastrophe when Judy's phone rings. *Tina Prentice*, says the screen. It's ten thirty p.m. Tina must be back from hospital. Thank goodness.

'Hallo. Tina?'

There's a pause and then a voice says, 'It's Denise. Tina's daughter. Mum passed away this morning.'

'Oh my God,' says Judy. 'I'm so sorry.' She stares at the TV.

Maddie has thoughtfully turned the sound off but figures in blue scrubs are moving purposefully round a pristine operating theatre. Judy can't help thinking that Tina's last moments must have been very different.

'I'm so sorry,' she says again.

'We weren't allowed to be with her because of Covid,' says Denise. 'I just hate to think of her dying alone.' She's crying now.

'I'm sure . . .' starts Judy but she stops because she isn't sure of anything any more.

'I'm ringing because when she went into hospital she was really struggling to talk. Struggling to breathe really. But she wanted to tell you something. She said, "Tell Judy. It was you."'

'It was me?'

'It didn't make sense to me but that's what she said. Liam, my husband, remembers it too.'

'Thank you for telling me,' says Judy. 'I do appreciate it. And, again, I'm so sorry. I only met Tina once, but I could see what a lovely person she was.'

'She really was,' says Denise. Her voice is choked and she rings off quickly.

Judy turns to Maddie and Cathbad, who are both looking at her with concern.

'It's started,' she says.

26

'"It was you",' says Nelson. 'What the hell does that mean?'

'I don't know,' says Judy. 'But that's how the daughter remembered it. Her husband too. I wish I could have spoken to Tina. It's so sad. She seemed fit and well when Tanya and I interviewed her.'

Although it's meant to be Tanya's day in the office, Judy has come in to discuss this latest development. Leah is back too, looking like a secret service agent in a black polo neck.

'Tina was in the dangerous age zone,' says Tanya. 'People over seventy are more at risk from Covid. Plus she was over weight. Petra says obesity is a contributory factor.'

'She wasn't obese,' says Judy. She feels oddly protective about Tina. She remembers the active figure bustling around her kitchen, feeding children and chickens, answering their questions with matter-of-fact kindness. *I'll relax when I'm dead.*

'You'd be surprised at the clinical definition of obesity,' says Tanya.

This reminds Judy of her Lean Zone theory. She fills Tanya in now. 'It's the only link between all the deaths.'

'Did Tina go to Lean Zone?' asks Tanya.

'I don't know,' says Judy. 'I'll find out.' She can't really go back to Denise on Tina's phone, but she can ask Jacquie and Barb to check their membership files.

'I keep going back to that third person's fingerprints on the door handle,' says Nelson. 'Someone was in Avril's house on the day she died. Or some time very close to it.'

'It might be worth talking to Avril's daughter again,' says Judy. 'Sometimes the shock of a death can wipe out recent memories. It's been a few weeks now. Something might have come back to her.'

A few weeks. It seems like years since she and Tanya visited the bungalow with the veranda around it.

'Good idea,' says Nelson. 'And let's keep trying to trace Joe McMahon. For his own safety as much as anything.'

'He hasn't done anything wrong though,' says Tanya. 'Apart from having pictures of Ruth all over his room.' She flicks a glance at Judy.

'Like I say,' says the boss, rather stiffly. 'I'm concerned for his safety. A fellow student mentioned that he might have had suicidal thoughts.'

'Which is more than any of our so-called suicides did,' says Tanya.

'You never know what people are thinking,' says Nelson. 'But we need to do some more digging on Avril. Good idea to go back to the daughter, Judy. Let's keep the other women in mind too. They might have taken their own lives but, then again, they might not. If so, there's a serial killer out there.'

It's the first time any of them have said these words. Judy wonders if they are all thinking the same thing. Lockdown could make life very easy for a serial killer.

Ruth is, once again, Zooming with her first-year students. There's no sign of Joe McMahon and, more worryingly still, Eileen does not appear. It's hard to engage them, online, with field methods in archaeology. Normally, this module is taught on site. Ruth had hoped to include Martha, the Tombland skeleton, this year. But today they have to make do with photographs of landscapes, spotting the topographical features – hillocks, dips or lines – that might be evidence of archaeological activity. Ruth's mind is slightly distracted and she's glad when the two hours are over.

Afterwards Ruth emails Eileen – *Just checking you're OK?* – but doesn't get any answer. Has Eileen gone home? Ruth hopes so. She wonders if Nelson has had any luck tracing Joe. She hasn't spoken to him since he left on Sunday morning. She wonders how he's getting on with Laura and whether seeing his daughter, who looks very like her mother, is making him miss Michelle. She also sincerely hopes that Laura is feeling better. She's very fond of Nelson's daughter and Kate adores her. It's all very complicated.

Kate has already finished the work set by the school and is embarking on another Lego construction. Ruth wonders if they should go out for a walk. Cathbad unexpectedly cancelled yoga this morning so they haven't had any fresh air. But she can't face disturbing Kate, so she goes back to her laptop and starts to prepare her next lecture. Excavating human remains.

Judy rings Bethany Flowers but there's no answer. She leaves a message and, keen to escape from the police station and Tanya's at-desk fitness regime – she stands up every fifteen minutes and performs lunges – decides to drive into Hunstanton. The library and the church are both shut. There's a note on the latter giving Mother Wendy's number *in case of emergencies*. Judy writes it down, wondering whether it's worth asking the vicar more about Avril's state of mind. *Of course she was worried. That's what the church is here for. For worried people.*

It's a sunny morning. Sunny Hunny, Judy's parents used to call the town, and it's certainly living up to its name today. Judy drives to the seafront and walks along the promenade. There are a few people walking along the beach, but the funfair is shrouded under plastic sheeting and there's police tape across the band stand. Of course, it's still only March. Will the tourists flock back in summer, even if everything is still shut? If so, it will be up to the local police to send them home. Judy walks back to her car, remembering trips to the sea-life centre and rides on the Tractor Train. However much she enjoys having the beach to herself there's something very sad about an empty seaside resort.

On impulse, Judy drives to Hugh Baxter's house. The garden is as neat as ever, now full of daffodils and tulips. Hugh Baxter answers the door almost before she knocks.

He's dressed, as before, in a neat shirt and tie, slacks and leather slippers.

'DI Johnson,' he says. 'How nice to see you again.'

Judy is touched that he's remembered her name (and got her rank right) but somehow sad that he's so pleased to see her. How many visitors does the old man get? she wonders. Vulnerable people are being told to shield which, in practice, means never leaving their house.

'I just wondered how you were,' she says. 'I can't come in, I'm afraid, and we should keep two metres apart.' She says this because Hugh has moved closer, peering short-sightedly.

'I'm fine,' says Hugh, backing away. 'I do my exercises every morning and go for a walk round the block. And I like watching the birds in the garden.'

'What about food?' says Judy. 'Are you managing OK?'

'The local Co-op delivers,' says Hugh. 'And I don't eat that much.'

Judy's heart contracts but the comment reminds her of the purpose of her visit.

'I know it's a strange question,' she says, 'but did Avril go to Lean Zone meetings? It's a slimming group.'

But Hugh answers immediately. 'Yes, she did. Not that she needed to lose weight. But you ladies are all the same. Even my late wife was, and she was as slim as anything.'

Judy doesn't argue with this although she's never dieted in her life. She knows that old people have different attitudes. Her grandmother keeps asking when Cathbad is going to make an honest woman of her.

'Do you remember if Avril had any friends in the group?'

'There was one woman. A nurse, I think. Avril used to talk about her sometimes.'

'Can you remember her name?'

'No, but it might come back to me. Sometimes things come back to me in the middle of the night.'

'Well, if it does, could you give me a ring? I'd be very grateful.' Judy hands over her card.

Hugh holds it very close to his face. 'Serious Crimes Unit.'

'That's just for show,' says Judy. 'I'm interested in non-serious crimes too.'

Hugh laughs, a surprisingly robust sound. Judy starts to say goodbye when he interrupts her. 'You don't know what's happened to Tina Prentice, do you? It's just that she usually rings me on a Sunday and she didn't yesterday.'

Judy takes a deep breath. 'I'm afraid I've got some bad news.'

When Judy gets back in the car, she breathes deeply for a few minutes. In for four, out for eight. Hugh had taken the news pretty well. He'd swayed for a minute and Judy had been afraid that he was going to faint, but he'd recovered himself, getting out a large clean handkerchief and wiping his face with it. Even this had seemed touching to Judy. Who has proper linen handkerchiefs these days? This one had been ironed too. Maybe Tina had done it.

'This Covid is a wicked thing,' said Hugh.

Judy agreed that it was. She also promised to check in again on Hugh in a few days' time. She wonders if she can contact social services but she's sure they are overwhelmed at the moment and, on the face of it, Hugh seems to be coping well. It's a lonely life though. She looks back at the house and sees the next-door-neighbour pruning her roses. Should she have a word, ask the woman to keep an eye on Hugh? As she ponders, her phone rings. Bethany Flowers. Avril's daughter.

'You left a message,' says Bethany.

'Yes,' says Judy. 'I just had a couple of questions. Nothing serious. How are you?'

'I'm OK,' says Bethany. 'As well as can be expected.' She gives a short laugh at the cliché. She sounds far more Scottish than Judy remembers. 'It's strange,' Bethany goes on, 'at any other time, I'd be able to keep busy, but I've been furloughed so I'm just sitting at home, thinking about Mum. James isn't much help.'

Judy knows that Bethany is married with no children. James must be the husband. She wonders why he isn't much help. Is he an essential worker or just generally useless?

'It must be very difficult for you,' says Judy. 'As you know, we're still investigating your mother's death.'

'That must be hard to do,' says Bethany, 'with everything locked down.'

'It's challenging,' says Judy, touched that Bethany is thinking like this. 'I was just wondering whether you'd had any further thoughts. Anything about your mum. However small. Anything that might be able to help us.'

'Not really,' says Bethany. 'I'm more thinking about the past. When I was a wee girl.'

'Your mum used to go to Lean Zone meetings, didn't she?' says Judy.

'Lean Zone? Oh, the slimming group. Mum was always dieting but she never seemed to lose any weight. She didn't need to anyway, in my opinion.'

'I've just been to see your mum's friend Hugh Baxter and he said that Avril had a friend at the group. A nurse, he thought.'

'I don't know about that,' says Bethany. 'Is Hugh all right? Mum was very fond of him.'

'He seems fine,' says Judy. 'I'll keep an eye on him.' She wonders if Bethany knows about Tina but doesn't feel up to delivering any more bad news.

They chat for a few more minutes and then say goodbye. The neighbour is still in her garden, poised with the secateurs. Judy is about to drive away when her phone pings. Cathbad.

'Judy. I'm really sorry but I think I've got Covid.'

27

Judy drives straight home. Maddie meets her at the door.

'Dad's in his bedroom. He thought he should isolate himself.'

Judy is halfway upstairs before she considers the significance of 'Dad'.

She opens the door of their bedroom. 'Cathbad?'

'Don't come in,' says Cathbad. His voice sounds reassuringly the same but, just as Judy is starting to relax, he starts to cough, a horrible racking sound that seems to go on and on.

'Shall I get you some water?' says Judy. Cathbad doesn't answer so she goes into the bathroom, pours a toothmug full of water and looks in the cabinet. Surely there's some cough mixture here? Eventually she finds an old and sticky bottle. Best before Jan 2018. Can linctus go off? Judy is bad with illness. Cathbad, as the parent at home, is the one who has had to cope with coughs, colds, ear infections, Michael's occasional bouts of asthma.

She slides the bottle onto the bedside table on her side,

without coming closer to Cathbad who is hunched on the other side of the bed, breathing heavily.

'Have you called the doctor?' she says.

'No,' says Cathbad, 'but I think it's Covid. I've lost my sense of smell and I keep coughing.'

'I'll call them,' says Judy.

Maddie, Michael and Miranda are all standing in the hall. Judy composes her face into reassuring lines.

'I think he's OK. Maybe it's just a cold. I'm going to ring the doctor just to be on the safe side.'

The surgery has a separate number for 'patients who think they have symptoms of Covid-19'. Judy speaks to a sympathetic-sounding nurse called Zoe.

'It's best to avoid hospital if you can,' she says. 'Tell him to take paracetamol and keep his fluids up. Ring again if you're worried.'

Judy finds some paracetamol and takes them up to Cathbad with a large glass of orange juice.

'Vitamin C,' she says.

'Thanks.' Cathbad is lying down, which looks so strange in the middle of the day that Judy feels quite sick.

'The nurse said to take paracetamol.'

'I will.'

'You'll be OK.' Judy stands awkwardly in the doorway. She wants Cathbad to tell her that everything will be all right, but he has his eyes shut and seems to be concentrating on breathing.

'Knock on the floor if you need anything,' she says.

'You should keep away,' says Cathbad. 'Keep the children away.'

Cathbad always wants the children with him. It's as if his body has been invaded which, in a way, Judy supposes, it has.

Nelson can't quite believe it either. If anyone could sail through the Covid crisis, he would have put money on it being Cathbad. He has an irritatingly healthy lifestyle, for one thing. Plus, he's probably protected by hordes of pagan gods and goddesses and all the saints of the Catholic church thrown in for good measure. Nelson thinks of his mother, who took a great fancy to Cathbad when they first met. Maureen is praying daily to St Carlo Borromeo, who was said to offer protection against the plague and so may well perform the same trick for Covid-19. He must ring his mother tonight.

Nelson sends everyone home early. Tanya is still checking CCTV for any sightings around Avril Flowers' bungalow. Nelson also catches her looking on Rightmove a few times. Leah is reorganising the filing system. Nelson tells her that she can work from home, but she seems keen to stay. 'I'll go mad at home.' But, by five o'clock, they are all on their way out of the building.

Nelson hardly recognises his house. Laura has been to the shops and has even bought flowers. There's a delicious cooking smell emanating from the kitchen and Radio 1 is playing upstairs.

'Hi, Laura,' he shouts. 'I'm home.'

Laura appears at the top of the stairs. 'I'm just doing some marking and I'll be right down.'

'No rush,' says Nelson. He wonders what Ruth is doing. Now that he knows their routine it's easier to imagine her and Katie in the cottage. Ruth will be at her laptop and Katie will be building something from Lego or writing her story about a cat. He wishes that he could ring them but doesn't want Laura to come in halfway through. Instead, he calls Judy.

'How's Cathbad?'

'Not too good. He's still coughing and I think he's got a fever.'

'Paracetamol,' says Nelson, drawing on his scant medical knowledge. 'And lots of water.'

'He's taking paracetamol,' she says. 'I hope he'll feel better soon.' There's a quaver in her voice that Nelson has never heard before.

'Of course he will,' says Nelson, hearing his voice sounding falsely hearty. 'He's as tough as old boots.'

'He is,' says Judy, sounding more like herself. 'It's just . . . I've never known him to be ill. Everything feels wrong. The kids and I don't know what to do with ourselves. And Thing's going crazy.'

The dog was always slightly crazy, in Nelson's opinion. The bull terrier does not have Bruno's superior intelligence. The house still seems very strange without Bruno. Nelson keeps thinking he can hear his claws clicking along the wooden floors or his tail swishing things off the coffee table. Maybe he's being haunted by Black Shuck, a spectral dog who crossed his path – in a non-corporeal sense – on another case. Cathbad would definitely say so.

'I'll pray to St Carlo,' he says. 'My mum says that he's good on Covid.'

'I'm praying too,' says Judy. 'I just wish he'd get better.'

'Me too,' says Nelson. 'Tell him get well soon from me.'

'I will. Bye, boss.'

'Bye, Judy.'

'Who's ill?' says Laura, coming into the room.

'Cathbad. He's got Covid.'

'Oh no!' Nelson had forgotten that Laura, too, has a connection with Cathbad. He'd been kind to her after Tim died and Laura had attended Cathbad's meditation classes for a while.

'Let's hope it's not serious,' he says, although something in Judy's tone tells him that this is a faint hope. 'Most people recover quickly.'

'Cathbad isn't most people,' says Laura. 'I've made stew for supper, but shall we FaceTime Rebecca and Mum first?'

'Where's Bruno?' is the first thing Rebecca says when she pops up on his laptop screen.

'He's staying with Jan for a bit,' says Nelson. 'I've got a lot on at work.'

'Why?' says Rebecca. 'Aren't all the criminals locked up in their houses?'

'Sadly not,' says Nelson. 'What's going on with you?'

Rebecca tells him about going for walks on Brighton seafront with Asif. 'It's so strange to have the whole town to ourselves. We walked around the Pavilion yesterday.'

'Take care,' says Nelson. 'Wear masks.'

'We've got matching masks,' says Rebecca. 'It's very cute.'

Michelle, speaking from her mother's immaculate sitting room, seems delighted to see Laura and Nelson side by side on the sofa.

'I'm so glad you've got company, Harry.'

It's really only Michelle and his mum who call him Harry these days. The name sparks an almost physical response, a twinge in his gut that's somewhere between love and guilt.

Georgie appears and the twinge becomes a wrench.

'Daddy! Laura!'

Georgie looks really well, tanned from all those trips along the Blackpool sands. Michelle, on the other hand, looks pale and rather drawn. Nelson asks if she's OK.

'I'm fine,' says Michelle. 'It's just hard being so far from home.'

'Surely you can leave Grandma soon,' says Laura.

'I don't know. I'm really worried about her with this awful Covid.' Michelle says it as if the virus were an unpleasant neighbour.

But, when Michelle's mother appears on screen, she seems in better shape than her daughter, immaculately dressed as ever, talking about online fitness classes and someone called Joe Wicks.

'Mum will be home soon,' says Laura when they ring off. 'Grandma looks very healthy to me.'

'She does to me too,' says Nelson.

'Don't worry,' Laura gives him a quick hug, 'Mum will

soon be back and Cathbad will get better. Are you ready for some vegetarian stew?'

The word 'vegetarian' always makes Nelson feel depressed.

Judy sleeps on the sofa. Thing is delighted and fetches his favourite squeaky toy so they can make a night of it. Judy manages to banish the toy but she can't do anything about the solid bulk of the bull terrier, who takes up most of the space and snores loudly in her ear. Not that Judy sleeps much. She can hear Cathbad coughing and twice goes upstairs to see if he needs anything. 'I'm OK,' comes the reply, 'don't come in.'

Judy lies awake, with Thing across her legs, wondering what to do. She wants to go into the bedroom but she can't afford to get Covid. She has to stay well for her children. It's as if the virus is lying in wait upstairs, as monsters of childhood are said to do. All she can do is hope that Cathbad's strong constitution will defeat the ogre. He's the fittest person she knows, honed by walking and yoga. Tanya says obesity is a contributory factor but Cathbad doesn't have an ounce of spare flesh on him. 'Irish peasant's physique,' he's fond of saying. He eats well and has never smoked, unless it's for hallucinatory reasons in his past life. 'As tough as old boots', that's what Nelson said. Surely Cathbad will defeat corona?

She must have fallen asleep because Thing wakes her at six a.m. by licking her face. She lets him out into the garden. The sun is coming up and the birds are singing in the trees. Judy puts on her mask and goes upstairs.

'Cathbad?'

There's no answer. Judy pushes open the door. Cathbad is lying on his back and, for a heart-stopping moment, Judy thinks he's dead. Then she hears a faint rattle of breath. She puts a hand on Cathbad's forehead and snatches it away again. The dry heat tells its own story.

Judy runs downstairs and phones for an ambulance. The operator is reassuring and says they are on their way. Judy looks up from her phone to see Maddie in the doorway, wearing only an oversized T-shirt saying, 'Grey Sloan Memorial Hospital'.

'Is he really ill?' she says.

'His temperature is very high,' says Judy. 'And I think he might need oxygen.'

Maddie puts her arms round her. 'He'll be OK. He's tough.'

'I know he is.' Judy hugs her stepdaughter. They both jump when Thing barks from the garden, keen to get inside and start his day.

The paramedics are in full hazmat suits. They carry Cathbad downstairs on a stretcher. Judy and the children watch from the hall. Miranda is crying but Michael is silent. Maddie has Thing on the lead and he pants to follow the strange procession. Judy knows how he feels.

'Can I come with you?' says Judy, knowing the answer.

'I'm afraid not, love,' says one of the suited figures. 'Covid restrictions.'

'How will I know how he is?' asks Judy, hearing herself sounding like a frightened teenager, not like a tough detective inspector, used to dealing with life and death situations.

The paramedic hands her a piece of paper. 'You can ring this number but give us time to get him to the Queen Elizabeth. We'll give him oxygen in the ambulance. His levels are very low. You and your family will need to go into quarantine too.'

Some of the neighbours have come out into their gardens, shivering in the early morning air. The ambulance moves away, lights flashing.

Thing starts to howl.

28

Nelson is on his way to work when he gets the call. He has his phone on hands-free so Judy's voice fills the car. Nelson finds it hard to take in the details, even as he drives through the empty streets. Cathbad is in hospital, on oxygen, Judy is in quarantine.

'I don't know any more,' says Judy. Nelson can hear her struggling to control herself. Judy, who is always in control. 'It's very hard not being with him.'

'I bet it is,' says Nelson, 'but he's in the right place. He's getting good care.' Even as he says this, he wonders if it's true. Is a hospital full of Covid patients really the best place to be during a Covid pandemic?

'Try not to worry, love,' he says. Then he spends the rest of the journey worrying about calling his most senior officer 'love'.

When he gets to the station, Tony is already there. Nelson groans inwardly. He doesn't think he can take a day listening to Tony's chatter. Sure enough, when Nelson explains about Cathbad, Tony launches into a long story about two cousins in China who caught, and subsequently recovered from, the virus.

'That's great, Tony,' says Nelson, when he can get a word in. 'Let's get on with our work, shall we?' In silence, he wants to add, like Sister Anthony used to say to his primary school class. 'I'm casting my cloak of silence over you.' But Tony seems to get the message.

Leah brings him a cup of coffee. 'I hope Cathbad's OK,' she says. 'Judy's so lovely. I can't bear to think of her being worried.'

Judy had been worried about Leah, Nelson remembers. What had she said? *She seems a bit quiet.* But Leah, unlike Tony, is not given to chatting. For which Nelson thanks God silently.

Thinking of God, as always, reminds him of his mother. He hadn't rung her last night so he does so now.

Maureen sounds bracingly the same. No, she's not ordering food online. She doesn't hold with things like that. She goes to the shops with her wheely bag. Of course she wears a mask. Maeve brought her a pack. Nelson's older sister, Maeve, lives near their mother, and visits every other day. 'She doesn't come in,' says Maureen, 'she stands in the garden and shouts up at me. It's a gas.' Nelson's other sister, Grainne, lives further away but apparently she did one of those Zoom yokes the other night.

'How are you, Harry?' asks Maureen at last. 'Are you still on your own? Is Michelle still in Blackpool with Georgie?'

'Yes,' says Nelson, 'she's a bit worried about her mum. Louise has diabetes, you know.'

'She's as fit as a fiddle,' says Maureen.

'She certainly seems it,' says Nelson.

'How's Katie?' asks Maureen. Nelson answers carefully. Maureen now knows about Ruth and Katie but he doesn't want to get into an ethical debate with her, if he can help it.

'She's fine. Her school's closed so Ruth's teaching her at home.'

A silence.

'Laura's back home with me,' says Nelson. 'She was finding it a bit hard to cope, living in the flat.'

'My prayers have been answered,' says Maureen but without much surprise. She always expects her prayers to be answered. 'Laura can look after you.'

'I can look after myself, Mum.'

'A home's not a home without a woman in it.'

Nelson thinks of the little cottage on the marshes containing two of his favourite women.

'We're taking turns cooking,' he says. 'I'm sure Laura will go back to her flat when all this is over.'

'Sure, it'll be over soon,' says Maureen. 'I don't know anyone who's actually got the thing, do you?'

'Cathbad. Remember him? He's in hospital with Covid.'

'Cuthbert? Of course I remember him. He's a good soul. I'll pray for him. I watch mass on the computer every day. Yesterday I went to the Vatican.'

'You do that, Mum. Give the Pope my love.'

'He's a good man, is Pope Francis. He understands about life.'

That makes one of us, thinks Nelson.

*

Ruth is also shocked by the news about Cathbad. Judy sends her a text, which is closely followed by a call from Nelson.

'I can't imagine Cathbad getting ill,' says Ruth.

'No,' says Nelson. 'I think it's thrown us all. I'll let you know if I hear anything.'

'Thanks,' says Ruth. 'How's Laura?'

'She's fine,' says Nelson. 'I expect she just needed a rest.'

Ruth is too proud to ask 'When will I see you again?' so she says, rather heartily, that she hopes Laura continues to feel better and she rings off. Kate is watching her.

'Is that Dad? How's Laura? Is she coming to see us?'

'I don't suppose she can. Because of lockdown.' Although that didn't stop her running home to Daddy, thinks Ruth. 'I heard from Judy earlier,' she says. 'Cathbad isn't very well.'

'Is it Covid?' says Kate, sounding disconcertingly like a much older person.

'Yes. They think so.'

'Tasha's mum had Covid but she's better now.'

'Most people do get better very quickly,' says Ruth. The words *but some people don't* hover unsaid. But they don't need to be said when every news bulletin is full of hospital wards crammed with the sick and dying. Is Cathbad in intensive care? Attached to tubes and drips? Ruth wishes she could ask Zoe about his possible treatment, but she saw her leaving for work earlier, wearing her blue scrubs and waving cheerfully. Ruth had waved back, channelling Mrs Grantham.

After a morning of pretending to work, Ruth and Kate go for a walk across the marshes. Ruth thinks of the first time she saw Cathbad. The archaeologists had planned to remove the henge timbers to the museum. The wood needed to be treated so that it could be preserved. But, when they arrived at the site that morning, it was to find a group of cloaked figures forming a protective ring around the original circle. The leader had been a youngish man with long black hair and a piratical beard.

'They belong here,' he had said. 'Between the earth and the sky. Part of the cycle of nature, part of the ebb and flow of the tides.'

Those, she thinks, were the first words she heard Cathbad say. Erik had been impressed with him, had stayed to argue his case, but Cathbad and his druid friends had refused to move. Finally, at sunset, and against Erik's wishes, the protestors were removed by the police. Ruth didn't speak to Cathbad then – they only became friends years afterwards – but he had, it transpired later, noticed her.

'Let's go back,' says Kate. 'It's boring and cold.' It's true that it's a grey day with a sharp wind. They haven't got near to the beach or the henge circle but Ruth agrees to turn back. 'Hecate knows her own mind,' Cathbad always says. 'But you don't seem to know her name,' Ruth sometimes answers. She can't, now, imagine a life without Cathbad.

Back home, they eat cheese sandwiches for lunch. Ruth will need to go food shopping again soon. Kate settles in front of the television but Ruth has a lecture at two so she props her laptop at a flattering angle and starts to upload her presentation. An email pops onto the screen, silhouetted against Avebury Ring.

I think I've found something. Can you come to Tombland?

Judy has never known a day like it. She has never realised before how much the house belongs to Cathbad. He's in every inch of it. His cloak over the banisters. His jams and preserves in the pantry. His bug hotel and hedgehog house in the garden. The hens squawking for him. Thing howling for him.

Maddie is a tower of strength and takes the children for a walk, before engaging them in several games of Mario Kart. Judy has to admit that the neighbours have also been very kind. Steve and Richard ('Whatsit' to Judy no longer) have baked a cake and passed it over the fence. Jill, on the other side, posted a card through the letter box. It showed a teddy bear looking out of a window and said, 'We're here if you need us. If you don't, we're still here.' She included her mobile number but not her husband's name, so Judy is still not sure if it's Fred or Ned. Did Jill buy the card specially? Where? All the specialist stationery shops are shut. Or does she have a stock of such things, a neat phrase for every occasion? This message strikes Judy as rather touchingly obvious. Neighbours are just *there*, you don't choose them like friends, they are simply the people who live nearby. But, today, their presence is definitely comforting.

Now it's afternoon and Maddie and the children are watching *The Lord of the Rings*. 'We'll watch all the films,' Maddie tells them, 'it'll take ages.' It's all a bit much for Judy; Frodo wondering why it's his fate to live through such times, Gandalf telling him to shut up and get on with it (or words to that effect). Cathbad loves Tolkien and once had a cat called Hobbit. Judy leaves the children in Middle Earth and retreats to her bedroom to ring the hospital. There's no answer on the number she was given by the paramedics but she goes through the switchboard and, eventually, after shamelessly using her police rank, she gets through to a nurse who tells her that Cathbad has been moved to Intensive Care.

'It's not necessarily anything to worry about,' says the kindly voice at the end of the phone. 'It just means that they can look after him properly.'

'And I can't see him?'

'I'm afraid not. No visitors allowed on the Covid wards.'

Judy sits at the workspace she created only a week ago. What would Cathbad do now? Pray to the healing spirits? Light a ceremonial bonfire? Bake some brownies? Instead Judy googles the hospital, planning to check the ICU success rates. If they are poor, maybe she can get Cathbad moved elsewhere. Along with complaints about parking charges and maps showing new building works, she sees news stories from the past, the hospital's name highlighted. One of them includes a photograph.

Nurse cleared of killing patients.
Nurse Dawn Stainton, 32, was yesterday cleared of killing patients Bill Grimes, 86, Edna Bates, 91, and Margaret Loomis, 88 . . .

Judy looks again at the photograph. She remembers the yoga picture and the slight unease she'd felt at the laughing face on the other side of Ruth's fence. Because Dawn Stainton is, without doubt, Ruth's new neighbour, last seen gatecrashing Cathbad's online class.

29

'Dawn? That's not her name. Can't remember what it is but it's something different.'

'It's the same person, Nelson. I'm sure of it.'

Nelson tries to recall Ruth's neighbour. He remembers the two women sitting in the darkness drinking wine, the face at the window when he left on Sunday morning. What was she called? One of those short names. Chloe? Zoe. That was it. Why does the name Dawn also strike a faint, but slightly sinister, bell?

'Zoe,' he says. 'Her name's Zoe. She is a nurse though. Ruth told me.'

'Zoe,' says Judy. 'Does she work at the surgery in Wells? Westway?'

'I don't know.'

'I think she does. I think I spoke to her yesterday about Cathbad.'

'Is there any news?'

'They're moving him to the ICU.'

'That's OK. He'll get good care there.'

'Yes.' There's a pause. Nelson thinks he can hear stirring filmic music in the background.

'It might be nothing,' says Judy. 'After all, she was cleared of any wrongdoing. I do remember the case though. It was before you came to Norfolk. There were several patients involved. I thought I remembered the woman's face when I saw it in that photo.'

It might be nothing, thinks Nelson, but the fact remains that Ruth and Katie are locked down in the middle of nowhere, next door to a woman once accused of murder.

'I spoke to Hugh Baxter yesterday,' says Judy.

'Who?'

'He was a friend of Avril Flowers. He said that Avril had a friend at Lean Zone who was a nurse.'

'And you think it could be this Dawn? Zoe? That's a bit of a stretch.'

'I know it is, but it might be worth checking up.'

'I'll certainly be having a chat with her,' says Nelson.

'Have you met her?' asks Judy.

'Just briefly.' Nelson still doesn't want Judy to know just how familiar he is with Ruth's house and her neighbour.

'I'll go around later,' he says.

'I thought you would,' says Judy.

Nelson doesn't know how to respond to this.

'Give Cathbad my best,' he says. 'My mum's praying for him. And she's got a hotline to the big man.'

'I'm praying too,' says Judy, 'and I haven't prayed for years.'

'Me too,' says Nelson. He has to stop himself saying 'God bless' when he rings off.

Nelson rings Ruth but there's no answer. Where can she be at four o'clock in the afternoon? That's the thing about lockdown. There's nowhere people *can* be. He's very jolted by the news that Ruth's apparently charming neighbour was once charged with murder. But didn't he always feel that the woman was a little odd, a little encroaching? He gets out his phone and finds the photograph of Ruth and Katie doing yoga in their garden. Ruth is laughing as she tries to stand on one leg. Katie is deadly serious. He loves the way her tongue is protruding slightly as she lunges forward. Zoe's face appears on the other side of the fence, her hair tied up in a spotted scarf. Is there something strange in her expression, something intent, almost greedy? Nelson looks on the Westway surgery website and learns that Zoe Hilton is the Lead Practice Nurse. He asks Tony to check whether Zoe was a member of any Lean Zone groups and the answer comes back that, for a while, she attended the same meetings as Avril Flowers. Could this be a link? One way or another, Nelson needs to speak to Zoe. And Ruth too.

'I'm off out,' he says to Tony. 'You can go home when you've finished there.'

'I'm just going through the reports on the suicide cases,' says Tony. 'Seeing if we've missed anything.'

'You keep on with that,' says Nelson. 'Leah! I'm off.'

As far as Nelson can see, the only people on the roads are those in some sort of uniform: delivery drivers, paramedics, nurses or carers. Nelson wonders idly how long it will take local drug dealers to don PPE before setting out to ply their trade. They can even wear masks. But there's no doubt that it makes driving easier. In less than fifteen minutes, he's driving over the Saltmarsh. It's one of those grey days when the land and sea merge together. Nelson thinks of the Golden Mile in Blackpool. Even in winter there is noise and colour, shouts from the Pleasure Beach, lights glowing on the piers. What crime did Nelson commit in a former life to be exiled here? 'Everything happens for a reason,' Cathbad always says but now Cathbad is seriously ill in hospital and nothing makes sense any more.

Ruth's cottage and its two neighbours are visible from miles away, bright spots in the gloom. Nelson sees immediately that Ruth's car isn't there. Where can she be? It's lockdown, for God's sake. She's not allowed to be anywhere. Nelson parks by the gate and hammers on the door. 'Ruth? Are you there?'

There's no car outside Zoe's house either. Nelson knocks on her door too. No answer. The marshland stretches around him, sullen and threatening. Nelson bangs on Zoe's window and has the fright of his life when a huge animal – surely far bigger than a normal cat? – appears on the other side of the glass. The beast has stripy fur and huge, yellow eyes. There's something very disconcerting about its stare.

Nelson turns back to the grey landscape.

Ruth and Katie have disappeared.

30

Ruth is still not sure whether she was right to come. Her journey can hardly be described as necessary. What if she's stopped by the police? Will name-dropping Nelson make it better or worse? But she is desperate for something to take her mind off Cathbad so, after her lecture – there's still no sign of Eileen or Joe – she turns to Kate.

'Fancy a drive to Norwich?'

Kate looks at her sceptically. 'Are we allowed?'

'Yes,' bluffs Ruth. 'It's for work. Janet – remember her? – thinks she's found a secret door into Steward's House. We won't have to go in. Apparently, you can see it from the road.'

Kate agrees. After all, she's bored too. There's a secretly festive feeling in the car as they drive along the coastal road, past the boarded-up pubs and the house with the mural of Rupert Bear. It's usually a long and frustratingly slow drive to Norwich but, today, they slalom through the round-abouts and encounter almost no traffic on the A148. It feels strange, too, to drive straight into the Close and park in front of the cathedral. Janet is waiting for them by the doors of the great church, now firmly shut, between the statues of Mother Julian and St Benedict. Ruth is not sure how to greet her friend, but they compromise on an awkward two-metres-apart wave.

'Is it shut?' Ruth gestures towards the huge wooden doors.

'Yes,' says Janet. 'So sad. It wasn't even closed during the plague, you know. I still come into the grounds to meditate. I'm living here.'

'In the cathedral?' says Ruth. She remembers the laugh in Janet's voice when she said that her new house was in the 'dead centre' of town. She wouldn't put it past Janet to be living in the cathedral with its multiple graves and coffin-filled crypt. People must still be living in the close, although there's no sign of life this afternoon. Kate runs across the manicured lawns like a captive freed from prison. Ruth and Janet watch her.

'It's good to have a child in the place,' says Janet. 'A few of the senior church-people live here but there are no young children.'

'Where are you living?' says Ruth. 'It's all very mysterious.'

'I'll show you,' says Janet.

They pass through the stone archway and cross the empty street. In front of them is the famously crooked façade of Augustine Steward's House, the timbers leaning so far to the left that you feel as if the earth has shifted on its axis. There's a shop downstairs saying 'Tourist Information' with a closed sign across it. Janet points to an upstairs window, where the house joins another to form Tombland Alley.

'There,' she says.

'You're living in Steward's House? Above the tourist centre?'

'Yes. They wanted someone to live there and keep an eye on the place. I volunteered. There are lots of empty houses in Tombland Alley.'

Ruth remembers Janet telling her the story of the Grey Lady, the woman who died after being locked up in this building. *I've often sensed something. A shadow, a presence, sometimes just a feeling of intense sadness. People don't like to work there after dark.* Ruth wouldn't live above Steward's House for a million pounds and an English Heritage grant.

'So what have you discovered?' she asks. She's still feeling rather guilty about being out in the open, talking to someone outside her tiny family group (which now seems to include Nelson).

'It's this way.' Janet leads them into the alleyway. The houses seem to lean in, as if glad of their company. A poster in the information centre offers 'The Top Ten Places to Visit in Norfolk'. Ruth wonders if any of them are open to visitors now. Perhaps the abbey grounds at Walsingham or the beaches of Hunstanton. But all the stately homes and historic churches will be closed. Norfolk is closed.

Janet stops by a low wooden-framed window. 'Look at the bricks there.'

Ruth peers down to examine the wall. She recognises the Tudor bricks immediately, shallow and uneven, filled with lime-rich mortar. Patterned brickwork was fashionable at the time and, for a moment, she thinks this is what she is looking at, but then she realises that the shape is actually that of a door, sunken into the ground.

'The strange thing is,' says Janet, 'I can't see where it comes out the other side. It should open into the undercroft but there's no sign. It did make me think. There are stories about people being bricked up, about tunnels leading to the cathedral. All that stuff.'

'The other side was probably just plastered over,' says Ruth. 'We can have a look inside when restrictions are lifted.' If they ever are, she thinks. Will there ever be a time when Covid-19 is as distant as the plague?

The alleyway leads into a grassy space, fringed by lilac bushes and surrounded by topsy-turvy houses. Are they really all empty? Kate has wandered away and is picking lilac. Should Ruth tell her to stop? Is anyone watching?

'I saw your student a couple of days ago,' says Janet.

'Which student?' asks Ruth. Though she thinks she can guess.

'The bearded one. Joe Whatshisname. The one you were asking about.'

'What was he doing?'

'Standing right here. Looking up at the houses. I waved but I don't think he saw me.'

Who knows what he thought if he saw a woman waving from one of the sightless windows, thinks Ruth. *Beware the Grey Lady.*

*

The car smells strongly of lilac on the way home. Kate seems energised by the outing, singing along to the radio and telling Ruth a long story about a boy in her class who makes rude noises during Zooms. Then she picks up Ruth's phone.

'Mum. You've got loads of messages from Dad.'

'Have I?' says Ruth. Now that she has Kate with her all the time, she keeps her phone on silent. She left it in the car when they were with Janet.

'Oh God,' she says. 'Is it about Cathbad?'

'I don't think so,' says Kate. '"Where are you?"' she reads. '"For F's sake, pick up the phone." Then there are lots of question marks and exclamation points.' Clearly the grammar lessons are paying off.

'Text him,' says Ruth. 'Say we went into Norwich and we're on our way back.'

Kate texts at lightning speed. Will skeletons of twenty-first century humans show enlarged thumbs?

'Shall I add a kiss?' she says.

'No,' says Ruth.

She can see Nelson from a long way off, a dark shape standing by her fence. Typical of him just to stand there like a thundercloud. Maybe she should get him a spare key, but would this make their arrangement, whatever it is, too official? Besides, Nelson has moved back home now. He's made his choice. Which means he can keep his disapproval to himself.

'Where have you been?' he says, as soon as Ruth gets out of the car.

'We went to the cathedral,' says Kate. 'We saw a secret door.'

'Sounds well worth breaking lockdown for,' says Nelson.

'Are you coming in?' says Ruth, opening the front door. 'Or are you going to stand there pontificating all night?'

Nelson glowers at her for a few minutes and then steps over the threshold, ducking as always at the low doorway.

'I've got something to tell you,' he says quietly, as Kate runs upstairs in search of Flint.

'OK,' says Ruth. 'Do you want a cup of tea?'

'You sound like my mum,' says Nelson. 'When in doubt, make tea.'

'Gee, thanks,' says Ruth.

Nelson, as always, looks too big for the kitchen. He folds himself into one of the chairs and says, 'How much do you know about your neighbour? The new woman?'

'Zoe? Not much. She's a nurse, divorced. She's got a lovely cat called Derek.'

'Is that the creature I saw at the window? It looked too big to be a cat.'

'It's a Maine Coon.'

'If you say so. Well, for a start she isn't called Zoe.'

For a moment, Ruth thinks he means the cat. She puts a mug of tea in front of Nelson.

'What?'

'Your neighbour. She isn't called Zoe. She's called Dawn Stainton and, in 1994, she was accused of murdering three patients in her care.'

Ruth feels her heart thumping. Various words rush into

her head – neighbour, murdering, patients – but one keeps bumping up against the sides: Dawn.

'Dawn?' she says.

Nelson looks at her in confusion. 'What?'

'Dawn. Is her name really Dawn?'

'Apparently so. She changed her name after the trial. You can't blame her really.'

'I take it she was found not guilty?'

'Yes,' admits Nelson.

'How old was she in 1994?'

'Why do you want to know?'

'Just tell me, Nelson. Please.'

Nelson gets out his phone and scrolls, much less efficiently than Kate, until he finds the relevant page.

'She was thirty-two when it came to trial in 1995. She would have been thirty-one in 1994.'

Ruth does the sum in her head, never an easy task for her. 'So, she was born in 1963?'

'Yes. I suppose so. Why?'

'Dawn 1963,' says Ruth. 'It was on that photograph I found in my mother's belongings.'

'I remember you saying something about it.' Nelson dismisses this, as she knew he would. 'The point is that your next-door neighbour is a murderer.'

'No, she isn't. I'm going to talk to her.'

'She's out,' says Nelson. 'I've been knocking all the time you were away. And a bloody long time it was too.'

'She's probably at work,' says Ruth. But it's six o'clock now and Zoe is normally home at half past.

'Are you staying?' she says to Nelson. For almost the first time since she's known him, he looks awkward.

'I'd like to,' he says. 'But it's difficult with Laura . . .'

'I understand,' says Ruth. 'Well, you'd better get back to her.'

Nelson stands up. 'Lock your doors,' he says. 'And if Zoe comes back, let me know immediately.'

But, although Ruth watches the window all evening, her neighbour does not return.

31

At first, she thinks that he'll be coming back. It's all a mistake, she thinks. He can't mean to leave her locked in the dark for ever. And it is dark. She doesn't have her phone. Where did she leave it? There are blanks in her memory which scare her even more than the locked room.

She tries to pace it out. Eight paces forward, eight paces across. When she reaches a wall, it's cold and clammy. There's no window. The door is metal. She heard it clang behind him. She can't remember entering the room. Did he drug her? She thinks, from the cold and damp, that she must be underground. She imagines earth above her head, fathoms of it. Is she in the basement of a house? Is anyone above her?

What did he say? That he'd be coming back later? Why can't she remember any more than that?

She sits down on the stone floor. Tries to breathe. In for four, out for eight. 'My breath is my anchor, my anchor is my breath.' But her mind keeps skittering away. She can't keep the rhythm going. Why is she here? What did he mean when he said he would see her later? She gets up again and, in her pacing, barks her shins against metal. *What is it?* She bends down and touches slippery nylon. *There's something familiar about it, something that takes her back to childhood camping trips. Of course, it's a sleeping bag. And it's lying on a camp bed, the old-fashioned metal kind that opens out like a concertina.*

For some reason, this discovery makes her more scared than ever. He must have planned this, she thinks. He's prepared a bed for her.

Does he, in fact, mean to leave her in the dark forever?

When Zoe still isn't home in the morning, Ruth starts worrying about Derek. She can hear him meowing from the other side of the wall. He hasn't got a cat flap because Zoe's worried about him getting lost. Zoe had mentioned giving Ruth a spare key but it never materialised. Is that strange? Ruth wonders. She and Zoe have become friends quickly, by Ruth's standards, but Ruth hasn't been inside the next-door house since its new occupant moved in. They've shared a bottle of wine; they've been for a walk and played tennis on the sand, but they've never been inside each other's houses. Lockdown, of course, is partly to blame but is Zoe actually slightly reluctant to let Ruth into her life?

'I'm going to try the back door,' she tells Kate.

'Can I come?'

Ruth is torn. If there's something terrible in the house next door, she doesn't want Kate to see it. But she doesn't want to leave her daughter alone either.

'OK,' she says. 'But stay with me all the time.'

They walk round the side of the houses. Ruth's cottage,

being in the middle, is the only one without side access. Zoe's back door, like Ruth's, is the stable kind with a lower and upper part. Ruth tries the top handle and it opens. She reaches in and opens the lower door.

'Perhaps it's an April fool,' says Kate. Ruth had forgotten that today is the first of April.

Ruth and Kate step inside a kitchen that looks bigger and brighter than Ruth's, partly because of the new, shiny, white units. Bob put them in, on orders of the agent, when he decided to rent out the house. But Zoe might have added the colourful posters, pot plants and orange kettle and toaster. There's a key hanging from a peg, helpfully labelled 'back door'. Ruth pockets it. Derek appears and meows accusingly.

Ruth opens several cupboards before finding cat food, apparently made especially for Maine Coons. Another animal with expensive tastes. She puts a generous portion in an orange bowl marked 'Derek'.

'Shall we look for Zoe?' says Kate.

Ruth hesitates. Zoe's car isn't outside but nonetheless there's still a chance that she's in the house. And, if she's there, it's unlikely to be good news. Nelson recently told her about another case where a woman was found dead on her bed. 'Verdict was suicide but I'm not so sure.' Ruth remembers the time she found a man dead behind his desk, the realisation that a human being can turn into an effigy. If there is a corpse upstairs, she does not want to be the one to discover it. But, on the other hand, does she owe it to her neighbour to look?

They go into the sitting room. It's so strange. Everything is exactly where it is in her house, just the other way around. The weekenders' place has been so extended and renovated that the resemblance isn't there any more. This could be Ruth's cottage, seen through the looking glass. This room, like its twin next door, has wooden floors and exposed beams but there are fewer books here and more ornaments. The sofa and chairs look newer and more comfortable and Zoe's cushions haven't been chewed by marauding animals. Ruth sees the chaise longue that she spotted being carried into the house on the day Zoe moved in. You can't imagine anyone ever sitting on it but there's no doubt that it does look rather cool. There's a book, face down, on the coffee table. *Atonement* by Ian McEwan. The staircase leads directly from the sitting room.

'Stay downstairs,' Ruth tells Kate. The stairs even creak in the same way hers do. On the landing, there are three doors. Ruth pushes open the first and sees an immaculate bedroom, bed neatly made, cushions all standing on their points. The next door is the bathroom and the third is a home office. All three rooms are completely empty.

'Mum!' calls Kate from downstairs.

Ruth rushes down the stairs to see Kate examining the photographs on a pine dresser. 'Look!' she says.

Ruth crosses the room to where Kate is holding a wedding photograph of a very young Zoe in a huge white dress holding onto the arm of a blond young man. But Kate is looking at the passport picture which has been inserted into the frame.

'Is that Grandma?' she asks.

Grandma. Mum. Jean Galloway.

Back in her own house, Ruth rings Nelson.

'You and Katie shouldn't have gone there on your own,' is Nelson's first, predictable, reaction.

'I was worried about the cat.'

'That's not a cat. It's a bloody leopard.'

'Anyway, Zoe's not there. I did find one strange thing though. A picture of my mum.'

'A picture of your *mother*?' Nelson sounds positively outraged. Is he at work? thinks Ruth. Are people listening to this through the thin walls of his office? Leah and whichever member of the skeleton staff is on duty today.

'Yes,' says Ruth. 'Remember that picture I told you about? Dawn 1963? Well, Zoe's name was once Dawn and she was born in 1963. Now I discover that she's got a picture of my mum tucked into her wedding portrait.'

'Don't do any investigating, Ruth,' says Nelson. 'Wait until Zoe gets back. Then you can ask her. But ring me first before you tackle her about any of this.'

'OK,' says Ruth although she knows that, if Zoe's car were to draw up outside, she'd be next door in a flash.

'And don't go gadding off into Norwich again,' says Nelson.

Ruth swallows her annoyance at Nelson's dictatorial tone. And the word 'gadding'. It occurs to her that she should tell him about the sighting of Joe McMahon.

This time Nelson seems about to spontaneously combust.

'She saw McMahon? Two days ago? After I'd visited his room at halls? Why didn't you tell me this before?'

'I forgot.'

'You forgot . . .' Nelson breathes deeply on the other end of the line. 'I'll give Janet a ring. Tell her to keep a watch for him. He might be dangerous.'

'I don't think he is,' says Ruth.

'His room had an altar to you, for God's sake.'

'An altar. You're still such a Catholic.'

Nelson ignores this. 'Well, let me know if anything – *anything* – happens. Promise?'

'OK,' says Ruth, crossing her fingers just to be on the safe side.

Nelson puts down the phone feeling deeply frustrated. For all sorts of reasons, this is an emotion that he often associates with Ruth. Now he finds that she's living next door to a woman once accused of murder. What's more, that woman seems to have disappeared off the face of the earth. Nelson decides to go in search of Dawn, aka Zoe. He'll make a visit to Westway surgery. But first he wants to speak to Janet Meadows.

She takes a long time to answer her phone. 'I keep putting it down,' she says, 'and forgetting where I left it. You know the feeling.'

'I can't say I do,' says Nelson. 'I'm ringing about a man called Joe McMahon. I understand you saw him recently.'

'Joe? Oh, Ruth's student. Yes, I saw him a few days ago. He was walking around Tombland Alley looking up at the houses.'

'Tombland Alley? Is that near the cathedral?'

'You must know Tombland Alley,' says Janet. 'It's by Augustine Steward's House. That's where I'm staying at the moment. I'm a kind of caretaker.'

Nelson doesn't think he would entrust a house to a woman who forgets where her phone is. He says, aware that he's sounding stiff and formal, 'I have reason to believe that Joe McMahon is dangerous. If you see him again, please contact the police immediately.'

'I'm sure he's not dangerous,' says Janet. 'I've spoken to him before and he seems perfectly nice. A bit of a lost soul, if anything.'

Nelson doesn't believe in lost souls, although his mother is always praying for them.

'I'll give you my direct number,' he says. 'And let me know if you see or hear anything suspicious.'

'Oh, I'm always hearing suspicious things,' says Janet. 'This is a haunted house, you know. Last night I heard the most tremendous bangings and crashings but I just turned over and went back to sleep.'

Jesus wept. 'Next time anything goes bump in the night,' says Nelson, 'let me know.' And he rings off before Janet can tell him any more ghost stories.

Nelson googles the address of the surgery. Normally he'd ask Leah but she's absent again. He hopes that she isn't sick too. He should ring Judy but he doesn't want to hassle her. He'll call after he's back from Wells.

'I'm off out,' he says to Tanya, who is on duty today. She's on the phone and just waves her hand in acknowledgement.

Nelson drives fast on the blessedly empty roads. He wonders if Zoe turned up for work yesterday and if her current employers know about her history. She must have filled in a DBS disclosure, he supposes, although those forms do rather depend on the applicant telling the truth. He thinks of the Soham murders where the school caretaker lied on his form and subsequently killed two little girls. Nelson grinds his teeth at the memory.

The first thing he sees as he steps through the automatic doors is a masked woman coming towards him holding out a small black object. For one crazy second he thinks it's a gun. Someone fired at him from close range last year and it's not something you forget.

'Just taking your temperature,' says the assailant.

The machine bleeps and the result must be satisfactory because Nelson is ushered in. The waiting room, like the police station, has been rearranged to allow social distancing. There's just one occupant, an elderly man in a mask. Nelson wonders what illness he has that has forced him to leave the safety of his home.

Nelson introduces himself to the receptionist. Normally he would ask to speak in private but the airy room seems the more Covid-safe option. He hopes that the elderly man is deaf.

'I'm looking for a Zoe Hilton.'

'Zoe? She's one of our nurses but . . .'

'Is she in today?'

'No. We were expecting her. I hope she's not ill.' That's the first assumption these days, thinks Nelson. Not skiving off.

'Was she in yesterday?'

'Yes, and she left at the usual time. Five thirty.'

'Is there anyone I can talk to about Zoe?' says Nelson.

'You'd better talk to Dr Patel. She's our senior partner.' The receptionist looks scared now.

Dr Rita Patel looks too young to be a senior partner, but Nelson is used to that now. She's a slight woman with black hair pulled back into a severe ponytail. Her eyes, above her mask, are dark and watchful. She's wearing blue scrubs which makes Nelson think of hospitals.

'They're the easiest and most hygienic option,' says Dr Patel. 'I don't think I'll go back to wearing ordinary clothes even after all this is over.'

'Must be a tough time for you.'

'It is,' says the doctor. 'We're doing lots of telephone consultations but there are some patients we really need to see. And I worry about the people at home who need medical help but are too scared to ask.'

'Scared of coming in?'

'Scared of wasting our time,' says Dr Patel. 'But people still get cancer in a pandemic.'

It's a very lowering thought. Nelson explains that he's looking for Zoe.

'She hasn't come in today,' says Dr Patel. 'We're a bit worried about her.'

'How long has she worked here?'

'Only since February but she's a very good nurse. We all like her.'

'I believe Zoe Hilton was once called Dawn Stainton,' says Nelson.

Dr Patel gives him a very straight look. 'Yes, she was. A very distressing time for her.'

'She told you about the case?'

'She was completely straight with us. She was found not guilty and the real perpetrator was caught and charged. Zoe was cleared to practise by the General Medical Council.'

'And you've no idea where she could be today?'

'No. As I say, we're a bit worried.'

When Nelson stands up to go, Dr Patel surprises him by saying, 'Is there any news of Cathbad?'

'No,' says Nelson. 'I'm going to ring Judy, his partner, in a few minutes.'

'Tell her we're all thinking of him,' says Dr Patel. 'I do his yogic breathing exercises every night.'

32

How long now? It must be morning although there's no change to the light in the room. Or, rather, the dark in the room. She doesn't wear a watch any more. She always has her phone with her. The loss of it feel like an amputated limb. She misses it, that comforting rectangle full of people. Even if she couldn't reach anyone, she would have a torch, she could play a game, read a book on the Kindle app. But all she has are her thoughts and these are not pleasant companions.

Last night he brought food and water, two biscuits and an apple. He pushed it through a grille in the door so, once again, she didn't get to see his face.

'A nice slimming meal,' he said, before closing the metal flap.

She tried to eat the biscuits slowly and kept the apple until later. She ate every bit, pips and all, but now she is starving, her stomach aching. In a way, she relishes the sensation. At least it proves she is still alive. At one time in the night – if it was night, everything is night here – she wondered if she wasn't already dead. Opening her eyes didn't help at all. She ended up pinching her arm until the pain made her believe that she was alive. But now, she wonders again. Is *she in the afterlife? If so, she has definitely taken the turning with the goats and the sinners and is in The Bad Place.*

Will he come and feed her again? If not, then she will certainly die, hungry and alone. She thinks of that story, The Grey Lady. She starved to death but, before the end, she had been so desperate that she had started to eat her dead parents. Without warning, she is retching. There's nothing much to throw up but, afterwards, as she is kneeling on the stone floor, she thinks: This is the lowest point in my life.

And then the grille opens.

Judy is expecting Nelson's call. She's only surprised that it took him until ten thirty to ring. There's no change, she tells him. Cathbad has been 'intubated', whatever that means. In the words of the ICU nurse, 'he's critical but stable'.

'Stable must be good, surely?' says Nelson.

'I don't know,' says Judy. 'I don't know anything any more.'

She can sense Nelson's frustration from the other end of the phone. He wants to do something, to drive to the hospital and make Cathbad better. But there's nothing anyone can do. Judy can't even go and sit at her partner's bedside. She thinks of Little Nell, of Beth dying in *Little Women*. Even these Victorian tearjerkers could not imagine a time when people had to suffer and die alone.

'He'll pull through,' says Nelson. 'He's tough.'

'So everyone keeps saying,' says Judy.

'Do you remember when he went into the dream world to rescue me when I was ill?'

'He said that's what he did,' says Judy. As she remembers it, Nelson has always dismissed this story as 'utter
bollocks'.

'I saw him,' says Nelson now. 'I saw him when I was in a
coma. And Erik too. I've never told Cathbad that. We talked
about murmuration.'

The world has gone mad, thinks Judy. Cathbad is dying
and the boss has turned into Mystic Meg.

'Trust to the flow,' says Nelson. 'That's what he told me.
He'll be OK. I'm sure of it.' Then, with an abrupt change of
gear, 'Zoe Hilton didn't come home last night. She's not at
work either. I went to the surgery this morning.'

How does he know Zoe didn't come home last night?
thinks Judy.

'Did they know at the surgery?' she says. 'That Zoe was
Dawn Stainton?'

'Yes,' says Nelson. 'She was very straight with them apparently. I spoke to Dr Patel.'

'Rita? I like her. She comes to Cathbad's yoga classes.'

'She sent her best to him,' says Nelson. 'And to you.'

'That's nice of her,' says Judy. 'But if Dawn – Zoe – was
innocent and they know all about it at the surgery, she's not
really a person of interest, is she?'

'I don't know,' says Nelson. 'Turns out that she knew Avril
Flowers. She went to the same slimming class. You were
right about that.'

Despite everything, Judy feels a faint glow of satisfaction.
'And you've no idea where Zoe is now?' she says.

'No. She seems to have disappeared. Joe McMahon too.

Although apparently he popped up in Tombland at the weekend.'

'What was he doing there?'

'God only knows,' says Nelson. 'But you don't need to worry about any of this. Concentrate on Cathbad and your family. Let me know if there's any news.'

That's easy to say, thinks Judy, putting down her phone. She can hear Maddie and the children downstairs. She knows that she should go to them. But instead she opens her file on the Avril Flowers case.

Nelson drives back to the station, feeling disturbed on many levels. He's worried about Cathbad. Much as he believes in the druid's powers of survival, it's no joke being in ICU during a pandemic. He wishes there was something he could do for Judy. Last time she had a crisis, when Michael went missing, the team had rallied round immediately. They had rushed to her side, not that they had received much gratitude for it at the time, and had worked night and day to find the kidnapper. Now Nelson can't drop in on Judy to give her an awkward hug and promise his support. The team can't career around the countryside solving crimes. Judy can't even visit Cathbad in hospital. All they can do is wait and waiting is not something that comes easily to Nelson.

He's concerned about Zoe too. She might have been found innocent of murder, but he doesn't want a person with such a chequered past living next door to Ruth and Katie. The two women have become quite friendly too. And is there some sinister explanation for Zoe's disappearance?

At the very least, it seems out of character. Her employers were expecting her to be in work today and she hadn't left instructions for feeding her cat. At the thought of Ruth and Katie going into the empty house next door, Nelson grinds his teeth again. He wishes that he could keep everyone he loves safe and under his eye but, even in lockdown, this is proving impossible.

And, finally, he's still worried about Leah. Should he call her at home, just to check that she's OK? Or would that seem bullying, as if he's insisting that she come to work even if she's ill? He wishes Judy was there to do it for him. But it's Tanya's day and, whilst his DS has many sterling qualities, empathy is not one of them.

Tanya is still working on the suicide cases. In his office, Nelson googles 'Zoe Hilton'. There's not much. She has a Facebook page but it's mostly pictures of that mutant cat. He tries 'Dawn Stainton' and the headlines spring up.

Killer Nurse

Angel of Death

Hospital Failures

Agony of families

He reads that Dawn Stainton, 31, was arrested when three elderly patients in her care were suspected of dying from insulin poisoning. The case came to trial the next year and Dawn was found not guilty, partly, it seems, because this type of poisoning is hard to prove. Chris Stephenson, Nelson's least favourite pathologist, gave evidence that the deceased showed signs of lower glucose which – counterintuitively – might point to insulin overdose. But Dawn had

no motive and there was no direct evidence of her involve-
ment. She was acquitted. Two years later another nurse,
Christine Sands, was found guilty of the murders but this
case does not seem to have generated nearly as many headlines. Nelson suspects that this is because Christine was not
as photogenic as the young Dawn.

So, on the face of it, Zoe is innocent, a victim of a miscar-
riage of justice. All the same, Nelson still feels uneasy about
her living next door to Ruth and Katie. And he'd very much
like her to turn up.

'Boss?'

Nelson looks up to see Tanya in the doorway, the lower
half of her face covered by one of her colourful masks.

'I may have found something.'

'Yes?'

Tanya comes closer but not too close. 'I spoke to Samantha
Wilson's adult children again. Just to see if anything had
come to them since their mother's death. The son, Brady,
mentioned that a neighbour had seen a man going into the
house a few times. A bearded chap, she said.'

A bearded chap. Nelson recalls the picture on Joe
McMahon's student card, the intense stare, the full black
beard.

'Did you talk to this neighbour?'

'That's the frustrating thing. She moved away, Brady says,
as soon as lockdown started. She was going to stay with her
grown-up son, but Brady doesn't know where he lives.'

'See if you can find her.'

'I will.'

Tanya seems to be expecting something but it's a few seconds before Nelson realises what it is.

'Good work,' he says.

Ruth finds it very hard to concentrate on her tutorials. These are final year students so her main job is to ensure that they finish their dissertations and to reassure them that, one day, they will have a graduation ceremony. She sympathises. It's hard writing a dissertation at the best of times but, when you can't get to a library and you're stuck at home in your childhood bedroom with no support from lecturers or fellow students, the task must seem monumental. Ruth gives all the help she can, whilst glancing at her phone to see if she's had a text from Judy.

When she's pressed 'leave meeting' for the last time, she thinks about Eileen Gribbon. She didn't appear for Ruth's last lecture. Is Eileen still in the empty halls of residence or has she gone back to the home where she doesn't feel welcome? She texts Fiona, who is Eileen's personal tutor.

'I was just about to message,' texts Fiona. 'Eileen hasn't turned up to the last two tutorials. I'm a bit worried.'

Me too, thinks Ruth. She texts David and asks if he's seen anything of Joe McMahon.

'No,' replies David, with what seems like breezy unconcern. 'I think he's dropped out.'

'Contact him,' Ruth texts back. 'ASAP.' She doesn't add 'please'. That'll teach him, she thinks. The truth is that David probably won't even notice.

Her phone pings. Nelson. *Cathbad in ICU. Tubes. Doesn't*

sound good. Ruth's heart sinks. She texts a quick *Thinking of you xxx* to Judy. What can she do to take her mind off her magical friend reduced to a body on an intensive care bed? Kate is absorbed in her cat saga, watched intently by Flint. Ruth goes to the window. Still no sign of Zoe although Ruth thinks that she hears faint meowing from Derek. Ruth gets out the yellow file marked 'House'. There are the photographs, the dray, the copy of the title deeds and the printout of the newspaper article.

Big-hearted Foster Mum Dies

Tributes have been paid to Dot Barton, of 2 New Road, Saltmarsh, who died of cancer at the age of 68. As well as being mother to two sons, John and Matthew, and grandmother of three, Dot also fostered more than a hundred children. 'Our door was always open,' says Dot's husband, Alf (70). 'Dot was so kind,' says Alma McLaughlin (21), who was fostered as a teenager. 'She really made a difference to my life.' Dot's funeral will be held at St Peter's Church, Gaywood, on Wednesday 17th June.

Ruth googles Alma McLaughlin and, at almost her first try, finds her on Facebook. She's the right age, early seventies, based in Cornwall and, by the looks of it, living an active paddle-boarding, scuba-diving existence. Ruth messages Alma and, a few minutes later, gets a reply. That's one of the only good things about lockdown. People are glued to their computers and have little else to do besides replying to random strangers. Yes, says Alma, she was fostered by Dot for a year in 1964 when she was fifteen. Her home life hadn't been easy but Dot – and Alf – had made all the difference. She has very happy memories of the cottage.

'I know this is going to sound strange,' types Ruth, 'but does the name Dawn Stainton mean anything to you?'

The answer comes back almost immediately. 'Yes! She was Dot's foster child too. But she was only a baby then. About a year old. She was living with Dot until she got a permanent adoption. Sweet little thing.'

'Do you know anything about Dawn's birth parents?' asks Ruth, typing so quickly that she almost misses out the apostrophe. She doesn't though; some things are still sacred.

'I think I overheard once that her mother was young and unmarried. The usual thing. You didn't keep your baby if you were an unmarried mother in the sixties. Makes you feel sad, doesn't it?'

It certainly does, thinks Ruth.

33

She crawls to the door. 'Let me out,' she says.

His voice is soft, almost kind. 'There's no way out.'

A plate is pushed through the grille. She reaches up to take it. Another two biscuits and half an apple.

'We don't want you putting on weight,' comes the voice.

'Can I have some water?' she asks.

He doesn't reply but, a few minutes later, a bottle of water is pushed through the slot. She drinks greedily then forces herself to stop. She doesn't know how long it will have to last.

'Please,' she says. 'Why are you doing this?'

'It's for the best,' he says. 'You're not happy. You've never been happy.'

'Let me out,' she says. Trying to make her voice sound authoritative and not pathetic.

'There's no way out. The only escape is to make your own exit. Take the narrow gate.'

She's silent then and, just when she thinks he's gone, something else comes through the grille. A pack of pills. She can't see what type

they are but, when she fingers them in their foil packet, the shape is
oddly comforting, like peas in a pod.

The only escape is to make your own exit.

Ruth looks around her sitting room, so comforting, so
familiar. The tatty sofa where Kate is now stretched out
eating an apple. The bookshelves, two-deep now, with
genres and authors jumbled together. The wooden staircase
leading to the upstairs rooms. The broken lightshade. The
chewed suffragette cushions. Is it possible that, some time
in 1963, Ruth's mother once visited this house with a baby
in her arms? That she handed the baby over to kind foster
mother, Dot, and departed, taking one last photograph to
remind herself of her daughter? Dawn 1963. And is it possible that Zoe, with whom Ruth did feel an immediate bond,
is actually her sister?

Ruth has always wanted a sister. It was something she
used to say to Simon when they argued. 'I wish I had a sister
instead of a stupid brother!' Had Ruth's mother overheard?
What had she thought? What had she thought when Ruth
announced that she was going to have a baby without a
husband in the picture? Ruth remembers when she told her
parents, walking in the grounds of Severndroog Castle on
Shooter's Hill. 'What do you mean, you're pregnant,' Jean
had said, 'you're not even married.' 'You don't need to be
married to have a baby,' Ruth had replied. But Jean had obviously felt that you did. Or maybe others had thought it for
her. She'd once told Ruth that her father had been strict but
Ruth, remembering a mild elderly man, had dismissed this.

But what if her grandfather had been a domestic tyrant, ordering his daughter to give up her illegitimate child? He wouldn't have been the first to do so.

'Oh, Mum,' says Ruth, aloud.

'What?' says Kate from the sofa.

'Nothing.'

Not for the first time, Ruth wishes that her mother was still alive. She wishes that she could ask her if this was where it all started: her disapproval of Ruth's life, her rigid Christianity, her hatred of Norfolk and this cottage in particular. Ruth remembers visiting her mother in hospital after her first stroke and having the distinct impression that Jean wanted to tell her something. But they had ended up talking about Kate, as usual. And Jean had adored the child whom Arthur, now a doting granddad, had once described as 'a bastard grandchild'. Ruth supposes that this represents closure of some kind.

Does Ruth's father know? She thinks not, remembering his genuine confusion over the Dawn photograph. Arthur and Jean met and married in 1964, Simon was born in 1966, Ruth in 1968. Ruth imagines that her mother simply left her past behind her. Something that her daughter, as an archaeologist, could have told her is almost impossible to achieve.

This explains, of course, why Zoe Hilton, née Dawn Stainton, came to rent the house next door. She must have known that this was where she spent the first year of her life. Did she also know that Ruth was her half-sister? You're allowed to trace your birth parents, aren't you, when you reach eighteen? Zoe had acquired a photograph of Jean from somewhere. It wouldn't have been hard to trace the line from Jean to Ruth. Ruth tries to remember what Zoe told her about her early life. Only that she'd married her teenage boyfriend, now white-haired but still cool, and that she thought they'd still be together if they'd had children. Her parents were both dead and her mother had been a keen gardener. Nothing about being adopted or the reasons for her child-free state. Jean would have been proud of Zoe, thinks Ruth. Nurse was top of her list of respectable professions. Archaeologist was near the bottom.

But where is her respectable nurse neighbour now? And does her disappearance have anything to do with the fact that her history is now known to Norfolk police? Ruth has not enjoyed the few instances when she has appeared on screen, as an expert witness in various archaeology programmes. She can only imagine how it would feel to have your face emblazoned across the papers, charged with the very worst of crimes. That Zoe was completely innocent doesn't seem to have affected the prurient tone that still accompanies her original name. Even Nelson called her a murderer.

Ruth goes to the window, hoping that Zoe will materialise in front of her. But all she sees are the marshes, the long grasses moving endlessly in the wind.

'We need to find Joe McMahon,' Nelson tells Tanya. 'His dad lives in London. Says he hasn't seen Joe for a year but maybe he'll turn up there. People do normally drift home in the end. Here's the number.'

'Do you think he's the bearded man the neighbour mentioned?'

'I don't know but he's got a bloody big beard and he's been acting suspiciously. That's enough for me. Try to find this neighbour of Samantha's too. Oh, and now Ruth's neighbour's gone missing.' He tells Tanya briefly about Zoe Hilton.

'I remember the Dawn Stainton case,' says Tanya. 'Deadly Dawn they called her.'

'You don't surprise me. She hasn't turned up for work today and apparently that's very out of character. I've put a trace on her car.' When Nelson had asked Ruth what car Zoe drove, she had replied 'I think it's blue'. The surgery had been more helpful and now they are looking for an electric blue Nissan Juke. The receptionist even knew the number plate, 'We need it for the parking permit.'

'Next of kin?' says Tanya.

'There's an ex-husband,' says Nelson. 'Patrick Stainton. She put him as next-of-kin on her personnel records, but I've contacted him and he hasn't spoken to Zoe in years. They divorced in 1994.'

'That must have been about when the court case was.'

'Yes, you're right.' Nelson is impressed, though he should be used to Tanya's powers of recall by now. 'Anyway, there's no one else.'

'That's a bit lonely,' says Tanya.

'I suppose it is,' says Nelson.

The thought doesn't make him feel any less troubled. Lonely people can be dangerous. When Tanya goes out of the room, bristling with purpose, Nelson rings Ruth.

'I've found out who Zoe is,' she says, without waiting for him to say anything. 'I think she's my sister.' Then she's off on a saga about photographs, foster parents and Zoe always reminding her of her mother. When Nelson can get a word in, he says, 'I take it she's not back yet?'

'No. I keep looking out of the window.'

'Keep your doors locked,' says Nelson.

'Why?' says Ruth.

'Because it's always a good idea to keep your doors locked. Especially when you live in the middle of bloody nowhere.'

'But do you think Zoe could be in danger?'

'I don't know but there's a lot that feels fishy to me. Joe McMahon having a room full of photos of you and then going missing. Those messages about the Grey Lady. Zoe disappearing on her way to work.'

'I'm a bit worried about Eileen too. You remember, the student who showed you Joe's room?'

Nelson remembers the girl shivering in the porch of the halls of residence.

'What's happened to her?'

'I don't know. She's not attending lectures. Her personal tutor hasn't heard from her in a while. I've asked the warden of the halls to check up on her today.'

'It'll be quicker to go myself,' says Nelson.

'That would be great,' says Ruth. 'I don't like to think of her in that place on her own.'

'Nor do I,' says Nelson. 'I'll call you later. And keep the doors locked.'

*

The halls look even bleaker today. It's April now and there's a real feeling of spring in the air but the blue skies and bright sun contrast with the general sense of abandonment. The grass grows high around the empty buildings and litter blows across the courtyards. Nelson has asked the warden, Jeremy Stokes, to meet him outside Vancouver House. He thinks the man looks nervous. He's wearing a surgical mask and backs away from Nelson even as he greets him.

'How often do you check on the students here?' barks Nelson from behind his own mask.

'They can call us whenever they need anything,' says Jeremy, tapping in a passcode to open the door.

'But you don't come here yourself?'

'No. I've been shielding. My wife has cancer.'

Nelson lets the man off but, all the same, UNN's student care leaves a lot to be desired. Eileen's room is on the second floor and, as soon as Jeremy lets them in with his master key, it's clear that it's been empty for a few days. There's mould on a coffee cup by the bed and an intricate spider's web across the en-suite shower.

'Maybe she's gone home,' says Jeremy.

'Have you got a number for her? Perhaps you could find out.'

Nelson goes into the corridor and starts knocking on doors. Before he's got to the end of the line, one of them opens.

'What's going on?'

It's Mei. The girl he met on his last visit, the one who said she'd keep an eye on Eileen.

'It's DCI Nelson. Have you seen Eileen?'

To his surprise, Mei nods. 'She put a note through my door on Monday night.'

'What did it say?'

Mei looks slightly alarmed at the urgency in his voice, but she says, equally enough, 'I think I've still got it. I'll show you.'

She disappears into her room and comes back with a postcard which she hands to Nelson.

I'm off! Thanks for everything. Love you Exx

Nelson stares at the rounded blue letters, the heart that follows the kisses. 'Does this sound like her?'

Mei smiles. 'It does.'

'Do you know where she was off to?'

'I assumed home.' Mei is starting to look worried.

'Can I take the card?' asks Nelson.

'Of course.' There are probably fingerprints all over it now, but Nelson gets out an evidence bag and inserts the card. Eileen wrote it on Monday. It's Wednesday now. Not that long for a teenager to go missing but long enough.

'How did she seem when you last saw her?'

'A little down. We all are. It's very hard, living here on your own, trying to keep up with your studies, worrying about Covid.'

'Are you on your own here?'

'There's one other girl. Lan. Her family are in China too.'

Nelson turns to Jeremy. 'You should be looking after these girls better.'

'I know,' says Jeremy. 'But what can I do?'

'You could check up on them sometimes,' says Nelson. 'Send them food parcels. Buy them a Netflix subscription. Show some bloody compassion.'

He thinks that the warden is about to burst into tears.

'It's OK,' says Mei kindly. 'We're all under pressure.'

Nelson leaves after a few more well-chosen words. He wishes he could find somewhere else for Mei and Lan to live but no one is going to be taking in lodgers during a pandemic and all the hotels and B&Bs are closed. Nelson gets back into his car feeling frustrated. He's about to text Tanya and ask her to put out a description of Eileen when a message appears on his screen.

Judy.

Cathbad worse. Think it's the end.

34

'You're not happy. You've never been happy.'

After he's gone, she ponders these words, wondering if they are true. Has she really never been happy? She thinks she has childhood memories of sunlight and laughter but maybe they aren't real. Just a delusion. Maybe there is nothing outside these four walls.

'Take the narrow gate.'

A phrase comes into her mind. 'Wide is the gate and broad is the way that leads to destruction.' Where did that come from? She still has the pills, in their comforting blister pack, in her hand. She pops the pod and two of the tablets are in her hands.

She swallows them with what's left of the water.

Nelson sits in his car staring at his phone. He watches Jeremy Stokes leave Vancouver Hall and stop to sanitise his hands, wringing them together for what seems like hours. Then he takes off his mask, revealing a short, grey beard. He rubs sanitiser over his face too, which seems excessive to Nelson, before walking off in the direction of his car, one of those smug hybrid makes.

Cathbad worse. Think it's the end.

Can this really be how it ends? Cathbad, the fearless druid, felled by a simple virus? Nelson thinks back to the first time he met Cathbad, then a suspect in a murder investigation.

'You're very abrupt. Are you a Scorpio?'

Nelson would cheerfully have killed Cathbad himself at that moment despite (or perhaps because of) him getting the star sign right. Later, he and Cathbad had crossed the marshes in a storm. Cathbad had stepped off the path and would probably have drowned if Nelson hadn't heaved him back to safety.

'I am in your debt,' Cathbad had said. 'The spirits of the ancestors are strong – they are all around us.'

Come on, ancestors, thinks Nelson, do your bit now. It was partly in repayment of this debt that Cathbad had – in his own words – travelled to the dream world to rescue Nelson. Clearer than the campus around him, Nelson sees the dark water, the steps, the stone boat.

'Don't let go,' he'd said to dream Cathbad.

'I won't.'

Since then Cathbad has fallen from a great height and landed on a stall selling Slush Puppies, he has saved his son from a kidnapper and accompanied Nelson to an earthquake zone. Surely, he has a few of his nine lives left?

Nelson can't face giving Ruth the news. She really loves Cathbad and would be lost without the old nutter. Nelson rubs his eyes, which have become strangely wet. The recently applied sanitiser makes them sting. Through a haze of tears, he drives back to the station.

*

Judy is moving in slow motion. 'You can FaceTime me,' said the nurse, 'and we'll hold the phone close to his head.'

Judy is dimly aware of the man's kindness even as she gathers her children together to speak to their father via iPad. They sit in a row on the sofa and Judy dials the number given to her by the nurse, whose name is Abbas. Her hands are shaking too much, so Maddie takes the tablet from her. After a few deft clicks, the screen shows a figure in scrubs, face hidden by a visor.

'I'm Abbas. I'm going to hold the phone next to Michael. Don't be distressed at his appearance. The tubes are to help him breathe.'

'Michael?' thinks Judy. But Michael is here next to her. She can feel him sobbing quietly, unlike Miranda on the other side who is almost howling. Then she remembers; Cathbad's baptismal name of Michael Malone must be on his medical records.

'Cathbad,' she says, 'everyone calls him Cathbad.'

'That's useful to know,' says Abbas. 'We'll call him Cathbad from now on. We won't leave him alone, I promise. There'll always be someone with him.' Judy can't see Abbas's face because of the mask and visor but his voice is calm and comforting. Judy wonders how many hours he's worked that day and how many deathbeds he has attended.

Then the screen shows a man with a mask covering most of his face, tubes snaking out from his mouth and nose. His long grey hair is spread out on the pillow.

'Cathbad,' says Judy. 'It's me, Judy. I'm here with Maddie, Michael and Miranda.'

'Hallo, Dad,' says Maddie.

'Tell Daddy how much you love him,' says Judy to her children. She has one thought in her head: the children must not look back on this moment with regret. With sadness, yes, but they must not regret what hasn't been said. They need to tell Cathbad that they love him. But Michael and Miranda are crying too much now to make any sense. It's up to Maddie to say, in her sweet clear voice, 'We all love you so much, Dad.' Maddie, who lost her little sister when she was still a child, is she about to lose her father too?

'Stay strong, Cathbad,' says Judy. 'I'm praying to all the saints and all the spirits. I'll even become a druid if it helps. Nelson sends his love and Ruth too.' Universal energy, Cathbad called it. Is it enough?

Do Cathbad's eyes flicker? Is he remembering travelling to the dream realm with Nelson?

'Abbas is looking after you,' says Judy. 'All the doctors and nurses.'

'Thing,' says Michael suddenly. 'He needs to say goodbye.'

Saying goodbye. Is that what they are doing?

Ruth has the strangest feeling, all afternoon, that someone is watching her. Corbyn is sitting on the fence, watching her out of his bright, dark eyes. Is he a warning or a messenger?

'Are you from Cathbad?' she says aloud. Then feels stupid. Corbyn takes flight but, a few minutes later, he's back, this time on the grass in front of Zoe's house. Zoe has succeeded in clearing away a lot of weeds but there's no sign of the cottage garden paradise that she planned. Will she ever come back? Will Ruth ever be able to have *that* conversation with her?

Ruth and Kate set out for their afternoon walk later than usual. It's another bright, sunny day but there's a sharp wind which makes the tall grass sway and whisper. What's it saying? Cathbad would know.

'Why do you keep looking back, Mum?' says Kate.

'Am I?' says Ruth. 'I didn't realise I was.'

'Help me look for unusual insects.' Kate has brought a cardboard box, with holes in the lid, in case she finds one of these creatures. Flint will think it's a takeaway.

Ruth can't resist one last look back. The grasses seem to close behind them, shutting off their escape, and the flat landscape offers no vantage point. After about half an hour, and an attempt to capture a damsel fly, they return to the cottage. There's still no car outside Zoe's house.

Ruth makes tea and finds some frozen crumpets which, toasted, make good comfort food. Neither of them feels like working so Ruth gets out the Norwich Cathedral jigsaw and they start the laborious work of filling in the blue sky and grey ramparts. It's curiously mesmerising. Steward's House is there too, a tricky vortex of black and white. Ruth manages to forget Zoe, Eileen, Joe, even Cathbad. When she looks up, it's almost dark outside.

'Just going to feed Derek,' she says. 'Don't answer the door to anyone while I'm gone.'

Who does she think will come knocking? Nelson? Zoe? The grim reaper? Kate leans over the puzzle, deep in concentration.

Ruth takes the key and opens Zoe's stable door. The kitchen is silent apart from a large station-style clock ticking on the wall. Ruth goes into the sitting room and, despite her wish to hurry back to Kate, is drawn to the wedding picture and the passport photo in the frame. It was taken in the days when you were allowed to smile but Jean has barely taken advantage of this; her expression is wary. Her hair is grey though, so it wasn't that long ago, in the shorter style that Jean adopted when she passed seventy. Where had Zoe found this picture?

A sound behind her makes Ruth jump. But it's only Derek, appearing from some secret hiding place in search of supper. Ruth puts cat food in his bowl, cleans out his litter tray and leaves the house, locking the door behind her. She's more certain than ever that Zoe would never have gone away without arranging for someone to take care of Derek.

Kate has almost finished the cathedral tower. Ruth goes into the kitchen to prepare supper and to lose herself in the wonderful pre-Covid world of *The Archers*. What will she do when they run out of pre-recorded episodes? She can't imagine a socially distanced Ambridge. Scrolling through the evening's TV on her phone she sees that there's a film called *The Cabin in the Woods*. She looks it up and learns that it's a horror comedy film directed by Drew Goddard. Can horror be funny? She remembers Peter's email about the original name of the house, The Cabin. *We used to joke about that.* The Evil Dead *and all those horror story tropes.* She remembers watching *The Evil Dead* at the cinema in Eltham, maybe even with Daniel. It's about a group of college students having a jolly vacation in an isolated cabin. There are, as Peter said, all the usual tropes: the porch swing moving on its own, the stopped clock, the 'Book of the Dead' conveniently left in a cellar, the tree branch breaking outside, the damaged bridge that means none of them can escape. It's not long before four of the students are possessed by demons. As Ruth remembers it, only one of them survives.

The wind is now blowing strongly. In the garden, the apple tree is whipped into a frenzy. Ruth double checks that both parts of the back door are locked. She jumps when Flint bursts in through his cat flap, tail puffed up in fright. 'What's the matter, Flint?' Flint meows, gazing meaningfully at his bowl. She jumps again when her phone buzzes. Nelson.

'It's Cathbad,' says Nelson.

'What?' Suddenly the room is as cold as if hosting a cinematic demonic presence.

'I'm sorry, love. Judy says it's the end.'

35

That night she sees the Grey Lady. She has no idea what time it is, drifting in an uneasy state between waking and sleeping. She opens her eyes. Or does she? There's a woman standing in front of her, dressed in long grey robes. Her hand is outstretched, as if she's offering something, but she can't see what it is. It's the eyes that she remembers most. They look so sad.

She must have fallen asleep because, when she wakes up, her sleeping bag is wet with condensation. Was the Grey Lady ever there, gazing at her with her sweet, sad eyes? He's left a bucket for her to pee in and she does that, gagging at the stench of ammonia. She can't be sick again because there's nothing in her stomach. She almost takes another pill, just for the sensation of swallowing, but she manages to stop herself.

She never hears him approaching. It's as if he has paws instead of feet. Like a cat. She's drifting in and out of sleep when the grille opens and she hears his voice.

'It's me,' he says. But who else would it be?

She takes the plate. It contains another apple and a tiny piece of cheese.

'You'll lose weight in no time,' he says from behind the door.

Will she continue to lose weight until she's nothing but a skeleton? There are more pills too.

'Why are you giving me medicine?' she says.

'Just swallow them,' he says, 'and then you'll be free.'

'Give me some water then.'

He pushes a bottle through. She takes a gulp.

'Have you taken a pill?' There's a new note in his voice. Excitement.

'Yes.'

'Good girl.'

Is that what the Grey Lady was doing? Holding out pills for her to take? But, no, she's convinced that the Lady was a friendly spirit. The way she'd looked at her was so sorrowful, so understanding. Our Lady of the Sorrows. But maybe this was just because she's dead too. Sometimes she imagines that everyone else in the world is dead, victims of the virus, and there's only her, battering on her prison door, shouting into the silence.

Ruth barely sleeps. She dreams about Cathbad, about walking with him on the Blackpool sands, about Cathbad climbing into the sky to rescue Kate. She sees a room with ballet dancer wallpaper, Cathbad weeping when Michael was born, his face when he performed Kate's naming ceremony. *May the gods keep this child perfect and let anything that is negative stay far beyond her world.*

Flint starts meowing outside the door at five a.m., just when Ruth has fallen into an uneasy sleep. Light is filtering in through the curtains. She might as well get up. Ruth checks her phone. Nothing from Judy. But would she tell

Ruth if the worst had happened? 'Think it's the end' is what Judy had texted to Nelson. What if the end has already happened? Is Ruth living in a post-Cathbad world?

She gets up and reaches for her favourite dressing gown. At least she is now free to wear this garment, which she considered too unsexy to show Nelson. It's very comforting though, towelling and threadbare. She puts on her slippers – equally ancient and not revealed to Nelson – and leaves the room, almost tripping over Flint who has positioned himself at the top of the stairs. Ruth goes into the kitchen to feed him and put on the kettle, in that order. The supply of gourmet cat food is running low. She will have to go shopping today.

Ruth takes her mug of tea into the sitting room. It's another stunning sunrise, the marshes turning palest pink and then deepest gold. Dawn, she thinks. Dawn 1963. Had her sister been named after this daily phenomenon? She can hardly ask her mother, and, at this rate, she'll never see Zoe again to ask her either. At six, she feels brave enough to text Judy. *How are you?* This seems neutral enough. She hopes that the message doesn't wake Judy.

But Judy texts back in seconds, clearly awake too. *OK. No more news. C still critical.* Critical, thinks Ruth, but still alive. Thanks be to the goddess. Despite spending years attending church with her parents, she doesn't know how to pray but she sends out a message to the wakening world, the waving grass, the swirling seabirds. *Please save Cathbad.*

Nelson, too, wakes early. His bed is bigger and more comfortable than Ruth's, but he hasn't slept well since he's been home. He misses sharing a bed with Ruth, he misses seeing Katie at breakfast, he even misses the yowls of the demon cat on the landing. He reaches for his phone. Six thirty. He can hear the radio playing softly in Laura's room. She doesn't sleep well either. Not for the first time, he wishes that Bruno were there. His primal needs – food and walking – would stop him thinking about Cathbad. Can it really be the end? Surely Cathbad is indestructible.

Nelson gets up and puts on his dressing gown. It's a Dad garment, bought by his daughters, with his initials on the pocket. Not something he would like Ruth to see. He puts on his slippers and pads downstairs. Once again, he imagines that he can hear Bruno beside him, panting gently, his tail battering Nelson's legs. Black Shuck again? Or a message from Cathbad the shape-shifter? Nelson is making tea when he sees that he has a message from Ruth.

Heard from Judy. No change.

'Thank Christ for that,' says Nelson, aloud. 'Where there's life there's hope.' He imagines the ghost dog wagging its tail.

Kate emerges at nine looking, for a scary second, like a mini teenager.

'How's Uncle Cathbad?' she says. She hasn't called him Uncle for years. Cathbad isn't Kate's uncle but he is her godfather – through the pagan ceremony and in the eyes of the Catholic church – and she loves him.

'He's still very ill,' says Ruth, 'but the doctors and nurses are looking after him. Judy says he's got a lovely nurse called Abbas.'

'We should pray for Uncle Cathbad,' says Kate. Ruth wonders again where Kate is getting this religious stuff from. 'I like Bible stories,' she'd said the other day. Ruth feels out of her depth although this would be familiar ground for Nelson. Last night he mentioned that he was praying to some entity called St Carlo, apparently on the advice of his mum. Ruth is always worried when Nelson takes his mother's advice. But, then again, what harm can praying do?

'Let's pray silently for Cathbad,' says Ruth. 'And we'll pray that Zoe gets home safely.'

'If Zoe doesn't come back,' says Kate, 'can we adopt Derek?'

Nelson has asked both Tanya and Tony to come in today. They have a lot to do, after all. Joe McMahon, Eileen Gribbon and Zoe Hilton are all still on the missing list. Then there's the witness who saw a 'bearded chap' visiting Samantha Wilson. Was this Joe McMahon? Nelson doesn't know but he would like to speak to the missing student as soon as possible.

Tony is in the kitchen and offers to make Nelson a cup of coffee. Nelson says yes although he knows he'll be buzzing after three teas. Still, the day he goes caffeine free will be the day they nail down his coffin lid.

'No Leah today?' says Nelson.

'I haven't seen her,' says Tony. 'Sugar?'

'No thanks.' Michelle made him give up last year.

Tanya floats in carrying her own box of special tea bags. 'This one's called health and well-being.' She waves a purple sachet at them.

'Don't know why the government bothers with all those health experts,' says Nelson. 'Send them a box and Covid will be finished. No more hands, face, space and all that bollocks.' This reminds him that he really shouldn't be in the small kitchen with two other people.

'Meeting in the incident room,' he says and goes to open some windows.

Tanya says that she's contacted Eileen's mother. 'She hasn't heard from Eileen in about a week. She didn't seem worried though.'

'Some people don't deserve to be parents,' says Nelson.

'Could Eileen and Joe be together?' asks Tony. 'They're in the same year at uni after all.'

'It's a possibility,' says Nelson. 'It was Eileen who first alerted us about Joe's disappearance, but he could have been in touch since.'

Tony opens his mouth and Nelson dreads an anecdote about his own university days, possibly featuring friends made in freshers' week and never forgotten, but he has underestimated the new recruit. 'I was looking at Judy's notes on the supposed suicides,' says Tony, 'and one of Karen Head's friends mentioned her having a boyfriend with an unsuitable age difference.'

Nelson is impressed. 'You think it might be Joe McMahon?'

'It's just a thought.'

'A good one. See if Joe ever attended one of those slimming meetings. Lean Machine or whatever they were called.'

'Lean Zone,' says Tanya, zipping through her notes as though keen to match Tony for insights.

'Ruth went to a Lean Zone meeting,' says Nelson. 'And McMahon seems to be obsessed with her. Her missing neighbour, Zoe Hilton, went too.'

'Good for Ruth,' says Tanya.

'Why?' says Nelson.

'No reason.' Tanya looks back down at her notes. 'Judy thought there was a link with Lean Zone, didn't she? I suppose we could ask her about it.'

'She's got enough on her plate at the moment,' says Nelson.

And that's the other reason for all the activity. To avoid thinking about Cathbad.

But Judy is, in fact, sitting at her home-office space in her bedroom. Maddie has taken the younger children to the beach and there is only one thing that can take Judy's mind off the possible death of her life partner: work. Although she's had messages today from Nelson, Clough, Tony and even Tanya, none of them have asked about the case. She wishes they would. She wishes that she could say something besides 'no news yet, in ICU, holding his own.' 'I used to hold my own,' Clough texted back, 'until I was told it would make me go blind.' She misses Clough.

There's something there, some link that she's not seeing. Judy leafs through her notebook.

She went to evensong at St Matthew's sometimes.

Avril and Tony loved birdwatching. It was one of the reasons they moved here.

She was very devout in her quiet way.

People do become very close sometimes. We've even had a few romances.

I was a bit worried. I wish I'd asked more.

What's the connection? She's got to find it. Nelson and co will never crack this case on their own.

'Mum!' She hears shouts from downstairs. Barking. Wails of, 'It's not fair. She said I could have it.' The children have become particularly demanding in the last twenty-four hours. Thing too. She knows she should go downstairs but she can't quite face it yet. Then she hears another voice, one that seems to come from another world, another life.

'I know I can't come inside but can you just say I'm here?'

'Clough!'

Judy runs to the top of the stairs.

Back in his office, Nelson takes out the postcard that Eileen Gribbon posted under Mei's door. It's still in its plastic evidence bag.

I'm off! Thanks for everything. Love you Exx

'Off,' says Nelson aloud. 'Off where, Eileen?' In theory, it should be easy to trace people during lockdown. After all, everyone is meant to be staying at home to save lives. But what happens when they have to leave home, maybe to save their own life?

Mei has given him her number and he rings it now.

'Just checking that you're all right.'

'I'm fine,' says Mei with the heartbreaking confidence of youth. 'Jeremy came to check on us today.'

'Jeremy? Oh yes, the warden.' At least he seems to be remembering his duty of care, albeit rather late in the day.

'Let me know if you're worried about anything,' says Nelson.

'I'm not worried,' says Mei, as if she's not alone in a foreign country in the middle of a pandemic.

After a cheerful farewell from Mei, Nelson turns the postcard over. The picture is of a lopsided black and white house with a cloaked figure standing in front of it.

'Augustine Steward's House, Tombland,' he reads, 'is haunted by the Grey Lady. This tormented ghost from the sixteenth century hides a terrible secret.'

36

'You shouldn't be here,' says Judy.

'Let's pretend I'm not,' says Clough.

They are walking on the beach, keeping the regulation two metres apart. Even so, Judy is meant to be in quarantine, Clough shouldn't be in Norfolk at all. 'Go for a walk,' Maddie had said. 'You're safe when you're in the open air. And it'll make you feel better. You can take Thing. You're allowed to go for two walks a day if you have a dog.' Judy doesn't know where Maddie gets her scientific facts from but one thing is certain; Maddie is becoming as wise as her father.

'I'm so pleased to see you,' says Judy.

'I thought you would be.' Clough sounds smug. 'Your last message sounded a bit . . . a bit like you needed company.'

'I do,' says Judy. 'I mean, I know I've got the kids but . . .'

'But you have to stay strong for them,' says Clough. 'You don't for me.'

They walk along the sand in silence. Thing doubles back to check that they're still there. His nanny instincts have become more pronounced in Cathbad's absence. Apart from another dog-walker at the water's edge, there's not a soul in sight. The multicoloured beach huts are empty, and the only sound is the hiss and sigh of the waves breaking.

'I just can't imagine a world without Cathbad,' says Judy.

'Nor can I,' says Clough. 'Do you remember when we first met him? Bloody great tempest raging on the Saltmarsh. Thunder and lightning. Cathbad gets out of the car and says to the boss, "I'll be your guide." And then they disappear into the night. I honestly thought it would be the last time I saw either of them.'

'Cathbad says Nelson saved him that night.'

'Something happened,' says Clough, 'that's for sure.'

'Cathbad likes you,' says Judy. 'He says that you're a positive life force.'

'Cassie says that I'm a pain in the neck,' says Clough. 'Maybe that means the same thing.'

'The boss misses you,' says Judy. 'Specially now he's stuck with Tanya and Tony.'

'Tony's the new boy, isn't he? I thought he seemed OK.'

'He's great. He's just very enthusiastic. Tanya's OK too. She's sent me some very kind messages.'

'The boss must be hating lockdown,' says Clough, 'especially if it stops him seeing Ruth.'

'I think he is seeing her,' says Judy. 'Michelle's in Blackpool. I think Nelson's been staying with Ruth. Or he was until Laura came back home.'

'He's taking a risk,' says Clough. 'If Super Jo finds out.'

'Jo hasn't been into the station since this started. She

keeps sending Nelson emails that he ignores. Tanya says that, with Leah off, Nelson doesn't answer anything from head office.'

'Leah's off? Is she sick?'

'I don't know. I hope not. Sometimes I think that everyone's going to get this thing eventually. I mean, if Cathbad can get ill, anyone can.'

'They'll find a vaccine,' says Clough. 'I was talking to someone at the university the other day. He says that Oxford are near to developing something. And that's quite something for a Cambridge man to admit.'

'It'll be too late for Cathbad,' says Judy.

'He'll pull through,' says Clough. 'And you know I'm always right.'

Once this remark would have induced actual physical rage in Judy. But, just for that second, her biggest regret about Covid is that it stops her from giving her ex-colleague a hug.

In the end Ruth takes Kate shopping with her but leaves her in the car when she goes into the supermarket.

'Text me if you're worried about anything,' she says. 'I won't be long.' Ruth looks at the line of socially distanced shoppers. 'Not that long anyway.'

'I'll be OK,' says Kate. She's playing a game on her phone that seems to involve a bird flying over a series of low hills.

Should Ruth lock the car? But what if Kate is trapped in it? But, if she leaves Kate with the keys, someone could steal her *and* the car. In the end she does lock it but tells Kate how to open the doors if necessary.

'I know, Mum,' says Kate, not looking up from the bird's aerial adventures.

Ruth queues, looking back at the car every few minutes. Kate's head is bent over the game. Would she even notice if an axe murderer tapped on the window? But axe murderers are in short supply in King's Lynn this morning. 'How would you know?' Nelson would say. Ruth looks at her hands on the handle of her shopping trolley. She's wearing plastic gloves today, which makes them look rather sinister. Maybe other people in the queue have hands that have been put to evil, murderous use. She stares hard at the elderly woman in front of her (surely, she should be shielding at home?) until the force of her scrutiny makes the woman turn and give her a timid smile, recognisable even behind her mask. Stop it, Ruth tells herself.

Once she is finally granted admission, Ruth throws food into her trolley without much regard for price or quality. She does remember the gourmet cat food though and scores the last packet of penne.

In the payment queue Ruth looks at the newspaper stand. 'Shambles,' says one headline. 'Get a grip Bozo,' says another. Ruth's beloved *Guardian* has, 'Virus patients more likely to die have ventilators taken away.' Ruth doesn't buy a copy. Eventually she is through the checkout, once again marvelling at the assistant's unruffled good humour, and zigzagging her trolley through the car park. Kate is still intent on her game. Ruth opens the boot and starts heaving the bags in.

'Did you get Jaffa Cakes?' asks Kate.

'Of course.' She's not about to forget the essentials.

'Dad rang,' says Kate. 'He said he was trying to get through to you. He said to be careful because there are lots of funny people in supermarket car parks.'

Ruth doesn't ring Nelson until she is home with a cup of tea and a Jaffa Cake. She knows he can't have news of Cathbad because she has just had a text from Judy saying, 'no change'. She assumes that he's just ringing to check up on her because she mentioned the perilous supermarket trip that morning.

But Nelson starts out with, 'What do you know about the Grey Lady?'

'The Grey Lady of Tombland?'

'How many Grey Ladies are there? No, don't answer that one. Bloody Norfolk is probably full of them.'

'Probably.' It's on the tip of Ruth's tongue to say, 'Ask Cathbad' but no one can ask Cathbad anything, possibly ever again. 'She's a ghost that haunts Augustine Steward's House by the cathedral,' she says. 'Why?'

'Eileen Gribbon left a note for her friend in halls. It was a postcard of the Grey Lady. I wondered if there was a link to Joe McMahon. Didn't you say he was obsessed with her?'

'I don't know about obsessed but my friend Janet said he was asking questions about her. And she'd seen Joe hanging around Tombland. I told you that.'

'I rang Janet Meadows,' says Nelson. 'She said she didn't think there was any harm in McMahon. Not that I trust her opinion. She kept going on about living in a haunted house. Practically said she was kept awake by ghoulies and ghosties.'

'Janet is perfectly rational,' says Ruth. 'Just because she believes in things you don't.'

'I might try ringing her again,' says Nelson. 'Just in case McMahon has turned up. Or the girl. Eileen. I don't like the fact that she seems to be a fan of this Grey Lady too.'

'Janet's actually living in Steward's House,' says Ruth. 'I can't say I'd like that very much.'

'Tombland,' says Nelson. 'The address is enough to put you off.'

Ruth doesn't tell Nelson the origin of the place name. Why spoil his fun?

'Joe was also very interested in the skeleton we excavated in Tombland,' she says. 'He insisted we call her Martha.'

'Martha was his mother's name,' says Nelson. 'It's in the case notes.'

'Eileen said that his mother committed suicide.'

'Did she?' says Nelson. 'That's interesting. No sign of your missing neighbour, I suppose?'

Ruth doesn't like the way his mind is working.

'No,' she says. 'I'm still feeding her cat.'

'That's not a cat,' says Nelson. 'It's bigger than Bruno.'

Ruth doesn't protest because she understands that Nelson is missing his dog.

'Any news from Judy?' she says, though she knows the answer.

'No,' says Nelson. 'But I think Cloughie might have gone to see her. He said he was thinking about it. I know I should have told him not to, but I didn't. I wouldn't often say this, but I think Cloughie might be just what Judy needs.'

Ruth thinks so too. She imagines Clough's tactless kindness blowing away some of the fear and embarrassment that surrounds serious illness. She sends out another message to the Gods of the Marshes. Just in case.

The day passes agonisingly slowly. Kate has almost completed the jigsaw, adding the lopsided roof of Steward's House and the dark entrance to Tombland Alley. Ruth gives a lecture on Skeletal Age Determination and checks to see if Eileen or Joe have been in contact. Neither of them has. Fiona, Eileen's tutor, is worried about her. 'I rang her mother, but she said she hadn't been in touch. She thought she might be staying with friends but couldn't think who they were.' Ruth doesn't judge Eileen's mother for this. She doubts if Jean could have named any of Ruth's university friends. David, Joe's tutor, is more abrasive. 'He's a troublemaker. I could tell that from day one. Always going on about plague victims.' Ruth rings off before David can start lecturing her about the Norwich plague pits.

Ruth goes to feed Derek, who now greets her affectionately. There's no sign of him running out of his special food. Had Zoe bought it in bulk specially? She said that she'd done a big shop just before lockdown started. But, surely, if she'd known she was going away, Zoe would have asked Ruth to feed her cat? But, Ruth reflects, shutting the stable door behind her, there were lots of things that Zoe didn't say.

Back home, Ruth switches on the television for the news.

With Boris Johnson still unwell, it's Health Secretary Matt Hancock's turn to give the daily briefing, himself just free from quarantine. Hancock has a curiously bland face, like a computer simulation. He leans forward on the lectern, which is adorned with a yellow and green flag saying, 'Stay home, protect the NHS, save lives.' 'We have listened,' says Hancock, 'and put the interests of healthcare staff first . . . These are unprecedented times . . .' The government now say 'unprecedented' so often that the word seems to have acquired the opposite meaning. The number of people with the virus who have died in the UK has risen by 569, taking the total number of deaths to 2,921. There is, seemingly, no way out of the Covid nightmare. No vaccine, no cure, just the soaring death rate. Ruth doesn't object when Kate wants to change channels.

Ruth checks her phone. She hopes that there will be something from Judy saying that Cathbad has made a miraculous recovery. But there's only a text message. From Janet Mcadows.

HELP ME

37

A shock of light makes her open her eyes. What's happening? She feels dazed and disorientated. She thinks she was dreaming about the Grey Lady again. Has she come to escort her into the other realm?

But then she realises that the door is open. He's standing framed in the aperture. His face is still in darkness and something about it makes her more scared than ever. She knows she should rush forward, to try to reach the light, but she's too weak and shocked to move.

He puts a plate on the floor. Why hasn't he put it through the grille like he usually does?

'It's nearly time,' he says.

'Time for what?' She doesn't even know if she said it aloud.

'You know what to do,' he says. But does she? She doesn't know anything any more. She shuts her eyes again.

When she opens them, he's left the room. But he's left something else too. Something that glows like a secret jewel. A phone. She waits but, as usual, she can't hear any retreating footsteps. She steps forward, knowing that she's shaking. Is it locked? Password protected?

No, the screen comes to life. She types two words but her hands are so cold that the phone falls to the ground.

'I'll have that.' He's back in the room, picking up the phone and putting it in his pocket. 'You didn't touch it, did you?'

'No,' she says. 'Please. Let me go.'

'There's no one who'll miss you,' he says. 'Just take the pills like a good girl.'

Should she? In their red and white packet, the painkillers look more enticing than the dry biscuits.

'I'll be back later,' he says. 'And we'll make an end to this.'

Nelson has had another frustrating day. They have been unable to trace Eileen Gribbon or Joe McMahon. There was no answer from Janet Meadows and no news from Judy. Nelson leaves at five thirty, leaving Tanya and Tony behind in the office. It's as if he's working part-time. At this rate, he'll be making Jo's dreams come true and retiring before the end of the year.

Nelson drives through the empty streets thinking about the missing students and the Grey Lady. He'd googled the legend after talking to Ruth. It was a particularly nasty story, he thought, even for Norfolk. The girl trapped in her house and then possibly eating her parents. It's no wonder the poor soul walks the streets at night. What would Cathbad say about it? Clear as day, in the quiet of the car, he hears the druid's voice, 'There are more things in heaven and earth, Horatio, than are dreamt of in your philosophy.' Cathbad sometimes calls him Horatio, after the original Nelson. He likes to have his own names for everyone. Ruth is Ruthie and Katie is Hecate. What does he call Judy? Nelson will probably never know.

'Hang on in there, Cathbad,' he says aloud. 'I don't want to have to come and rescue you again.'

He's several miles outside Lynn before he realises that he's driving to Ruth's. The journey has become second nature to him. It's almost an effort to remember the route to his own home, the place he has lived for over twenty years. The sea is sparkling in the distance. Why shouldn't he drive to see Ruth and Katie? It's not exactly in the Covid rules but last week he was practically living there. Why not see Ruth while he can? On the phone last night Michelle said she might be home soon. 'George misses you,' she'd said. Nelson drives even faster, trying to escape guilt.

He's practically at the Saltmarsh turning when there's a call on his phone, which is in hands-free mode. He half hopes, half dreads that it'll be from Judy. But instead, there's a voice message from Leah.

'Help,' is all she says.

Ruth rings Janet back. 'This is Janet Meadows. Leave a message and I'll get back to you. Peace and love.' The cheerful, self-mocking tones almost make Ruth think that the original message must be a joke. But something about the capital letters make it seem real. HELP ME. Ruth thinks of Janet alone in Steward's House. 'She kept going on about living in a haunted house,' said Nelson. 'Practically said she was kept awake by ghoulies and ghosties.' But what if it wasn't the undead who kept Janet awake but actual human intruders, people who could do her harm? Crime doesn't stop because there's a pandemic, Nelson said once, it just goes underground. 'It's Ruth,' she says. 'I'm a bit worried. Please call me back.'

Kate is watching *Friends*. Ross is dressed as an armadillo. 'There were these people called the Maccabees . . .' Ruth remembers Janet telling her about the Grey Lady, in the cheerful fluorescent light of the cafeteria. 'The house was boarded up. That's what they did in those days. Sealed the house with the occupants still inside. They'd draw a cross on the door and sometimes the words "Lord have mercy" and they'd leave the household to die. I suppose it was a way of containing the outbreak. When they opened the house again, they found the bodies of a man, a woman and a young girl.' Things are not always what they seem.

Ruth phones Nelson. She can hardly believe it when she doesn't hear his voice on the end of the line. Nelson always answers his phone. But maybe he's driving and has forgotten to put it on hands-free. Maybe he's home with Laura and has switched his phone off, the way she does when she has Kate by her side. What should she do? After pacing the room for several minutes, watching Father Christmas and Batboy join the Armadillo, Ruth looks through her contacts at the Serious Crimes Unit. She can't ring Judy, for obvious reasons. Clough is no longer on the team. In the end, she clicks on the name 'Tanya'.

'Tanya Fuller.' The no-nonsense voice is a relief.

'Tanya. It's Ruth. I've had a rather worrying message and I can't reach Nelson.'

'That's weird,' says Tanya. 'The boss left an hour ago. I'm still at the station,' she adds, rather self-importantly.

'That is strange,' says Ruth, feeling the first stirrings of real concern. She tells Tanya about the message from Janet Meadows. 'I've tried to ring her, but the message goes straight to voicemail.'

'Where does she live?'

'She's staying in Steward's House in Norwich.'

'Have you linked to her location via Find My Phone?'

'No,' says Ruth. Her phone is only linked to Nelson's because Kate did it.

'Shall we go to Norwich? Have a look at this Steward's House? You can meet me at the station.'

'I'll have Kate with me.' Ruth isn't about to leave Kate on her own at night.

'That's OK,' says Tanya. 'Tony can babysit.'

Nelson stops the car in a lay-by and rings Leah. No answer. The voice on the phone had been high and frightened. The plea had been genuine, he's sure of it. He looks in his contacts to see if he has an address for Leah. She lives in Gaywood, which means going back the way he came. He considers calling for back-up but thinks it might be better to check out the situation for himself first. Nelson starts the car again and performs a screeching U-turn.

Ruth half expects to see Nelson on the road but the only vehicles she passes are delivery vans. Kate is excited by this change in their routine.

'Why can't I come with you to Norwich?' she asks.

'It's against the rules when the police are involved,' Ruth extemporises.

'There are a lot of rules now,' Kate mutters.

'They're to keep us safe,' says Ruth. She's noticed a tendency in Kate to flout regulations. She doesn't get this from Nelson, who believes strongly in the rule of law, even if he flouts it when it suits him. It must be from Ruth's side of the family.

She reaches King's Lynn in thirty minutes, which must be a record. The town centre is quiet but there are lights in the upstairs rooms of the police station. It's half past seven.

Ruth texts Tanya, who comes down to let her in.

'Still no word from Nelson?' asks Tanya.

This was going to be Ruth's first question too. 'No,' she says, trying to squash down her anxiety.

'Well, let's go and see what's going on,' says Tanya. Tony appears behind her. Ruth has only met the DC a few times but he seems pleasant enough. Very young, of course, but isn't that what all middle-aged people say about police officers and doctors?

'Hi, Ruth,' says Tony. 'Hi, Katie.'

'It's Kate,' says Ruth.

'Hi, Kate,' Tony grins at her. 'Do you want to play battle-ships with me?'

'OK,' says Kate, allowing herself a slight smile.

'We won't be long,' says Tanya. 'It's probably nothing.'

Ruth doesn't know whether to be reassured or offended.

*

Nelson has keyed Leah's address into his satnav but still gets lost in the suburban streets of Gaywood. Eventually, the smug voice tells him, 'You have reached your destination.' Nelson parks outside a semi-detached in a cul-de-sac very like his own. The curving street, like every other street he has passed, is completely deserted. It's not yet dark but the street lamps have come on, casting unnatural, theatrical shadows across tidy lawns and neat hedges.

Nelson marches up the garden path and raps on the door. After a few minutes' delay, the door is opened by a man Nelson vaguely recognises as Leah's husband. He has picked her up from a work a few times, an inoffensive-looking sandy-haired chap. Nelson thinks he has an inoffensive job too. Something to do with banking or insurance.

'DCI Nelson,' says the man. What's his name? Something short, Nelson thinks. Lee? Ian? Jay, that's it. 'To what do we owe this pleasure?'

'Is Leah in?'

'I think she's taking a bath.'

Nelson's antenna are now on full alert. Who takes a bath at six thirty on a Thursday evening? A shower, maybe, but a bath?

'Can I talk to her?' he says.

'She's in the bath,' repeats Jay, sounding slightly less genial.

'All the same,' says Nelson, 'I'd like a word.'

Jay looks as if he's about to refuse. For a moment he and Nelson stare at each other then Jay turns and shouts up the stairs, 'Leah! Your boss is here.'

After a few seconds, Leah appears, fully dressed, at the top of the stairs.

'Hallo,' she says. Her voice sounds odd, as if she's trying to warn him about something.

'Hallo, Leah,' says Nelson. 'Can we have a word in private?'

'Now look here,' says Jay, 'this is my house. And we're under lockdown. I can't allow it.'

'Let me in,' says Nelson, 'or I'll arrest you.'

Tanya doesn't talk much on the drive to Norwich. She drives fast and well, arms braced at the wheel. Judy drives like that too. Maybe it's how they are taught on police training courses. Tanya is wearing a red mask with blue and white stars on it. The effect is incongruously cheerful. Ruth has forgotten to bring a mask and surreptitiously opens her window slightly, trying not to breathe in Tanya's direction. She checks her phone repeatedly. No messages from Janet or Nelson. The A47 is dark and empty but, when they drive through Dereham, the streetlights illuminate people standing by the side of the road and framed in open doorways. It seems almost sinister, as if they are waiting for a signal. Then a siren sounds. Ruth opens her window completely and hears a ripple of applause punctuated by the clatter of pots and pans.

'Clapping for carers,' says Tanya, without taking her eyes off the road.

38

Nelson takes a step forward. Jay takes one back. Leah is now halfway down the stairs.

'Want to step outside, love?' says Nelson. 'So that we can talk.'

'You can't talk to my wife behind my back,' says Jay.

Leah flashes her husband a look and, in that second, Nelson sees it all: the fear, the days off work, the polo necks.

'Pack a bag,' he says to Leah. 'And I'll take you somewhere safe.'

'Now look here . . .' Jay grabs Nelson's arm. Nelson spins round and knocks him out with one punch. Leah screams.

'Hurry up and pack that bag,' says Nelson, breathing slightly heavily.

'Is he dead?' says Leah.

'No such luck,' says Nelson, although the man does not seem to be moving much.

By the time Leah descends the stairs carrying a small suitcase, Jay is making groaning sounds. Nelson takes the case and ushers Leah out of the door. She almost runs to the car. Nelson resists the temptation to deliver a farewell kick to Jay's ribs. As he shuts the door, the next-door neighbour opens his, like a cuckoo clock.

'Everything OK, Leah?' says the man.

'Yes,' says Leah.

'You should have asked that a bit earlier,' says Nelson. 'Weeks earlier. Months earlier.'

'I beg your pardon?' says the neighbour.

'I forgive you,' says Nelson, wondering if he can forgive himself. He clicks open the car and puts the suitcase into the boot. Leah gets into the passenger seat. Nelson sits beside her and keys the postcode of the women's refuge into the satnav. The neighbour is still watching from his front porch.

Tombland is silent. All the clapping has stopped. Tanya parks in front of the cathedral, which looms above them, a huge expanse of darkness. As Ruth looks up, a bird – or perhaps a bat – circles the tower. Another night bird calls. The Close is deserted, just a few lights shining in the houses around the green, but somehow it seems expectant, a darkened stage waiting for the curtain to rise. Ruth's unease is starting to feel very much like fear. Also, where the hell is Nelson?

'Right,' says Tanya briskly. 'Where's this haunted house then?'

Ruth leads the way through the gateway. A fox saunters across the road, lord of all it surveys. Most of the shops are boarded up but there's a light on the upper floor of Augustine Steward's House.

'Someone's in,' says Tanya.

But who? thinks Ruth. The information centre is in darkness, but Ruth remembers that there's a bell for Janet's flat. For a moment she has a vision of the Grey Lady herself gliding down to answer their summons. But, when the door opens, Janet is framed in the lopsided beams.

'Ruth! What are you doing here?'

'I had a text from you,' says Ruth, feeling suddenly foolish. 'It sounded like you were in danger.'

'A text?' says Janet. 'I haven't got my phone. I must have left it somewhere.'

'Looks like someone's found it,' says Tanya. She shows Ruth's phone to Janet.

'"Help me",' reads Janet aloud. 'What *is* this?'

'I don't know,' says Ruth. 'But it sounded serious. I thought it was you.'

'Is there anyone who has access to your phone?' asks Tanya.

'No,' says Janet. 'I'm completely on my own.'

Ruth shivers. She is grateful for Tanya's slightly bored efficiency.

'Well,' she says, 'while we're here, we might as well have a look around.'

Nelson waits until Leah is booked into the refuge and then he checks his phone. Ten missed calls from Ruth and several text messages. The last one says, 'Where are you??' It's very unlike Ruth to use two question marks. He calls her but the phone goes straight to voicemail. Then he sees that he has a voice message from Tanya. Nelson listens impatiently for a few minutes, sitting in his car outside the anonymous house on the outskirts of Norwich. Then he starts up the engine.

Janet brings a torch and a stout stick.

'What's that for?' says Tanya.

'Just in case,' says Janet.

'Just in case you're charged with grievous bodily harm,' says Tanya. But Janet still brings the stick.

They walk through the dark alleyway where the houses close overhead. Then they are in the space of grass. Ruth can smell the lilac. She remembers Janet showing her the hidden doorway while Kate picked flowers. She looks at the wall where the bricks form a rectangular shape and, just for the moment, she thinks she hears something. A scuffle followed by a faint whining sound. Has an animal got trapped in there?

'Look!' Tanya points.

In one of the higher windows Ruth sees a flickering, uncertain light. It's not electric but something older and more elemental.

She's often seen in the alley, walking through walls, opening doors that aren't there. Sometimes you just see the light of her candle reflected in the windowpanes.

Judy is with her family, watching *The Return of the King*, the last of the *The Lord of the Rings* films. She read the books years ago and has rather lost track of the plot. There are more battles than she remembers, lots of aerial shots of horses galloping towards each other and orcs having their heads chopped off. But this is a rather sweet scene between one of the many bearded men and – unusually for Tolkien – a woman. They are waiting for news and waiting is now all that Judy does. She savours the moment of calm, Michael leaning against her and Miranda with her head on Maddie's lap. Both younger children seem to want constant physical reassurance. Thing too, who is staring unnervingly at Judy. Does he know something? Cathbad always says that he has a psychic bond with the dog.

Judy remembers Clough saying, that morning on the beach: 'He'll pull through.' For those few minutes, Clough's certainty had carried her, the way the waves sometimes do when she's bodyboarding with the kids. But as soon as he roared away in his smart Land Rover Discovery, the doubts and fears came flooding back. Everyone says that Cathbad is tough, immortal, etc, etc. But what if he isn't?

Judy checks her phone. Abbas has her number and has said that he will call if there's any change. Deep down Judy knows that change can only be for the worse. Instead there's a text message from Tina Prentice's daughter, Denise, thanking Judy for her condolence card. Judy thinks of the family preparing for the funeral. She is sure that Tina had many friends but none of them will be able to pay their last respects. She will be shown to her grave by her daughters and their husbands, even her grandchildren won't be able to attend.

A winged creature appears on the screen, to general dismay amongst the goodies, and – clear as day – Judy hears Tina's voice, as she busied herself making lunch for children and dogs.

I went round to Avril's at eleven as usual. I remember it was a lovely day and there was a heron by Avril's pool. I took a picture of it.

Judy texts Denise. *Know this sounds odd but is there a heron pic on your mum's phone? If so, cd you possibly forward? ty*

As she presses 'send' another message flashes up.

It's from Abbas.

39

'Looks like someone's at home,' says Tanya. 'Is that where you're staying, Janet?'

'No,' says Janet, still clasping her stout stick. 'It's the house behind. I've got a key to it though. I've got keys to all the houses in the alley.'

'Let's get it then,' says Tanya.

Janet leads them back to Steward's House and into the shop on the ground floor. There, amongst leaflets extolling the wonders of Norfolk, she opens a safe and takes out a key. Ruth and Tanya wait by the door. Tanya still looks calm, almost bored, but Ruth notices her checking her phone. Is she wondering why she hasn't heard from Nelson?

Armed with the key (and the stick) they make their way back through the alley and round to the road on the other side. There are more Tudor houses here, bulging out into the street. Janet goes up to a small oak door.

'This is the one, I think. Yes.' The door creaks open, with full Hammer House of Horror sound effects.

'Shall we go in?' says Tanya, as if offering a great treat.

Ruth almost asks to stay behind but the thought of being left alone in the silent street is almost worse than climbing the stairs and facing whatever entity will be revealed by the flickering candlelight.

Tanya goes first, holding out her phone, its torch app illuminating low ceilings and heavy beams. Janet follows. Ruth wishes she wasn't at the back.

It's almost nine o'clock when Nelson reaches the centre of Norwich. Tanya said that she was parked by the cathedral, so he drives through the gateway and stops in front of the huge wooden doors. He's never given much thought to the church before and has never been inside. 'Protestant,' his mother would say, before adding, 'but it was ours once.' In the dark it seems rather ominous, such a solid edifice of wood and stone. A fitful moon spotlights battlements and leering gargoyles. Nelson gets out of his car. Where is Tanya and, more importantly, where is Ruth? 'Steward's House,' Tanya said in her message. Nelson remembers Eileen's post-card. *Augustine Steward's House, Tombland, is haunted by the Grey Lady. This tormented ghost from the sixteenth century hides a terrible secret.* Where the hell is this cheery place?

He walks back through the gateway and surveys the street opposite. The lopsided house with its parallelogram of beams is unmissable. It's leaning in towards its neighbour, squashing the windows inwards. The place is clearly unsafe. Surely it should have been knocked down years ago?

Nelson crosses the road and sees that the ground floor is a shop, one of those tourist centres. 'Norfolk,' declares a poster, 'Nelson's county.' Nelson smiles thinly and knocks on the window, wondering if he'll set off an alarm. But there's nothing but an echo, amplified by the silence. Then he sees a door with bells for several flats. He rings them all. No answer. Nelson walks around the corner, through a small alleyway. It's even darker here and there's a soapy scent, both familiar and rather unpleasant.

When he's felled to the ground his last coherent thought is that the building has collapsed on him.

'Can you call me?' That was Abbas's message. Judy goes into the hall to do so. From the sitting room, the battle music is rising to a thrilling climax.

'I think we might be reaching a crisis point,' says Abbas.

'What does that mean?' asks Judy, amazed that she is still able to speak. She feels oddly calm, as if her mind has left her body and is floating somewhere above her, amongst the cobwebs that Cathbad won't remove because he respects spiders too much.

'Cathbad's immune system's in overdrive which means his body is starting to attack the healthy tissue.'

'What can you do about that?'

'We're doing what we can but his temperature's very high and we're concerned about his heart rhythm.'

'Can I see him?' says Judy.

'I'm afraid not. I'm so sorry.'

'What can I do then?'

'Pray,' says Abbas.

*

'Who's there?' shouts Tanya. Ruth has to admire her nerve. They are on a small landing, facing several closed doors. Light clearly shows under one of them.

'Hallo?' comes a quavering voice. To Ruth's surprise, she thinks she recognises it.

The door opens and a thin figure in a grey hood stands in front of them, holding a candle.

'Mother of God,' says Janet, reverting to her Catholic upbringing.

'Eileen?' says Ruth.

Eileen Gribbon, who is wearing a grey UNN sweatshirt, says, 'Dr Galloway? What are you doing here?'

'I might ask you the same thing,' says Ruth, rather breathless from the stairs and the fright.

'We're living here,' says Eileen. 'Me and Joe. Joe was looking round Tombland one day and he saw all these empty houses. We broke in. We're not doing any harm,' she adds, obviously seeing Ruth as an authority figure. 'It's just that we didn't have anywhere to go, and I couldn't stand halls any more.'

'You should have told me,' says Janet. 'I would have let you in. There's no one else here.'

'I think there is,' says Eileen. 'I can hear someone crying at night.'

Ruth's blood runs cold, especially when Janet answers calmly, 'That's just the Grey Lady. I've heard it too.'

'Eileen,' says Ruth, 'where's Joe?'

'I'm not sure,' says Eileen. 'He went out about an hour ago, just for some fresh air. I wish he'd come back.'

And, echoing through the walls, comes the terrible sound of sobbing.

Nelson is, once again, floating on a dark sea. The waves are breaking, white against black and, somewhere far off, he can hear music playing. It sounds like the slot machines on Blackpool pier. Then he's on the beach, miles and miles of sand interspersed with strange shapes that look both ancient and threatening. There's someone waiting for him at the water's edge and, for a second, he thinks it's Tim. Then there's a swirl of cloak and he knows.

'Hallo, Cathbad,' says Nelson.

40

'That was no ghost,' says Tanya.

Once again, Ruth is grateful for Tanya's presence though she could have done with some of Judy's sympathy and Nelson's comforting bulk. Where *is* he?

'That's the sound I heard,' says Eileen, sounding very young and very scared.

'Where's it coming from?' says Ruth, retreating a few steps down the stairs just to be on the safe side.

'From down below, I think,' says Janet. 'Maybe the cellars? The undercroft?' How can she be so calm when it's her own – temporary – house that she's talking about?

'I thought I heard something earlier,' says Ruth. 'When we were passing the bricked-up doorway. It sounded like an animal.'

'Let's go back that way,' says Tanya. 'It must be in the right general direction.'

They must make a strange procession, thinks Ruth, as Tanya leads them back into the enclosed garden. Tanya with her phone held out in front of her, Janet with her stick, Eileen shivering in her hooded sweatshirt, Ruth in her TV-watching attire of jumper and loose trousers. It's much colder now and she wishes she'd brought her anorak.

'Where's this doorway?' Tanya points her phone torch at the wall.

'Here.' Ruth turns on her own torch app. 'Where the bricks are different.'

As they go nearer, they hear the sound again, louder this time and definitely human.

'Police!' shouts Tanya. 'Who's there?'

Her words echo around the stone square. *There, there, there . . .*

And a faint voice answers them.

'Help.'

'What are you doing here?' says Nelson. The waves crash against the shore but the fairground music is still playing.

'I might ask you the same thing,' says Cathbad in his usual maddening manner.

'This is my dream,' says Nelson, rather annoyed.

'I think you'll find it's mine,' says Cathbad. He hums gently as he gazes out towards the horizon.

'What the hell am I doing in your dream?' says Nelson.

'I think you've come to save me,' says Cathbad.

Tanya kneels on the uneven ground by the wall.

'Who's there?' she calls.

'Me,' comes a voice. Just as she did earlier, Ruth thinks that it sounds somehow familiar.

'Are you locked in?' says Janet.

'Yes.' There's something unintelligible then, 'Underground . . . he locked me in.'

'We'll get help,' says Tanya. She stands up and speaks into her phone, calling for back-up using impressive-sounding code words.

'Hallo?' Ruth presses her face to the wall. 'It's Ruth.'

There's no answer.

'Ruth,' says Tanya. 'You go around to the house and wait for back-up. Nelson might already be there. Tell them where to find us. Janet and I will wait here. See if we can find a way in.'

'Here's the key to the shop,' says Janet. 'Are you sure you don't mind?'

'Not at all,' says Ruth. Frankly, Tanya had her at 'Nelson'. Ruth sprints back through the alleyway. Eileen starts to follow but Tanya calls her back, presumably wanting to question the girl further.

Ruth lets herself into the shop and switches on all the lights. She's had enough of the darkness. She prowls around, sending carousels of fridge magnets spinning. She knocks over a pile of calendars showing the Beauties of Norfolk. She imagines Nelson striding in, shouting 'Jesus wept' at the scenic images of his adopted county. When she hears footsteps, she almost shouts out, but she stays silent, hidden behind a life-size replica of Seahenge.

Between the papier-mâché timbers she sees the door opening and an elderly man entering the shop, blinking in the glare of the lights.

*

Tanya leaves Janet and Eileen trying to find a way into the hidden room and walks towards the alleyway. She'll speak to the back-up officers herself. If Nelson isn't already there. Where is the boss? He left the office at five thirty. Normally, they'd all assume he was with Ruth but Ruth is here, in Tombland. And Joe McMahon is missing too which is why Tanya wants Eileen to stay close, where she can see her.

Tanya jumps when her phone buzzes. 'Judy' says the screen.

'Judy! How's Cathbad?'

'He's dying,' says Judy in an odd, tight voice. 'But that's not why I'm ringing. I think I know who killed Avril Flowers. I'm sending you a picture of him.'

Tanya looks expectantly at her phone. She's still walking, which is why she almost falls over Nelson's body.

Why is this old-age pensioner here? thinks Ruth. Has he got confused and wandered in to do some late-night shopping? But it's lockdown. Surely, he should be shielding at home. He looks extremely feeble. And he seems to be wearing his slippers. Maybe she should go and help him. But something – maybe the ghost of Erik hidden within the ersatz Seahenge – makes her stay hidden.

The man goes to the safe Janet used earlier and extracts a key. As Ruth watches he walks towards a door at the back of the shop, almost hidden by packing cases. Edging around the fake timber posts, Ruth follows.

*

'Nelson!' Tanya kneels beside him. 'Boss!'

Nelson mutters something. It sounds a bit like 'Cathbad'. At least he isn't dead, thinks Tanya. She picks up her phone to call for an ambulance. 'Tombland Alley,' she says, thinking how ridiculous the address is. Nelson is showing signs of life now. Tanya touches his shoulder.

'Boss. It's me. Tanya. I've called for help.'

'Cathbad,' says Nelson again. 'Where is he?'

And Tanya remembers what Judy said on the phone. 'Cathbad's dying.'

The old man descends some stairs. He doesn't put on a light. Maybe he can see in the dark, like a cat. He's certainly as silent as a cat. Ruth follows, trying to tread quietly in her trainers. The man stops and so does Ruth. 'Don't look round,' she prays. He doesn't. Maybe he's deaf, even though he seems to have X-ray vision. She hears another key turn in a lock and the man says, in a pleasant, slightly quavery voice.

'Well, Zoe? Have you decided?' Is it time to kill yourself?'

41

Ruth thinks it's time to act. Surely, she will be a match for this ancient jailer?

Ruth turns on her phone torch. 'Zoe?'

'Ruth!' comes the reply. The man turns, holding up his hand against the light.

'Zoe,' Ruth steps forward into the doorway, 'are you OK?'

Zoe is in a windowless room. Ruth can just make out a camp bed and a bucket. It reminds her so much of another underground room, discovered fourteen years ago, that her head swims and she thinks she's going to faint. The man takes full advantage of this. With a surprisingly swift movement he grabs Ruth's phone from her hand and backs out of the room, slamming the steel door behind him.

Ruth is left alone with her sister.

Nelson struggles to sit up. 'Cathbad,' he says again.

'Take it easy, boss,' says Tanya. 'I've called an ambulance.'

'I don't need an ambulance,' says Nelson. He supports

himself on his elbow, breathing hard. 'What's happening?' he says.

Tanya is not quite sure where to start. 'Ruth got a message,' she says. 'She thought it was from Janet Meadows, who lives here. We came to investigate, and we discovered two students living in one of the empty houses. Then we heard someone sobbing. It seems like there's someone stuck in an underground room. I've called for back-up. Ruth's waiting for them now.'

'Ruth . . .' Nelson rubs his eyes. 'Where is she?'

'She went back to Steward's house.' This is Janet, appearing out of the shadows with the student – Eileen – at her side. 'What happened to you, DCI Nelson?'

'I think I was hit on the head,' says Nelson. He manages to get to his feet although he looks very pale and sways slightly.

'You should stay here,' says Tanya. She doesn't want him collapsing on her.

'I saw Cathbad,' says Nelson. 'He was on a beach.'

'You're delirious,' says Tanya. Just her luck to be stuck in the middle of Tombland with a bunch of crazies.

'No,' says Nelson. 'It was a dream. It was his dream.'

'You're not making much sense, boss.' But thinking of Cathbad makes Tanya remember why Judy called in the first place. *I think I know who killed Avril Flowers.* She was sending a photograph. Tanya clicks on the link, squinting to see in the dim light. She can hear Janet telling Nelson to rest and Eileen babbling about the Grey Lady. What wouldn't she give to have someone sane with her? Judy or Clough. Even Tony.

The picture shows a white bird by a pond and a man in the distance, slightly blurred as if he is walking fast.

Ruth bangs on the door. 'Help!'

'It's no good,' says Zoe. 'I keep calling and nobody comes.'

She's still in her nurse's scrubs and has a sleeping bag round her shoulders. Her hair is loose and matted. Ruth hardly recognises her stylish neighbour.

'There are people here,' says Ruth. 'We heard you crying.'

'He left a phone here earlier,' says Zoe. 'Just for a second. It was on the floor. When his back was turned, I managed to send a message. I hoped it was to you. Did you get it?'

'Yes, I did,' says Ruth. 'And I brought the police.'

'DCI Nelson?'

'I hope he's here somewhere but I'm with an officer called Tanya. She's very sharp. She'll find us.' Ruth says this with confidence but a few minutes in the underground room have already had their effect. She's beginning to feel that they will be there for ever, starving to death in the darkness, ending up as ghosts like the Grey Lady.

'I thought I heard someone saying "police",' says Zoe. 'But I thought I might be imagining it.'

'What happened?' says Ruth. 'How did you end up here?'

'I got a call from a patient,' says Zoe. 'He said that he was taken ill while working at the information centre. He's an old man so I was worried. I should have thought that all the tourist places are closed because of lockdown. Anyway, I drove here on my way home. He tricked me. He said he felt faint, so I got him to sit down. Then he said he'd left his inhaler in the cellar. I went into this room and he locked me in. That was Tuesday night, I think. What day is it today?'

Ruth has to think. 'Thursday.' It seems years since they heard people clapping for the carers. 'They're clapping you,' she'd said to Zoe that first time.

'It seems longer,' says Zoe. 'I think he might have drugged me. He's been coming to see me, every day, bringing me food and telling me to kill myself. It's really creepy.'

Ruth is shivering and not just from the cold. 'What's the man's name?'

'Hugh Baxter. He always seemed a nice old thing.'

'Yeah, he sounds a real sweetie,' says Ruth.

Zoe laughs but then the laugh goes on too long and she starts to sob. Ruth puts her arm round her. 'It's OK,' she says, hoping that it is. Where is Tanya? Where is Nelson? Ruth peers at the metal door. Never has anything looked more closed. What if the man – Hugh – comes back? Ruth looks around for a weapon. Could she throw the noxious-smelling bucket at him?

'Shall we . . .' she begins, not knowing what to suggest. Shall we hide? Shall we get ready for hand-to-hand combat? But, before she can finish the sentence, the steel door opens and a bearded man stands in front of them.

Nelson still looks slightly unsteady on his feet but he dismisses Tanya's suggestion that he sit on the grass and wait for the ambulance. 'I'm coming with you,' he says, in the tone that means he's not listening to reason. So Tanya leads the way back to Steward's house followed by Nelson, Janet and the weird student girl. Tanya wishes that she could shake them all off. The road is deserted apart from an elderly man walking towards the gateway to the cathedral. The shop lights are on and the door is open.

'Ruth!' shouts Nelson, barging in front.

'Be careful, DCI Nelson,' says Janet. 'DS Fuller, do tell him to be careful.'

But Tanya is off, sprinting after the old man.

'Joe?' says Ruth.

'Dr Galloway,' says Joe. 'I've come to save you.'

'Thank you,' says Ruth. All the same, she thinks she will only feel safe once she and Zoe are out of the underground room. Joe seems friendly enough, but she can't forget that he had a noticeboard full of pictures of her. *Stone walls do not a prison make.* She grabs Zoe's hand and tries to edge towards the door.

'I saw him,' says Joe. 'The man who locked you in. I hit him over the head with my torch. Burly, dark man.'

'That wasn't ...' begins Ruth. Zoe had described her captor as an old man. A burly, dark man can only mean one person. Is that why Nelson hasn't arrived? Because Joe has knocked him out, maybe even injuring him badly?

'How did you get the key?' says Zoe.

'It was in the safe,' says Joe. 'I wasted a bit of time trying to get in by the cellars. I knew this room was here. I saw it on the old plan of the house.'

'Very interesting,' says Ruth, in her lecturer voice. 'Now, if you'd just let us past ...'

But, before they can go further, there are thunderous footsteps on the stairs and Nelson bursts in. He's at Ruth's side in seconds.

'Are you OK?'

'Yes. Fine. Zoe's here. She was locked in by a man called Hugh Baxter . . .'

'Hugh?' says Janet from the doorway. 'But he's one of the volunteers. A nice old thing.'

'I saved you, Dr Galloway,' says Joe, sounding rather plaintive. 'I saved you from *him*.' He points at Nelson.

'Did you?' growls Nelson. 'Well, you're under arrest for assaulting a police officer for a start. Come on, Ruth, let's get out of here.' He steers Ruth towards the door. Eileen is standing there looking rather lost. Ruth hears her say, 'Where were you, Joe? I was scared.'

They emerge into the shop where the flashing lights of the emergency vehicles are reflecting on the glories of Norfolk.

And, in a King's Lynn hospital, Cathbad opens his eyes and says, 'Nelson?'

42

After that, it's all rather chaotic. Tanya appears, leading Hugh by the arm. He keeps asking what's going on, in a plaintive voice, but Tanya tells Nelson not to be fooled. 'Judy's got evidence of him at Avril Flowers' house on the day she died.'

It's quite a shock to see the paramedics wearing masks. For the last few hours, Ruth has managed to forget the pandemic altogether. They want Nelson to go in the ambulance with them, but he refuses. 'The hospital's full of Covid patients. They don't need more work.' In the end, he agrees to go with Zoe and promises to drive her home afterwards. Zoe's car is presumably parked around here somewhere. One of the uniformed police officers takes Nelson's Mercedes. Hugh is in the back of the police van. Despite his threat, Nelson doesn't seem to have charged Joe McMahon with anything and Ruth hears Janet offering him and Eileen a bed for the night. Ruth and Tanya walk back to the cathedral close.

'How did you know about Hugh?' Ruth asks Tanya.

'Judy sent me a photo of him. I don't know how she got it. It was a bit blurred, but I recognised the white hair.' Tanya is silent for a few minutes as she starts the car and performs a sharp three-point turn to exit through the gateway. Then she says, 'Ruth . . . Judy said Cathbad was dying.'

'What?' Ruth realises with horror that she has forgotten Cathbad too in the excitement of rescuing Zoe. 'Why didn't you say?' she whispers.

'I suppose I put it to the back of my mind,' says Tanya, sounding rather defensive. 'I had a job to do, remember.'

'I'll text Judy,' says Ruth, although she'd rather throw her phone out of the window. Tanya had recovered it from Hugh Baxter and Ruth has already texted Kate to say she's on her way.

But, when she activates the screen, there's already a message there.

Good news! Cathbad has come round. Docs say a miracle.

Ruth relays this, tears running down her face. Tanya, too, is wiping her eyes as they take the road for King's Lynn.

It's ten thirty by the time they reach the police station. Kate is asleep on a sofa in the custody suite, Tony is watching *Brooklyn 99* on his phone.

'She's only just gone to sleep,' he tells Ruth. 'She's seriously good at battleships.'

'Thank you so much for looking after her,' says Ruth.

She'll have to buy Tony a present tomorrow. She wakes Kate who opens her eyes and says, 'I'm leading thirty games to twenty-five.'

Ruth hugs her. 'Have you thanked Tony for looking after you?'

'He didn't mind,' says Kate. 'He loves playing battleships.'

But she does thank Tony who says it was a pleasure. Ruth knows that he and Tanya are keen to get on with their work. Hugh Baxter is being booked in at the front desk but Ruth doesn't know if they'll question him now or tomorrow morning. She and Kate exit through the back door and are soon on their way home. Kate is suddenly wide awake and Ruth winds down the windows to keep them both that way. She puts on her favourite Bruce Springsteen CD and they race through the dark Norfolk roads telling each other that they were born to run.

Flint is waiting by the front door, looking outraged. Ruth feeds him and tells Kate to get into bed. When she goes up to kiss her goodnight, Kate is already asleep, clutching a cuddly chimpanzee, an old birthday present from Nelson. Somehow, the sight of it makes Ruth want to cry again. She has told Kate the good news about Cathbad, but her daughter was not surprised. 'It's all the praying I've been doing,' she said. Ruth now mutters one of Cathbad's own mantras, 'Goddess bless, Goddess keep.' Then she goes downstairs to wait for Nelson.

Ruth is dreaming about underground prisons when headlights illuminate the room. She hears voices and then

Nelson is at the door. For a moment, they stare at each other and then Nelson wraps his arms round Ruth, as solid and comforting as ever.

'Zoe's next door,' he says, into her hair. 'I think she'd like a chat if you're not too tired. I'll be here with Katie.'

'Will you be here when I get back?' asks Ruth.

'Of course I will.'

It's midnight now but suddenly Ruth isn't tired at all. On impulse, she takes a bottle of wine with her and knocks on the stable door. Zoe answers immediately, Derek in her arms.

'Thank you for looking after him,' she says.

'That's OK.' Ruth pats the cat's silky head. He shuts his eyes, enduring her.

'Nelson says you know,' says Zoe, 'about us being sisters. Half sisters.'

'I guessed some of it,' says Ruth. 'I saw the photograph of my mum next to your wedding picture.' She supposes that she should say 'our mum', but that seems a step too far.

'Let's have a drink,' says Zoe. She leads the way into the unfamiliar, familiar sitting room. Slightly too late, Ruth remembers social distancing and sits on the chaise longue, which is as uncomfortable as she imagined, rather than joining Zoe on the sofa. Zoe pours them both a glass of red.

'I always knew I was adopted,' says Zoe. 'Mum and Dad must have told me when I was very young. We celebrated my adoption day as well as my birthday. But I didn't have any urge to look for my birth parents while they were alive. Then I got divorced and Mum and Dad died within months of each other. Then there was the court case. Do you know about that?'

'Yes,' says Ruth. 'It must have been awful.'

'It was a nightmare,' says Zoe. 'I knew I was innocent but, at times, I even thought I must be guilty because everyone else seemed so certain. That feeling didn't go away even when they found the real culprit. I changed my name and I thought: maybe it's time to find out who I really am.'

'Did you send off for your adoption records?' Ruth has been doing some research.

'Yes. And there it was. Mother: Jean Finch. It didn't take long for me to find her married name. I wrote to her.'

'When was this?' asks Ruth.

'Six years ago,' says Zoe. She takes a sip of wine and strokes Derek, who is stretched out beside her.

'Jean wrote back,' she says, after another pause. 'It was a kind letter, but she didn't want to see me. She said she hadn't told her husband or her children about me. But she did say she hoped we could meet in the future. But she sent me a photograph. And she told me my father's name.'

'What was it?' asks Ruth.

Zoe laughs. 'Derek. I named the cat after him, but I haven't tried to get in contact. I suppose I felt a bit bruised after Jean's response. Apparently, Derek was someone Jean worked with at the bank. She was in love with him but he was married.'

And, once again, Ruth hears her mother's voice. 'What do you mean you're pregnant? You're not even married.' If only you'd told me, Mum, she thinks.

'Jean didn't feel able to bring up a child as a single mother,' says Zoe. 'They were different times, that's what she said. I'll show you her letter. I did hope that we would meet but . . .'

'But she died the next year,' says Ruth. 'How did you find out?'

'There was something in her local paper,' says Zoe. 'I'd put a search link on the name Jean Galloway. It was a shock but then, I'm afraid, I turned my attention to you. I've always wanted a sister.'

'Me too,' says Ruth.

'It was quite difficult to stalk you,' says Zoe, with a slight smile. 'You don't have any social media presence, but I read your books and watched your TV programmes.'

'Oh God,' says Ruth.

'I thought you were wonderful,' says Zoe. 'I was in awe of you. Then this house came up for rent and I had a chance to be your neighbour. I grabbed it.'

'I'm glad you did,' says Ruth. 'Did you realise that your foster mother had lived next door? In my house?'

'No,' says Zoe. 'Did she really? I don't really remember her, but I was always told that she was very kind. Maybe that's why these houses always felt so homelike.'

'It was the same with me,' says Ruth. 'I wanted to live here as soon as I saw the cottages. Maybe I sensed that it had been a safe place. That's what Cathbad would say anyway.'

'Cathbad?' says Zoe. 'He's one of our patients. I'd heard he was in hospital. Is he OK?'

'I think he will be,' says Ruth, reluctant to talk about it for fear of jinxing the miracle. 'I found a picture of my cottage

when I was going through my mum's things. *Our* mum. On
the back it said, "Dawn 1963".'

'I was born in 1963,' says Zoe.

'I know,' says Ruth. 'You're five years older than me.'

'I've got a little sister,' says Zoe with a smile. 'It's been
wonderful getting to know you. I didn't count on being
locked down together though. Or being kidnapped by a
murderous pensioner.'

'To be fair,' says Ruth, 'those were hard things to predict.'

'I'll get you the letter,' says Zoe. 'And then I'll make us
both a cup of tea.'

Ruth is sure that this is an excuse to leave her alone with
her mother's words and she's grateful.

Dear Dawn (I know you are Zoe now but wanted to call you
that name just once),

I can't pretend it wasn't a shock to hear from you. I've
always thought about you, though, and I'm glad that your
adoption was a happy one. I'm afraid I don't feel able to
meet with you just yet. I haven't told my husband and
children about you and I still don't feel ready to do so.
One day, I'm sure, our time will come.

You deserve to hear the story of your birth. I met
Derek at the bank where I worked. He was older than me
and seemed glamorous and sophisticated. We started an
affair (an awful word but what's the alternative?) but I
didn't know he was married. I only found out when I fell
pregnant with you. Derek refused to leave his wife and I
couldn't face life as a single mother. They were different

times then. My daughter is a wonderful single parent but I didn't have her courage. My parents were furious and I went into an 'unmarried mother's home' to have you. I was only allowed to see you once. You were a beautiful baby and it broke my heart to say goodbye to you. I named you Dawn after Sleeping Beauty. I was told that your foster parents were good people and I managed to find out where they lived. I even went to their cottage one day but wasn't brave enough to knock on the door. I took a photograph of the house – little knowing how important it was going to be to my family – and have often looked at it over the years.

Shortly after your birth, I met Arthur and married him. He was already a Christian but we were both Born Again fourteen years later. God has been such a comfort to me. I hope He is in your life. We have two children. Simon is married with two grown-up sons. Ruth is a very successful archaeologist (she has written books!!) and she has a lovely daughter, Kate. I do hope you can meet them all one day.

God bless you.

Your mother

Jean

Ruth finishes this letter in a haze of tears. *Our time will come. A wonderful single parent. It broke my heart to say goodbye to you. She has written books!!*

She thinks she loves her mother more for those two exclamation marks than for anything else.

43

The next morning, Tanya interviews Hugh Baxter in the largest custody suite. His solicitor, Shobna Harris, is present only via Zoom, which is the way they have to do things these days. But Tanya is taking no chances and there's an 'appropriate adult', a social worker called Belinda Carter, sitting two metres away from Hugh. Shobna is on screen wearing a neat white blouse and black jacket. Tanya wonders if she has her pyjamas on underneath. Tony is also in the room and everyone is masked except Hugh who says he is exempt for medical reasons. Nelson is watching through the two-way mirror.

'This is DS Tanya Fuller. With me is DC Tony Zhang. We're interviewing Hugh Everard Baxter under caution in the presence of his legal representative, via Zoom, and Belinda Carter, acting as an appropriate adult.'

Hugh Baxter blinks at her. He has mild blue eyes, but Tanya is not taken in by this or by his sparse comb-over. When she'd apprehended Baxter last night, he had flashed her a look that was pure evil.

'Do you understand that this is an interview under caution?' she says. 'You have the right to silence but it may
harm your defence if you do not mention something when
questioned that you later rely on in court. Anything you do
say may be given in evidence.'

Hugh looks towards the screen and Shobna nods. He says,
'I understand.'

'Do you know Zoe Hilton? She's a practice nurse at
Westway Surgery.'

'I do go to Westway. I have angina and high blood pressure.' Hugh gives Tanya a pathetic look, which she ignores.

'And do you know Zoe?' Tanya pushes a photograph
across the table.

'I think I recognise her.'

'On Tuesday, thirty-first of March, did you telephone Zoe
and ask her to meet you at Steward's House tourist information centre? I should remind you that we have your phone
records.'

'I can't remember,' says Hugh.

'And, when Zoe arrived at Steward's House, did you
imprison her against her will in the cellar?'

'No!' Hugh sounds shocked. 'I wouldn't do that.'

'We have CCTV footage that shows you entering Steward's
House on Wednesday the first and Thursday the second,'
says Tanya.

'CCTV?' Hugh sounds as if he's never heard of it.

'You're on camera,' says Tanya. The footage arrived that
morning. She thanks God for the cathedral's security system.
'We have photographs.'

'I don't remember,' says Hugh.

Tony leans forward, his voice full of sympathy. 'Would you like a glass of water?'

'Yes please,' says Hugh quaveringly. Tony pours a glass from the jug on the table.

'Mr Baxter,' he says, 'you were good friends with Avril Flowers, weren't you?'

Tanya sees that Hugh prefers this form of address. He says, almost proudly, 'Yes. We were very close.'

'Did you visit her house on the morning of Tuesday the twenty-fifth of February?'

'I don't remember,' says Hugh. 'So much has happened since then. This terrible Covid . . .'

'We've got a photograph,' says Tanya.

Hugh shoots her a look of dislike. 'So many photographs.'

'Did you visit her that day?' asks Tony.

'It's possible.'

'We've got a picture of you by the pond,' says Tony. 'There's a heron there. I remember that you like birds.'

'I do like birds,' Hugh admits.

'Did you go into the house?' says Tanya. 'Did you lock the door of Avril's bedroom?'

'Why would I do that?'

'You were Avril's boyfriend, were you?' says Tony.

'Hardly boyfriend at my age.' But Tanya thinks Hugh sounds flattered. 'We were companions.'

'Were you also Karen Head's boyfriend?'

'Karen . . .?'

'Karen was a teacher who killed herself in November 2019,' says Tanya. 'Did you know her?'

'I don't think so.'

'Her friend sent us a photograph of you together,' says Tony. 'Do you want to see it?'

Hugh doesn't answer but Tony puts the photograph, emailed by Sue Elver that morning, on the table anyway.

'What about Samantha Wilson?' says Tanya. 'Did you know her? Samantha's daughter Saffron identified you from a photograph we sent her.'

'That's him,' Saffron had said. 'Creepy old man. Always talking about his wife who committed suicide. Almost as if he was encouraging Mum to do the same.'

'I can't remember any of these people,' says Hugh. 'I'm tired. I need a break.'

'Interview suspended at eight thirty-five a.m.,' says Tanya.

'He remembers, all right,' says Nelson, when they gather in his office. Super Jo is there too, wearing a see-through visor that makes her look as if she's about to perform dental surgery.

'I'm sure he does,' says Tanya.

'He'll put in a plea of temporary insanity if we're not careful,' says Nelson, 'but the way that he kept Zoe locked up, bringing her food and drink – not to mention pills in case she wanted to top herself – shows planning and forethought.'

'What about the other women?' says Jo. 'He didn't lock them up, did he? It seems he just talked to them about suicide.'

'That's what Saffron Evans said,' says Tanya. 'Hugh went to Samantha's slimming club and they became friends. Saffron said he kept making disparaging comments about her weight and talking about ending it all.'

'Nice,' says Nelson. 'Hugh must have been the bearded man the neighbour saw going into the house. The one the son mentioned.'

'That's right,' says Tanya. 'It's funny how you don't notice a beard so much when it's white.'

'And he knew Karen Head too,' says Nelson. 'That was bright of you to see the connection, Tony.'

Tony looks modest. 'I remembered that she had a boyfriend with an unsuitable age difference. I thought it might be a younger man, perhaps Joe McMahon, but it turned out to be an older man. Hugh Baxter.'

'But none of this adds up to anything,' says Jo. 'He didn't imprison those women. He just talked to them.'

'If his fingerprints are on Avril Flowers' door, we'll have some evidence,' says Nelson. 'The picture Judy sent Tanya shows that Hugh was at her house that morning.'

'Why did he do it?' asks Jo, who always feels offended if criminals don't act in the way she expects. Nelson expects nothing so is rarely disappointed.

'I spoke to Madge Hudson earlier,' he says. He sees Tanya and Tony exchanging looks. They know that the forensic psychologist is not on Nelson's list of favourite people, though he'd admit it's not a long list. 'She said that it might be a form of Munchausen's by proxy or whatever it's called these days.'

'Fabricated or induced illness,' says Tanya.

'Hugh's wife committed suicide,' says Nelson, 'and he may have enjoyed the attention he got in the wake of that. He enjoyed comforting women who felt bad about themselves even though he was the one who'd made them feel that way.'

'It was quite a leap kidnapping Zoe Hilton,' says Jo.

'Criminals escalate,' says Nelson. 'We know that. It may just have been that he had the means to hand – the underground room – and saw a way to lure Zoe here.'

'It's amazing that the woman living there didn't hear anything,' says Jo.

'Tony and I spoke to Janet Meadows this morning,' says Tanya. 'She says she heard noises, but she thought it was a poltergeist.'

'Jesus wept,' says Nelson.

'I can't believe I'm talking to you,' says Judy.

The iPad seems too small for the joy it contains. Cathbad still has a tube coming out of his nose but his eyes are bright and his voice is the same, just a bit croakier.

'I can't believe it either. I'm a medical miracle, Abbas says.'

'Abbas has been brilliant.'

'He's an earth angel,' says Cathbad. 'His aura is pure light.'

'You're embarrassing me,' says an offscreen voice.

'When can you come home?'

'It'll be a while, they say. I still need oxygen and antiviral drugs.'

'We've been so worried,' says Judy. 'Everyone has. Ruth, Nelson, Tanya, all the team. Clough even came to see me, breaking all the rules, of course.'

'He's a good soul.'

'The boss has been fretting. You know how he hates it when he can't do anything.'

'Tell him he did do something,' says Cathbad. 'He was in my dream. He guided me back to life.'

The children are clamouring to talk so Judy relinquishes the device. Afterwards, she feels restless. The children are running wildly round the garden, using up their pent-up energy. Thing is barking his accompaniment. Maddie says she's going to bake a cake. There's only one thing Judy really wants to do.

'I'm going into the station,' she says.

'Is that allowed?' says Maddie, squinting at the recipe on her phone.

'I'll socially distance,' says Judy. 'I'll wear a mask.'

The desk sergeant greets her with a wave, but Judy isn't prepared for the reception she gets in the incident room. Tanya and Tony burst into applause. Nelson comes to the door of his office, grinning broadly, and even Super Jo emerges from her inner sanctum, wearing a visor and a rather sinister Joker mask.

'I wish I could give you a hug,' says Tony, over-sharing as usual.

'What news of Cathbad?' says Tanya. She doesn't look as if she is disappointed at the lack of physical contact, but Judy can tell that she is smiling broadly underneath her multicoloured mask.

'It's incredible,' says Judy. 'He's awake and talking. I was able to FaceTime him this morning. He asked after you all. He said you were in his dream, Nelson.'

Nelson says nothing but Tanya pipes up, 'You said the same thing, boss. When you came round after being knocked out.'

'You were knocked out?' says Jo. 'I didn't hear about this.'

'I tripped over something,' says Nelson. 'Bloody silly thing to do. I missed all the fun while Tanya rushed around solving the crime and arresting people.'

'It wasn't *quite* like that,' says Tanya but Judy can tell that her colleague concurs completely with this description of events and, for once, she doesn't feel irritated or envious. More important things were going on last night.

And, it seems, she has underestimated Tanya. 'It was Judy who cracked the case,' she says. 'She sent me the picture of Hugh Baxter in Avril's garden.'

'How did you get that, Judy?' asks Nelson, sitting on one of the desks, which is the cue for everyone else to sit down. Jo looks as if she is missing her yoga ball.

'Tina's daughter sent it to me,' says Judy. 'Tina was Avril's cleaner and she mentioned taking the picture of the heron on the day that she found Avril's body. Tina tried to contact me, saying that someone had been at Avril's house that day. But, before I could speak to Tina, she was taken ill with Covid and died later. Her daughter said that Tina had sent me a message. "Tell Judy it was you." Last night I realised she was saying, "It was Hugh." I wondered how she'd guessed and thought that the evidence must be in the picture.'

'Great work, Judy,' says Nelson. 'We've been finding out a bit more about friend Hugh, haven't we?'

'Yes,' says Tanya. 'It turns out he specialised in befriending women and then belittling them, putting thoughts of suicide into their heads. Saffron Wilson said that he was creepy, always going on about women's weight.'

Judy remembers the picture of Hugh and Avril on Cromer pier. 'She said that dress made her look fat.' She remembers too the dead wife who was 'as slim as anything'. She should have seen the warning signs, but she'd been taken in by the elderly man with his interest in local history and touching friendship with the dead woman. She says, 'I think Hugh locked Avril's door to make sure she didn't escape. If his fingerprints are on the handle, we'll have evidence.'

'That's true,' says Nelson. 'The rest is almost impossible to prove, sadly. If he hadn't kidnapped Zoe Hilton, we'd have nothing on him.'

'Is he in custody?' asks Judy.

'Yes,' says Tanya. 'We're holding him for twenty-four hours. We've done an interview under caution but haven't charged him yet.'

'We need to get this right,' says Nelson. 'I don't want Baxter claiming that he was just confused, playing the Alzheimer's card. He locked Zoe in that underground room at Steward's House and kept her there for two days. He brought her painkillers and tried to persuade her to take an overdose. She said she almost gave in.'

'That's horrible,' says Judy.

'Janet Meadows says that she heard noises but she put it down to ghosts,' says Nelson. 'Like you do.'

'It is a very haunted place,' says Judy. 'Cathbad says so.'

'I can't wait until Cathbad's better so I can tell him what I think of his lunatic ideas,' says Nelson.

'Weren't you in his dream?' says Judy slyly. 'You could have told him then.' She has the pleasure of seeing the boss colour up behind his mask.

'Joe McMahon heard voices too,' says Tony. 'He said he thought it was unquiet spirits.'

'Who's talking about spirits?' says a voice. 'Mine's a double brandy.'

And there in the doorway, wearing a Chelsea scarf over his nose and mouth instead of a mask, is Clough.

Ruth hardly notices Nelson leave. She sleeps until nine and is woken up by Kate and Flint, both demanding breakfast. It's another lovely day so she and Kate take their toast into the back garden. This is one of the only good things about lockdown, thinks Ruth – no six-thirty starts, waking in the darkness with the radio alarm flashing, no drive through the rush hour to deposit Kate at school or childminder. The sun is warm on her face and she has just had a text from Judy saying that Cathbad is sitting up in bed and talking. Flint is testing his claws on the apple tree and Kate practising crow pose. The real thing, Corbyn, is sitting on a fence post as if carved in wood.

'Tell Cathbad we're thinking of him,' Ruth tells the bird.

The crow watches her for a moment. His bright, dark eyes

reminding her of something. Of someone. Then he caws once, spreads his wings and rises into the air.

'Hi!' Zoe appears at the fence. She's in her smart pyjamas and her hair is skewered in an artless bun on the top of her head. She's been imprisoned underground with only bread and water for three days and she still looks better than Ruth. Only the dark shadows under her eyes betray her.

'You're back!' Kate rolls onto her feet and skips over. 'We looked after Derek. Where did you go?'

'It's a long story,' says Zoe.

'I like stories,' says Kate. 'I'm writing one about a time-travelling cat.'

'I'd love to read it,' says Zoe.

'Actually,' says Ruth. 'Zoe and I have got a story to tell you, Kate.'

'Heard you had some fun last night,' says Clough.

'You shouldn't be here,' says Jo, but mildly. She's always had a soft spot for Clough, thinks Nelson.

'Too boring for you in Cambridge?' says Nelson.

'Yeah,' says Clough, miming a high five with Judy. 'Nothing going on. McDonald's is shut. All the students have left and the criminals are all sitting at home watching box sets.'

'It's not *too* boring here,' says Tanya. 'I, we, have just caught a kidnapper. Possibly a murderer too.'

Nelson leaves Tanya recounting the events in Tombland and retreats to his office. He wants to check up on Leah and, though he wouldn't admit it to anyone, his head is aching badly. He tried to find some ibuprofen in Ruth's bathroom cupboard that morning, but it was full of tea tree shampoo and old bottles of Calpol. Ordinarily, he'd ask Leah and she'd tactfully bring him some coffee with a couple of aspirins on the saucer. But Leah is elsewhere. Nelson sends her a text, 'How r u?' and, seconds later, his phone rings.

'Hi, Leah. How are you doing?'

'OK. They're very kind here. Even so I can't quite relax. I keep thinking that Jay will burst in and drag me home.'

'Has that happened before?'

'Once. I left to go to my sister's. Jay came after me. He even persuaded my sister that I should come home with him. Said it was all in my head.'

'Bastard,' says Nelson. 'You should press charges against him. Coercive control.' He remembers Jo making him go on a course about it.

'He's more likely to press charges against you for hitting him.'

'Let him try.'

'I can never thank you enough,' says Leah. 'I really think you saved my life.'

'I wish I'd known earlier,' says Nelson.

'I wanted to tell you,' says Leah. 'But I was ashamed.'

'You've got nothing to be ashamed of,' says Nelson.

'I know,' says Leah, 'but I was, all the same.'

'Your job's waiting for you,' says Nelson. 'Whenever you want to come back.'

'I'll be back,' says Leah. 'You'll never be able to work out the new software that Jo's ordered.'

Judy appears in the doorway. Nelson beckons her in and says goodbye to Leah.

'Are you OK?' says Judy. 'You look a bit rough.'

'I'm fine,' says Nelson. 'I've just got a bit of a headache from last night.'

'Here.' Judy rifles through her handbag. 'Have some Nurofen.'

'Thanks. You're a lifesaver.'

'Was that Leah on the phone? Is she still off sick?'

As succinctly as possible, Nelson tells Judy about Leah and Jay.

'I should have guessed,' says Judy. 'I knew something was up. She was clearly afraid of going home. I should have known. I've done the training on spotting signs of domestic violence.'

'Don't beat yourself up,' says Nelson. 'I was the one who saw her most and I didn't realise until I saw her in the house with him.'

'She won't be the only one,' says Judy. 'Lockdown will mean lots of women locked away with abusive husbands.'

'That's what they said at the refuge,' says Nelson. 'We need to think of ways for women to ask for help. I've heard of giving coded messages to pizza delivery guys.'

'Steady on,' says Judy, 'or Jo will recommend you for a modern policing award.'

'I don't think so,' says Nelson. 'I knocked Leah's husband out last night. That's old-fashioned policing for you.'

'And what was all that about you being knocked out too?' says Judy. 'What happened?'

'Joe McMahon hit me over the head with a Maglite,' says Nelson. 'I'm not pressing charges though. He thought I was the one who'd kidnapped Zoe. Got it into his head that he was protecting Ruth. Mind you, I will be having a little chat with Mr McMahon later. He's a little too obsessed with Ruth for my liking.'

'How is Ruth?' says Judy. 'I hear she was involved last night.'

Nelson gives his DI a sharp look, but Judy's face shows only polite interest.

'She's OK,' he says. 'It's been an emotional time for her. Turns out Zoe's her half-sister.' He explains, as briefly as he can, about 'Dawn 1963'.

'It's funny,' says Judy, 'when I saw the picture of them together, I thought they looked slightly similar.'

'I can't see it myself,' says Nelson, 'but I think it will mean a lot to Ruth. And she was really happy about Cathbad. She's very fond of him.'

'Cathbad says you saved him,' says Judy.

'He's delirious,' says Nelson. He's not going to tell anyone, even Ruth, about the dark beach and the fairground music.

Despite the Nurofen, Nelson's headache gets worse. Cloughie seems to have re-joined the team and even sends out for pizza at lunchtime. This reminds Nelson of women ordering pizza in a coded cry for help against domestic violence. He googles it and finds that it's only an urban myth. There is, however, a scheme in bars and restaurants called 'Ask Angela' where, if women use the name Angela, it alerts staff to abuse or to a date that is going dangerously wrong. There ought to be more, thinks Nelson, picturing Leah's face when he'd appeared at her house last night. If she hadn't had the courage to text him, what would be happening to her now?

In the afternoon, Nelson drives back into Norwich. He parks outside the cathedral and crosses the road to Steward's House. It looks even less stable in the daylight, as if the whole edifice would topple over with one push. Nelson leans on the doorbell, trying his luck.

Janet Meadows opens the door. Nelson remembers her telling him that she'd heard crashing and banging in the night but had turned over and gone back to sleep. *I'm always hearing suspicious things. This is a haunted house, you know.* Presumably the noise had been Zoe Hilton being imprisoned in the room downstairs. If only Janet had called the police rather than assuming paranormal activity, it might have saved a lot of trouble. But Janet isn't charged with any crime. Tanya seems satisfied with her answers. And, if Janet hadn't left her phone lying around, to be picked up by Hugh Baxter, Zoe wouldn't have been able to call for help. Nelson gives Janet a curt nod. 'Afternoon. Is Joe McMahon still with you?'

'Yes. He and Eileen are staying until they find somewhere else. I've got plenty of room.'

'Can I have a word with Joe?'

'Yes. Do you want to come in?'

'I'd better not.' Nelson gestures to his mask thinking that Janet might be up to date on the plague but she seems to have forgotten the more recent health crisis. 'Could Joe join me out here?'

The young man looks rather scared when he sees Nelson on the doorstep. He doesn't look any less wary when Nelson suggests a walk in the cathedral grounds. They walk past the church and across a green bordered by hundreds of archways. Cloisters, he thinks they're called. There are private houses here too, smugly looking out across the smooth lawns. Who lives here? Bishops? Priests? Well, none of the residents are in evidence today. Nelson and Joe walk in silence until Nelson says, 'You know I could charge you for assault?'

'I didn't mean to hit you,' says Joe. 'I thought . . .'

'I know what you thought. You thought you were protecting Ruth. Dr Galloway.'

'I'd heard a woman crying. I knew she was locked in somewhere. I thought you'd locked her in.'

'Is that what you normally do? Hit first and ask questions later?'

'No. I'm morally opposed to violence.'

'I'm glad to hear it. Dr Galloway is one of your lecturers, isn't she?'

'Yes.' They are walking two metres apart, but Nelson catches the quick, sidelong glance. 'She's the best in her field.'

'Is that why your room is full of pictures of her?'

Joe is silent for a moment and then he says, 'It was the body.'

'What?' says Nelson. Is he going to have to hit Joe after all?

'The body we found in Tombland,' says Joe. 'The medieval

woman. Ruth said she had dark hair and blue eyes like my mum. That's why I wanted to call her Martha. After my mother.'

'Let me get this straight,' says Nelson. 'The body that was excavated in Tombland, that reminded you of your mother, so that's why you're obsessed with Ruth?'

'Sort of,' says Joe, looking down at his feet. He's wearing black DMs. 'Bovver boy shoes,' Nelson's mum would call them. 'But I already admired her.'

Nelson thinks the young man's feelings go way beyond admiration. 'Did you send Ruth those emails telling her to beware the Grey Lady?' he asks, trying to keep his tone neutral.

'I just wanted her to be careful,' says Joe. 'Tombland is a dark place. I knew she was friends with Janet, but I wanted her to stay away.'

'Yes,' says Nelson. 'Janet said she saw you sneaking around her house.'

'I wasn't sneaking,' says Joe. 'I was keeping watch. Like the Watchers in plague times.'

'Whatever you call it,' says Nelson, 'it has to stop. You can't keep prowling around, sending sinister messages to your lecturers. You have to change universities.'

'But I like it at UNN.'

'I don't care if you do,' says Nelson. 'I'll be checking up and, if I don't hear that you've switched courses, I might just remember that you hit me over the head with a large torch.'

'I'd never harm Ruth,' says Joe. 'I think she's wonderful.'

'We all do, son. We don't all cover our walls with pictures of her.'

Joe gives him another quizzical look but doesn't say anything more until they are back at Steward's House.

'Well, goodbye and good luck,' says Nelson. 'I hope our paths don't cross again. Can you send Eileen out to me?'

Eileen appears, looking slightly more cheerful than when Nelson last saw her. Their discussion is brief.

'Eileen,' says Nelson. 'Go home to your mum.'

As he walks back to his car Nelson suddenly feels very tired. His head is still pounding, and he feels slightly dizzy. He texts Judy to say that he won't be going back to the station and he drives straight home. He wants to sleep for about ten hours.

As he turns into the cul-de-sac, he realises that something is different. There's a new sound in the air, as there was when he first heard the clapping for carers. But this is louder and somehow more heart-warming. Barking. He opens the door and is hit by a solid wedge of fur and muscle.

'I got him back from Jan's,' says Laura, who is sitting on the stairs. 'I hope you don't mind.'

'Of course not.' Nelson squats next to the dog, patting him and pulling his ears.

'I'm going to be working from home next week,' says Laura, 'so I can take him for walks. He's so happy to be back.'

Bruno licks Nelson's face and goes in search of a present. He comes back with Michelle's bra, which is still hanging over the banister.

'He misses Mum too,' says Laura. 'Here, you stupid dog. Give that back.'

Nelson gets to his feet. 'I need a shower.'

'What happened to you last night?' says Laura.

'I texted,' says Nelson. 'I got caught up in a case. I slept in the station. On one of the sofas in the custody suite.' Tony had told him that Katie slept there last night. Katie made Tony a thank you card with one of her special pictures of Flint on the front. Nelson forgot to hand it over and it's still in his pocket.

'Did you catch the bad guys?' says Laura, going into the kitchen.

'I think so,' says Nelson.

'There's a postcard for you from Grandma,' says Laura. 'I think she's the only person on earth who still sends post-cards.'

The card shows an illuminated Blackpool tower and the message on the back reads: 'Having lots of fun (joke!). Wish you were here Mumxx'. Nelson feels strangely tearful. His mother misses him, that's the reason she took the card from her stash, stuck on a stamp and braved the walk to the post box. And, strangely enough, he misses her too.

After his shower, Nelson comes downstairs to find Laura heating something up in the microwave. She's in the garden with Bruno and he can hear the dog's excited barks. Thank God there's a can of beer in the fridge. Nelson drinks it while the plate revolves in the microwave. He thinks of Samantha Wilson and her Weight Watchers' meal. When did she decide to kill herself? Between the defrosting and the eating? Did Hugh Baxter really persuade her to take her own life? Sadly, that will be impossible to prove but they should be able to get him for Zoe's kidnapping. Even so, with a good lawyer and considering his age, Baxter might get away with a suspended sentence. How many people are there, thinks Nelson, who kill without using a lethal weapon? 'He just talked to them,' said Jo earlier. How many people whispering poisoned words in their victims' ears? How many men like Jay, outwardly respectable, yet fiends of cruelty in their own home?

This line of thought is making Nelson very depressed. He takes his beer into the sitting room and switches on the TV. But there's no sport because of lockdown and all the other programmes seem to be repeats. He's looking for an American cop show, something like *Colombo* or *Kojak*, when his phone buzzes. It's Michelle.

I'm coming home.

44

Monday, 20 April

Three weeks after he was rushed into hospital in an ambulance, Cathbad leaves in a wheelchair to a rapturous round of applause from the ICU staff. Cathbad is embarrassed about the wheelchair – he's perfectly able to walk – but is told that this is hospital policy. He's overwhelmed too that the doctors and nurses are actually cheering *him*. 'It's a success for us all,' Abbas told him, 'when someone who was so sick goes home again.' Cathbad thanks Abbas by the main doors, pressing his hands together in a namaste although he would love to be able to give the nurse a hug. Abbas bows back, eyes smiling behind his mask. Cathbad remembers looking into those same eyes during the many hours when he couldn't speak and was scared that his next breath would be his last. 'Keep going' – that was the message Abbas sent him silently. Cathbad also has a confused memory of Nelson saying, 'You're not dead yet, Cathbad.' Was this an actual memory of the night on the marshes or did Nelson visit Cathbad in a dream? He doesn't know but he hopes to find out one day.

A week earlier Boris Johnson also left hospital. He credited two nurses, Jenny from New Zealand and Luis from Portugal, with saving his life. 'They kept vigil,' he said, 'when things could have gone either way.' Hearing this, Cathbad experienced a rare feeling of kinship with the Prime Minister.

Judy drives him home. Cathbad thinks that the sky has never looked so high and blue. When he sees the sea, sparkling away like a tourist poster, he almost cries again. He's always prided himself on being in touch with his emotions but, in recovery, he's found himself laughing and weeping at the smallest things. Yesterday, Abbas told him a joke about David Beckham that almost killed him.

The tears flow again when they reach the house and Cathbad sees his neighbours lining the road: Steve and Richard, Jill and Barney, Vikram and Elsa, Donna, Sue and Dorothy. Across the porch is a banner saying, 'Welcome home, Dad'. Ruth and Kate are standing by the gate, waving madly, and Maddie, Michael and Miranda are in the doorway. As Cathbad approaches, wiping his eyes, they run towards him, but Thing is too fast for the humans. He flings himself on Cathbad, almost knocking him to the ground. Cathbad remembers the day he first met the dog, at his friend Pendragon's cottage on Pendle Hill, when the bull terrier's exuberant welcome had succeeded in flooring him.

'It's all right, Thing. I'm home now.'

Judy pulls Thing away and Cathbad is embracing his children, a scrum of love and relief and tears.

When they pause for breath, Cathbad turns to Ruth, who is still keeping her socially approved distance. She and Kate are both smiling and suddenly seem radiantly alike.

'It's wonderful that you're home,' says Ruth.

'I prayed for you,' says Kate.

'Thank you, Hecate,' says Cathbad. 'It helped. A lot.'

'Go into the house,' says Ruth, 'and carry on getting better.'

Cathbad raises his hand and it seems that even the seagulls, high above, are welcoming him home in raucous chorus.

Ruth and Kate drive home still elated by the hero's return. Kate talks excitedly about Cathbad. 'Do you think it's a miracle, Mum?' Ruth doesn't feel qualified to judge but she's glad Kate is happy when she's had so many disappointments recently. It's become clear over the last few weeks that the Year 6 trip is not going to happen. 'We hope to have the children in school for a week in June,' said Mrs Obuya, 'and we'll have some socially-distanced celebrations.' But it's not the same as a trip or a disco or a prom. Ruth finds Kate's stoic acceptance of this almost heartbreaking.

But Kate does have the excitement of a new aunt and, as they near the little cottages, they see Zoe in the garden. She has cleared the ground and has sown seeds with witchy names like salvia, scabious and zinnia. Sunflowers are growing in pots and Zoe is busy preparing hanging baskets for the summer. Derek and Flint are watching with interest from their respective doorsteps. They need no government directive to maintain social distancing.

Zoe has gone back to work, physically none the worse for her ordeal, but she's told Ruth that she's having night-mares about the underground room and Hugh Baxter's soft voice urging suicide. Ruth finds it both stressful and touching to be receiving confidences of this kind. Is this what it means to be a sister? Simon has never confided in her and most of her friends have families of their own. Now Ruth has gained another close family member. It's rather a responsibility.

Ruth told Simon of Zoe's existence via Zoom. It was another one of those occasions where the discussion would have been easier face to face. Ruth looked at her brother's baffled face on the screen and wished she had been able to give him a hug, or at least a hearty pat on the back. It's been a hard time for Simon. Covid turned out not to be a government conspiracy and he's locked down at home with his wife and adult sons. No wonder he looks greyer than when Ruth last saw him.

'Mum had a daughter,' he kept repeating. 'Before I was born.'

Ruth was glad when Cathy appeared beside Simon. 'These things happen,' she said briskly.

'You'll like Zoe,' Ruth assured Simon who, foregrounded against his record collection and abandoned teenage acoustic guitar, suddenly looked rather pathetic.

'Does Dad know?'

'No,' said Ruth. 'I think we should tell him later. When we can see him in person.'

She has no idea when that will be.

Zoe comes over to meet them, her hands dark with earth. 'How was Cathbad? Everyone at the surgery is so happy that he's out of hospital.'

'He looked a bit frail but he was obviously delighted to be home,' says Ruth. 'He's got nine lives, but I think this has used up one of them.'

'My time-travelling cat has got ninety-nine lives,' says Kate.

'Have you written any more?' asks Zoe. Ruth listens to Kate telling her aunt about Whittaker's latest adventures. It takes her mind off the fact that Nelson is, probably at this very moment, being reunited with his wife.

Nelson has taken the day off work but now he wishes he hadn't. The time seems to pass so slowly in the silent cul-de-sac. He can't stop thinking about Cathbad coming home from hospital, about Ruth and Katie, about the team back at the station.

Hugh Baxter has been charged with unlawful imprisonment but he's pleading memory loss and incipient dementia. Nelson has an awful feeling that he'll get away with it all. There's no evidence that Hugh persuaded Samantha, Avril and Karen to kill themselves. His fingerprints were on the handle of Avril's bedroom but Hugh is sharp enough to say that they got there on one of his many visits to the house. 'We were friends,' he tells Tanya,

'I loved Avril.' Nelson, watching on the video link, isn't convinced for a moment.

Hugh can't deny trapping Zoe in the room below the information centre but he is saying that he was confused and didn't know what he was doing. Against this is the fact that he visited Zoe several times, bringing food and pills and urging her to put an end to her life. He had obviously planned the whole thing, discovering the underground room when he was working as a volunteer in the shop. Kindly Hugh, with his interest in local history. Who would have thought that, not content with telling visitors the story of the Grey Lady, he seemed determined to re-enact it?

Zoe will be a good witness for the prosecution although Nelson knows that she's worried about the earlier case being resurrected. 'I don't think I can quite face being the angel of death again,' she said, with a brave attempt at a smile. Ruth will be a witness to the fact that she found Zoe in the cellar and was locked in by Hugh herself. Nelson doesn't know why Hugh went to such extreme lengths with Zoe. He obviously knew her through the surgery. Did he know about the Dawn Stainton case too? Is this why he targeted her? Nelson has wondered if Hugh was the elderly man in the waiting room when he visited the surgery to enquire after Zoe. At the time, he had seemed a harmless, anonymous presence. The mask had helped too.

Leah is back at work, helping Nelson through the latest interactive nightmare devised by Jo, something called Teams. Leah is still living at the refuge but hopes to get her own place soon. Nelson is trying to force through several initiatives about domestic violence. If Jo is surprised at this sudden interest in community policing, she doesn't say so. On the other hand, she hasn't stopped reminding Nelson that it could be time to retire. 'After the shooting last year and whatever happened at Tombland, you deserve a rest.' Jo clearly hasn't bought the story about Nelson tripping over and banging his head. 'I'm fine,' Nelson told her, 'never better.'

Joe McMahon is transferring to Birmingham. Nelson mentally sends the university his best wishes and hopes that Joe will not feel the need to keep in touch. Eileen has gone home. She sent Nelson a postcard thanking him for his help and saying that she hoped to be back in Norfolk next year. Eileen, like Nelson's mother, is clearly a fan of postcards. This one, rather tactlessly, showed an artist's impression of the Grey Lady, midway through a wall.

Laura is in the kitchen, preparing a welcome-home meal. Bruno is with Nelson, restlessly pacing the parquet floor, toenails clicking. Suddenly the dog's ears seem to become even more pointed. He barks and goes to the door. Nelson can't hear anything, but he knows that the dog has sensed something, a change in the space-time continuum perhaps. Minutes later, Michelle's car pulls into the drive. After a day of waiting, suddenly Nelson is not ready. Bruno whimpers excitedly but Nelson waits in the sitting room until the very last moment, until he hears Michelle's key in the lock and Georgie's shout of 'My Doggy!' Or maybe it's 'My Daddy'. Nelson's not sure. He comes into the hall and swings his son into the air. At least this bit is easy, he thinks. It's never been difficult to summon his love for his children.

Laura is hugging her mother. 'I'm so glad you're back. We've missed you so much.' Nelson meets Michelle's eyes. She looks tired from the drive, but he's struck, once again, by her beauty. Surely, she's more beautiful now, at fifty-one, than she was at twenty-one when he first saw her in the Blackpool rock shop. Laura envelops George in a hug. Bruno runs up and down the stairs in a frenzy of welcome.

'Hallo, love,' says Nelson.

'Hallo, Harry,' says Michelle.

Nelson kisses her cheek and they get through the next few minutes somehow, talking about the drive and the children, against a background of Bruno's barks and George's squeals of joy.

It's only later that Michelle says, 'Harry, we need to talk.'

EXTRACT FROM
WHITTAKER THE TIME-TRAVELLING CAT

The grass was so long that the girl didn't notice the cat at first. It was only when he spoke to her that she stopped and stared.

'Be careful where you're walking,' said the cat.

'I'm sorry,' said the girl. 'But I've never met a talking cat before.'

'Apology accepted,' said the cat, who was bright ginger with a long tail and very green eyes.

'I'm Whittaker,' said the cat.

'I'm Laura,' said the girl. 'Why don't you tell me how come you can talk?'

'I'm very busy,' said Whittaker, 'but I suppose I could spare you a few minutes. Have you got any tuna?'

'No,' said Laura, 'but I could get some.'

When Whittaker had eaten his tuna he told Laura that he was born in the Garden of Eden but decided that trees were boring and that he wanted to see the world. He lived in the Tower of Babel and that's where he learnt to speak every language on earth. Then he was one of the cats on Noah's Ark. Whittaker lived in a pyramid for a while and was worshipped by the Egyptians. But Whittaker didn't like being a god and stowed away on a ship to Rome. He became friends with the Emperor, a nice man who was very fond of his horse and went to Britain with him. The Romans had a fight with Boudicca who had red hair and a chariot. In Norfolk Whittaker made friends with a druid and he taught him cat language although the druid never became really good at it. Whittaker stayed in England because he liked rain and he lived in a henge which is lots of wooden sticks in a circle. When that got too cold he moved in with someone called Mother Julian who lived in a garden next to a church. She was very wise and said all shall be well. Whittaker was excellent at catching rats but there was still a plague. He helped rescue other cats during the Fire of London. He was Queen Victoria's favourite pet and he was the cat in Dick Whittington.

'You've done so many amazing things,' said Laura. 'What are you doing here?'

'This is my most difficult mission of all,' said Whittaker. 'Do you want to hear about it?'

Headlines from the *Cathbad Chronicles* on 20 April 2020:
Sunrise: 5.53 a.m.
Sunset: 8.07 p.m.
High tide: 12 a.m. (flood warning for Wells)
Education secretary Gavin Williamson said that he didn't know when schools would reopen.

The government has lost a boat full of equipment for hospitals.

Thing ate a cuttlefish on the beach.

Cathbad came home.

All shall be well and all shall be well and all manner of thing shall be well.

ACKNOWLEDGEMENTS

I thought long and hard about setting a book in lockdown but, having written a book a year about Ruth for the last thirteen years, it seemed wrong to miss out 2020. The events of that terrible year are taken from various sources but mostly from my own diary.

Tombland, Norwich Cathedral and Augustine Steward's House all exist although the characters that people them in this book are imaginary. The Queen Elizabeth Hospital in King's Lynn is also real and, although Abbas is invented, I'm sure that all its staff showed similar courage and compassion during the Covid-19 crisis. The story of Dawn Stainton is completely fictional as is Westway Surgery.

Congratulations to Eileen Gribbon for winning the CLIC-Sargent auction to have a character in this book named after her. All proceeds go to the charity, which supports teenagers with cancer, so huge thanks to Eileen and to anyone who took part. Eileen, I hope you like 'your' character, especially the dancing. Thanks to Jan Adams, a previous winner, who appears again. Thanks also to Mary Williams for her insights into university life in lockdown and to Francesca Lewington for her memories of home-schooling. My heart goes out to all those involved in education during this time. Thanks to Aoife Martin for her help and advice.

Thanks, as ever, to my wonderful publishers Quercus Books and especially to my matchless editor, Jane Wood. It's not easy to produce books in lockdown but I have felt supported all the way. Huge thanks to everyone at Quercus, especially Florence Hare, David Murphy, Hannah Robinson and Hannah Winter. Thanks to Jon Butler for always believing in me and in this series. Thanks also to my fantastic agent, Rebecca Carter, and to all at Janklow and Nesbit in the UK and the US. Thanks to all the publishers around the world who publish these books with such care. Thanks to Ghost Design for the amazing cover and to Liz Hatherell for her meticulous copy-editing.

The Locked Room is dedicated to the friends who helped me through lockdown, first with Zoom chats then with garden croquet, distanced walks and chips under the arches. This one is for you: Frauke Dingelstad, Julie Williams, Lesley Thomson, Melanie Lockett, Nancy Weibel, Robert and Stephany Griffith-Jones, Veronique Walker and William Shaw. Also remembering Sam Brittain and the Zoe Way.

Love and thanks always to my husband, Andrew, and our children, Alex and Juliet. And to Gus, of course.

Elly Griffiths
2022

WHO'S WHO
IN THE RUTH GALLOWAY MYSTERIES

Dr Ruth Galloway

Profession: forensic archaeologist

Likes: cats, Bruce Springsteen, bones, books

Dislikes: gyms, organised religion, shopping

Ruth Galloway was born in south London. Growing up she had a difficult relationship with her parents, who were Born Again Christians, but excelled at school and went on to study archaeology at University College London. As a postgraduate student at Southampton University, she met Professor Erik Anderssen who became her mentor and friend. In 1997 she participated in Professor Anderssen's dig on the north Norfolk coast which resulted in the excavation of a Bronze Age Henge. Ruth subsequently moved to the area to take up a post at the University of North Norfolk. She's now head of the archaeology department. In 2007, she met DCI Harry Nelson and her life got a whole lot more complicated. As well as involving her in several murder cases, Nelson is the father of Ruth's beloved daughter Kate.

Pets: a ginger cat called Flint

Surprising fact about Ruth: she collects pony books and would love to own a horse.

Harry Nelson

Profession: Detective Chief Inspector

Likes: driving cars, solving crimes, his family

Dislikes: Norfolk, the countryside, management speak, retirement

Harry Nelson was born in Blackpool. He came to Norfolk in his thirties to lead the Serious Crimes Unit, bringing with him his wife, Michelle, and their daughters, Laura and Rebecca. Nelson has a loyal team; they have been through a lot together and are a close unit, despite Clough's recent defection. Nelson thinks of himself as an old-fashioned policeman and so often clashes with his boss, Superintendent Jo Archer, who is trying to drag the force into the twenty-first century. Nelson is fiercely protective of his family, which now includes his son George and the daughter he insists on calling Katie. He knows that whatever decision he makes in the future will result in hurting someone he loves.

Pets: a German shepherd dog called Bruno

Surprising fact about Nelson: he's a huge Frank Sinatra fan.

Michelle Nelson

Profession: hairdresser

Likes: her family, exercising, socialising with friends

Dislikes: dowdiness, confrontation, talking about murder

Michelle married Nelson when she was twenty-four and he was twenty-six. She was happy with her life in Blackpool – two children, part-time work, her mother nearby – but encouraged Nelson to move to Norfolk for the sake of promotion. When her daughters were old enough, she took a job managing a hair salon. The last few years have been challenging for Michelle: Nelson's affair with Ruth; her own tragic relationship with Tim Heathfield, a detective on Nelson's team; an unexpected pregnancy in her mid-forties. She loves her son, George, but sometimes feels that her life is travelling very fast in the wrong direction.

Surprising fact about Michelle: she once played hockey for Blackpool Girls.

Michael Malone (aka Cathbad)

Profession: druid, teacher, house-husband

Likes: nature, mythology, walking, following his instincts

Dislikes: rules, injustice, conventions

Cathbad was born in Ireland. He was brought up as a Catholic but now thinks of himself as a druid and shaman. Cathbad came to England to study first chemistry then archaeology. At university he came under the influence of Erik Anderssen, though they found themselves on opposite sides during the henge dig. Cathbad's friendship with Ruth came later and he's a devoted godfather to Kate (whom he calls Hecate). Cathbad has a grown-up daughter, Maddie, from a previous relationship and two children with Judy, his life partner. He's happy looking after the children and teaching meditation classes, but sometimes still hankers after the nomadic life.

Pets: a bull terrier called Thing

Surprising fact about Cathbad: he can play the accordion.

Shona Maclean

Profession: lecturer in English Literature

Likes: books, wine, parties

Dislikes: being ignored

Shona is a lecturer at the University of North Norfolk and one of Ruth's closest friends. They met when they both participated in the henge dig in 1997 and their friendship has survived Shona's marriage to Phil, once Ruth's head of department. Shona and Phil have a son, Louis, who is the apple of their eye and one of Kate's least-favourite people.

Pets: none

Surprising fact about Shona: as a child she won several Irish dancing competitions.

David Clough

Profession: Detective Inspector

Likes: food, football, his family, his job

Dislikes: political correctness, graduate police officers

David Clough ('Cloughie' to Nelson) was born in Norfolk and joined the force at eighteen. He was a loyal member of Nelson's team until he was promoted to detective inspector and moved to Cambridge. Clough's star seems to be in the ascendent: he has a new job, a beautiful wife, Cassandra, and two adored children. He has also, in Nelson's opinion, started dressing like a teenager. Clough still misses Nelson though.

Pets: a bulldog called Dexter

Surprising fact about Clough: he can quote the 'you come to me on my daughter's wedding day' scene from *The Godfather* off by heart.

Judy Johnson

Profession: Detective Sergeant

Likes: horses, driving, her job

Dislikes: girls' nights out, sexism, being patronised

Judy Johnson was born in Norfolk to Irish Catholic parents. For a while, Judy's life proceeded along cautious, conventional lines: she joined the police at eighteen and married her childhood boyfriend. But then she met Cathbad and discovered an unexpectedly wild and passionate side to her nature. Judy now lives with Cathbad and their two children. Judy is an excellent police officer and has passed her inspector's exam but she knows that, if she wants to progress in her career, she will have to leave Norfolk.

Pets: half-share in Thing. Judy also once inherited two hamsters called Sonny and Fredo.

Surprising fact about Judy: she's a keen card player and once won an inter-force poker competition.

Tanya Fuller

Profession: Detective Sergeant

Likes: sport, succeeding, being called 'ma'am'

Dislikes: history, being overlooked

Tanya studied Sports Science at Loughborough University. She joined the police as a graduate trainee and moved to Norfolk shortly afterwards. Tanya is fiercely ambitious and often clashes with Judy, although a grudging respect exists between them. Tanya recently married her girlfriend Petra, a secondary-school teacher.

Pets: none

Surprising fact about Tanya: she enjoys knitting and once made Petra an Inca-inspired alpaca cardigan.

Tony Zhang

Profession: Detective Constable

Likes: chatting, socialising, art

Dislikes: family expectations, silence

Tony Zhang was born in London to first-generation Chinese immigrants. As a child, Tony lived through tragedy when his sister, Lily, died of meningitis. Tony studied economics at the University of East Anglia and joined the police force as a graduate trainee. He's a good officer, keen, hard-working and sensitive. He has to learn to stop whistling though.

Pets: none

Surprising fact about Tony: he has a Blue Peter badge